D1215946

Citadel of God

Citadel of God

A Novel about
Saint Benedict

by
Louis de Wohl

IGNATIUS PRESS SAN FRANCISCO

First edition published by
J.B. Lippincott Company
Philadelphia and New York

Cover by Christopher J. Pelicano

ISBN 0-89870-404-9
Library of Congress catalogue number 91-77212
Printed in the United States of America

Book One

1

"ROME IS FINISHED", said Senator Albinus. He sipped his wine, then held up the goblet carved from amethyst. "Very pretty", he approved. "I wonder where they find stones large enough to be cut like this. Very pretty."

Senator Boethius frowned. "They come from India, I believe", he said, with a warning glance towards his wife.

But Rusticiana was beyond taking notice. Her face was drained of blood, and her hands twitched. "Rome is indeed finished", she said breathlessly, "if there are no Romans left. And I see there aren't."

The boy Peter gazed at her with rapt admiration. She was as beautiful as a goddess when she was angry. She was a white flame burning.

"Romans", Senator Albinus drawled. "I wouldn't say there aren't any, Domina Rusticiana, but they are few, you know. The city prefect tells me he had great difficulty in getting the men together for the escort of honor."

"The escort of honor for a barbarian tyrant", Rusticiana said icily. "Indeed, I hope it was difficult. It is bad enough that anyone at all would comply."

"Oh, it wasn't for that reason, I'm afraid", Albinus said dryly. "They didn't want to wear armor all day. So heavy, don't you see, and standing on the walls and in the streets in it for hours on end. The city prefect had to grant them three sesterces for special duty. They asked for five, at first." He smiled at Rusticiana's disgust. "The trouble with you, Domina, is that you were born five centuries too late. On second thought, make it a thousand years. You ought to have been a contemporary of Cloelia, Virginia, and Lucretia."

"I wish I could return the compliment", Rusticiana snapped.

"Don't you see that he talks like that only because he, too, is suffering?" Boethius asked with gentle reproach.

"Talking seems to be all that is done", she said. "If there were one true Roman left, he would act."

"What would you have him do, Domina?" Albinus asked, mockery in his tone, but not in his eyes. "Have a nice, hot bath and open his veins? Old Scaurus did that, last week, when he heard that the King was coming to Rome."

"He was eighty", Rusticiana said, her eyes blazing. "And at that age the only veins a man can open are his own. But at least he did do that."

Albinus looked at Boethius. "Do you know, I begin to believe your wife wants me to go and kill the King." He laughed. "As her husband, I trust she has given you first chance."

"A thousand years ago," Rusticiana said, "at the time of Lucretia, we threw out our own King, and not even the maddest of the Caesars dared to assume that title again. Now we are to give it to an Ostrogoth."

"Just as I thought." Albinus gave a nod. "No denial. No contradiction. I wonder what you told her when she suggested it. But whatever it was, it doesn't seem to have been very convincing. Very well, I'll have a try." He turned to Rusticiana, the mask of amused banter gone. The clever little face with its small, almost womanish mouth was tense. "What do you think would happen in such a case?" he asked softly. "Not that I could succeed—there are clusters of his brawny giants around him all the time, and they'd cut me down as soon as they saw a sword or dagger in my hand. But let's assume I succeed before they cut me down. What would happen? First, they'd massacre everybody in sight. I am a senator, so is your husband and so, of course, is your noble father. They'd kill every member of the Senate, Domina, and they would not choose an easy death. Nothing would convince them that this wasn't a conspiracy, and they'd torture all of us to get the names of other conspirators. King Theodoric isn't coming here alone, you know. He'll have a small army with him, and *his* men don't mind wearing armor. They would have to elect a new king, naturally.

Theodoric has no son, only a daughter, and she is little more than a child. They'd choose a soldier-king. Young Tuluin, perhaps, or his cousin Ibba or someone of that kind. Theodoric is a barbarian, but at least he has some respect for our culture and civilization; and he's practically the only one who has. His successor's first great action would be to avenge Theodoric's death. There is no Roman army on whom he could avenge it, so he'd have to find a scapegoat. There is only one: Rome itself. He'd burn it down, destroy it. No one could stop him. Do you want this to happen, Domina? You would lose your husband, your father, your friends, your wealth, and your home, and Rome would be in ashes. And Italy would still be ruled by the Ostrogoths, under a king worse than Theodoric. You'd gain nothing."

"I?" Rusticiana asked. "You don't think I would survive my husband's death, do you? But we would all die as free Romans. And history would record it."

"History would do no such thing", Albinus returned to his easy, almost playful tone. "And that for the simple reason that there'd be no one left to write it down, except perhaps Cassiodor. The King has made him his private secretary, I'm told."

"Magnus Aurelius Cassiodorus", Rusticiana said bitterly. "A man of his family and upbringing, the secretary of Theodoric. Freedom has no meaning any longer, it seems."

"Nothing has any meaning when you're dead", Albinus said, with a shrug. "Forgive me, Rusticiana—you and your husband are known to be good Christians and therefore you believe in a good many things. They baptized me too, but . . . well, never mind. As for Cassiodor, he wouldn't survive the King's death either, I'm afraid. But no historian worthy of the name could possibly record that Rome was burned because the Romans rose against the tyrant and fought for their freedom. It wouldn't be true. It may be extremely regrettable, but on the whole they are not opposed to Theodoric's regime at all."

"Albinus!"

"I'm afraid he's right, Rusticiana", Boethius said sadly.

"You're living in a dream world, Domina", Albinus went

on. "You seem to forget that the man has been the ruler of Italy for seven years. True, this is the first time he's come to Rome. But what of it? He's been ruling Rome from Ravenna, just as some of our own emperors did in the past. This is no more than a visit, a ceremonial visit, of course, with everyone present in his best clothes to greet the great royal illiterate."

"He can't write? He's as crude as that!"

"He does quite well, nevertheless. He's not a stupid ox as so many of them are. He likes erudite people, I'm told. He's an organizer, too; and for a German he's remarkably mild."

"True", Boethius agreed quietly.

"His laws are not without a kind of down-to-earth wisdom", Albinus continued. "He's shrewd. Twice within the last five years he has lowered the taxes. And those of my colleagues in the Senate who visited him in Ravenna, say that he has great dignity and even that he is a great ruler in his own barbarous way."

"He bought them, no doubt", Rusticiana said contemptuously. "Not all senators are as wealthy as you are, Albinus. And if it weren't for that and for the fact that you are an old friend of my husband's, I would be tempted to ask what he has done for you that you defend him so eagerly."

"Rusticiana," Boethius said severely, "you forget yourself. Do not pay any attention to this, Albinus, I beg of you. My wife is very young and very much upset by this . . . royal visit."

"I'm not offended." Albinus smiled. "In fact, I admire your wife's spirit. And there is no harm in saying what one feels . . . here, in the great house of the Anicians. Elsewhere, of course, it might be a little dangerous. The Anician family knows how to choose its slaves, too. Besides, we're among ourselves, in this room, the three of us—the four of us, I mean", he corrected himself, still smiling. "I almost forgot our young friend here. But you won't give us away, Peter, I know that."

"I'm a Roman", the boy Peter said, staring at Rusticiana.

"Exactly", Albinus said.

"Peter had a Roman father and a Greek mother", Boethius

explained. "She was a great and gracious lady. We are happy to have him with us."

"I well believe that." Albinus gave the boy a friendly nod. Intelligent little face, he thought. He wondered for a moment whether Boethius might be the boy's father and dismissed the thought. Boethius was a paragon of virtue. Besides, Domina Rusticiana was not the kind of woman who would consent to have her husband's natural son under her roof. The boy adored her, obviously. "How old is he?"

"Thirteen", Peter said quickly.

"He will be thirteen next month", Boethius corrected. "His birthday is almost the same as my wife's. We celebrate them together."

"You make me sound like a child, too", Rusticiana said reproachfully. "I shall be eighteen."

"As old as that, are you, Domina?" Albinus asked gravely. "Then there will be silver in your lovely hair in only forty years' time."

She could not help smiling. "I'm glad you are not offended, Albinus. My husband often tells me that I'm hasty and too impulsive. But I do feel strongly—"

She was interrupted by the chant of a beautiful voice, coming from somewhere high up. "The ninth . . . hour."

"As late as that", Albinus said. "We must go, friend. The Senate is assembling."

"The . . . ninth . . . hour", sang the slave at the sundial on the roof.

"The King hasn't come yet", Boethius said. "I have posted slaves at the gates where he is most likely to arrive. None of them has come back so far."

"The . . . ninth . . . hour", came the third call.

"Even so I think we'd better go", Albinus said. "They'll be on horseback and they love galloping through the streets. Once they're within the city gates all the streets to the Forum will be blocked."

Rusticiana gritted her teeth. "Rome has been invaded by barbarians before", she said. "There was Brennus and Alaric and Genseric of the Vandals. But what I cannot bear is that instead of resisting we open our gates to this brute, this great, organizing, tax-reducing brute; that the greatest assembly on earth, the Roman Senate, consents to receive a barbarian as their lawful ruler. We no longer feel the shame of slavery. We're content to lick the boots of a Goth."

"They won't taste very different from those of Nero and Domitian", Albinus replied bitterly. "We have become accustomed to slavery. That's why I said Rome is finished, Domina. The spirit of a few of us won't help. Only if a couple of hundred thousand Romans would share it and act accordingly . . . by all the gods and saints, you'll have me daydreaming too, if I listen to you long enough. Boethius, we *must* go."

"My litter is waiting beside yours in the courtyard." Boethius embraced his wife. "Don't take it so hard", he said gently. "It's only a formality. I shall be back for the night meal. The official banquet is not until tomorrow." But she was stiff and unyielding in his arms, and her bow to Albinus was cool.

When the men had left, she sank down on the couch and buried her face in her hands. "Rome is finished", she said. "Finished. Finished."

"I'm a Roman", the boy Peter said fiercely.

Perhaps Albinus was suffering, too, as Boethius seemed to think, but what if he were? As a Christian one could offer up one's own suffering to Christ—Deacon Varro always said that. But could one offer up the shame of one's country?

And to think of the finest mind and the greatest person in the world, of Anicius Manlius Severinus Boethius, bowing and scraping to a barbarian chieftain and a heretic to boot . . . it was too much.

She burst into tears. But almost at once she remembered that she was not alone in the room, the boy was there, it was not seemly that she should let herself go like this before his eyes. He had said something, a little while ago, what was it?

She wiped her eyes. "What was it you were saying, Peter?"

There was no answer. She looked up. The boy had gone.

2

THE BOY PETER walked swiftly through the atrium and out into the garden. All that mattered now was whether Corax or Marullus was in charge of the gate. Corax was slow and dull-witted, but Marullus was a sharp one. It was Corax, his bald pate shining like a pink moon. Good.

"Young master? You're not leaving, young master, are you? You mustn't go into the streets alone."

"My tutor is coming with me, Corax, he'll be here any moment."

The slave wagged his head. "Better wait till he is, young master." He grinned. The spear in his enormous hands looked like a thin reed.

"There he is now", Peter said, pointing to the entrance of the house, half hidden by a cluster of trees. As Corax turned, he leaped past him, slipped through the gate and ran down the street.

"Stop!" Corax yelled. "Young master, stop at once. You mustn't . . . I can't let you . . . "

Peter stopped at a distance of about twenty yards, as if he were undecided, and Corax promptly came after him. When he was near enough, the boy ran off, not too quickly. If he discouraged Corax he would only go back and give the alarm. Then they would send swift runners after him. Instead he allowed his pursuer to come almost within reach before he made another spurt. He succeeded in doing that twice again, before the slave gave up and ran back. It would take him some time to get to the house.

Peter ran as fast as he could, till he reached the maze of streets that was the Trans Tiberium district. Let them send out runners *now,* he thought. All around him crowds of people were walking, most of them in the same direction, towards the center of the city. He let himself be swept along with them. No one could find him now.

A plan, he thought. I must have a plan. The King was coming from Ravenna. Therefore he was bound to arrive at one of the northern gates, the Porta Salaria, the Porta Nomentana, or the Porta Aurelia, near the mausoleum of Hadrian. All of them were a long way off, right at the other end of the city. Before he could reach any of them, the King would have passed and be . . . where? Where would he go? The Forum Romanum most likely. There the officials usually assembled for a state reception. Then they would lead him to the Palatine. They had been working day and night for weeks, to get the ancient palace ready, so that the Goth could sleep where the emperors used to.

To the Forum then. But there would be masses and masses of people there, one would be wedged in like a tiny piece of a mosaic floor. No chance of moving as much as an inch in any direction. They'd keep room free for the royal progress, of course, but that would be a narrow lane, flanked by the municipal guards, the only troops Rome still had, tailors and shoemakers and stonemasons, dressed up as soldiers. A man had no chance at all to get anywhere near the King. A boy might, though. . . .

Still walking, Peter took the writing tablet out of the belt of his tunic. A few words in Greek were written on it, a line from the *Iliad.* He detached the stylus from the tablet and wiped the words off with its flat end. Then he gazed at the other, the sharp one. Julius Caesar was killed by a stylus in the hand of Brutus. If such a thing could kill Caesar six hundred years ago, it could kill a Goth now.

"I shall be grateful to you to the end of my life", said the old man in the dark robe. "How *kind* people are here in Rome! It is quite different where I come from, I assure you. It cannot be much pleasure to one as young as you are to show an old man like myself the wonders of this city, this unbelievably beautiful city. You know all about it, of course, you have seen it a thousand times, yet here you are, giving me your time. And you don't even know my name. . . . "

"I know you are a holy monk", his guide replied. "Surely that is enough. I'm only a student."

"A monk I am, yes. I am Abbot Fulgentius of Carthage, alas, an abbot without a monastery, an abbot without monks, a fugitive from persecution. The Vandals are cruel masters; you would not believe me if I were to tell you what they have done to the men of our Faith. They killed fourteen of my monks, oh, most abominably; only a few of us managed to escape. A monk I am, but not a holy monk, or else I would have stayed and died a martyr's death, instead of fleeing and saving my useless old life. But even so I am thankful to God that I am still allowed to walk on earth a little longer and to see this city. There is nothing like it on earth, I am sure of that."

"Careful, venerable Father", his companion warned. "There are chariots coming." But the old man went on staring at the cascade of marble palaces that was the Palatine Hill and had to be pulled back sharply, with the hooves of the first four horses almost upon him.

The horses thundered past them, drawing five, ten, twenty chariots—grays, roans, piebalds, and a magnificent foursome of white horses, whose charioteer was wildly applauded by the crowd.

"Who is that?" the old man enquired.

"I'm sorry, venerable Father, but I don't know."

A fat man beside them gave a chuckle. "Where do you two come from that you don't know that?" he asked. "That's Spirax, thrice victor at the Great Games. No man ever sired a better charioteer. I never lost a copper piece on him. Typhon with his piebalds cost me a small fortune. If you really never heard the name of Spirax before, you can't be Romans, either of you."

"I've only just arrived from Africa," the old men explained, "from Carthage. But my young friend here is a Roman, I believe."

"I have been here for several years," the young man admitted, "but my home is in Nursia."

"You don't mean to say that in several years you never saw a chariot race?" the fat man asked incredulously.

"Didn't you hear him say he's from Nursia?" another man interposed. Grinning, he showed the seven teeth left to him. "And don't you remember what Cicero said?"

"Who's he?" the fat man asked. "And who are you?"

"I'm Quintus Verrius, the Rhetor, at your service. I'm a good rhetor, but not as good as Cicero used to be; or not quite. But then no one is. And Cicero said of the Nursians that they are the most austere of all men, *severissimi homines.* No wonder then that this excellent young man does not indulge in betting and the like."

The young Nursian did not like to have his shoulder patted condescendingly by an extremely dirty hand; he liked it still less when he saw the rhetor's left hand snaking up to the old abbot's belt where, next to his writing tablet, a withered old purse was hanging dejectedly.

"Come along, venerable Father", he said, shook his shoulder free, and pulled the Abbot away.

"Everybody is so friendly here", the old man said, "and so cheerful. It is as if one were among good friends all the time. The Vandals are cold and hostile, God forgive them—Oh, look, whose is the great statue over there?"

"It is the Emperor Constantine."

"Ah, the great Emperor . . . where would we all be if it hadn't been for him. But how strange that his horse has only three legs."

The young Nursian answered somewhat dryly that the fourth leg had been stolen and that half of the statues in Rome were lacking legs, arms, and even heads for the same reason, but the Abbot could not hear a word of what he was saying because the whole crowd had begun to shout as the municipal guards came marching along, resplendent in their scarlet tunics and brass helmets.

"How lucky I am", the Abbot said, "that I should still be allowed to see brave Roman soldiers. In Africa . . . "

"They are the guard of honor for King Theodoric", his companion explained, when the shouting subsided a little.

Abbot Fulgentius nodded eagerly. "What a wonderful thing that Romans and Goths are getting on so well together. But what a city, what a city! Where is the poet who could describe this vision of marble and silver and gold and ivory! Where are you leading me? Oh, oh, this must be the Forum Romanum. What crowds! And those grave-faced men in their snow white togas with the broad purple stripe, they are the senators, of course. How much I heard about them, when I was a boy; the noblest assembly on earth, my father used to say. What dignity! Hundreds of kings to greet the King of the Goths. I must thank God every day to the end of my life that he allowed me to see all this." The wrinkled old face was radiant. "How beautiful must be the heavenly Jerusalem, if earthly Rome can shine in such glory!"

The young Nursian's gray eyes widened. Suddenly he understood that the old man was not looking at Rome as it was now, shallow and thoughtless, loose-living, corrupt, and enslaved by its own vices even more than by an alien conqueror, but at the great city across all centuries, the Mistress of the known world, the city of Saint Peter and Saint Paul. And God was good to the old man, he would not let him see the dirty hand of the pickpocket who quoted Cicero. He would not let him hear about the shame of Romans, robbing their own statues for the sake of a few bits of old metal. God allowed him to see only beauty and glory.

"And next to God, I am most grateful to you", the Abbot said. "I will pray for you. That reminds me . . . I don't know your name."

"Benedictus."

"You were given a blessing for a name. Pass it on to others and you will be the richer for it."

The young man bowed respectfully.

"I think I have seen enough for today", the Abbot said with a sigh. "If you agree, I shall go back to my abode in the Via Portuensis." He tried to turn about and found that he could not. A large crowd had assembled behind them as well as all around them. They could not move at all.

"We shall have to wait until the royal procession has gone past", Benedictus said. With a worried look he added: "I hope you will be able to stand it, venerable Father."

The Abbot smiled. "We won't have to wait very long", he said. "I can hear trumpets. I think the King is coming."

There was a slight commotion on their right. A woman gave a shriek, a few men cursed, and others laughed.

"What is it?" the Abbot asked. "My old eyes can't see that far."

"It's a boy", Benedictus said. "He's crawled through to the front line. On all fours. There he is now—just behind the line of soldiers. A small boy, ten years old or a little more. They must have cuffed him badly. The poor little fellow looks quite white and ill."

The trumpets sounded again.

From afar came the shouting of vast crowds and the muffled thunder of many hooves.

The sentinels at the Mausoleum of Hadrian had been the first to see the cloud of dust approaching, and messengers sped away to inform the city prefect and the Senate that the royal progress was in sight. Half an hour later the vanguard of the Goths passed the mausoleum, swung sharply to the right, and on the Aelian Bridge crossed the lazily flowing Tiber, large men on large horses, with leather helmets and metal-studded leather cuirasses, with small shields, short-shafted spears, and huge swords, twice as long, almost, as the Roman sword that had conquered the world between Britain and Persia. They rode in a triple row, a thousand and again a thousand, and the bridge trembled under them.

Before them opened the huge wings of the Porta Aurelia, and they passed into the city, an army of silent giants.

After them followed a swarm of commanders, each dressed as he pleased, but all in armor. Some had bull's horns on their helmets, some the wings of birds or animal figures made of metal six inches high or more, wolves, elks, ravens, or cranes, crudely fashioned, most of them, the emblems of tribes or petty principalities of the past, before the Ostrogoths had become a people under a single king.

Behind them came Theodoric. The man on his right, boy-faced Visand, carrying the blue banner with the Amalung lion on it, was at least a foot taller than the King and had the knotty, bulging muscles of a Hercules. The girl on his left, a child of ten, was of exquisite beauty, a fairy princess with tawny hair and large, green eyes, dressed in gold cloth and riding a milk white horse, an Arabian filly, the gift of the King of the Vandals. But neither Amalaswintha, Theodoric's only daughter, nor Visand, the strongest man of all Goths, could draw attention away from the King for more than a moment.

He was forty-five. The hair showing under the low helmet, circled by a twelve-rayed golden crown, was the color of dark amber and so was the beard which formed a half circle across cheeks and chin. He wore no moustache. The mouth was firm, the nose short and aquiline. The eyes under thick, blond eyebrows were of an icy blue, and he had a trick of shifting his gaze only by moving his head. Perhaps it was that which gave cause to the rumor that no one could tell the King a lie when he looked straight at a man. Over his armor of countless tiny silver rings he wore a purple cloak. The harness, reins, and saddlecloth of his black horse were dyed purple. He was armed only with his sword. Behind him, Count Leuthari carried his shield and Count Gerbod his spear.

"That building on the left is where the Emperor Hadrian was buried, Father", Amalaswintha said.

The King nodded, without turning his head. He knew that the large, round tower was the strongest outer bastion of the city but now had a garrison of only twelve soldiers. In the case of a siege, there ought to be two hundred. Strange that an effeminate aesthete like Hadrian should have a citadel for a tomb.

"The Aelian Bridge, Father. And the Porta Aurelia."

Ten feet of water in the Tiber at this time of the year. Enough for small warships, branders, perhaps. But why think of that? This was his city, though he had never before set foot in it.

Count Tuluin was waiting at the gate, bowing and holding up the hilt of his sword, the sign that all was well and no trouble in sight.

And this was Rome. Get those walls up again, man them with those new ballists, put fifty thousand men into the city and stocks of food, and it could outlast any siege. How difficult it was to think of Rome as a city of peace. Its great past came up, flooding the mind. Hannibal had never seen this gate from the inside.

"The Campus Martius, Father."

The Field of Mars. That's where they used to train their soldiers, little brown men, heavy with armor and packed like mules yet agile and quick, under the best discipline in the world. Lack of discipline was the main worry of a Gothic commander in the field. Would they ever learn it? I learned it, he thought grimly. Seven years as a hostage in Byzantium could teach a man a lot, if he kept his eyes open. Not exactly what the Greek Buffoons learned, though.

No one was training now on the Field of Mars, and no one had to. An army of two hundred and fifty thousand Goths was ready to defend Rome and Italy.

But what a flood of buildings, towering over each other, covering all the hills, a man-made world in itself, no comparison at all with Byzantium where everything was graceful and glittering. Byzantium was a woman. Rome was a man, an old man. The corpse of an old man. A man just slain was often still capable of some kind of feeble movement, a twitching, trembling. Rome, political and military Rome, was dead. But in all other aspects it could be revived, and this he would do, this he must do, for that was kingship.

The people in the streets gave ragged cheers. A poor-looking lot. The statue of Trajan on a horse. The horse had no tail. The statue of Agrippa on a horse with damaged legs. The statue of Augustus on a horse, with half the horse missing. Enough bronze and marble horses here to equip the entire Gothic cavalry. But only the bronze statues were damaged. Metal thieves.

"That's the Theatre of Pompey, Father, that rubble heap on the right. They say it would cost too much to restore it."

"You seem to know your Rome, daughter."

"I do, Father. Cassiodor explained it all to me, so that I could be your guide."

She was riding well, too. Six hours in the saddle and no signs of being tired. He reached over and patted her on the head. "Pity you're not a boy", he said with a little sigh. "Cassiodor!"

A young man in Roman dress emerged from behind Leuthari and Gerbod. He was riding a dun horse. "My lord King?"

"Make some notes. First: the Theatre of Pompey is to be rebuilt, plans and costs to be forwarded to Ravenna for my approval." Watching with some amusement how Cassiodor struggled to deal all at once with his writing tablet, his stylus, and his horse, the King did not see that Amalaswintha was on the verge of tears. She struggled hard to regain control of herself, and she succeeded as she had many a time before. It was a pity that she was not a boy. Her father always said that. Gerbod said it and Riggo and many others, when they thought she could not hear them. A girl was nothing, a useless thing, except to be given in marriage to some foreigner, for the sake of an alliance. Only her mother had never said it, but she was dead. And Cassiodor didn't; perhaps he was too courteous.

"Secondly," the King said, "any further damage to the statues of Rome must be prevented not only by sharp punishment of the culprits, as a deterrent, but by constant patrolling at night. They'll get the thieves. Breaking off metal is noisy work."

Cassiodor's lean, intelligent face bent eagerly over his tablet. "An excellent solution, my lord King. Thus the statues themselves will be able to add to their own protection. No longer mute, they will defend themselves as their metal protests against the hammer of the attacker."

"You have a rare talent", the King said dryly. "You can speak with the elegance of a poet about petty thieving."

Cassiodor was too much of a courtier not to laugh at a royal joke.

"You are teaching my daughter well", Theodoric added with a nod.

Count Tuluin came up again. "The Roman Runts have posted troops on the main square, lord King", he reported. "Six to seven hundred men, all in armor."

"Report again, Count Tuluin", the King said curtly.

The young commander looked surprised. "I said the Roman Runts have . . . "

"Report again, Count Tuluin", the King interrupted.

Tuluin's face flushed. "The *Romans* have six to seven hundred soldiers in armor assembled on the main square, my lord King."

"That's better", Theodoric said. "The escort, no doubt. You will now repeat to the leaders of the vanguard my strict order, given when we set out, that my Italian subjects are to be treated with special courtesy."

"Yes, my lord King." Count Tuluin turned his horse and sped off, sparks flying.

Theodoric smiled. "A very good fighter", he said aloud. Count Leuthari was Tuluin's uncle. It was better to let him know that Tuluin was not out of favor. No need to say anything to Cassiodor. He was too intelligent to feel offended by Tuluin's tactlessness. He was probably accustomed to it, too. Gothic warriors would never learn to be tactful, which put a constant strain on their relations with the Italians all over the country. But better that than the softness that went with pretty manners. No one could behave more elegantly and charmingly than the people in Byzantium, and no people was so false and so corrupt. The Goth was rough, but he could fight. No need for him to hire foreign mercenaries to fight for them. Let the Runts—the Romans—call him uncouth and barbarian. It was the minor evil. Today, however, everything was to go smoothly. The visit to Rome must be a success.

"The Theatre of Balbus, Father. And the next one is the Theatre of Marcellus." Amalaswintha's voice was quite steady. "That's the Aemilian Bridge on the right."

The crowds were growing thicker and thicker, but the cheering, though louder, seemed to come from groups among them. Paid groups, most likely.

The street broadened as the royal progress turned left, towards the Forum Romanum, "the main square", as young Tuluin called it. The sight of the Palatine Hill on the right was a thing never to be forgotten. There was something almost superhuman about the noble grandeur of those ancient palaces and temples, rising to the sky.

"To think that men built that", Count Gerbod said with awe, and Leuthari murmured something about Valhalla. He was not a Christian; nor was young Tuluin. Visand was goggling like a country yokel. They were all a little too much impressed.

"Visand!"

"My lord King?"

"The Roman troops on the square will lower their *vexilla* when I pass. You keep the Amalung Lion up. Don't dip it an inch."

"Wouldn't dream of it, my lord King." Visand grinned hugely.

Trumpet signals sounded, again and again.

The Forum was in full view now. Three hundred senators in gleaming white togas, with Symmachus, the Princeps Senatus, in front. Municipal soldiers in scarlet tunics. The representatives of the Equestrian Order. The delegations of the trade unions. The city prefect with his personal guard.

The cheering of the crowd became deafening. They could not very well have paid all those yelling people. Too expensive. They liked a show, the King thought. Always did, always would.

A small boy broke into the open between two municipal soldiers.

"Hey, keep out of the way, youngster", Visand said. His huge foot shot out and the eager little fellow crumpled up, right before the hooves of Count Gerbod's horse. Quite mechanically, Gerbod drew his sword.

"It's only a little boy", Amalaswintha cried. "Don't hurt him. Help him, Cassiodor. He'll be trampled to death."

But before Cassiodor could dismount, a young man stepped out of the crowd and helped the dazed boy to his feet.

Gerbod just managed to force his horse past. The young man resolutely carried the boy back into the crowd. The royal progress flowed on, slowly, inexorably. Another fifty Gothic nobles rode by, scions of the great and ancient families, some of which claimed Wodan, Berahta, and other gods and goddesses as their ancestors, like the Volsungs and the Velands, and men who had won their rank and title in battle, like Valamir and Tagila and Tota. Behind them came a long line of wagons, each drawn by four horses, carrying the royal luggage and household goods, a carriage with two ladies-in-waiting of Princess Amalaswintha, a larger one with a dozen maidservants, and then three thousand more Gothic cavalrymen.

"Silly little idiot", Gerbod growled, sheathing his sword. "Somebody must have sent him to have a petition granted—he was carrying a writing tablet, I think."

"Amalaswintha", the King said.

"Yes, Father?"

"Your compassion was out of place. No emotions must be shown at a state function. When incidents occur, the King's servants will deal with them. If they don't know how, the King will tell them."

"I'm sorry, Father."

The Gothic vanguard, on the Forum, had divided into two formations of a thousand men each, with a narrow lane in between.

Through that lane the King, Amalaswintha, Leuthari, Gerbod, Cassiodor, and the nobles rode up to the gleaming white cloud that was the Roman Senate house. The King reined his horse at a distance of six yards from Symmachus, the Princeps Senatus, who bowed to him and began to read the official welcome of the city of Rome.

The King listened attentively. His Latin was good enough to understand the most intricate phraseology, and it had to be.

Amalaswintha did not take in a word. The great, rolling sentences passed by like waves of the sea. Fixed in her mind, bewildering, incomprehensible, and frightening was the terrible hatred in the eyes of a little boy.

3

A NUMBER of the Young Lions of Rome often met at the palace of the Anicians in the Trans Tiberium. Known by that nickname they carried it with a pride based on the high flight of their minds rather than on deeds. Most of them came from the great families of Rome who could claim the heroes of twelve centuries of history as their ancestors. Some, although baptized and even devout Christians, still maintained that Venus and other Roman or Etruscan divinities had a place in their family tree. To all of them the palace of the Anicians was a natural center. Here one could talk freely.

The eldest of those present was Senator Albinus, and he was in his early forties. Boethius, their host, was not yet thirty, Equitius and Florentius were in their twenties. There was no banquet, and no slaves were present. The young men themselves filled their goblets from pitchers and the pitchers from four amphorae, standing in a row on a large table of precious citrus wood that was worth a king's ransom. One contained Falernian, the second Massican, the third Caecuban wine, and the fourth water. Unwatered wine was only for sots and foreigners.

"The three wines of the heroes, by Jupiter", exclaimed young Equitius. "Marius drank of one of them before he decided on his battle plan against the Cimbri; Caesar did, before he crossed the Rubicon and when he celebrated his victory over Pompey. . . . "

"And Constantine, when he convoked the Council of Nicaea", Florentius added, with a grin.

"That's a bad example. What's so glorious about a council?" Albinus asked.

"At that council", Florentius said, "the heresy of Arius was condemned for all time. And our glorious masters, the Goths, are Arians, therefore heretics and therefore condemned. Right?"

"By Saint Peter and Saint Andrew, the man is right", Equitius said. "One can see that you're studying for the priesthood. You still are, aren't you, Florentius?"

"Well, yes. I'm not in too much of a hurry about it, though."

"I know the reason for that, I think", Albinus said, smiling. "I even know her name. I congratulate you, Florentius. The lady is very beautiful."

"Too beautiful", Florentius said, refilling his goblet.

"Well, why don't you marry her?" Equitius asked innocently.

"Marry Lelia? I'd be a poor man within six months. Not that that would frighten me. But it would certainly frighten her."

"I am not sure whether a priest does well to marry at all", Boethius said pensively. "Many of them are married, good ones, too. But a priest is a man set apart, isn't he? A man dedicated, ordained . . . he should not have to think in terms of everyday life, he should not have to think of wife and children first, but of his flock. It is easier for me to think of a priest as a saint than as a married man."

"Easier for you, Senator Boethius," Florentius said gravely, "but not for the priest, I fear."

Boethius smiled as the younger men laughed. "Saint Peter was a married man," he said, "but he left his wife and home when he followed the Master. Saint Paul never married—and he had much to say for the unmarried state."

"Yet he said: 'It is better to marry than to burn' ", quoted Florentius. "As I said, it is easy for you to talk like that. You have a beautiful and charming wife."

"I am not a priest", Boethius replied gently. "And I am not sure whether you—no, I mustn't say that. There are limits, both to reason and to intuition."

"Meaning that both your intellect and your intuition tell you I shouldn't be a priest, but that a vocation is something not necessarily measurable by either, I suppose", Florentius said.

Boethius looked at him. The forehead of a god, the nose and mouth of an animal, he thought. But was that not, ultimately, or at least penultimately, the description of every human being?

A slave entered. "Deacon Gordianus to see you, Master."

Boethius frowned. "Old Gordianus? At this hour?" Then he saw that the slave knew more but would not speak out in front of his guests, and he rose. "I had better go to see what he wants", he said. "We must postpone our little argument, Florentius."

Outside, the slave said: "Young master Peter is back, Master."

"What? Thank God for that. My wife will be so glad. Did you tell her?"

"The Domina is with him now. He must have had an accident, Master. Deacon Gordianus—"

But Boethius was already on his way to the boy's room. At the door he met Rusticiana just leaving. She put a finger to her lips and drew him away. "I've sent for the physician", she said. "His right hip seems badly hurt. He said a very terrible thing. . . ."

"What do you mean?"

"He said: 'I failed you, Domina.' Again and again he said that, nothing else. And he was crying. I have given him some poppy seed in wine. He'll sleep soon. Boethius, what can have happened to him? What does he mean?"

"I don't know. Perhaps old Gordianus can give us an explanation. Where did he find him?"

"He didn't find him. It was the student."

"A student?"

"They're both in the library. I didn't want to leave them in the atrium."

"You were quite right, of course. I must see what this is all about."

In the library Deacon Gordianus said in Greek: "The joy of God to you. Please permit me to introduce this young man to you. His name is Benedictus. He is a student in Rome. He is also a somewhat distant relative of ours. From Nursia."

"Of both of us? He must have some Anician blood then. Nursia..." Boethius' phenomenal memory went to work. "Nursia... an aunt of my father's married somebody from Nursia, who was it? Aulus... Aulus Eupropius, that's it."

"Eupropius is my father's name", Benedictus stated.

"Then he must be the grandson, no, the great-grandson of Domina Severina Marcia Anicia. You should have come to this house much sooner, young man. I might have been able to do something for you."

"I am not in need of help, noble Senator."

Boethius laughed. "We are all proud when we are twenty."

Benedictus thought that over for a moment, frowning. "I did not speak from pride", he decided. "I meant just what I said. And a man in your position has to assist so many people that it would be wrong to add to your burden."

"You are right, in a way." Boethius eyed him curiously. "But it's unusual to hear that from one so young. At your age one rarely thinks of others."

"To eat my dinner twice would be doing myself wrong," Benedictus said cheerfully, "and to let somebody else go hungry for it would make a second wrong."

The work of the intellect was Boethius' main joy in life. Contact with a good brain invariably set off a spark in his own. He completely forgot the reason for meeting this pale, lanky young man. Perhaps it was one of the many traps and dangers in the life of the rich, he thought, that they almost invariably felt no one could get on in life without their assistance. Just one little step farther, and one lost interest in those who needed no help, simply because they did not need it. This was reducing the personality of others to mere objects, a kind of ownership, a rather egocentric attitude. It could become downright tyrannical....

"How did you come to find little Peter?" Rusticiana asked impatiently.

But Benedictus was still looking at Boethius. "I am most grateful for your generous thought, noble Senator", he said, and Boethius blinked as he realized that the astonishing young man must have followed the trend of his unspoken thoughts and was trying to make him feel better.

"On the contrary," he said, rather lamely, "we are much indebted to you for bringing Peter back to us. We are fond of the boy. He ran away, you know. The fool of a slave at the gate saw him, but was too clumsy to stop him and then too cowardly to tell us . . . with the result that we only found out the next day that he was gone. I sent out a dozen slaves, but no one seemed to know anything. But here I am, digressing again. I always seem to do that. How *did* you come across him and where?"

"On the Forum Romanum", Benedictus said. "The southern end of it. I was there with Abbot Fulgentius of Carthage. A great crowd had assembled to see the arrival of the King of the Goths."

"You wanted to see that?"

"No, noble Senator. I was just showing the holy Abbot the city—he had never been in Rome before. But we got stuck in the crowd and could not move. When the King passed by, the boy suddenly ran forward, and one of the King's men kicked him."

"The brute", Rusticiana exclaimed. "But why—" She broke off.

"I saw that he could not get up," Benedictus went on, "and there were all those horses coming, so I went after him, picked him up and carried him back."

"They could have arrested you both", Boethius said tonelessly. "Impeding the royal progress; causing a public disturbance; perhaps even . . . " His voice trailed off. He looked thoroughly miserable.

"I thought they would", Benedictus admitted evenly. "But the boy might have been trodden on by those horses. . . . "

"You are not by any chance trying to apologize for having saved Peter, are you?" Boethius asked.

"In any case they didn't arrest us," Benedictus went on, "and I think they didn't because Abbot Fulgentius fainted. He is very old, and he had been forced to stand there a long time. So when the soldiers came—"

"Romans?"

"The city soldiers, yes. They came and fussed over the boy and over Abbot Fulgentius, and I helped to carry them both. The soldiers have a horrible way of making room in a crowd, though. The officer in charge seemed to think only of getting us all out of the way as quickly as possible. He even found a litter for us, near the Circus Maximus."

"He didn't ask for your names and addresses?"

"No, noble Senator. I think he was rather glad to get rid of us, and then went back in a hurry. In the litter, Abbot Fulgentius came to and did not know where he was and who the boy beside him was—which I did not know either. We took him back to his abode, and then I tried to find out the boy's home address. He had a writing tablet in his hand, but he was holding it so tight, I could not get it out of his fingers. He had no letters or anything else to show where he was living, and *he* did not regain consciousness so quickly. So I took him to my own quarters and stayed with him. I sent Cyrilla to fetch a physician—she is an old servant of my family's and is looking after me here in Rome. The physician came, Dylon is his name, a Greek from Corinth. He put compresses on the boy's hip and gave him some medication, too."

"The boy was conscious by then?"

"Yes, but he wouldn't speak."

"He would not speak?" Boethius asked.

"Not a word. But this afternoon the venerable Father Gordianus came to see me. . . ."

"You have known each other before?"

"We are old friends, Benedictus and I", Gordianus said, caressing his short gray beard. "He wanted me to interpret Holy Scripture for him. He's a great one for asking difficult questions."

"I can well believe that. And you, of course, recognized Peter."

"I did, though I had seen him here only a couple of times, and when he was much smaller. But he refused to come with me. He wanted to stay where he was. He wouldn't say why."

"What on earth has happened to the boy?" Boethius exclaimed. Looking at Rusticiana, he saw that she was very pale and near crying.

"I asked myself the same question", Gordianus said. "Frankly, I have no explanation ... the less so, as my young friend Benedictus did not seem to be very communicative either."

"What more do you know about this, Benedictus?" Boethius asked.

"I know nothing more, noble Senator."

I should leave it at that, Boethius thought. He felt, dimly, that nothing good would come out of any further attempt to clarify the situation, and yet to clarify it was what he wanted. He blundered on, relentlessly. "You know nothing more," he repeated. "But perhaps there is something you guessed ... is there? Didn't the boy convey anything to you—in one form or other?"

"He would not speak to me about it, noble Senator", Benedictus said stolidly.

"Nor to others? That servant of yours? The physician?"

"No, noble Senator."

"Very well. But have you an idea, a theory perhaps of his behavior?" When there was no answer, Boethius went on: "Listen, Benedictus. This boy is an orphan. His mother died when he was five, his father when he was nine. Ever since then he has been living in my house, and when I married, my wife accepted him as if he were my own son. It is a terrible thing to us that he should have lost confidence in us as he seems to have. If this means failure on our part in some way ... and it must ... we must make amends. But to do that we must know what happened. Every clue that you may have is important. Think it over, and I am sure you will stop being evasive."

After a while Benedictus said curtly: "He spoke in his sleep."
"Ah. What did he say?"
"It may have been just a nightmare."
"Quite. Therefore there is no reason to withhold what he said."
Benedictus nodded reluctantly. "He said: 'I failed you. I couldn't kill him. I failed you.' "
Rusticiana gave a low moan.
"He said that several times", Benedictus continued. "Then he added: 'I can't ever go back. They would punish them for it.' "
Sobbing, Rusticiana left the room.
Boethius made a move to follow her, stopped and sank on a chair. "Poor boy", he said hoarsely. "Good God in heaven. Poor boy." How could he have been so . . . so dense. It was all clear, clear as sunlight. Little Peter the Roman, the tyrannicide, a new Brutus. He had been in the room when Albinus interpreted Rusticiana's words as an incitement to kill the King of the Goths. The writing tablet served to conceal the stylus. The weapon of Brutus. No one in the Forum seemed to have thought of his real intention, not even those who saw the incident. He himself had been in the Forum, with the other senators, and he had seen nothing. It was not so surprising, really, in such a huge square. For the first time he remembered that Senator Sulpicius, several hours later, in the Curia, mentioned something to a group of his colleagues about "somebody trying to hand the King a petition". That was all Sulpicius knew and more than the others had known. Very fortunate, of course.
But to think that such a terrible idea could have been born in his house! He should have stopped Rusticiana from talking like that in front of Peter but, like her and Albinus, he had clean forgotten that the boy was present. Peter worshipped Rusticiana, of course; whatever she said was gospel truth to him. How quickly guilt could slip into a man's life. Guilt and . . . danger.
He looked up. "Benedictus," he said, "you were quite right to refuse my help. Of the two of us it is I who will always

remain the debtor. And I must further increase my indebtedness to you by asking you to keep silent about this."

"Don't worry about that", Gordianus interposed. "Neither my friend Benedictus nor I talk about . . . other people's nightmares. We came to put an end to your worries, not to start or to prolong them. Now, if you will kindly excuse us, we shall go back where we came from. We want to argue about the meaning of some passages in Saint Augustine's letters."

"I wish you'd stay, both of you", Boethius said. "I have some friends here, and they must wonder by now what has happened to me.

"I saw Florentius' litter outside", Gordianus said. "They say he wants to become a priest. I wonder . . . "

"So do I", Boethius said. "But one never knows for sure, does one?"

"I don't think we should intrude on your friends", Gordianus said. "So, if you will forgive us . . . "

"Just one more thing", Boethius said. "I must at least try to settle the smallest part of my debt, the material one. There is the physician who looked after Peter and . . . "

"Leave it to me", Gordianus said, "I'll arrange it all, and you can refund me later, if you wish."

But at that moment one of the atrium slaves appeared in the door.

"The Royal Protonotary Magnus Aurelius Cassiodorus to see you, Master."

Boethius paled. Cassiodor . . . who had been with the King when it happened. So they had followed it up after all. They knew. "Lead him into my study", he said stonily.

4

WHEN THE SLAVE had withdrawn, Boethius said: "I am glad I kept you here just a little longer—you might have run straight into him, and he is one of the few who must have seen the incident from very near. He might have recognized Benedictus. Besides . . . he may not have come alone. You had better leave by the garden door. Come and see me again soon, Gordianus, and bring your young friend along with you. I like him. I only hope I shall be able to receive visitors", he added, with an uneasy smile. "Go, friends. Gordianus, you know the way, I don't have to ask one of the slaves to show you out."

After they left Boethius stood immobile, breathing slowly, relaxing. Then, with slow, measured steps, he walked towards the study.

"I am sorry to disturb you at this hour, Boethius", Cassiodor said politely. "But as you know, I am no longer master of my own time; and I am here on the command of the King."

"I thought you might be", Boethius said.

A gust of laughter came from the adjacent room.

"You have guests, of course", Cassiodor said. "Do I know any of them?"

"You know Albinus, I think . . . he's a senator."

"I do."

"Then there are a few younger men—Equitius, Florentius, Tertullus, and others."

"Some of the Young Lions", Cassiodor said, smiling.

"So you know that nickname."

"We know a good deal, in Ravenna. I would like to meet your friends, if I may."

Boethius raised his brows. "I thought you had a message for me."

"Not a message, an invitation. The King wants to see you tonight."

Boethius nodded slowly. "You are a very courteous man, Cassiodor. A king's invitation is a command. Under the circumstances, we had better go at once. I shall tell my friends to come back on another day."

"There is no hurry", Cassiodor said. "The King is busy with the Roman clergy, at present. Some complaints of the Bishop of Nuceria and a number of other matters. We don't want a repetition of what happened before, do we?"

A few years ago Deacon Laurentius had been nominated antipope by a very belligerent minority, and the position of the lawfully elected Pope was in grave danger. Rioting took place not only in the streets, but in the churches, and in the end King Theodoric had had to settle the matter by upholding the authority of the true successor of Saint Peter. The antipope was given the See of Nuceria.

"Bishop Laurentius should be glad to be where he is", Boethius said. "He might have fared much worse."

"I quite agree", Cassiodor replied. "But then the King is often very clement. He is hard only where he has to be."

Was it a hint? Cassiodor's face was not easy to read and he was a master of words.

"In any case, Boethius, the dignitaries of the Church will occupy the King's time for quite some while. He does not expect us till midnight, and I have a fast carriage outside. So there is no reason why you should send your friends home now. Let's join them instead, shall we?"

"As you wish."

When they entered the room young Equitius cried: "Where have you been all the time, Boethius? We are dicing for—" He broke off. Like everyone else in the room, he rose.

"Magnus Aurelius Cassiodorus, Protonotary of the King, gives us the honor of his company", Boethius said quietly. Some of them might not know Cassiodor, others might be drunk. Now they all knew that they had to measure their words.

"Welcome, Cassiodor", Senator Albinus said. "Does your Royal Master approve of such nocturnal outings?"

"Certainly", Cassiodor replied, smiling. "He trusts me so much he even permits me to go into a den of Young Lions."

"At least the man is witty", Florentius said in a low voice.

Boethius gave his new guest a cup of Falernian and then filled his own.

"Excellent vintage", Cassiodor said.

"I suppose by now you have become accustomed to drinking mead", Equitius suggested. "Or *ael* or whatever the stuff is called that the Goths drink." Nudging his neighbor, young Tertullus, he giggled.

"Oh, the *cave* at Ravenna is fairly well stocked", Cassiodor replied. "The King likes a good wine. But he never gets drunk."

Florentius came to the aid of his friend. "A good answer," he said, "but let me ask you something. We know you are doing invaluable work for the King of the Barbarians. You are doing his reading and writing for him. You are probably teaching him how to behave—not to belch or pick his nose in public and so on. And no doubt he's paying you a good salary for all that. But is there anything he has ever taught you?"

"Yes", Cassiodor seemed quite unruffled. "He has taught me a great many things. For instance that a ruler, unpopular on account of his race and descent acts wisely when he keeps his interference with the customs and habits of his subjects to a minimum. Theodoric has been King of Italy for seven years, and none of you has seen much of him and his Goths, is that not true? Yet at the same time his system of constant patrols has made our roads more secure than they have been for several centuries. All civilian administration is left to us Italians. But stern measures were taken against anyone trying to make excessive profits from the necessary imports of grain, with the result that bread is cheaper than ever before. The famine at the end of the war with Odovacar he dealt with at once—it was the very first thing he did. Italy is no longer dependent upon a good harvest in Apulia, Calabria, and Sicily, for all the silos are full and new ones have been built and filled all over the country.

He has taught me that a man without culture and erudition can still foster these qualities; that a barbarian conqueror can have the greatness to honor and respect the ancient institutions of the land he conquered by force of arms; the Roman Senate first and foremost, of which you, my gracious host, and you, Albinus, have the honor to be members. Mining has been begun again in Dalmatia and in Bruttium, the Pontine Marshes and those of Spoletium have been drained, shipping has been encouraged and service to and from the provinces has been extended. The income of the average citizen has more than doubled, yet money has not lost even a fraction of its value. Not since Trajan and Valentinian has Italy enjoyed so many blessings, and that is why I feel that a Roman of noble descent should collaborate with such a ruler rather than sit back and jeer, as some do, feeling themselves great patriots for doing so."

There was a pause. None of the Young Lions had an answer ready.

Albinus cleared his throat. "You must forgive our young friends, Cassiodor", he said silkily. "At their age one is usually a little . . . impulsive, and you cannot expect them to be a match for a man as wise and experienced as you are. But permit me to say this, just for argument's sake: everything you have pointed out is quite true, as I will be the first to acknowledge. But all of it would apply also if we Italians were slaves. Well-kept slaves, mind you, the slaves of a benevolent and generous master, but slaves just the same. We are told what to do and as long as we do it, we are kept well-fed, well-clothed, and all the rest by our master. All we miss is that little thing called freedom. And when one is young and not yet accustomed to taking things as they come, one is inclined to rebel against slavery, however comfortable it may be. That, I think, is what our Young Lions feel, even if they have not been able to put it in so many words . . . which is due, I think, to the excellence of our dear host's wines."

"Long life to you, Albinus", Equitius cried.

"I drink to you, Albinus."

The Senator smiled thinly. Detaching himself from them, he had yet been able to ward off Cassiodor's attack.

"Freedom", Cassiodor said slowly. "When did we last have it, we Romans? The days of the great Roman Republic are so far away, that its history sounds like a myth. We used our freedom for a series of civil wars, Marius against Sulla, Caesar against Pompey, Octavian against Anthony. Then Augustus reintroduced the monarchy in all but name, and after that only the ruling Caesar was a free man in the empire—until he was murdered and replaced by another. Freedom . . . to do what? To wage war? If so, against whom? Does anybody in his senses wish to reconquer Britain from the natives there, or Transalpine Gaul from the Franks? What for, in the name of sanity? All we ever got out of Britain was tin and oysters, and we paid heavily for them. Now we get the same commodities by trade, for a fraction of the costs of occupation. Why live in a land of fog, rain, and moors when one's homeland is Italy? As for Gaul, we liked its climate so well that we used to send people into exile there in the pious hope that they wouldn't survive it for long."

"There is Africa . . . " Tertullus interposed.

" . . . which we lost to the Vandals a hundred years ago and could not reconquer. On the contrary, King Genseric paid us a visit here in Rome which was very different from the one we are having here now, despite Pope Leo's valiant effort to repeat his miraculous feat against Attilla. As it is, we have an alliance of sorts with both the Vandals and the Franks while trade with Africa and Gaul is improving year by year. As for defensive war: Who would dare to attack us today and face a Gothic army under Theodoric? Besides, there is no law I know of against Italians joining the army. In fact, there are Italian contingents. Thus any of you who wants to be a Young Lion in more than name can carry sword and shield whenever he wishes to."

"You weren't present when we talked about what has happened in Rome since the arrival of the Gothic Trajan", Equitius said. "His mild, benevolent Goths have looted several shops near the Baths of Caracalla and beaten up Roman citizens trying to resist. The municipal guards did not dare to interfere. Complaints were made to the city prefect who shrugged his shoulders and said that, for the time of the royal visit, any such complaint must be made to his Gothic counterpart, Count Ringulf. Unfortunately Count Ringulf was too drunk to receive any visitors."

"That's quite true," Cassiodor admitted, "but I'm afraid your report is somewhat incomplete. Let me complete it for you. This morning, twenty-two Gothic cavalrymen were put on trial for looting, with the King himself presiding over the tribunal. Five of them were condemned to death and executed on the spot. Eleven others were fined twenty-five solidi each, to be deducted from their pay. The others were acquitted. Count Ringulf was severely reprimanded and sent back to Ravenna. He has been replaced by Count Addo, one of the sternest disciplinarians of the army. It is said the Gothic soldiers are more afraid of him than of the devil. All loot was restored to the shops—there were six of them—and a substantial sum was paid to the owners for damages. Now tell me, friend, do you think that Roman citizens would have received equally swift retribution and compensation under Roman jurisdiction?"

"No", Equitius admitted. "But I still wish Rome were Roman."

"So do I", Cassiodor said.

"You do?"

"How can you doubt it? How can anyone born in the Eternal City feel otherwise? But whose fault is it that a King of the Goths can be the ruler of Italy, if not ours? If Rome were still Roman, no Alaric, no Genseric, no Odovacar, and no Theodoric would have ever set foot on our soil. He who wants to be free, friend, must deserve his freedom."

"And we don't?"

"We quite obviously don't. And the proof is that we don't have it. Can you imagine a Roman uprising against the Gothic rule? Who will rise? Who will fight? Why, it's like the attempt of a child to kill a giant."

Boethius darted a quick glance at the speaker. But Cassiodor was not looking at him.

"I wish I had been born some centuries earlier", Equitius said miserably. "Under Trajan, perhaps . . . or under Augustus. Or, better still under no one—in the times of the Great Republic."

"An easy way out." Cassiodor shrugged his shoulders. "And not a particularly courageous one. It is better to face the problems of your own time and deal with them as best you can. As for me, I have no wish to live in a pagan Rome, whether it be in republican times or under Augustus. And under Trajan, though he was a good ruler, I would have had to face persecution as a Christian. There is no persecution under Theodoric—or I would not serve him."

"Still, he's a heretic, and you're supposed to be a Catholic. That doesn't seem to disturb you much, does it?"

"No, it doesn't", Cassiodor said. "And I don't see why it should, as long as no attempt is made to interfere with my religion, in which I believe at least as much as you do. I can say that, because I believe in it implicitly, and no one can do more. Therefore I wish, I must wish, that Theodoric and his Goths too would share my faith. Unfortunately the sad spectacle of disunity even among our higher clergy is not likely to impress the King. And where morality is concerned, we could learn a few things from the Goths. They cannot, most of them, read or write—but they do not commit adultery. They don't know who Homer or Virgil was, but they also do not know prostitution. There are errors in their faith, but they are morally cleaner than we are. My desk, on the Palatine, is swamped with petitions to the King, and it's my business to sort them and report on them. Do you know what most of our Roman petitioners want? The reintroduction of the Lupercalian festival, fertility rites, coarse mummery, obscenities, and all! The very thing the late Pope Gelasius after hard efforts finally succeeded in abolishing. Now they want a heretical king to reestablish it for them."

Cassiodor rose. "I must go", he said. "Will you come with me, Boethius? Much as I hate to break up the party—"

"I promised friend Cassiodor to accompany him on his way", Boethius said. "Don't let that disturb you, I beg of you.

The night is young, and you may wish to resume your dicing." He gave them no time to ask questions, but walked out quickly. Outside the room he hesitated for a moment. "I wonder whether I should not tell my wife; she'll be asleep by now, I think, but . . . "

"Then why wake her?" Cassiodor said lightly. "You can tell her more when you come back."

Yes, *if* I come back, Boethius thought.

"You didn't take much part in our little discussion", Cassiodor said, as they walked through the atrium.

"I don't suppose I did. But I think most intellectuals talk too much and listen too little."

"I did talk a great deal, I'm afraid", Cassiodor admitted.

"I wasn't referring to you, of course. . . . "

"No, no, I know. But a good deal can be learned also from watching the reaction of one's listeners."

"I see. And what was it you learned?"

"That . . . forgive me, but it would be wrong for me to discuss it at this stage."

Boethius nodded. "I only hope you're not taking them too seriously. I should have warned you beforehand that they would be a little . . . that they might say things which . . . "

"That they might regard the King as a barbarian and me as a traitor to Rome? I never expected anything else from the Young Lions. Perhaps some of what I said may have sunk into their somewhat woolly minds, and perhaps not. No harm in trying."

"Then you won't . . . hold it against them, officially, I mean?"

"They were only *talking,* friend. What I am interested in are men who act."

Almost the same thing that Rusticiana had said the other day, Boethius thought. Then it had led to little Peter's action. This time it might lead to his own arrest, perhaps his death.

Cassiodor's carriage was waiting at the main gate. Four horses, Boethius thought, Numidians. Lines built for racing. No wonder Cassiodor called it swift.

They mounted, and the charioteer set off immediately. They

could not talk much during the drive, not with the thunder of hooves reverberating in the narrow streets and the wind of their own speed beating against their mouths. Twice they were stopped by Gothic patrols, but each time a single word whispered by the charioteer opened the way again. They raced across the Sublician Bridge and up the Palatine Hill. They drove through a side gate into a huge courtyard and stopped at one of the many doorways. Large men with flowing hair and naked shoulders took care of the horses. Someone came up to them with a burning torch, an officer, tall, blond, blue-eyed, with a long moustache and a jutting, shaven chin.

"Senator Boethius to see the King", Cassiodor explained.

"The King is still busy with the holy incense swingers", the officer said. "Go find somebody to show you to the anteroom. I don't know anything about this imperial rabbit warren. Ye gods, what a place." He walked away without further ado.

"Count Tuluin", Cassiodor said, "is the type of man who conforms to your young friends' conception of a Goth, isn't he? Fortunately I know exactly where to go."

Silently Boethius followed him along the marble pavement of the corridor, up some stairs and into a fairly large room. A group of Gothic officers broke off their conversation, stared, and resumed talking again.

"Do you understand their language?" Cassiodor asked.

"No, and frankly I don't feel I'd want to. It sounds very ugly."

"Most languages do when we cannot understand them", Cassiodor said, with a shrug. "I used to think so myself. One gets accustomed to it after a while, I suppose."

But Boethius was angry, and as usual his anger turned first and foremost against himself. How could he have listened to Cassiodor's fine speeches about the great King of the Goths and all the good he had done and was doing and would do, when barbarians were stalking about in the ancient Imperial Palace and some blue-eyed lout could treat a Roman senator as if he were a sandalmaker from the Subura? Cassiodor seemed to have become accustomed not only to the language of the barbarians but also to their manners and to the humiliation they inflicted on the conquered. The Young Lions could not stand up to his glib tongue, but they were right. Very well then: if this King of Louts and Boors wanted to have him arrested and killed in vengeance for a child's pitiful attempt to play Brutus, let him. Boethius would not give him any satisfaction by showing fear or even regret. In a way it was a relief to be angry, to have cause for anger. He drew a large chair closer and sat down, crossing his legs.

The Goths did not take any notice, but went on gabbling gutturally. Cassiodor also showed no reaction to his gesture of defiance. A pity really. It would be joy to give him a piece of one's mind.

But wishful thinking was no use. That damned traitor had given him hints enough about what the King knew; it could mean nothing but arrest and death. Quite clever, really, to get him here in the middle of the night. In a rabbit warren, as that insolent Goth called the palace, a man could so easily disappear without leaving a trace, and tomorrow the King could pretend that he did not know anything about a visit of Senator Boethius, and Cassiodor could say that he had only taken a drive with him and that the Senator had insisted on returning on foot. Perhaps he had had an accident on his way back, or, more regrettable still, had been attacked by some cutthroat who robbed him of his money and threw the body into the Tiber. Such things could happen, despite the great King's many measures to make all roads and streets safe. . . .

I should have refused to come, Boethius thought grimly. I should have forced the barbarian to have me arrested in my own house so that the Senate could demand an orderly trial. Only the Senate could sit in judgment over one of its members. Theodoric could not break that rule and yet go on posing as the benevolent respecter of Roman laws and customs. Instead, like a fool, I have walked straight into their trap.

A door opened and a veritable mountain of a man emerged. Boethius remembered having seen him carrying the King's banner.

"The noble Senator Boethius to the King", Visand said. He remained where he was, holding the curtain back, and Boethius rose and walked through, into a small room, where the King was sitting behind an ebony desk. There were some papers on the desk, and, despite anger and worry, Boethius wondered what the King was doing with them, as he could not read or write.

"Welcome, noble Senator", Theodoric said. "Please be seated."

Boethius hesitated.

"Be seated", the King repeated, smiling broadly. "You don't expect a Goth to stand on imperial ceremonial, do you?"

Boethius sat down.

"Besides," the King went on, "I have always found that men who work with their brains talk much better when they can sit—just as soldiers think at their best while standing . . . if they think at all, that is. Now then, Boethius, I must start by apologizing for dragging you out at such an hour. There is a good reason for it, though."

Exactly, Boethius thought. He was not going to be taken in again by a false geniality. "The ruler has no need to apologize", he said curtly.

"I disagree", Theodoric replied. "You weren't even told the purpose of this audience. The least of my soldiers has a right to know why when I send him into battle. How much more a Roman senator, the scion of one of the most ancient families of Rome and the best brain in Italy as well."

"The King is very courteous", Boethius said coldly.

"Courtesy," Theodoric said, "like many other things, is something about which we have much to learn and in due course may learn from your people. But that will take time. You Italians too had to learn it. You too started as simple men, warriors and peasants. And I doubt whether a Roman of the time of, say, King Tullus Hostilius had the accomplished manners of a modern Roman senator like Boethius, Symmachus, or Albinus—whether he was not, in fact, as rough as some of my nobles, Count Ringulf, for instance, or Count Tuluin."

Boethius looked up sharply, but the great leonine face, made still larger by the semicircle of beard around it, showed no expression.

"Some of my Goths have little liking for Romans", Theodoric went on. "They feel that Italy is much better off under my rule than it has been for centuries and that we receive little thanks for our efforts to bring that about. That is very natural—just as it is natural that some Romans have equally little liking for us. How can I expect an Anician, a Cornelian, a Licinian to accept with indifference that his country, the Mistress of the World of ages past, is being run by the crowned chieftain of what must be to him a barbarous people."

Boethius said nothing.

"I am not so blind and not so stupid", the King said, "to take the niceties of official speeches at face value. The Princeps Senatus was good enough to call me a second Trajan." He smiled. "But I am not sure whether the noble Symmachus remembered that Trajan, one of Rome's most successful rulers, was not a Roman at all, but a Spaniard. Which reminds me that Diocletian was an Illyrian, as were several other emperors. And quite a number of them could not either read or write. To an erudite man like you that may be quite shocking."

There was a glint of humor around the King's mouth.

"Few erudite men would make good rulers", Boethius said and immediately hated himself for having said it.

"Enmity exists on both sides", Theodoric resumed calmly. "And its motive is pride in the virtues and ways of life of one's own people. Our pride is hurt, because we feel inferior to you in culture and civilization, because we are clumsy and awkward where you are self-assured and at ease. Your pride is hurt because we are stronger and by our strength have conquered this country of yours. And those who feel like that are often the best and the finest men in your ranks and in ours. That means I cannot count on them for constructive work, and that I will not tolerate. So I decided to act. You, Boethius, are not only an Anician and a senator, you are also the friend, and your house is the center, of the Young Lions."

"Cassiodor mentioned that name to you, I suppose", Boethius said, not without bitterness.

"On the contrary, it was I who mentioned it to him. It is my duty to know what is going on in Italy. Boethius, you are far too intelligent to believe that your young friends will ever be a danger. They grumble and swear, but it's all talk and talk will change nothing. In its own way it is as silly and hopeless as the attempt of a boy, a child, to attack a man. I hope your adopted son will soon be well again. He had the misfortune to encounter the largest foot in the Gothic army, Visand's. No, don't say anything, Boethius. You cannot possibly have known about it beforehand, or you would have stopped it."

"That is quite true", Boethius said, and he tried hard to keep his voice from trembling.

"Such a childish thing," the King went on, "and yet born in the great house of the Anicians. Even if you didn't know anything about it, it is clear that the boy didn't think of it all by himself, without any—let's call it stimulation. Tell me: What would a Roman Caesar do to the head of a family whose son had tried such a thing? No, you don't have to answer that. Instead I shall give you *my* answer, the answer of a barbarian, a Goth, but a king. I want you to be a minister of my government."

Boethius stared at him, speechless.

"You will stay here in Rome", Theodoric went on calmly, "and report to me in Ravenna only from time to time. Your duties will be many, but they can be expressed simply and, therefore, the way I like. You are to look after Rome as a son looks after his mother. Naturally, you will be the highest official in the city. The city prefect will report to you. The commander of the municipal guards will report to you and so will the heads of the organizations in charge of food stocks, food supply, street security, and various others, including two new organizations I created yesterday: the committee for the preservation of Roman statues and the committee for the reconstruction of the Theatre of Pompey. Ecclesiastic matters will be dealt with by your office only inasmuch as they concern the city of Rome. That is what I propose to you, Boethius, and I think it is a better role for a man of your integrity, intelligence, and culture than that of presiding at banquets and little meetings of patriotic young fools whose influence on the history of the Eternal City will be exactly nil."

I can't do it, Boethius thought. I mustn't do it. But, God forgive me, I'd like to.

Theodoric calmly watched him struggling with himself. After a while he said: "I promised I would let you know why I called you at this unseemly hour. I have thought of the possibility that you might refuse. If you do, Cassiodor will take you back to your house and your audience will be kept a secret. You won't have to explain anything to your friends and not even the most hotheaded will lose confidence in you for having conferred secretly with the Gothic tyrant. You will then remain the head of the Young Lions, and that suits me. I'd rather know a sensible man is the leader of malcontents, than some irresponsible idiot who might force me to take stern measures. But I would regret a refusal very much. I want Italy to flourish, and for that I need the help of the best men in the country. There is just one other thing. I know that by inclination you would rather keep out of all state business. You would prefer to sit in your library—I'm told it's a very lovely one, with glass windows and ivory-lined walls and many precious and rare books. You are a writer and a philosopher at heart. But ask yourself whether you can take the responsibility before your conscience of living the life of an exile in the very city that needs your service. I want you to serve *Rome,* her greatness, her beauty, and her many needs. What is your answer?"

There was a long pause.

"I would love to say no", Boethius said in a strained voice. "I wish to God I could say no, for how can a city and a country be great unless they are free? But when my mother is a prisoner, held captive by an honorable foe, and that foe charges me to look after her . . . can I answer him: No, you have taken her prisoner, therefore it's up to you to look after her, I will not lift a finger to make her lot easier? You have appealed to my conscience. It is my conscience that makes me accept what you suggest."

"The honorable foe", the King said with a broad smile, "is glad of your decision. Cassiodor tells me that according to a wise Greek called Plato—you've heard of him, I suppose, I hadn't—a philosopher would be the best man to lead public affairs. So I thought, I'd try to find out whether the man was right."

"It has been tried before", Boethius said, and for the first time he could smile a little. "Marcus Aurelius was both emperor and philosopher. And Seneca—the younger Seneca—was minister under Nero."

"Was he successful?"

"For some years, yes. But in the end Nero forced him to commit suicide."

"Theodoric is not Nero", the King said.

"And Boethius is not Seneca", Boethius said. "As a Christian I cannot claim the Stoic's privilege to end his own life. It would be necessary to have me killed outright, my lord King."

They both laughed, cheerfully, contentedly, as men do when they have come to terms and want to break the tension of a struggle concluded.

5

IT WAS TWO HOURS after midnight when Boethius returned home; he could see from the faces of the slaves that the house was in an uproar.

Rusticiana came running up to him, her hair disheveled, and

threw herself into his arms. "You're safe", she sobbed. "Oh, thank God you're safe."

"Why are you still up?" he asked, caressing her with awkward fingers. "I thought you'd gone to sleep long ago. And where are the . . . where are my guests?"

"I sent them away", Rusticiana admitted, wiping her eyes. "I couldn't stand them any longer, drinking and singing, when you were in danger. So I told them that little Peter was very ill and would they please come back another day, and Albinus invited them to his house and they left."

He smiled down at her. "What made you think I was in danger?" he asked.

"Cervax told me that Cassiodor arrived and you went away with him. I knew that could only mean trouble. What did he want? Where did you go? Why did he come at such a time?"

"There is no trouble," he said slowly, "though I really don't know how to tell you about it."

"You look so tired," she whispered, "so dreadfully tired. Won't you have some wine?"

"No, thank you, I think not. How is little Peter? What did the physician say?"

"He'll be well again in a few weeks, but he may always limp."

"Poor boy."

"I was so worried about him, but that was nothing when I heard that you had left with that awful man. Then I really found out what fear means. I didn't know what to do, I . . . "

"He isn't awful at all, you know. And he's very intelligent. You should have heard him dealing with our friends here. He did it all so elegantly and . . . "

"Never mind that. What did he want of *you?* He is always around the King. If he ever finds out that Peter—"

"I told you there is no trouble", Boethius interrupted her. "But I think he has found out. And the King knows it all and it doesn't matter."

She stared at him, wide-eyed. "Are you mad or am I?"

He gently led her to a nearby couch and sat beside her.

"Neither, child", he said. "Will you please get it into your mind that there is no trouble? And no danger? I have met Theodoric. We had a long talk. He said he hoped Peter would soon be well again—our adopted son, he called him. And he asked me to accept the office of a minister in his government."

"I was wrong, then", Rusticiana said. "You're not mad; neither am I. The King is. He must be."

"No, he isn't", Boethius told her patiently. "On the contrary, he is wise and a great statesman. He used Peter's silly attack to appeal to my conscience. I am to look after Rome."

"You . . . you don't mean to say you accepted?"

"I did."

She froze into immobility. After a long silence she said: "This is the darkest day of my life. I wish I were dead."

He frowned. "Stop being a child, Rusticiana. Wild talk will get us nowhere. It is precisely because of your wild talk that poor Peter tried to play the great Roman hero and tyrannicide. You must listen before you form your judgment. I've said that to you many times." He told her briefly about his audience on the Palatine Hill. "I couldn't refuse him", he said in the end. "Not under the circumstances. And I will look after Rome. Can't you see that I had to do it?"

"What I can see is that I underrated that barbarian", she said bitterly. "He is very shrewd. He's as wily as Satan himself. He's taken you in completely."

"The formula is not quite that simple", Boethius said.

"He threatened you . . . "

"On the contrary, he made it quite clear that he would let me go in peace even if I didn't accept."

"That's exactly the kind of threat that would work with you. If he had told you he was going to have you killed or thrown into jail, you would have resisted. But he threatened you in a far more subtle way. He was going to let you depart in peace, laden with the burden of his generosity. He knew you wouldn't be able to bear that. A Boethius could not be outdone in generosity. That's how he got you, the rogue."

"I'll try to give you the real formula", Boethius said. "Neither of us was entirely frank with the other. But nevertheless we knew each others' thoughts."

"That's too much for me."

"I accepted", Boethius said quietly, "because it meant that I could do Rome a good service, and I said so. I did not add: And I can accept, because there isn't the slightest chance of fighting you. If there were, I'd fight you for all I'm worth. But I think he knows that's what I was thinking."

"There is still the Emperor in Byzantium. . . . "

"Child," Boethius said mildly, "Theodoric came to Italy with the full knowledge, the approval, and assistance of the Emperor, to take this country away from the usurper Odovacar."

"The Emperor didn't intend the Goth to establish himself in his own right. He was to be the Emperor's governor, or vice-regent."

"That was the original intention," Boethius admitted, "but you forget that two years ago Emperor Anastasius sent Theodoric the regalia of Rome. That is an open acknowledgment of Theodoric's independent kingship."

Rusticiana sucked in her breath sharply. "He told you that, I suppose. . . . "

"He showed them to me", Boethius said. "The Emperor has acknowledged him. We Italians have no army to drive him out. *He* is our army against potential invaders. Shall I leave the administration of Rome, the welfare and the cultural interests of the city to a Gothic count, high-handed, ignorant, and loutish? I shall serve Rome. And as it can't be done in any other way than by being Theodoric's minister, I will be just that."

She nodded, stony-faced. "Your thoughts are fine and logical, and my brain is not good enough to contradict you. All I can say is: I know in my heart that no good will come from this."

"That will be as God wills it," he answered, "but I wish you were on my side."

Fear and fierceness left her as she turned towards him. "I am," she cried, "of course I am. You called me a child, but it's you who are a child, a wise, honorable, much too credulous child, and I love you."

Peter was slow in getting well. Physically, he recovered sufficiently, after a few weeks, to get up and hobble about. But he was shy and strangely reticent.

Boethius took him aside and talked to him, lovingly and gravely. "You did a very foolish thing, Peter, and it might have endangered us all. Didn't you hear Senator Albinus say so? It was a bad thing, too. We are not allowed to kill, except in war."

"There *is* war", the boy said.

"No, there isn't. War must be declared and . . . " He stopped. Who in Italy could declare war on the man who was the country's rightful ruler? "We mustn't take the law into our hands", he went on. "Even if the King were the tyrant you thought him . . . the fate of those who have tried to kill tyrants has never been fortunate, whether they succeeded or not. Rome was not grateful to Brutus and Cassius for assassinating Caesar, and the end of those who killed Domitian and other emperors was swift and bitter."

But the boy remained sullenly silent, and Boethius wondered whether he was justified in evading the main issue. Perhaps he should have told him that women, even great and highborn ladies, were often more vehement than correct in their political views and must not be followed blindly. But somehow he could not talk to Peter like that. It did not seem right. Maybe Peter himself had guessed something, though . . . he seemed to avoid Rusticiana's company and he was as monosyllabic towards her as everybody else. Quite different from his former attitude. The best thing was probably to let the boy outgrow the whole thing. He would mope for a while, but it could not last very long. A pity that he now had so little time for the boy. The old tutor, Pharicles, was a gentle old man and cultured, like so many Greek slaves, but Peter needed younger company, other boys, or better still a young man, just sufficiently older to influence him in the right way.

This led to an idea, and the idea led to sending for Gordianus. The venerable old man came and listened. "I may be able to persuade Benedictus," he said, "but I'm not at all sure. That young man has a mind and will of his own."

"Obstinate, eh?"

"Not a bit of it. But he's out for something . . . I don't honestly know what it is, and I'm not even really sure that there is anything, except that he seems to be following a particular course or purpose . . . "

"The oracle of Delphi was considerably more lucid than you are, friend."

"That's because I'm not clear about it in my own mind."

"I gathered that much, Gordianus!"

The old man smiled good-naturedly. "Whatever it is, he wants it badly, I feel, and he won't submit to anything that may keep him from it. Remember how he refused to accept any favors from you? Still, I may be able to persuade him that tutoring little Peter might do them both good."

"Do persuade him. I liked him. Something clear about him. Clean, too. Rather exceptional brain, I should say. I could get him somewhere, if he'd let me."

"He won't let you", Gordianus said. "He'll go his own way, and God alone knows what that will be. You can't *teach* him anything, you can only put your thoughts before him as if you were selling them, and he may or may not buy. But you never need repeat anything. Until I met him I thought young Agapetus was the most intelligent youngster I had ever known . . . though he's my own son . . . but now I'm no longer so sure. Benedictus can ask the most amazing questions. Last week he wanted to know how one could please God on a sliding surface. . . . "

"What did he mean by that?"

"He seems to regard the whole world around him as a sliding surface, with everything giving way and nothing fixed."

"An Archimedean idea", Boethius said, smiling. " 'Give me a fixed point, and I will unhinge the world.' "

"Come to think of it, it's the exact opposite of your Archimedean idea", Gordianus replied. "He's got his fixed point anyway. God. And he doesn't want to unhinge anything. He wants to stand firm and finds he can't do it properly in these surroundings."

Boethius laughed. "He'll fall in love, one of these days, and then everything will look different."

"That might unhinge him," Gordianus admitted, "but somehow I can't see it happening. I shall let you know what he has to say to your idea."

A little to Gordianus' surprise Benedictus accepted, and from then on came every afternoon to look after Peter.

They got on astonishingly well. Peter soon talked. He talked almost too much, and Benedictus was careful not to stop him.

"You're such a patient donkey, Benedictus", the boy said. "The things you permit them to cram into your head all day long! Rhetoric, dialectic, grammar, music, law . . . *ars aequi et boni* they call it, don't they? The noble art of what's right and good. Piffle, more likely than not. Yet there you go, day after day, so early in the morning that it's still pitch-dark and you have to carry your little oil lamp with you because they're too mean to light the schoolrooms. How do you stick to it and why?"

"There are times when I wonder myself", Benedictus admitted wryly. "Much of it, even most of it, is rather artificial."

"Then home to your worthy Cyrilla," Peter went on, "and long discussions with Papa Gordianus about philosophy and things . . . "

"That's different", Benedictus said. "There's substance to that."

"But what is it all for? Do you want to be a philosopher? Only very rich people can afford that. It's a breadless art, they say. Uncle Boethius is very good at it; of course, he's good at everything and he never loses his temper, not even with me."

"I hope I won't, either", Benedictus said.

"Why do you bother about me?" Peter asked point-blank. "You did quite enough, dragging me away from those horses, thought I'm not sure you did the right thing. I may turn out to be a frightfully nasty man, and then it will be all your fault."

"No, it won't. And I would have done the same thing even if I had known for sure that you would become a nasty man." By now he was accustomed to the boy's odd ways, voracious for learning when he felt like it and then suddenly bored and cynical like some of the students at the Athenaeum, sleepily sidestepping questions, with eyes half closed, or grinning faintly, as if he were playing some secret game of his own.

"You'd save just anybody, would you?" Peter shrugged his narrow shoulders. "I wouldn't. It was dangerous, wasn't it? Why risk one's life, unless it's worth it?" He spoke jerkily, his eyes mere slits. "And now you have to play at being my teacher. *That* can't be much fun."

"I like it", Benedictus said, unruffled. "And I'm not here for fun."

"Then you might as well have stayed in Nursia. I mean to say . . . what are we learning all this nonsense for, you and I? Can you imagine a successful man needing any of it for his career?"

"It depends what the career is."

"Oh, anything, as long as it is successful . . . no, don't! Don't pin me down on that one, I know you can tear it to pieces. I wonder why you don't bore me, Benedictus . . . you should, really."

"And I wonder why you don't exasperate me, Peter. You should, really."

"I do, but you won't admit it", Peter said, grinning. "I'll tell you something. You'll never get anywhere. And do you know why? Because you want to be something one can't be *and* get somewhere. You want to be a *good* man. Don't deny it! I know. And who's the best man who ever lived?"

"Our Lord, of course."

"Exactly. And what did they do to him? Beat him, tortured him, crucified him."

"That was not the end of it", Benedictus said.

Peter shook his head. "I don't want to wait until after my death. I want to succeed here. I shall, too."

"You won't, unless you learn something."

"I agree, Benedictus, but what? Not what I've been taught so far . . . except for one thing."

"And what may that be?"

"That one must never do what others want", Peter said. His voice sounded brittle. "One must do only what is good for one's own purpose, for one's own success."

"Success", Benedictus said slowly, "is just another name for Mammon."

"No, it isn't. Mammon's money, and I don't care for money at all. I mean, not very much. I mean, only so far as I need it for *real* success."

"And what is that?"

"To do what one wants", Peter said shrilly. "And never what . . . others want. To use others and not to be used by them."

"But what is it you want?" Benedictus asked. "You haven't told me that yet."

A veil went over the boy's face. "I won't tell you", he said, falling back into his sullen manner. "I won't tell anybody. Not even you."

Benedictus said nothing. He was aghast at what was going on in the boy. He could not fathom it. That speech about "using" people . . .

"Women are the worst", Peter said suddenly.

Benedictus could not help smiling. "Who told you that?"

"No one. But I *know.* Don't laugh, Benedictus. If you want to be a friend of mine, don't laugh."

"I want to be a friend of yours", Benedictus said gravely. "So I won't laugh. But . . . how do you know?"

"It's the only thing I know", Peter told him in a low voice. "And you mustn't ask questions. Let's go back to . . . what was it? History, that's right, the history of Rome. Do you think it's worth while learning about that? Rome is finished . . . they say."

"It can't be", Benedictus replied. "Rome is where Saint Peter is . . . your patron saint. The first Pope. His tomb is here. His successor is here."

"He doesn't have to be," the boy said lightly. "And neither need I. The Pope, you say. Which one? The one in the Lateran or the one in Nuceria?"

"You know quite well that there is only one, and he is here in Rome."

"That's how it is now. A couple of years ago there were two here. Tomorrow there may be two again."

"God forbid", Benedictus said.

"I heard something", Peter whispered. "They may start quarreling again. There's something going on in the Senate, and elsewhere, too. The old man in Nuceria won't give up so easily. Can't blame him either. To be Pope means to have real power, doesn't it? He can bind and loose."

"You are quite insufferable today", Benedictus said, half-amused, half-angry. "I think we'd better go for a walk, to get the cobwebs out of your mind."

There was little pause.

"You forget that I'm a cripple", Peter said between his teeth. "I'm still limping badly. I don't want people to laugh at me."

"They won't", Benedictus said firmly. "And the physician says you will get completely well, so don't you call yourself a cripple."

"I think the man's lying", Peter said. "He probably wants to put hope into us, so that he can come for many more visits and charge for them."

"Peter, Peter . . . not everybody is evil."

The boy's eyes narrowed. "Perhaps not", he said. "Uncle Boethius isn't and you aren't, I think. But the good ones always lose, and I want to win."

6

As usual, Florentius came to fetch the Lady Lelia at Eunike's shop, and as usual he had to wait for an hour before she emerged, with her beauty repaired and brought to full magnificence.

"My dear, you look absolutely divine. I never—"

"Nonsense", she cut in. "The fool of a girl didn't get the curls right. Up, I told her, up, but no, she insists on having it her own way. Never mind." She put a tiny, pale foot on the step of her litter. Her sandals were of gilded leather, studded with opals. "I'm afraid I can't ask you to get in with me", she said. "I don't want to have my robe crushed." She swung herself in and settled down on the cushions, carefully smoothing her robe of green silk. She smiled at his crestfallen expression. "Tell them to go slowly," she said, "and walk beside me, so we can chat."

He obeyed and the six negroes lifted the bars on their shoulders and began to walk.

"A shop like Eunike's shouldn't be in this district, really," she said, "but she won't move. She says if the Anician Palace is here, it is good enough for her, too. I suppose Rusticiana pays her huge fees or something. That's it, over there, behind the pine trees, isn't it? Or is it the larger building on the left?"

"They both belong to it", Florentius replied. "There's a pergola between them, but you can't see it from here."

"So that's where the Young Lions gather. . . . "

"Not any more", he said. "Not since Senator Boethius chose to become a minister to Theodoric."

"Really? So you're ostracizing him for that."

"Oh, we're doing nothing so obvious. One's got to be careful, you know, so we still go there occasionally, some of us, but we mind what we say. I was there last week, or was it the week before? That's a new emerald on that bracelet of yours, surely?"

She laughed. "What if it is?"

"I was only admiring it", he said dryly.

"I bought it at Chrysaphios' shop", she said. "It isn't paid for yet. Now, don't tremble, my Florentius, I know you can't do anything about it. Fifteen hundred solidi Chrysaphios wants for it. Who is the young man?"

"What young man?"

"The one leaving the Anician Palace, of course."

"I don't know. Yes, I do. That's little Peter's new tutor. I met him the last time I was there. Fearfully serious young fellow. When they told him I'm studying for the priesthood, he talked theology to me for half an hour until somebody rescued me."

"He's very handsome", the Lady Lelia said.

"He won't pay for your emerald either", Florentius told her and was given a slight slap with her fan.

"I wish to make his acquaintance", the Lady Lelia declared. "Call him to me, please." She tugged at the silk cord whose end was attached to one of the litter bearers' fingers. At once the man lifted his free arm, and the litter came to a halt.

"My dear Lelia," Florentius protested, "the boy isn't even a Roman. Comes from some dreadful little provincial town . . . "

"There are moments when you make me quite angry", she said. "Will you call him?"

"Oh, very well. Hey, Benedictus!"

A minute later Benedictus found himself introduced to a richly dressed lady of indisputable beauty.

"Florentius has told me about the interesting conversation he had with you last week," the lady said, smiling, "and that made me curious to know more about you."

"We were talking about Saint Augustine's writings", Benedictus said, "and of his studies . . . "

"Yes, yes, quite so. Florentius is going to be a priest some day. You too, perhaps?"

"I have not decided yet. I'm only a student, noble lady."

"What a wonderful thing to be . . . with the whole of life in front of you."

"You'll be late for your party, Lelia", Florentius drawled. "And you're the hostess. Don't you think . . . "

"Who cares? If my friends can't wait for me, they're no friends, I always say. Tell me, Benedictus, what are your plans, I mean for the next few hours?"

"The same as usual, noble lady. To go home, to sup, to work a few hours, and go to sleep."

"All necessary and important things," she said with mock reverence, "but I can't see any reason why you should have to sup at home. Come to my party instead."

"But, noble lady . . . "

"I insist. You will have time enough for your work later on, and a bit of a change will do you good. Also I can promise you that you will meet interesting people. Florentius can vouch for that, can't you, Florentius?"

"Lady Lelia's house is famous for its hospitality", the young man said with reluctant obedience.

"That's settled, then", the lady said sweetly. "And as we're late, you two better had get yourselves a litter. There's one for hire over there; get it, Florentius."

The young man whistled, and the litter approached. Next to Lady Lelia's elegant vehicle with its ornaments of burnished brass, its pale green cushions, and its well-groomed bearers the other looked very shabby.

"In you go, then", Florentius said with ill grace.

"But, look here . . . "

"Oh, come on now. She wants it, doesn't she? No good behaving like a boor."

"Just follow me", Lelia cried cheerfully, and she tugged again at the silk cord.

During the drive Florentius was silent and seemed to be as sullen as little Peter in his worst moments. Benedictus wanted to ask him a dozen questions, but did not. After all, Florentius was several years his senior, he would be a priest in a year or two, and it was he who had made the introduction.

They were late. The party had started without the hostess, and the Lady Lelia was running from one guest to the other, apologizing prettily and exchanging merry courtesies and jokes with the men and barbed courtesies with the women.

"I am so sorry, Sulpicius, what a thing to do to the City Prefect! I know I should have received you at the door, with all my slaves assembled, and given you the kiss of reverence."

"You can give it to me now, Lelia, but I won't insist on the reverence."

"Ye gods! You're much too young to say things like that in public. Pisania, my sweet, that is the most becoming dress I ever saw you in . . . gold everywhere! You must have King Midas for your lover."

"Kind and charming as always, my Lelia; and don't you worry about being late, I told everybody that you were sure to be at Eunike's. She's by far the best beautician in Rome and can do something even with the most desperate cases."

"I only go there for the stories she has to tell", Lelia said, "there's no one like her for little scandals."

A woman with the face of a vulture, topped by a red wig, said pointedly: "I don't think a lady should go to such places at all. One's got one's own slaves for that kind of thing."

"It is a bit of a risk . . . if one doesn't want the world to know one's physical shortcomings, I admit", Lelia said. "Ah, Jubal! I'm so glad you came. When are we going to win lots and lots of money from you again?"

The slender Numidian played with his necklace of gold charms. "Next month, noble lady, when the winter games start."

"Not if you're training in this house, Jubal", Sulpicius said.

The great charioteer showed teeth that would have done honor to a leopard. "I don't have to run", he said. "My horses do that for me, and they aren't being trained here. Don't let them upset you, my lord Prefect."

"No one wants to upset him", Senator Faustus said soothingly. "We're all good Venetans here. At least I think we are. There's a young man I've never seen before. Yes, I mean you. Are you a Venetan or, heaven forbid, a Prasinan?"

"I'm from Nursia", Benedictus said, and his eyes widened when his answer was greeted with a roar of laughter.

"Excellent answer", shouted a young man with his hair set in shiny waves. "So we have three factions now. What's the Nursian color, if I may ask?"

Benedictus had no answer to that. A fat lady, on a couch near his own, stopped nibbling away at a plateful of delicacies to look at him attentively. "What's the matter with you, Apollo?" she asked. "You don't mean to say that you don't know about the Blues and Greens in the circus? Why, they're the only colors that matter, or one of them at least!"

"He looks like a strong boy", the Numidian said, flashing his teeth again. "Come and see me one of these days, and I'll teach you the art."

"He won't be a charioteer", Florentius said. "He's a bookworm."

"Come all the same", Jubal said. "In exchange I'll read a book . . . if you'll teach me how to read."

"Why should you want to read, Jubal?" Senator Faustus said. "Leave that to bookworms and senators. People with real power don't read nowadays. Try this Massican, Count Agila. It tastes like the lips of your first love."

The young Gothic noble said gravely: "You have spoken truth, grayhead. Men of power don't read. They don't have to. And they write only with a stylus five feet long. But there's never any doubt about the meaning of their writing." He belched contentedly and made the muscles of his sword arm move like live animals.

"A grand brute", the fat lady said. "He could lift you with one arm and hold you in midair until you starved to death, my Apollo."

"My name is Benedictus."

"And who cares?" the lady said. "You look like Apollo to me." She was a woman of forty, and she had painted her face in such a way that one could scarcely guess what it was really like. "Are you strong, Apollo? Let me feel your muscles."

The Lady Lelia arrived in a hurry. "My poor boy," she said, "no one's looking after you. But I had to go round and make my apologies. Syrus, come here with that dish. Wine, Timaon. Quickly."

"Another silk dress", the lady next to Benedictus said acidly. "That's the fifth I've seen you wearing in as many weeks."

"So this is silk", Benedictus said naïvely. He wondered whether it was the kind of thing the Lord meant when he spoke of people in soft garments who were to be found in palaces.

"Yes", the Lady Lelia said. "Feel how soft it is."

"Don't tempt Apollo", the fat lady said, laughing. "He's a virginal god. Look, he's blushing."

"What *is* silk?" Benedictus asked.

"It's the fur of some strange, catlike animal that exists only in silk-land, east of India", Lelia explained. "Some people believe it isn't fur at all, but a thread spun by a caterpillar. That's the funniest thing I ever heard. Caterpillars! It's amazing what stupid things some people will believe. Here now, have some of these little birds, stuffed with figs; they're delicious. You have some too, Viria."

"I've eaten far too many of them", the fat lady sighed. "I do believe you give us such lovely food only to spoil our figures so that you can rule supreme. One of your better tricks, my dear."

"There's gratitude for you", Lelia laughed. "Here's Timaon at last. Massican for the noble Benedictus, Timaon. You mustn't leave it all to Count Agila, friend. That's going too far in paying tribute to our fair-haired conquerors."

Benedictus tasted the wine and looked up in surprise. "It's strong", he said. "There can't be any water in it at all. But it's very good", he added politely.

" 'But I believe in wine and not in water' ", Lelia quoted from a poem very much in fashion. " 'I believe in fire and not in warmth. I believe in ardor and not in sweet talk . . . For that is the way of purest passion.' "

"Quiet everybody, Lelia is reciting her Credo", an elderly man at an adjacent table said, grinning. "I'd believe in passion too, Lelia, if you would consent to teach me. . . . "

"I doubt whether any woman could teach you anything,

Servilius", Lelia answered. "And I could call a number of witnesses who would vouch for that."

To Benedictus it seemed that these people had a secret language of their own and yet they were each other's enemies. A kind of sweetish and perfumed hatred hung over the entire room, an invisible cloud, yet they inhaled and exhaled it as if it were their natural element. What was he doing here? What was Florentius doing here, who was studying for an office in which he would be able to call the living God down on his altar and give him to the people?

At the house of Boethius they loved thought and writing—almost too much, perhaps, they seemed to love them for their own sake—but here they seemed to love words only when they hurt and to enjoy things glittering and soft—soft like that silk stuff—mainly because they aroused envy.

He sought Florentius with his eyes, but he had vanished in a swarm of laughing people who were eating and drinking and talking all at the same time.

"You would like to be far away, wouldn't you, my earnest little student?" the Lady Lelia whispered close to his ear. She too was perfumed, but there was nothing sticky and sweet about the smell, it was fragrant and . . .

"I understand", she went on. "This isn't your world, I know, and, believe me, it isn't mine either."

"Then why . . . "

She silenced him, putting a finger to her lips. "Not all of us can live the way we want to. I wonder whether anybody does. Do you?"

"I don't know yet," he said staidly, "but I don't think that is what matters."

"In this room nothing matters", she whispered. "Don't go, I beg of you. You want to, don't you? I can see it in your eyes; they have gone already. Don't go. You're real and these people aren't. They're illusions, nightmares. I must talk to them now, but I beg of you: stay. Stay for my sake. I need you."

She left him, and he could see her resume her game of approaching this table and that, exchanging banter, laughing, ordering slaves about. . . . What did she mean? How could she possibly need him?

They were dicing at the elderly man's table. Two women were standing behind him, leaning over his shoulders, as he threw the dice.

"Nine! Halfway between Venus and the Dog. Next time better", one of the women shouted.

"My turn now", said a cadaverous-looking Greek, shaking the dice in a silver goblet. "Here . . . nine as well. No decision. Tell you what, Servilius. Let's raise the ante to a thousand solidi for this throw."

"Very well", Servilius said with a shrug.

The sums they were betting on! A thousand solidi was the price of a house. A house with a garden.

"Ten", said the Greek. "It isn't too much, but you might have less."

"Hear my prayers, O Mercury", Servilius said, lifting his eyes to the mosaic ceiling in mock worship. "Here I go—one, two, three. . . . "

"Twelve", one of the women shrieked. "Oh, good for you, Servilius."

Scowling, the Greek scribbled a note on a wax tablet, signed it, and gave it to the winner. The women both stretched out their hands, and Servilius drew some gold solidi from his purse for them.

Music shrilled from the end of the room, and everybody turned to look, as a curtain was drawn aside and a woman tumbler began to show her art, walking on her hands, turning cartwheels, and somersaulting in mid-air. She was a young negress, dressed in a few bits of orange-colored cloth; lithe and sinuous, with a large gold ring in her nose.

The Greek liked her. He beckoned his hostess. "Is that animal yours, Lelia, or did you hire her?"

"She's one of Changar's troop", Lelia explained. "He's also got some new ones from India, wizards and magicians and fire-eaters."

"Blackest girl I ever saw", the Greek said. "I'll talk to Changar about her. He usually sells them when they've lost the gleam of novelty."

There was a crash as one of the guests fell under the table, dead drunk. Four slaves hastily lifted him and carried him out.

"Much too early for that sort of thing", the fat lady next to Benedictus said disapprovingly. "That comes from having the wine served neat. Upstart ideas. Lelia should know better. Who's your present love, Apollo? I know it isn't Lelia—not yet. She must be a great talker. She's made you forget how to speak."

What was he doing here? How could she possibly need him? In this whirl of noise and movement and color one could not think.

"Two thousand solidi." Servilius and the Greek were dicing again. There was a juggler on the stage now, a young man in Gallic trousers, filling the air with gold and silver balls and catching them without fail.

The sport enthusiasts were back at race talk and began to lay bets on Typhon and Spirax, Diocles, and, of course, Jubal. The Numidian grinned at them. He was munching grapes.

"I know nothing of all this", Benedictus said aloud, and the fat lady immediately became maternal. "My dear boy, why anybody should drag you into this, I'm sure I don't know. Who picked you up and where? Was it Lelia? Are you a relative of hers, perhaps? You're really from the country, aren't you? Nola, you said; or was it Nursia?"

Somebody said: "Faustus is all for Nuceria, of course."

"He got a lot of money from you-know-where."

"What do you mean?" came the irate voice of the Senator.

"Not you, Faustus. The dear Bishop of Nuceria."

"Nonsense", a voice shrilled. "Byzantium isn't in the least interested in the matter."

"I never said it was Byzantium. Anyway, how do *you* know they're not interested?"

"Why don't you ask Boethius", Senator Faustus suggested with heavy irony. "He's in charge, isn't he?"

"Not of that kind of ecclesiastic affair. He wouldn't know

anything. But I can tell you, there's going to be quite a fight. The Pope can't tolerate . . . "

"Who cares about popes and bishops. Our Gothic friend here must be bored with all this. Well, Count Agila, what about trying this wine for a change? It comes from the slopes of Vesuvius. Fire was its father and molten lava its mother. What do you say?"

But the fair-haired Goth was beyond taking any interest. He was staring into his cup, bleary-eyed and humming a dreary little tune to himself. As they watched him he began to hiccup violently. One of the ladies imitated his expression, then the noise, and Servilius and his two ladies joined in the fun. The others laughed. The young Goth let his head drop forward, strands of his long hair hanging down into his wine. He snored, and they promptly imitated that too.

"That's one conqueror defeated", Senator Faustus said, grinning. "We ought to collect an army of amphorae and send all Goths to sleep. A novel way to regain one's freedom."

"Freedom", Servilius said, shrugging. "Who wants to buy that commodity? We would have to rearm our own population to protect our frontiers. Somebody must pay for all those helmets and swords and all the rest of the military nonsense. Taxes would go up in no time. What's wrong with having the Yellow-hairs as watchdogs? We had them before, by the tens of thousands, and called them the Roman army, and for that bit of misstatement we had to pay them heavily. Now they make their own arms and pay their own way. They don't disturb our way of life too much, do they? Let them stay. It's better for you and me, and what's better for you and me is better for the country."

"Servilius," Senator Maximus said, "you're a great patriot. Be still, Faustus, he is. He's got a good case, a very good case. And that way we can keep our wine for ourselves, too."

"I can tell you where the real trouble is", the Greek said. "It's Boethius and Cassiodor and their crowd."

"Why?"

"Because they stand in the way of good business. I could

have made a marvelous bargain with the city of Capua last month, eleven shiploads of wheat from Sicily. What does the idiot do? Steps in and fixes the price. Naturally, the Capuan city fathers licked his feet for it. Cost me . . . cost me . . . never mind. It's a scandal, really, the whole system of fixed prices."

"I entirely agree", chimed in a senator with a brick red face. "My worthy colleague Boethius is getting a little too big for his boots, and we all know why. King Ox-head has promised him that he'll be Consul one of these days, I mean, years. Consul under King Ox-head, a singular honor. So he must show himself as incorruptible as Marcus Porcius Cato. Last week Flavia's bracelet was stolen. Did the police recover it? Of course not. That's what Boethius should concentrate on. Crime! Not the business affairs of other people."

"Flavia's bracelet?" a lady asked in joyful horror. "Not the new one, the one with the large rubies? She got it from . . . "

"My dear, we all know who gave it to her, I'm sure."

"No, it wasn't Domitillus, it was Count Ludolf."

"Now that's a remark in very doubtful taste, my dear Marcia. Let a girl have as many lovers as she wants. But when it comes to a barbarian . . . "

"Quiet, Servilius."

"Oh, nonsense. That fellow Agila is in the seventh Valhalla or whatever they call the place where their gods drink themselves silly."

"Did you know there's been a petition to King Theodoric to have the Lupercalian festival reintroduced?"

"But of course, my dear, I happen to be a member of the Senate and even King Ox-head is good enough to put petitions signed by a very considerable section of the city's population before us before he decides what's good for us and what isn't."

"Come to think of it," the Greek said, "the city has never been the same since the Lupercalia was abolished."

"But surely that was done because the Church insisted on it. The old fertility rites . . . "

"The Church! That's the trouble with having a heretic as the head of state. He doesn't know how to deal with the Church.

He should have told the Pope to keep his nose in his missal and leave ancient Roman customs alone."

"Ah well", Senator Faustus said, with a shrug.

Benedictus sat motionless but for his fists, clenching and opening. I mustn't hate them, he thought. I may hate the evil in them, but I mustn't hate them. He tried to concentrate on something else and could not. They were mad and horrible, and the best they could offer was indifference. How fond they were of shrugging their shoulders. He had always disliked that movement, he discovered, just because it showed indifference and perhaps even contempt. One should not shrug at all.

"The whole thing is so childish", said the red-haired lady with the vulturelike face, and of course she shrugged, too. "All that running about of naked men, chasing women in the streets, and performing their silly fertility rites . . . after all, that's what it boils down to. So crude, and always the same thing."

"My dear Pylia, it is always good to let the common people enjoy themselves as they understand it, I always say. Besides at your age you are perhaps a little prejudiced against the finer points of the whole thing. Those were the only days when ordinary men could permit themselves certain liberties which on other days . . . "

"Come with me", a voice said near Benedictus' ear, and he rose at once, only too glad to leave the room. The air was stale and reeking of wine and an intolerable cloying sweetness, but there were stronger poisons too, and he wondered how he could have endured it so long.

"You're staggering", the Lady Lelia said. "My poor lamb, the wine was too strong for you."

"I only had one cup", he heard himself say as if from a distance.

This was not the atrium, it was a much smaller room, but the curtains were not drawn and the night lived in it. But even the night air was mild and caressing, not cool and bracing as in Nursia.

Lady Lelia looked quite different, no longer as tense and

drawn and artificial as when she was with those people, but almost serene and just a little sad.

"You didn't like them, did you?" she asked.

"Do you, noble lady?"

"They amuse me, at times. Most of the time they bore me to distraction. And they, too, are bored. Yet so many of them, most of them, are among the richest and the most powerful people in the land. Perhaps . . . you understand better now why I wanted you to come tonight."

"I don't understand at all, noble lady."

"Don't you?" She busied herself with a decanter and some goblets. "Now you and I are going to have a sip of wine together all by ourselves", she said. "No one will disturb us." She put the goblets down very gracefully. Her dress rustled.

"Didn't you know any of them?" she asked.

"Only Florentius."

"Oh, Florentius. Do you know there was a time when I seriously thought I was in love with him? He was very young and fresh and he was going to be a priest, a holy man. That attracted me. I shouldn't tell you that, really."

Did she want him to answer something to that? He could not think of anything.

"Here's your wine", she said. "Drink, my boy, you look as if you needed it."

He said slowly: "It is terrible to hear these people talk of Rome. No wonder God permits us to be ruled by the Goths, if the rich and powerful think only of their pleasures and money affairs, and the poor of bringing back the worst of pagan customs."

"Well put," she remarked lightly, "oh, very well put. You should have a wonderful career, as a lawyer perhaps, or a rhetor, or a priest."

He was speaking of Rome. She was speaking of his career. "Why should a man build a career in such a world?" he asked bitterly.

"Because he has to live", the woman replied, and suddenly she looked older and haunted. "It isn't so easy to live, my

Benedictus, believe me. People try to keep you down, they want to tread on you and use you as a stepping-stone towards their own goal. If you succeed, they jeer at you for not always having been on top, and if you don't succeed, they'll jeer at you for that. Life is dirty, Benedictus, you don't know that yet. I wonder whether a saint could keep clean if he lived in Rome."

"From what I have seen and heard today . . . "

"That was nothing. You've no idea what these people are capable of, what they have done and are doing to each other. Remember Pylia, the awful woman with her red wig? She's done away with two husbands. Poisoned them. It could never be proved, of course, trust her for that, but I know she did it. One's got to invite her—everybody does—because otherwise she'd launch a campaign against one, anonymous letters, bribe government officials, make lying accusations in court or in private, anything to ruin you. And Servilius! He cheated his wife out of her money and loses it all to Lukides—that's the Greek with whom he was dicing tonight. Lukides lets him win at dice, occasionally, and then wins a hundred times more from him in some shady business deal. He has a dozen senators in his pocket, *and* the city prefect as well."

"You mean . . . "

"Yes, my innocent, I mean that he bribes them."

"It is not possible, it can't be. . . . "

"That's how it is, you great big child. Why do you think I'm telling you all this? I watched you. I saw you look so horrified, so disgusted—so that's the world the Lady Lelia lives in! But you live in it, too! These people are your senators and high officials and administrators. It is the world of Rome. And don't think you can change it. No one can."

"God can."

"Then why doesn't he? He must have given us up."

"Too many of us are giving *him* up."

She sighed. "My sweet friend, I just want you to understand that one needn't be horrible in order to put up with a horrible world . . . however difficult it is to keep oneself untouched.

When you think of these people, I don't want you to regard me as one of them. And that's what you would have done. You would have thought 'Such is Lelia's world, and I hate it and hate her, and thank God I have nothing to do with it.' After all, you know very little about me."

"That is true."

"I'm a Sempronia, on my mother's side", she said, and she drew herself up a little. "We have given great men to Rome in the past. My father, Titus Lelius, was a shipowner. He lost most of his money to Lukides. To pay his debts I had to marry a wealthy man. But my father died three days after my marriage; and my husband two years later. He was then seventy-six." She closed her eyes. "I haven't been very lucky, have I?"

Deep compassion welled up in him. She was still young and she looked frail and unhappy. There was no one to protect her. . . .

"I told you about Florentius, and that I thought I was in love with him, didn't I? I believed in him, at the time, I thought he was good and pure, but I soon found out that he was no better than the others, just greedy and out for his own advantage, a talker of fine words. . . . "

He began to understand how safe and protected his own life had been, and his sister's, back in Nursia. And even here in Rome, as long as he saw nothing but the Athenaeum and his own dingy room.

She smiled at him helplessly. "I can't get away from all this by myself", she said. "I only wish I could . . . "

"What can I do to help you?" he asked almost gruffly.

"Nothing . . . and yet everything", she said. "It does make a difference, I know, that a decent, clean man believes in you. And I feel you are just that, Benedictus; I knew it as soon as I set eyes on you." She let her head drop on her folded hands. "Florentius didn't like it when I invited you", she added, smiling. "He was afraid . . . "

"Afraid?"

"But of course. He knew you were what he only pretended to be. He knew he was going to lose me. Will you help me,

Benedictus? Will you come and talk to me, be with me, protect me . . . not against *them*"—she moved her head a little in the direction of the banquet room; the sound of music was coming from there and gusts of shrill laughter—"but against myself. I don't want to become as they are. Will you help me, my sweet friend?" She stretched out her hands to him. "Now you know why I need you", she whispered.

Her slender fingers began to draw him towards her.

"My lady," he stammered, "if I am to help you . . . " But he felt his strength ebbing. Her lovely face was coming nearer and nearer, time itself began to recede as her arms went around him. Her lips sought his mouth in hungry submission. "I love you", she said breathlessly. "O God, I love you. . . . "

God. She said God. But this was not the love God wanted, this was a different thing, hot and greedy and overpowering, the sweetness was deadly peril, the bones of a death's-head were behind it, and he gasped and struggled to free himself.

"How charming", a thick voice said.

Instantly she released him and swung round to face the intruder.

"I thought as much", Florentius said. His face was swollen with rage and drunkenness. "Can't you be faithful to any one man for more than a few months, you . . . "

"Go away", she snarled. "Go back where you came from, you drunken animal."

"So you're supposed to save her now", Florentius said contemptuously. "She always wants to be saved, it's such a convenient habit with a certain type of man. I thought she might try it on you, too. Did she tell you the same story she told me? The old husband she had to marry to save her father? The poor, misunderstood young widow, delivered to the beasts of society? A pack of lies, all of it. She never . . . "

"Beast yourself", the Lady Lelia shrilled. "I'll ruin you for this."

Suddenly Florentius burst into tears. "I can't do without you", he sobbed. "It's hell to be away from you. I don't know how you've done it, but I must be with you. Have pity on me. . . . "

"You go and be a priest", she snapped. "That's all you're good for."

At long last Benedictus could move again. Trembling, pale as a sheet, he turned and walked away.

"Stay", the woman's voice rang out behind him. "Don't leave me, Benedictus . . . come back to me . . . come back . . . can't you see that he's lying? . . . come back. . . . "

There was a burning urge in him to turn once more and look at her, frail and beautiful and in need of help; and another that forbade the very thought of it, hard and cold like a sword, and he knew them both and which must be obeyed. He walked out and through the atrium and into the street and on and on, unthinking, his steps quickening. The only thing that mattered was to increase the distance between him and the woman and her world.

7

HE WALKED AND WALKED and there was no end to the city, stretching into a murky, eyeless eternity. Two-legged rats were scurrying by, and litters passed, like whitish cocoons in the starlight. Columns and arches stood boasting silently of long past victories. Drunks vomiting . . . street girls emerging from dark houses, like beetles crawling from under a stone, painted, bewigged, and smiling. They all looked like her and were her. The enemy's world was loosed, and he must escape.

His head ached and his legs seemed leaden, as in a nightmare.

The streets became darker and dirtier, the houses ramshackle and threatening: Come in and be buried, we are all rubble and so are you. Then they were houses no longer, only rubble, a mass of stone and broken things. Pottery broke under his feet, hundreds of broken pots and other vessels, hills of it, a mountain of it, and it came to him, dimly, that this was a place of which he had heard, although he had never seen it before: Mons Testaccus, the Hill of Shards, the place where were dropped all broken things. The Hill of Shards, the eighth hill of Rome.

He stumbled over debris; the sour smell of age and decay, of staleness and filth in his nostrils. Broken bricks and broken marble, rot and disintegration, and everywhere the powdery dust from which all matter came and to which it must return, eyes and lips and smiles and graceful movements, skin and hair and bones, to this they would all come in the end. The world without blessing.

He threw himself headlong into a thicket of sharp splinters and jagged debris to tame the beast the enemy had roused. The body, so ready to surrender, must be forced into subjection again. And by that act, rough and wild and almost mad, he regained detachment, he was no longer part and parcel of a world condemned. With blood flowing from many wounds, he was able to pray again.

"Where am I to go?" he prayed. "Where can I go so that I may serve you as you wish to be served? I am not a saintly sage like Abbot Fulgentius, so full of heaven that, of your grace and of his charity, he can see it everywhere, even in Rome; a man who can look back on his life and see it as an offshoot of heaven itself. I am young and have only just seen something of the power of the enemy; I have seen the dance of the living dead, and it has led me to the Hill of Shards. I know now that the city itself is no more than this hill, a place of broken ambitions and of futile successes, and that only three things in it are holy: the blood of its martyrs, the tomb of the apostles, and the presence of the Church. Give me a sign, Lord, in what way you want me to serve you and, whatever it is, I will do it."

He returned home just before dawn, dirty, disheveled, and with bloodstains all over his body.

Three days later old Father Gordianus came to see him. "It's only for a very short visit", he said, "to tell you that I won't be able to come again this week or next—But you're looking pale, you're not ill, I hope?"

"I was ill. I am all right now."

Gordianus nodded. "Roman air is not healthy these days", he said. "There's trouble brewing. Bishop Laurentius has been seen in Rome—you know, the Bishop of Nuceria."

Nuceria. They had been talking about him . . . there. What had they said? Money . . . something about money from Byzantium.

"You perhaps remember the trouble we had with him a few years ago", Gordianus went on, "when he almost caused a kind of civil war. Heaven preserve the Church from such scandals."

"I had only just arrived at the time, venerable Father, and I never quite understood what was happening."

The old man sighed. "A minor part of the clergy decided to proclaim Laurentius pope", he said. "The entire city was split into two camps. There was fighting in the streets, in the very churches. Both parties appealed to the King and the King settled it—or so we thought at the time. But apparently the Bishop of Nuceria has been in Rome several times since then and he seems to have support from outside Italy. . . . "

"Byzantium?" Benedictus asked, and he bit his lip.

"It is possible." Gordianus nodded. "But a number of our senators are supposed to be great friends of his as well. Now we hear that he has launched an official accusation against the Holy Father, in Ravenna, and that Theodoric has sent another bishop as his judge to deal with the case." The old man was near tears. "It is a terrible thing", he said, "that worldly power should interfere with the Church in such a way. What times we are living in, Benedictus! What good is it to think and meditate about holy things when our very house is falling down upon us."

"But the Church cannot perish", Benedictus said. "Our Lord himself said so."

"That is true, son, but the Church would still be alive if only you and I were left in it to regain other souls, and I cannot think of anything more frightful than kings and emperors using the bishops as pawns in some game of their own."

The dance of death was still going on, the game of the enemy was spreading. Life is dirty, the woman said. Don't think you can change it. No one can. And you, too, are living in it.

"There will be another synod", Gordianus said. "Bishops are coming in from all over Italy, from Gaul, and even from Spain. I have heard dreadful speeches made by men who should proclaim the Gospels: that the Pope was upheld only because King Theodoric believed Laurentius to be supported by the Emperor of Byzantium and that all the accusations, or some of the accusations, made against him were true."

"And . . . are they?"

"By my soul's salvation, no", Gordianus broke forth. "I *know* they're not. But it's all so subtly done, so devilishly put together that it has the ring of truth. Angels themselves could be led into doubt. And all the signs of discord are here again, people whispering and conspiring, clashes between neighbors . . . as if it were a quarrel between the factions of the circus."

The Venetans. The Prasinans. We're all good Venetans here. What are you?

"Evil lies ahead", Gordianus said sadly. "I even fear for the Holy Father's life. You don't know what these people are capable of."

You don't know what they have done and are doing to each other.

"The new synod is going to take place next week", Gordianus said. "In the Basilica Julia in the Trans Tiberium. My son and I will be present. Not at the actual assembly, of course, but to accompany the Holy Father and protect him on his way there and back . . . if we can. Anything could happen."

Was that the answer to his question on the Hill of Shards?

Could there be anything more pleasing to God than to protect the successor of Saint Peter?

Benedictus took a deep breath. "I shall come with you", he said.

8

THE BISHOPS WERE WALKING in a double file, one hundred and fifteen of them, with Pope Symmachus in their midst, under a swaying canopy. On either side two rows of men marched, many of them ecclesiastics, mostly of the lower orders, doorkeepers, lecturers, exorcists, and acolytes, though some were priests, like Gordianus. But there were laymen too.

Benedictus was marching beside a young coppersmith; just in front were Gordianus and his son Agapetus, a young man of twenty-three or -four who would be a priest himself soon.

The streets were strangely quiet. Far fewer people were there to watch the papal procession than on the day when King Theodoric entered Rome, Benedictus thought. And those who had turned up, seemed to behave in an extraordinary way. Instead of lining up in rows on both sides of the streets, they clustered together in groups of a hundred, or two and three hundred. Some of these groups cheered, others remained sullenly silent or shouted insults.

Twice hostile groups clashed, and the municipal guards had to separate them. A rumor ran along the procession that two men had been killed and several severely injured.

Benedictus prayed for the dead and the wounded and so did Gordianus and his son. Disunity within the Church . . . it was almost unthinkable. And now it had led to bloodshed. What would the martyrs say, looking down from high heaven, they who had shed their blood to confess and confirm the Faith? What sort of age was this when people could kill each other and think they were doing it in the service of the Faith?

It had happened before, he knew that. But then the conflict had been between Catholics and Arians, or Donatists, Valentinians or whatever their names were. Now Catholic was fighting Catholic in the name of the Faith. It was unheard of.

The Basilica Julia loomed up before the procession and absorbed it, a long trail of learned, zealous, and holy men, each of them a successor of the Apostles. The men who guarded them stayed outside to keep watch at the door. Only the bishops were allowed to be present at the unique and frightening trial of a successor of Saint Peter himself.

Could they really try him? Did they have the power, legally and spiritually, to do so? Most likely they would have to debate that, before they could commence the case itself.

A few of the two hundred-odd men outside went home for their noon meal. The others sat down on the steps, relieved that the first part of their task was over. None of them spoke, and into their silence came from time to time the sound of muffled voices from within the basilica. They were tired and thirsty and at least some regretted that they had let their sense of duty prevail over their appetite, instead of joining those who were now munching away at their *pulsum* and meat and washing it down with good red wine. The year was late, but it was hot, and Father Gordianus said, frowning, that he did not like the feel of the sky. "What do you mean, Father?" Agapetus asked, and the old man said crossly, "What I said"; but after a while he added, "The truth is that I don't really know what I mean . . . except that there is something leaden and heavy in the air. If we were near Vesuvius, I would know what it is." As young Agapetus looked up to him fondly, Benedictus saw for the first time how much they resembled each other.

Just then the Noise came.

At first it sounded like low and distant thunder, and some of the men looked up. But the sky was clear and cloudless. The thunder grew, there were screams, and then, terrified, they saw a mass of people bursting into the square, a mob of a thousand, of two thousand and more, intermingled with a few hundred municipal guards who were trying in vain to form a solid line. Wherever some of them succeeded, the chain was broken a moment later.

"Great God in heaven", Gordianus said in a shaken voice, "they are going to storm the basilica."

As if an order had been given, the watchers stood up as one man to form a tight mass around the church door.

An officer of the municipal guards raced onto the steps. He was a small man, but wiry, with a jutting chin and a firm mouth. "Soldiers, to me!" he shrieked and fifteen, twenty, thirty of his men managed to join him. The others were still caught in the thick, ugly flood of people like scarlet dots on the flanks of a large, twitching fish.

The entrance was guarded. The mob had filled the square, but there was no attack as yet.

"Attilius!" the officer said. "Probus! Off with you to the station post at the Circus Maximus. Ask for reinforcements. Two hundred men at least. Three hundred would be better. Avoid all fighting. You must get through. Move slowly through the crowd or they'll stop you. As soon as you're out of sight, run as fast as you can."

The two soldiers obeyed in a casual manner.

The officer turned. "Anybody here who knows whether there are other entrances to the basilica?" he asked.

"There are three more", a priest answered, "one on each side and a small one in the rear."

The officer cocked his head, listening. "There are more of 'em coming from the Via Minervina and the Amphitheatre", he said. "Lucius! Rutilus! Trebonius! Collect a dozen men, each of you, and guard those other doors. Be quick about it. Report here only in case there's real danger."

In a quarter of an hour he received a report that a mob of two hundred was trying to storm the small door in the rear, and almost immediately afterwards the same thing was reported from the eastern door.

"I can't hold this building much longer", he said. "It'll take at least half an hour before I get reinforcements, perhaps more. We must tell the holy bishops that they'll have to go elsewhere. If they stay, they'll be massacred. I can protect them on the way . . . I hope. Who's the senior priest here?"

"I think I am", Gordianus said. "But . . . "

"Then come with me into the basilica."

Gordianus stared at him. "No one is allowed to enter—" he began, but the officer cut him short.

"You don't understand", he snapped. "We've *got* to get in . . . or the mob will be, in fifteen minutes. It's a matter of life and death. Death probably, *but* outside there'll at least be a fighting chance."

As he was speaking, stones began to fly at the defenders of the main door. The municipal soldiers blocked most of them with their shields, but even so a few found their targets, and there were screams and shouts. The officer took Gordianus' arm, and they entered the basilica.

Benedictus and Agapetus looked at each other. The son of Gordianus was slim and not too sturdily built; he had the eyes of a dreamer. "I never thought I would have to wage war", he said with a timid smile. Benedictus smiled back at him, encouragingly. "Anything can happen in this service of ours."

Agapetus' eyes lit up. Neither of them had done any soldiering, and neither had been in physical danger before. Now they began to find it exhilarating in a strange, sharp-edged way.

"This is not the moment to turn the other cheek", Agapetus declared. "These people are not out to insult us, they want to insult and hurt the Holy Father."

"And we are here for the purpose of preventing it", Benedictus added. "But I wish I had a stick; a big one."

"So do I. Perhaps we could seize a couple from the enemy. Look at that . . . there are some fellows carrying burning torches. Heavens above, they intend to set fire to the basilica!"

"And they call themselves Christians!" Benedictus exclaimed.

"Some of them may be. But there are a good many types from Subura among them who don't look baptized to me."

A burning torch flew over their heads, crashed against the wall and fell into the swarm of defenders. There were shrieks of pain, but the torch was trampled underfoot and put out.

The officer emerged from inside, with Gordianus behind him, and as he bellowed orders, the municipal soldiers began to take up a new formation. He drew his sword and raised it. "Men of Rome," he roared, and the mob fell silent for a moment. "The procession will leave this church and go elsewhere", he shouted. "I'm in charge. And my men have orders to use their swords, if there's any nonsense from you. Give way, then, and go home. There's nothing for you here."

The mob roared angrily.

"Draw swords", the officer ordered. Benedictus caught a glimpse of his eyes and saw with a shock that the man was frightened and trying hard to hide it.

Agapetus was looking at his father. Gordianus was very pale, and his eyes were filled with tears. The young coppersmith came up. "We won't be together, this time", he told Benedictus. "We are to march in a single file. The soldiers will be on the outside." He looked at Benedictus obliquely to see whether he was afraid.

"Very sensible", Benedictus said soberly. "They have shields, and we haven't."

"I should have brought my hammer", the coppersmith said with profound regret.

The first miters appeared in the entrance, and the mob surged forward, only to be pushed back vigorously by the soldiers.

"Out of the way", the officer yelled, and he gave the sign to advance. Slowly the procession began to push itself into the milling, throbbing mass of the square, with twenty soldiers as the spearhead. More and more miters appeared from inside the basilica. The bishops looked wan and upset. Benedictus tried in vain to get a glimpse of the Pope. Were they trying to get him out through another door?

"Now you." The officer pointed to Gordianus and his group, and they took up their places next to the mitered men. The procession was again six deep, with a double file of bishops in the middle, and the lower ecclesiastics and laymen in a single file on each side, each flanked by a single file of soldiers. Now the canopy appeared.

Progress was slow. The soldiers had to push and more than once cut their way through. Stones were still being thrown, and two bishops were wounded and had to be supported; but they moved on.

"The plague on you, you scum", shouted the young coppersmith. "Can't you leave these holy men alone?"

He saw the stone, ducked, and it flew across the procession and crashed into the mob on the other side, causing yells and fury.

"They must walk quicker, Attilius", the officer in charge said out of the corner of his mouth.

The soldier gaped at him. "Am I to tell the Pope how he ought to walk, tribune?"

"Yes, if he wants to stay alive."

Frightened, Attilius obeyed, and the bishops complied, walking as quickly as dignity and the pressure of the mob would allow. The soldiers clearing the way, lunged at the assailants with their swords.

"There has never been a procession like this", Agapetus ejaculated. "Father, where are we going? Is it far?"

"To the Church of the Holy Cross of Jerusalem, son. That, they can assail for weeks without success. The Holy Father himself suggested it, and the bishops agreed."

"How did he take it?"

"He was quite calm. But he said he was sorry for the people who were stirred up to such crimes by evil men. He asked all the bishops to pray for them."

Benedictus' eyes lit up.

"But the accusers—" Gordianus said and then broke off.

"What about them, Father?"

"They said terrible things against him . . . and in his defense terrible things were said against them. I only heard a few sentences . . . before we could make our presence known . . . but it has bitten into my life."

"But the accusations were lies, surely?"

"Of course they were. I should know. I have been the Holy Father's friend for more years than you carry. I know his heart. But to hear such words from consecrated lips . . . "

At that moment the storm broke loose. A swarm of wild-eyed, determined men rushed straight at the middle of the procession, just behind the canopy over the Pope's head, which was now weighted down by a dozen stones, and so fierce was the impact that the procession broke in two.

The officer shouted and pointed with his sword, but more men threw themselves in the way of the soldiers trying to run towards the breach, and around the canopy all was in upheaval.

"The Holy Father", Gordianus cried. "Save the Holy Father!" He struggled like a madman to get back. Agapetus and Benedictus tried to keep pace with him, but were forced to exchange blows with a number of ruffians who were pressing them back. The canopy pitched, rolled, and in the end fell like a dying animal, and for the first time Benedictus saw the Pope, an elderly man, hook-nosed, austere, standing immobile, with his hands folded, he alone quiet in the maelstrom of movement.

A stone whirred past him. He did not move his head. Around him a thin wreath of bishops was trying to shield him as the petals of a flower shield the calyx.

When a one-eyed man lifted a stone and threw it ferociously, Benedictus instantly saw that his aim was true. Throwing himself forward he knew instinctively that he was too late. He saw Gordianus raise himself to his full height, his arms outstretched. The stone hit his skull with such force that Benedictus could hear its impact despite the noise around him. Then at long last he and Agapetus were there, covering the gap with their own bodies, hitting out mechanically. From somewhere came the sound of a voice praying aloud the prayers for the dying: it was the voice of the Pope; a stone had knocked the miter from his head, and he was holding up his folded hands.

Trumpets sounded and for one wild moment Benedictus thought this was the call of Judgment Day, surely this was the day for it. Then suddenly the attack welled back, a great shout went up, and there was a new sound, a clattering of hooves; it was the mounted guards from the Circus Maximus.

The mob wavered, recoiled, and ran. One strong detachment of mounted soldiers drove off the stragglers, another surrounded the shaken ecclesiastics. It was all over in a few minutes.

Benedictus bent down to Gordianus in Agapetus' arms. "He is safe," he cried, "and it was you who saved him."

Then he saw that the old man was dead. The missile had broken his skull. Agapetus' face was like stone.

Benedictus stood, transfixed. Gordianus, the venerable, the wise, had left the earth. The pain in his heart was hot and searing, but it was enshrined in a feeling much greater. There was sorrow for the dead, still greater pain for poor Agapetus. But Gordianus had died the most glorious death, laying down his life for another man, and that man the Father of Christendom and his friend. He was the true victor of the battle, triumphant, taken up to the throne of God, a martyr, whose blood was sacred as the thing most fertile on earth. This was the fertility rite of Christ, the Lupercalian festival of the New Testament.

And yet, even that was not the ultimate. Still higher, still deeper the thought stirred and came alive that there was only one victory and one triumph for a man, to come as close to God as grace and will could lead him. Gordianus had taken heaven by a single assault. But his way was not granted to all. And Benedictus prayed that by the blood of Christ's martyr Gordianus he, too, would be shown his way to God.

He did many things, then, that had to be done. He helped Agapetus carry the martyr's body away, to find a litter, and to take him home. He spent the night with the bereaved young man.

When he returned home at last, Cyrilla rushed up to him, with the indignant relief of an old woman who discovers that all her fears were unnecessary, but she stopped short before him. "Dear young master . . . what has happened to you? You . . . you look so different."

He passed a weary hand over his forehead. "I am leaving Rome", he said.

"What? You are not giving up your studies?"

"Yes, I am."

"But . . . why?"

"There must be a shorter way and a more direct one."

"Where to?"

"To God."

9

To escape from Rome was not as easy as he had thought. At first, Benedictus considered disappearing overnight. But that would not have been right towards a number of people. A man who knew that he was dying must put his house in order. A man who knew he was dying to the world must do likewise. He wrote a letter to his father, and that proved to be the first difficulty. How could he explain what to himself was still a hazy and unformed plan? "I must be where I can be as near to God as possible", he wrote. "I found I did not get any nearer by my studies here. The world of Rome is one long chain of dangers, and much of it is held in captivity by the enemy. People here think that the enemy is the Goth, or a rival in business or another faction in the games of the circus; they do not look for him where he really is, within them, ruling their desires and inciting them to wrong action. I thought of the priesthood. But to be a priest in Rome makes one part of many currents whose very nature opposes tranquillity of mind and makes close and constant union with God possible only for those of a very exalted state of soul. I am not holy enough to meditate while all around me stones are thrown. The body grows without our will, but the soul does not, I think. I must be alone with God to find out what he wants of me and how I can best serve him." He did not add that for exactly that reason he could not return to Nursia, however much he missed his father's grave courtesy, the deep tone of his voice at prayers; the tomb of his mother; his sister's boundless joy in life and in learning—she had been christened quite differently, but everybody called her Scholastica, because she always had her little nose in a book; yes, and the picture over his bed, the Virgin holding the Child, and the Child holding a Cross. When he was six, his father gave it to him. "This is something you must learn early, Benedictus. Never think of the Blessed Mother of God without thinking of her Child; and never think of the Child without thinking of the Cross." But all this meant not only sweet memories, but also protection; and he must have no protection where he was going.

The next difficulty was leaving Agapetus, still deep in mourning for his martyred father; and another was that he had to inform Senator Boethius that he would be giving up his visits to little Peter. And there was Peter himself.

Agapetus understood at once. "You must go, Benedictus, just as I must stay and in due course take my father's place in the priesthood." He was filling another breach.

"You'll do that", Benedictus said, and to his own surprise he added: "You will do more, and your way will lead you to the wheel of the ship." Whatever made him say that? The words were out before he was aware of their presence in his mind.

Agapetus looked at him strangely, but said nothing.

There was no need, at least, to worry about the safety of the Pope. The bishops had exonerated him of all accusations, and Laurentius had fled back to Nuceria.

Senator Boethius received Benedictus' news with kind equanimity. He was sorry to hear that he was leaving, but he had always known that such a gifted young man could not go on for long wasting his time on a boy like Peter. What exactly did he intend to do?

"I am not sure yet", Benedictus said slowly. "I think I shall have to live as a hermit. I am not ready for anything else . . . perhaps I never shall be."

"A hermit", Boethius repeated. "My dear boy, are you sure you're ready for *that?* Forgive me for asking, but it is not only a hard life, the hardest of all, I should think, it also has its own set of laws and dangers, and you are very young."

Benedictus smiled. "That shortcoming at least diminishes a little every day."

There was twinkle in Boethius' eyes. "I am glad you haven't lost your sense of proportion", he said. "It is the basis of that invaluable thing, a sense of humor. But where do you intend to go?"

"To some solitary place in the mountains . . . the Sabine mountains, perhaps, or the Abruzzi."

Boethius nodded. "At least it's a healthy climate, though it can be very cold in winter. And you'll be near places like Tibur or Enfide. You'll find some very fine people living in the hills. They may be able to assist you. Now, don't tell me again that you have no need of assistance. God uses men to help men. I feel rather sorry for Peter. It will hit him badly, I fear. You'll say good-bye to him, won't you?"

Little Peter took a deep breath when Benedictus told him, and for one moment it looked as if he might be going to cry. He did not. His eyes were oddly clear and hard as he said: "Of course you must go. Everyone must do what he thinks is good and useful for him. You want to be a monk or something like that. So a monk you'll be."

"I don't know what I shall be, Peter."

"I also shall do what is good and useful for me, when the time comes", Peter said, and his voice sounded high and cracked. "So I suppose I cannot expect you to act differently than I would act myself."

"There is only one service overriding all others—"

"Yes, yes, I know. But how do you know you're really

doing what God wants? Maybe you only think so, and what you're doing is really what you want yourself."

"Your thoughts are older than your age, Peter, but are they good? There is bitterness in them and, I think, mockery. Yet I will answer you. The fact that I want a thing, does not make that thing either better or worse. What God wants must be good. To do what he wants is duty and sacrifice only when I don't want to do it, but when I do, it's joy. In fact, there is no greater joy. There can't be. When the day comes for you to decide about your aim in life, ask yourself first whether it *can* be what God wants, and if the answer is an honest yes, go and do it and you will be happy, whatever comes."

Peter grinned. "You and Uncle Boethius are the only good people who have an answer to everything. Whether the answer is true, life alone can show. Good-bye, uncle monk. I don't think we shall ever meet again."

"We shall when you need me", Benedictus said, and once more he did not know what made him say this.

But the greatest difficulty of all was Cyrilla, and here he failed. That her young master was leaving Rome was quite all right. That he was giving up his studies was of course a great pity, but it was not for her to remark on it. She knew her station, although she had carried him in her arms when he was a baby. But to go alone, without her, that was impossible, that was out of the question. She had promised her master, Eupropius, to serve his son faithfully and look after his needs and that she was going to do. If he were going to enter a monastery, where she would not be allowed, that would be a different thing, for there he would be provided for, however badly. But as long as a monastery door had not closed behind him she was going to stay with him or go with him wherever he went, even to the two-headed men on the faraway Islands of Spice or the one-footed people in India.

No arguments, no pleadings, and least of all an attempt to be severe made the slightest impression on her, and she watched him with Argus eyes, to make sure that he did not slip away in secret.

He left the city by the Tiburtine Gate, carrying a staff and a small bundle with a spare tunic and a few other things.

He never looked back, but he knew that Cyrilla followed not far behind him and he walked slowly, lest she get tired.

The Tiburtine Gate was magnificent, triumphal. One would never think that the Emperor who had it built almost a hundred years ago, Honorius, had been no more than a plaything in the hands of his German minister, Stilicho, who virtually ruled Rome and the Western Empire. And after Stilicho had come Alaric of the Visgoths, Athaulf, Genseric of the Vandals, the Suevian Ricimer, the Herulian Odovacar, and now Odovacar's conqueror, Theodoric of the Ostrogoths.... Germans, all of them.

For a hundred years one powerful German after another had ruled Rome and the Roman world. Who would come after Theodoric? Yet the Romans went on as if their rulers did not exist, or rather, they pretended not to be aware of their own position.

Benedictus remembered the cry of the holy Bishop Martin of Tours: "Who, in the face of captivity, can think of the circus? Who can go to his own execution, laughing merrily? We are living in fear of slavery, but we go on playacting; we are threatened with death, but all we think of is amusement. One would think that all the people of Rome had eaten Sardinian herbs... dying and laughing at the same time."

The landscape before Benedictus did not laugh. The campagna looked like a huge lake whose waves had been turned into stone in the midst of a storm. The stone was lava. Volcanoes had ruled here before either Romans or Germans, and the signs of their reign might well outlast the Tiburtine Gate in all its glory.

After an hour and a half he reached the Anio River at the Mammaelian Bridge and turned towards the chain of blue hills in the faraway upriver country.

In the plain the air was foul with sulphur fumes, born from the deep craters of the volcano Sulfatara, now filled with gloomy, stinking water.

But after a while the scene changed. Green prevailed, and the silvery gray of olive groves on the slopes of the first hills. High up on the summit lay Tibur, the city of the rich. The hill was dotted with villas, the refuge of the wealthy families, when summer made Rome an ill-smelling mass of stone, scorchingly hot, and permeated by the fetid emanations of the sewers and Subura.

And here, almost untouched after four centuries, were the monumental buildings of Emperor Hadrian, the great aesthete, the magnanimous protector of the arts, the paragon of pagan Rome. Himself a divinity, he was courteous enough to erect temples for other deities, both Roman and foreign, for Apollo, Hercules, and Serapis. But these were only part of the grandiose scheme to build, on a single hill, a small but exquisite reproduction of the entire Roman world. Here was the Academy, hall and garden for Peripatetic philosophers; the Lyceum, the stadium for circuses and games; the Prytaneum, the public dining hall; the perfect imitation of the Poecile, the market hall of Athens. Here were the reproductions of the famous Vale of Tempe in Thessalía and of a Serapeum of Egypt, a hall of columns, three theatres, a palaestra for fencing and wrestling, a library. There were large barracks for the Praetorian Guards and, in the midst of it all, there was the imperial palace.

Benedictus, slowly ascending the road towards the mountains, saw the whole magnificence of pagan Rome, the essence of it in pure marble, the empire compressed in such a way that its Emperor could see it all in a single glance, as Benedictus now did. But now there was no life in it. The merry eaters, the worshipers of Serapis, the courtiers and philosophers, the Praetorian Guards, and the imperial aesthete himself with his pretty friend Antinoüs were dead, as dead as pagan Rome.

And here was a tiny chapel. Benedictus remembered Gordianus telling him about it, the chapel in memory of Symphorosa and her seven sons. They were Christians and they had been living here when Hadrian decided to dedicate his new palace. The priests of Apollo, god of Art, told him that the god would remain silent forever and the place be accursed, as long as people were living there who denied him adoration. Hadrian had a strong dislike for curses. He ordered the woman and her sons to renounce their faith. They refused. Hadrian was not, on the whole, cruel, but he was not going to have a pleasant life interfered with by the stupid obstinacy of common people. He decided to have them killed in a style that would placate any god he knew. He was not sure whether the gods existed, but he would not take unnecessary risks. He had the woman first tortured and then drowned in the Anio. The seven young men were chained to seven stakes, placed at mathematically exact distances around the temple of Hercules and killed, each in a different way. Even when he was forced to be cruel, Hadrian remained an artist.

The little chapel had been built on the remains of the temple of Hercules, the only building in ruins, due to a local earthquake.

Benedictus prayed in the chapel for a while and then walked on, with his shadow and Cyrilla's lengthening behind them as the day aged.

He reached the height of the pass and left Tibur behind him. The large villas of the rich, too, were deserted, except for skeleton staffs. "Everybody" was in Rome at this season. But the great Anio Falls were there, cascading down into the plain as they had done in Hadrian's time and a thousand years before Hadrian or any Roman Caesar. The air was filled with the dance of a host of diamonds, spraying in all directions and uniting again to quick-flowing water in the river bed. There was nothing lifeless about the Anio.

Beyond Tibur, the Via Valeria led through rough valleys past Varia, and on the right, across the river, hewn high up in the rocks were the cells of monks.

Benedictus stopped. For a long time he stood, looking at them, waiting. But nothing spoke in his heart, and he went on. He reached Sublacum, the city in the Simbruvian hills, and left it after a short rest and a meal of bread, cheese, and fruit which he shared with Cyrilla. "Tired?" he asked her.

"Not a bit", she declared defiantly. "Would be the first time in my life that I got tired before you did, young master."

He smiled. To Cyrilla he was still the child she had put to bed every night and then gone on with her housework.

"Nevertheless," Cyrilla said, "it would be nice to know exactly where we're going . . . in case you know yourself."

By way of answer he rose and walked on. About an hour later they came to a village very different from those they had seen. It was a village, not a town. But unlike others, there was nothing rough or primitive about it, and it was amazingly clean. The houses were built in a triple circle around the church and every one of them had a little garden of its own. None of them looked as luxurious as the smallest of the villas of Tibur, but all looked comfortable and snug. Cyrilla gave a deep sigh. "Young master," she said, "I lied to you. I was tired in Sublacum. Now I'm *very* tired. We've been on our feet for seven hours on end. So unless the place you want to go to is very near . . . "

"We shall spend the night here", Benedictus said. "But we must find an inn."

"There is no inn in Enfide", a voice said.

Benedictus turned. The speaker was a man in his fifties with a fine, high forehead, and a graying, well-kept beard. His tunic was without embroidery, but made of excellent cloth. "There is no inn," he repeated, "but there is always room for a stranger, and it needn't be a stable either." He smiled cheerfully. "My name is Sebastianus," he added, "and that is my house, the white one, behind the pear trees. If you will do me the honor of spending the night there, I shall be very pleased. And a suitable room will be found for this good woman as well."

Benedictus bowed. This was the kind of reception his father would have given a stranger who looked as if he could be trusted; he would have received Sebastianus this way if Sebastianus had come to Nursia.

"You are very kind", he said. "We accept with joy."

As they were walking together towards the house, Benedictus remarked: "That is a beautiful little basilica you have here. What is it called?"

"Saint Peter's", Sebastianus said.
Benedictus began to feel at home.

10

CYRILLA CAME TO LOVE Enfide. She had been so worried about the young master's sudden decision to leave Rome and go into solitude, a monastery perhaps or, worse still, a place where he would live as a hermit. In a monastery they would look after him, but how could one look after a hermit? She would try, of course, but hermits always lived far away from any human habitation, in rough little huts or in caves. Where could she go to buy food?

But now all these problems were solved. Life in Enfide was most agreeable, in fact much more so than it had been in Rome, where everybody was out to cheat everybody else. How careful she had had to be when buying a chicken! The poultry men had a trick of blowing water into their chickens with a little tube, quite disgusting, and then sealing it off and thus a meager hen could pose as a well-rounded pullet. Here in Enfide no one had even heard of such tricks. The people were decent, like the people in Nursia. Duilius, the priest, was a learned man, the young master said so himself. And Sebastianus and his wife were friendly hosts. The only drawback was that their household was so well organized that there was no work for her, no real work anyway. True, they allowed her to help a little here and there, but she could not help realizing that they did so only because they knew she could not bear feeling useless.

Her happiness was complete when the young master, after a week, rented rooms in a new house, and she could look after him again. He was earning money, too, by teaching the children of a number of villagers how to read and write, and all that business with figures which educated people thought was important. He was a teacher. Everybody knew that that was a great and honorable profession, and at his age, too!

The priest Duilius told Sebastianus: "I am glad you could stop young Benedictus on his way. He is that very rare thing: a thoroughly good man."

Sebastianus nodded. "Fortunately my old friend Boethius forewarned me that he might show up, and he described him so well that I recognized him at once."

"Does he know that you were expecting him?"

"No. Boethius wrote that he had mentioned Enfide to him quite casually. Well, I agree with your judgment. Boethius, too, is right: he's too young for a hermit's life. Frankly, I can't see why anybody should live like that. What good are these people doing, living like animals in the wilderness?"

Duilius closed his eyes. "I disagree", he said. "They are a great force for good. Their prayers are a living chain between God and the earth. They are doing what most of us can no longer do since the Fall in paradise: they live for God alone. In fact, if I were younger and in better health—"

"I know", Sebastianus interrupted. "It's your oldest wish, and the people of Enfide are glad that God won't grant it to you. But you know as well as I do that far too many of these people are not as they ought to be. Many are lazy, and some are downright vicious. And just as you are no longer young enough, Benedictus is too young. . . ."

"That is true", Duilius said. "And that's why I could dissuade him with a good conscience . . . I think. Mind you, it took some dissuading."

"I wonder how you did it."

"I pointed out to him that a hermit must have knowledge of

a great number of things. One can't jump from an apartment in Rome into the wilderness and stay whole."

"He would have perished. The snow in winter . . . and it's coming now; the wolves of the Abruzzi mountains . . . "

"Yes, and ignorance about which roots and herbs and mushrooms are edible and which are not. Some of them are poisonous. So we agreed that I would teach him all I know about such things, as well as about liturgy and ascesis, and that our learned friend Varro would teach him about the writings of Basilius and others—and that in exchange he would teach the children of the village."

"In other words, he hasn't given up his plan; he has only postponed it."

"I don't know," the priest replied, smiling, "but it seems to me that he fled from Rome not so much because he wanted to become a hermit as because he could not find an inner peace there—and no wonder, Rome being what it is."

"In that case he could not have come to a better place than Enfide."

"Exactly. I am glad he is staying. I—" Duilius broke off. After a while he said in a low voice: "I hope I have done the right thing."

Sebastianus opened his mouth for a question, but the priest shook his head. "Don't", he said. "I can't explain. I . . . I don't want to."

Benedictus was happy in Enfide. In Rome, Gordianus had introduced him to Saint Augustine's writings. Now Varro, a layman of noble family like Sebastianus, but far more erudite, taught him about Saint Basil whom he regarded as "the greatest teacher the Church has produced in its five centuries".

Obese and bald, with cheerfully twinkling eyes, Varro loved quoting from the vast store of knowledge and wisdom. "Here's what Saint Basil says himself, my Benedictus: 'I have already been trained through many experiences and indeed also have shared sufficiently in the all-teaching vicissitudes of both good and evil fortune, so that I can indicate the safest road, as it were, to those who are just entering upon life.' See what I mean? No better teacher for you, or for anybody else."

"I still wonder—often—whether I've done the right thing, settling down in this peaceful place, Varro."

Smilingly, the fat little man quoted: "Best is the man who sees of himself at once what must be done; and excellent is he, too, who follows what is well indicated by others; but he who is suited for neither is useless in all respects.' "

"Did Saint Basil say that?"

"No, Hesiod did. But Saint Basil quotes him in one of his addresses to young men. I have the manuscript here, it's quite a good copy, too, with only five pages missing. I'd give my eyeteeth if I could get hold of those pages. Do you want to read it?"

Benedictus read and reread it. In two short sentences the saint gave him the solution of his problem: "Now it is said that even Moses, that illustrious man whose name for wisdom is greatest among all mankind, first trained his mind in the learning of the Egyptians, and then proceeded to the contemplation of him who is. And like him, although in later times, they say that the wise Daniel at Babylon first learned the wisdom of the Chaldeans and then applied himself to the divine teachings."

There was his answer. First, learning. Then, contemplation. First, knowledge, even when it was alien and strange. Then, the direct service of God.

He was right, then. And he had not, after all, made a vow to become a hermit. It was no more than a plan that he had given up because of the counsel of good and wise men. No one could say of him what Euripides said (as quoted by Saint Basil): "The tongue is sworn, but the mind is unsworn."

The air was cool and clean, the library full of book rolls, each one more precious than the next and Varro, Sebastianus, and the venerable Duilius knew the answer to many questions which even the blessed Gordianus might not have known. Life was good. God was good.

There was not much choice in the fruit market, and the women returned in a group, chatting about the cost of oranges and olives from Sicily.

"Have you finished with the bolter I lent you, Cyrilla?" old Trabia asked.

"Yes, this morning. It's an excellent bolter."

"I should say it is", Trabia chuckled. "Nothing like it to clean the wheat, not in Enfide there isn't. My mother used it before me and her mother before *her.* An heirloom, you might call it, but I always have to lend it to somebody. Eugenia is waiting for it now, aren't you, Eugenia? Then Aglae wants it and then, God willing, I shall have it back myself. Always the good neighbor, that's me, if I say it myself."

"I'm most grateful to you", Cyrilla assured her. "I shall bring it back to you this afternoon."

"No need for that", Trabia said. "We'll pass your house on the way, and you can give it to Eugenia. You'll be careful with it, Eugenia, won't you?"

"But of course, Trabia. You know I will."

When they reached the house, Trabia said disapprovingly: "You left the window open, Cyrilla. I shouldn't, if I were you."

"I can't imagine that things aren't safe in Enfide", Cyrilla said.

"Nothing's safe anywhere, my good woman. Take the brats of Widow Farria, always out for mischief and—Oh no! Oh my goodness! Now look what's happened."

The women crowded around her. The bolter was on the floor, broken.

Cyrilla broke into sobs.

"There you are", Trabia said hoarsely. "My mother had it and her mother before her. A pity, I call it. A great pity."

"It must have been the wind", one of the women said. "Or a stray cat."

"The wind could never move it, it's much too heavy for that", Eugenia cried. "I'm sure Trabia is right. Those brats of Farria's . . . "

Cyrilla ran into the house, into the kitchen. She picked up the broken pieces and stared at them in anguish. Two pieces. The bolter was broken into two irregular halves.

Outside, old Trabia took a deep breath. "I am very sorry, Eugenia", she said pointedly. "But you won't be able to have it for your wheat."

"That's the least of it", Eugenia said magnanimously. "Though I really don't know what I shall do. But you've lost your bolter, Trabia."

"It's in two pieces only", the other woman said. "Perhaps one could glue them together."

Trabia gave a bitter laugh. "Don't be a fool. The thing is ruined."

"I am so terribly sorry, Trabia", Cyrilla stammered.

The faces of the women at the window were hard and set under a show of compassion.

"Never mind," Trabia said coldly, "but you shouldn't have left the window open." They left in an uncomfortable and uncomforting silence, and Cyrilla sat down heavily, buried her face into her hands and cried her heart out.

That was how Benedictus found her when he came home from Varro's house, half an hour later. With some difficulty he got out of her what happened.

A broken bolter. Yet the poor old woman cried as if it were a grave and irreparable loss. He wanted to smile and found he could not. However small the matter appeared to him, it was obviously a terrible thing for Cyrilla. The neighbors . . . her honor as a housekeeper. Something that did not belong to her and which apparently could not be replaced. She suffered to the depths of her being. A noble who had lost the royal citadel in battle, a king who lost his finest castle in a fire could not suffer more . . . or a child when its favorite toy was broken.

Perhaps one could repair it? He took it with him to his room, to examine it. Pottery. Very old. He put the two broken pieces together. A clean enough break, yes, but no hope of repair, not with this kind of vessel. Poor Cyrilla.

Turning away he felt his own eyes go moist. He knelt down

at the table and began to speak to the Lord about it. Thoughts welled up—he did not know, at first, whether he willed them to the surface from the recesses of his own mind or whether they were put there and asked to be heard. He knew later on.

A vessel, destined to clean wheat, was broken. Christ came to men under the form of bread. He was the manna of the New Testament. He also was the Lord of the earth, every Christian praying the Our Father asked for the kingdom to be established on earth as it was in heaven, and of earth was the vessel that was broken, the vessel to sift the wheat from the chaff. A small thing, Lord, and yet not a small thing, because the suffering of the Lord's humble servant Cyrilla was great and because no suffering was small to him who took upon himself all human suffering and wore a crown of thorns. A sparrow could not fall from the roof without his awareness. He changed water into wine to save the host of the house from humiliation in the face of his guests. He made all things new and he made all things whole. For he was the Lord not only of all people and of all other living creatures, but also of all things, and no one and no thing was either great or small in his eyes, but was what it was. And as he prayed, it came to him that he was being answered all the time, up to the last thought, and that those very thoughts were the answer. And that last thought was: "Did I not tell you that the Father would grant you everything you asked for in my name?" So he bowed his head in gratitude and rose and took the bolter off the table, went back with it to the kitchen, gave it to Cyrilla and then returned to talk to the Lord again. And that was all there was to it.

But not for Cyrilla. She put the bolter on the kitchen table. With a trembling finger she tried to feel the line of the break and could not find it. She went on trying, murmuring to herself, and sobbing a little. Then, summoning all her courage, she held it up and peered, and turned it and peered again, and shook it and peered some more.

She put it back on the table, gasping. Then she snatched it, as if somebody might try to take it away from her, and ran out of the house.

Old Trabia was having her supper when Cyrilla marched in, carrying the bolter as if it were an altar vessel.

"What's it now", the old woman asked sullenly. "Don't tell me you've been trying to glue it together. It'll never—Good Lord! Good Lord in heaven. How did you . . . "

"I didn't", Cyrilla said in a strangled voice. "It's the young master."

It was Trabia's turn to test the vessel with thumb and forefinger. When she looked up, her face was gray. "How . . . did he do it?"

"I don't know", Cyrilla said helplessly. "All I know is he was praying. I could hear him, in the kitchen."

Trabia got up heavily. "I promised it to Eugenia", she said dully. "I must take it to her . . . I suppose."

"I'll come with you", Cyrilla said.

"He prayed, you said?"

"Yes."

"It's a miracle."

"That's what I've been thinking", Cyrilla said. "But . . . he's never done anything like this before. He's my young master. I carried him in my arms. He was a sweet child, he and his little twin sister. Sweet children. But this . . . I'm going crazy, Trabia."

"You better have some wine", Trabia said. "Here . . . take this goblet. Can do with one myself. Wait till Eugenia hears about this. And Aglae. And Farria! I still think it's her brats who done it. I must tell Farria. Promise me you won't tell anybody without me. After all, it's my bolter."

"I have no other explanation", Sebastianus said. "What do you think, Duilius?"

"You have no other explanation because there is no other", the priest said. "Great Lord in heaven, what else can it be but a miracle?"

"Yes, but think of it . . . a miracle in our day! Why, it's unheard of. We no longer live in the times of the apostles, do we? Christ no longer walks on earth, does he? One's heard of all kinds of strange things, occasionally, of course, but . . . "

"We're all talking a lot of nonsense", the priest said. "Has God been limited to any particular period when he wishes miracles to happen?"

"You're quite certain of it, Duilius? I mean . . . it couldn't be, for instance, that the women saw a broken vessel and thought it was old Trabia's famous bolter and it wasn't at all, and later that woman Cyrilla produced . . . "

"That would mean that both Cyrilla and Benedictus are lying", Duilius said. "That's hard to accept. It would mean also that old Trabia didn't recognize her own bolter at a distance of four feet, which is even harder. That's the trouble with miracles, Sebastianus—in order to explain them away you have to introduce theories so nonsensical that they are less believable than the miracle itself."

"But if it is a miracle . . . "

"It is. I have no doubt about it."

"Then young Benedictus . . . "

The priest slowly shrugged his shoulders. He said nothing.

Varro came to join them. "Enfide's standing on its head", he told them. "This thing's spread like wildfire. No one talks about anything but Trabia's bolter. I had just made up my mind to go and see Benedictus about it, when he came to see me. Wanted to know something about Saint Ignatius of Antioch. Imagine it! What's he made of? And he isn't playacting, you know."

"I don't know anyone as unlike an actor as he is", Sebastianus said. "He's the quietest, the most reserved young fellow I ever met. Shy. Almost awkward, sometimes. There's no wit, no brilliance. . . . "

"He is very intelligent", the priest said.

"Undoubtedly, in a scholarly sort of way. Boethius, too, said so, in his letter. But he doesn't show off his knowledge. In fact, he doesn't talk much."

"Except when it is worthwhile", the priest said.

"Right again, Duilius. What is one to think? A shy, reticent, studious young man, extremely devout . . . he would make a good priest, I should think, though I suppose he'd hate preaching sermons . . . "

"Preaching is mingled with vanity, more often than not", the priest said. "Benedictus has no vanity."

" . . . and he prays over a broken bolter and it puts itself together again. To the village people he's a saint, of course."

"What is he to you, Varro?" the priest asked in a low voice.

"That's a hard question, Duilius." The fat little man wriggled uneasily on his chair. "I don't know, I really don't. Only yesterday he mispronounced two Greek verbs and today he's a saint. What *is* a saint, anyway?"

"Something that hasn't much to do with the correct pronounciation of Greek verbs", Sebastianus interposed dryly. "But I admit it is a little . . . frightening. I mean . . . he's a very lovable and good young man. I liked him from the first moment. But this thing . . . how does one behave towards a saint? How does one even address a saint?"

"He may not be a saint", the priest said, and the others looked at him, bewildered.

"But you just said it could only be a miracle. . . . "

"So well educated", Duilius went on. "So erudite. Yet you don't know your New Testament. Or have you forgotten it?"

"What do you mean?"

"The Gospel of Saint Matthew," the priest said, "the seventh chapter. It's part of the Sermon on the Mount, of which so many people remember only the Beatitudes. 'The kingdom of heaven will not give entrance to every man who calls me Master, Master; only to the man who does the will of my Father who is in heaven.' "

"But what has that to do with young Benedictus?" Varro asked.

Quietly, Duilius went on quoting: " 'There are many who will say to me, when that day comes, Master, Master, was it not in thy name we prophesied? Was it not in thy name that we performed many miracles? Whereupon I will tell them openly, You were never friends of mine; depart from me, you that traffic in wrongdoing. . . . ' "

They were silent.

"God may show his power through a man, yet that man may not be a saint", the priest said, "though no man may be pronounced a saint, unless God has shown his power through him. I believe, I am convinced, that a miracle has taken place, in which young Benedictus was God's instrument. But whether or not he is or ever will be a saint, I don't know. Only God knows that."

"Maybe so", Varro said after a pause. "But I can't see that boy trafficing in wrongdoing, although Greek verbs—"

"What does he think, himself?" Sebastianus interposed. "Did you ask him?"

"Yes. I asked him why he thought God had chosen him for such a miracle."

The two men looked at him expectantly.

"He pondered over that for quite a while", the priest went on. "Then he said: 'I asked for help and I was given help. He has done for me and for Cyrilla what he has done for the blind, the lame, and the lepers.' "

"Good answer", Sebastianus said.

"Is it?" Varro asked. "It was old Trabia's bolter that was made whole; not Benedictus or Cyrilla."

The priest said sharply: "That is exactly what I wonder about. It's such a small matter, isn't it? A broken pot or sieve or whatever it is. And what will be the result? They're all goggling at the boy. Old Trabia's asked him to bless her house. So did Eugenia and Aglae and Damas and a lot of others. They stand in groups around his house. The woman Cyrilla is going around with her eyes down and her hands folded, almost bursting with pride. Poor Turbo told everybody he's going to ask the saint to cure his leg by praying over it. 'What he's done for a bolter, he can do for my leg, can't he?' What will it do to Enfide?"

"What will happen if he does not perform another miracle?" Varro asked thoughtfully.

"Or if he does", Sebastian said. "They'll send us their cripples and invalids from all over Italy."

"What will it do to *him?*" the priest said. "Or perhaps even what has it done to him? It could turn anybody's head, couldn't it?" He rose stiffly. "I don't know what to do. I suppose I ought to inform his bishop. But before I do, I must have another talk with our young thaumaturge. I will go to see him tomorrow morning."

On his way to Benedictus' house Duilius encountered a swarm of people who were also looking for him. At first they all shouted together, and he could not understand what they were saying, but after a while it became clear that they wanted him to hang up Trabia's bolter at the church door, as a permanent reminder of the miracle of Enfide. Old Trabia had consented, though at first she demanded that her name should be written on it as the donor.

"Did Benedictus suggest it?" the priest asked severely. When they denied it, he asked: "Did you tell him?"

"We haven't seen him yet."

"Very well. I shall ask him what he thinks of it", Duilius said, and he walked on. They did not dare accompany him, but they followed him at a distance.

He had to knock several times before Cyrilla opened the door. She looked haggard, and her eyes were red from crying.

Duilius decided not to take any notice. "I have come to speak to Benedictus, Cyrilla."

"He has gone", she said in a whisper.

He frowned. "What do you mean, gone?"

"He's left", she said. She began to cry again. "Left . . . by . . . night", she sobbed. "Didn't . . . tell me . . . anything."

A wail went up from the people behind Duilius.

"Where has he gone?" the priest asked.

"I don't know. I don't know. I found this on his table. . . . " She showed him a thin strip of parchment with a few words scribbled on it. "I can't read", she added helplessly.

Duilius took the parchment. "He asks us to look after you", he said rather sadly. "To let you stay here or to help you to get back to Nursia, whichever you may prefer. I'm afraid he won't come back to Enfide."

Cyrilla dissolved in tears.

"We'll talk about it later", the priest said, gently enough.

Some of the people behind him came up. Their speaker was a tall, gangling artisan. "The saint has left us", he said sadly. "Will you let us hang the bolter on the church door now so that we may remember him and his miracle?"

There was a pause.

"Do so", Duilius said in a strained voice. He would have to see it every day, when entering his own church. It was a lesson; the least he could do was to accept it.

11

THE ANIO was a gleaming ribbon, far down in the plain. The town of Sublacum, fully visible only half an hour ago, had vanished completely, and the small lake high above it, too. There was nothing left but bushes, rocks, and sky. There was no voice of man or animal, only the song of the wind in the treetops and the rustling of branches.

Here he stayed.

And here the monk Romanus found him, by accident, as ignorant people would say, on his way down to Sublacum, where he was to buy oil for the lamps of his monastery. He had taken this way before, but not very often, for although it was a shortcut, it was not without peril from small landslides or the sudden fall of stones. Romanus was a man nearing fifty, with a straggly, gray beard and large, round eyes like an owl's. He wore the melote of sheepskin and rough sandals, as all monks did.

When he saw Benedictus, he stopped. "You can't have been here very long . . . Brother."

"Seventeen days."

"Where do you get food?"

"I haven't had any."

"Even hermits must eat, Brother."

"Our Lord fasted forty days in the desert."

"But after that he was hungry, Brother." Romanus' smile contained no trace of mockery. "When the fast is over, you will go back to Sublacum, or wherever you came from, I take it?"

"No. I shall stay here."

"As a hermit?"

"If it pleases God."

After a pause Romanus said: "I'm a monk of the monastery on the other side of Mons Talaeus. It is not far from here. Our abbot, the Venerable Adeodatus, is a good man, a friend of God. If you wanted to join us, I think he would accept you gladly."

"You are kind. But I must be alone with God. It may not be forever, but it will be for a long time yet. After that, I don't know."

Romanus nodded. "I shall come back. Pray for me as I will pray for you."

He came back twenty-three days later and found Benedictus at the same place. "The forty days are over", he said. "Now you must eat. And do not fear that I may tempt you as our Lord was tempted. All I can offer you is bread, and not very much of that."

Benedictus thanked him, took the bread, prayed over it, and began to eat, very slowly, tiny morsels at a time.

Romanus said: "You must eat regularly from now on. You are sure you won't come with me to our monastery?"

"Quite sure."

"Then I shall bring you your daily bread."

"God reward you."

"Your tunic is in a bad state, Brother."

"It is true, but I have no other with me."

"A few more weeks and the holes will have won their battle with the enemy encircling them."

"It's the thorns."

"I know. What you ought to wear is a melote. A hermit is a monk, Brother, and a man becomes a monk by wearing the melote."

"I am new."

"So you are, or you would not have chosen this place as your abode."

"Why not?"

"Because winter is coming, and the place is unprotected against rain and snow. If you do not want to live in a cell, you should have a cave. I can show you one, not far from here."

Benedictus rose, not without reluctance.

"I know how you feel", Romanus told him gently. "You were growing roots here."

"It does not matter", Benedictus said, biting his lip.

They ascended to a barren plateau, surrounded by rocks and large trees. "The cave is in there", Romanus said, pointing to an entrance, more than half-hidden by bushes. "Mind you, it's small—only just large enough for one man to stand up in and to lie down."

"There is no need for more."

"Enter then, Brother, and see how you like it."

Benedictus obeyed. When he came out again, a minute later, he was carrying a large, shaggy fleece on his arm. "The cave is good", he said. "I found this in it. Did you put it there?"

Romanus nodded. "I tested you," he said solemnly, "and you stood the test."

"How so?"

"You kept the forty days' fast. When you broke it, you prayed before you started eating, and you ate slowly and without greed. Take off your tunic and put on the melote I brought you. From this day on you are a monk."

Book Two

12

ARMY COMMANDER COUNT WITIGIS was reporting to the King, and Cassiodor, whose report was next on the list, had time to look, from under half-lowered lids, at Amalaswintha who was sitting beside her father on a low chair. She was a mature woman now, and more beautiful than ever. The year of mourning for her husband, Prince Eutharic, was over, so she had shed her widow's weeds. Her robe of brilliant blue matched the glory of her hair, a golden-yellow brown like the skin of a lioness, and she did look a little like a lioness, or rather like a princess in a story Ovid had forgotten to tell in his *Metamorphoses,* a princess whose mother had succumbed to Jupiter under the form of a lion.

From where Cassiodor was sitting he could see her profile in line with Theoderic's. The resemblance was there, of course, in forehead, nose, and chin. But the King was an old lion now.

Count Witigis, a brawny, flaxen-haired man with fists as large as a human head, rambled on with his report. The production of the helmet factories at Mantua and Florentia. The introduction of Spanish steel for sword blades. The import of horses from Illyria.

The King was an old lion, but he had not mellowed with age. Several times he interrupted Witigis, questioning his figures. The large vein on his forehead and the muscles of his neck stood out.

Cassiodor sighed inaudibly. At the best of times it was no pleasure to report bad news to the King. It was worse when the King was in an ill mood, and worst of all when Amalaswintha was present to witness a stormy audience. At court, a man must learn to be elastic and to bow as a tree bows in a storm. He had done so often enough. But when Amalaswintha was present his very nature rebelled against humiliation. She knew it and felt sorry for him, and her compassion was more difficult to bear than the king's rage.

The King bellowed that he wanted horses to be bought in Spain and not in East Roman territories. "We have given far too much trade to the Buffoons."

Count Witigis grinned delightedly. He was one of the King's favorites and had done extremely well in the war against the Gepids, in the Gothic style, by splitting enemy heads, helmet, skull, and all. Perhaps the King was right to make him an expert on helmets and their resistance and durability.

"Pleases you, does it?" growled the King. "*You* don't have to receive speechifying Byzantine ambassadors. Very well. Anything else? Right. You may stay on and hear what Cassiodor has to say. It's bad news. I always know when he's got bad news. What is it this time? Still no answer from Byzantium?"

"Worse, I'm afraid, my lord King", Cassiodor replied. He spoke fairly loudly. The King was getting a little deaf. "The Emperor's answer is negative."

Theodoric's brows contracted. "What's he say? Where's the letter?"

Cassiodor produced it.

"That's not an imperial letter", Theodoric snapped. "And don't you tell me it is. No purple ink. No big seal attached. Just because I can't read, you can't cheat me. The Emperor, God blast him, can't read or write either. Doesn't have to. What's this scrap of ass' hide about?"

"It is a letter from the Emperor's nephew. . . . "

"Justinian. Can't wait till the old man is dead, eh? He's the man to watch, daughter, remember that."

"Prince Justinian seems to be in charge of all important foreign affairs", Cassiodor went on. "His letter is addressed to the Royal Secretariat—quite correctly so, as he is not in a position to address the King directly, on state affairs."

"All Byzantines love formalities", Theodoric explained to Amalaswintha. "And they hate everything that is straight and simple. When a Buffoon wants to scratch behind his right ear, he'll use the left hand just to make it a little more complicated. *Will* you tell me what the young man says, Cassiodor?"

"He refers to the King's letter to the Emperor about the edict against the Arians."

Theodoric's face was dark. "I wrote to the Emperor", he said between his teeth. "Is Justinus incapacitated that his nephew must answer for him, or is he trying to insult us?"

"The letter is couched in very polite terms", Cassiodor replied, somewhat evasively. "Prince Justinian expresses his regret for having been directed to reply that the edict cannot be withdrawn, as the King suggested. Also there can be no restitution of former Arian churches to that sect . . . "

"Wants to keep stolen goods."

" . . . for the reason that most of these churches were Orthodox before they were taken over by the Arians and . . . "

"Go on, man. Let's have it."

" . . . and that it would be wrong to foster and assist a heretical belief. The Church should be one, and the Emperor's policy is to make it so with all the means in his power and especially by his prayers."

Theodoric gave an angry laugh. "So he can pray and steal in the same breath . . . that's a Byzantine for you. Mark it well, daughter, when the time comes. Make the Church one! Ever since they settled their quibbles, the Roman priests are getting all cock-a-hoop. We are Arians, we Goths. Or most of us. And we intend to remain what we are. What's more, we're not going to sit back idly, while they persecute those who believe as we do. And 'with all the means in his power', eh?" The King's eyes narrowed. "I'm a simple man," he said, "but perhaps not quite as simple as they think. We have a little power too, eh, Witigis?"

"Yes, my lord King."

"We shall give the pious Prince and his uncle Emperor proof of that. And some other people as well. But first tell me, Cassiodor . . . what is the news from Rome?"

"Nothing today, my lord King."

"Nothing at all? I see. And the Senate? What's your opinion

of that great and honorable assembly, Cassiodor? All loyal to us? No suspicious activities? No secret activities?"

"If there were," Cassiodor said quietly, "I feel sure the King's minister, Senator Boethius, would have reported it."

"You do, eh?" Theodoric remained silent for a while. "What about other parts of the country?" he asked suddenly. "Nothing to report to us, Cassiodor? From the North? From Padova, Pavia, Verona, Milan?"

"Nothing of importance, my lord King."

Theodoric turned his huge head to look his minister full in the face. "We hear a great deal more than official reports", he said. "For instance, that the priest of the church of Saint Stephen in Verona preached a sermon in which he called all Arians heretics who did not give Christ his due honor and said that the Emperor was right in condemning them as the Church had done. And that he would rather destroy his church than give it up to Arian priests."

"Priests are apt to feel very strongly about such matters", Cassiodor dared to say. "I am sure that in Arian churches . . . "

"When I want your opinion I shall ask for it, Cassiodor. I have decided to make an example of Saint Stephen's. The priest shall have his wish. Saint Stephen's will be burned down."

"Father," Amalaswintha pleaded, "don't give such an order, I implore you. They will say . . . "

"Quiet, daughter. I let you hear what is going on in matters of state because I want you to learn, not because I want your advice. You can spare yourself the effort in any case. My messenger to Count Ibba, Governor of Verona, rode off last night. The church of Saint Stephen no longer exists."

"The Pope will regret it deeply, my lord King", Cassiodor said.

"And so do I", Theodoric replied. "You will report to His Holiness about it. Tell him, Saint Stephen's is a token of what will happen to a hundred, to a thousand of his churches, if I give the order. Only three months ago I gave him two candelabra for Saint Peter's, as a sign that I respect and honor a faith even when I do not share it. But when my tolerance is answered by intolerance, my clemency by impudence and rebellious sermons, I have my answer ready. Tell him *all* of that, Cassiodor. And add that I wish him to keep his priests in order, unless he wants worse things to happen."

"Very well, my lord King."

"Write to Senator Boethius, too. I wish to be informed about any man of importance and especially any senator who shows sympathy for Byzantium."

"Sympathy, my lord King?"

"You heard what I said. And you know exactly what I mean. Make it clear to Boethius in whatever terms you like, *but make it clear.*" He rose and stalked out.

Count Witigis bowed to Amalaswintha, grinned broadly at Cassiodor, and clanked out, too.

"What does all this mean?" Amalaswintha asked anxiously.

"Nothing good, Princess", Cassiodor said in a low voice. "I'm afraid the King believes that the Emperor's edict against the Arians was made purely for political reasons."

"How so?"

"To create the feeling in Italy that the Emperor regards himself as the protector of all Catholics. Prince Justinian used rather strong words, for an official communication to another power. If the content of his letter became known, it might make people—some people—look towards Byzantium, when they ought to look towards Ravenna."

She nodded. "And do you think my father is wrong?"

"I don't know for certain, Princess", Cassiodor admitted. "But I do think that the order to destroy a Catholic church is not likely to be the best answer."

"I would never have given such an order," Amalaswintha said emphatically, "and I think it is perfectly natural that Romans should have sympathy for other Romans. One cannot blame them for that. And poor Senator Boethius is supposed to inform on his own colleagues. It isn't right."

"What a brave Gothic warrior feels is always right", a child's voice shrilled. A boy, seven years of age, came in, skipping. "I heard everything", he declared. "Why do you always side with the Runts, Mother?"

"The Romans, you mean, Athalaric", Amalaswintha corrected calmly. "Who says I side with them?"

"Uncle Tuluin, and Count Witigis and lots of others. Why do you, Mother?"

"I don't side with anybody", Amalaswintha said. "Both Goths and Italians are your grandfather's subjects. And eavesdropping is not worthy of a prince. Where is Theron, your teacher?"

"I don't know, Mother. I ran away from him. Greek is *awful,* Mother. It's a language for Buffoons, and all Buffoons are actors and trollops. What's a trollop, Mother?"

"Who spoke that word to you, Athalaric?"

"Uncle Tu . . . never mind, Mother. What's it mean?"

"Greek", the Princess said, "is the language of civilization and therefore of all educated men. It is also the language of the greatest of all poets. A prince who wants his actions to be remembered after his death must be the friend of poets."

"I don't care what happens to me when I'm dead", Athalaric said sullenly. "Trollop, trollop, trollop. I'm glad Grandfather had that silly old church burned. So is Uncle Tuluin and Uncle Pitza, too."

"Don't talk about things you don't understand", Amalaswintha told him. "Why don't you go and play with your sister Mataswintha?"

"What? She's only a girl! Girls are no good for anything."

Amalaswintha bit her lip. "You will go back to Theron this instant", she said sharply. "And if I ever catch you eavesdropping again, you will stay in bed for a whole week, with nothing to eat and drink but bread and water. Go!"

Looking up doubtfully, Athalaric saw that his mother was in dead earnest. He turned away and walked off. After half a dozen steps he began to skip again. "Burn the church, burn the church", he sang.

"I shall see to it that in future he is kept away from . . . certain people", Amalaswintha said firmly. "It isn't easy to be both mother and father to a boy, Cassiodor."

"He is only a child, Princess", Cassiodor said gently.

She sighed. "He has all the faults of Eutharic, and none of his good qualities. He's willful and obstinate and he can be cruel."

So her marriage had not been happy, he thought. He had never really known. People talked, of course; they always did. Eutharic was a great prince, a good-looking man, tall and proud. Many people had thought he would be Theodoric's heir and successor, at least until Athalaric came of age. His premature death, quite suddenly, from a rare heart ailment, was a terrible blow for the King. Was it a blow for Amalaswintha? It was said that the two did not see eye to eye on a number of issues. But then, these Goths expected a woman, a wife, to remain in the background, to be a mother and a housekeeper, and no more. A princess who could speak several languages, who could write letters in Latin and compose poetry in Greek seemed to them almost a freak. Perhaps even her husband shared that opinion, despite his many good qualities. On the other hand, it may very likely have been the Princess' influence that made Eutharic appear to be one of the more moderate men at court.

"Cassiodor . . . "

He woke up. "My princess?"

"Cassiodor, I am worried. I'm worried about the future. The King is getting old. And I am very much alone. They don't trust me."

They. The Goths were "they" to Theodoric's daughter.

"Now the King is taking measures the Italians won't like. There will be hatred. I feel it. Promise me that you won't resign."

So she had guessed. How well she knew him and the thoughts of his heart. All of them, perhaps, except the one that concerned her most.

"It does not depend upon me alone, Princess."

"The King will not dismiss you, whatever happens. He trusts you. You and Boethius are perhaps the only Romans he trusts. And I trust you—more than I trust myself. You . . . you love me, don't you, Cassiodor?"

When his heart began to beat again he said: "Yes, Princess, I have always loved you. It never occurred to me that you knew."

"I am a woman. It is perhaps a pity that I was born Theodoric's daughter and a Gothic princess. They would never permit us . . . never mind. You and I are so many things. We are philosophers and statesmen and people who love everything that is beautiful and noble and right. Promise me you will never leave *my* service, Cassiodor."

He looked at her. "I promise I shall never leave your service, most noble Princess", he said. "Not as long as you love what is beautiful and noble and right."

"God forbid that there should be a day when I don't", she said with a slight shudder. "Though Sophocles says that a man must never forswear anything."

"You are the only person in the world who makes me believe that I was right to serve the King of the Goths", he said gravely.

"I know. Oh, I know. And you are my guardian angel and friend. Will that be enough for you, Cassiodor?"

"As a mortal man I could not think of anything more, Princess."

13

WHEN THE MAJORDOMO made his announcement, Rusticana stared at him incredulously. "Peter?" she asked. "It isn't possible. He is in Athens or Ephesus or somewhere. It can't be Peter."

"It is, Domina", said Peter, entering. "May all the saints, gods, nymphs, and apostles bless you and make you feel kindly disposed towards a poor traveler."

"Peter," Rusticiana said. "My little Peter . . . a great, big, good-looking man, and how elegant! And I have known you since you were *that* high. I must be old . . . as old as Troy."

"If you had said as beautiful as Helen when nations quarreled and warred for her, I would agree, Domina", Peter said, and there was something in his tone that startled her a little.

"The nonsense you talk", she said lightly. "Better tell me how it is that you're here in Rome. Where do you come from? How did you get here? Why aren't you in Athens? Why haven't you written to us? We haven't heard from you. What has happened to you?"

"Stop it, Domina", he laughed. "You're worse than the city prefect interrogating a particularly suspicious individual. I've arrived from everywhere. I've been to all sorts of places. The ship that brought me to Ostia came from Messana. The ship that took me to Messana came from Rhodes. And the ship that took me to Rhodes came from Byzantium."

"Heavens above, Byzantium! What were you doing in Byzantium, Peter? But sit down, Odysseus, and have some wine. Glabrio! Cervax! Wine! You look marvelous, Peter. What a long coat . . . and such heavy yellow silk. And onyx buttons on your sandal tops!"

"That's the latest fashion in Byzantium, ever since Prince Justinian made the Lady Theodora a patrician."

"We have heard of *that.* Who hasn't! None of my women friends could talk of anything else for weeks on end. Is it true that she used to be . . . "

"Quite true. Whatever they said is true and however much they said I could add to it. I have the latest gossip—no more than three months old, that is. She's a guttersnipe, Domina, but she'll go on up and up, you may count on that. Nothing but the best will be good enough for Patricia Theodora."

"But they say she's the daughter of a lionkeeper . . . "

"Bearkeeper, Domina. The man's name was Acacius. A Cypriot. But her mother must have been Aphrodite."

"Bearkeeper, then. But you don't mean to say Prince Justinian is going to marry her?"

"He certainly will. He would have done so six months ago, if it hadn't been for old Empress Euphemia who protested so shrilly that poor old Justinus gave in. The protest was rather funny, considering that both Justin and Euphemia come from peasant stock. So, of course, does Prince Justinian. His father's name was Sabbatius . . . think of it . . . and his mother's is practically unpronounceable. The best I can do: Biglenitza. Sounds like a sneeze, doesn't it? *And* breaks your tongue at the same time. Unique. I'm glad to see that Uncle Boethius' Falernian is as good as ever. The graces and archangels be with you, noble Domina."

Rusticiana laughed. "Graces and archangels! A minute ago it was nymphs and apostles."

"That also is the latest fashion in Byzantium", he told her, twinkling. "Justinian is a devout Catholic, and it's he who is behind all those laws against pagans and heretics—you've heard that, I suppose—so out of a spirit of sheer contradiction 'high society' swears by a mixture of Christian and pagan entities or powers. They make all kinds of jokes about the new Pope, too . . . John the First. They say he thinks he was given that name after John the Apostle who lived to be a hundred, but he will find he was really named for John the Baptist, when King Theodoric has him beheaded."

"What awful people those Byzantines are."

"Not really, Domina. They love a joke and they pretend to be irreverent—some of them are, too, but the majority believe sincerely enough. Theodora does, I think, and Justinian, definitely."

"His edict against the Arians has caused us a great deal of trouble here", she said. "Boethius is rather worried about it. But never mind our troubles. . . . "

"Oh, but I am most interested. . . . "

"I'll tell you about them later, then. Now you tell me . . . I haven't seen you for . . . how many years?"

"Seven, Domina."

She sighed. "How time flies. You find me the mother of two young men, in the service of the state . . . "

" . . . and only last year both consuls, at an age at which the average Goth doesn't yet know the facts of life."

"We evidently have no secrets from Byzantium."

"You can't keep consulships secret, Domina. But it's true, they are remarkably well informed there."

"But what have you been doing all these years?"

"Oh, everything and nothing", Peter said lightly. "I studied in Berytus and in Athens and then drifted towards Byzantium. I felt that I might find some scope for experience there. As you know, I was well off . . . thanks to the fact that Uncle Boethius paid me my heritage in full and told me to spend it in my own way."

"He gave it to you because you asked him for it. We were both a little worried about what you would do with it. It was a very great amount of money your parents left in trust with us."

"Fairly so. Well, I invested the major part of it. I have property in various provinces of Asia Minor, houses, all kinds of things. I've almost tripled the original amount."

Rusticiana laughed. "Clever Peter! Who would have thought you'd develop into a businessman. How pleased my husband will be."

"I'm not so sure whether he'd approve of some of my deals. Where is he, by the way, and where are your sons?"

"The boys are in Sicily at the moment. My husband is still in the Senate. He is Princeps Senatus now, you know. Not that it means too much, nowadays. My father also still retains his seat, but he's no longer young enough to be as active as he used to be."

"Symmachus has always been a sensible man. Most men seem to find it difficult to retire in time; they want to go on and on. It's always like that in periods when one can make a great deal of money, I suppose."

"Part of my husband's activity is concerned with the curbing of speculation."

"Naturally", Peter said. "Bound to be."

"What do you mean?"

"Simple, Domina. Speculation means large gains for somebody—usually at the expense of a town, a city, or a province. When large bodies of men lose out to a few, they become disgruntled, and from being disgruntled there is only one step to disloyalty. Yet the chief duty of Theodoric's minister must be to keep the people loyal to the regime he represents. Ergo: he must curb speculation."

Rusticiana said nothing.

"I see", Peter said slowly. "You are still not quite reconciled to the fact that Uncle Boethius is working for the King of the Goths."

"He is working for Rome", Rusticiana said angrily.

"No doubt he is, Domina. Or thinks he is. And you . . . do you think so, too?"

"I am his wife."

"The wife of a man of consular rank and the mother of two sons of consular rank", Peter said, his tone just a shade too bland.

She made a gesture of annoyance. "I see you can still be quite insufferable when you feel like it, Peter. You ought to know that rank and honors make no difference to anybody in this house, and least of all to a philosopher like my husband."

"I of all people ought to know that", Peter admitted courteously. "Please, forgive me, Domina. Remember I've been in Byzantium, where most idealistic ideas are regarded as hopelessly old-fashioned. At least that is so in what is called 'high society'. It is good to discover that old-fashioned people still exist in Rome, and in high positions, too. Am I forgiven? I shall drop down on my knees, if I'm not."

She could not help laughing at his mock contrition. "You're a rascal, Peter, you always were and now you're worse than ever. Your pater confessor can't have an easy task, nor your guardian angel, either."

"I don't know about that", Peter said. "I haven't been in touch with either of them."

"And your conscience? What does it say to all this?"

"My conscience is as good as new", Peter declared cheerfully. "I've never made much use of it."

"Peter! I thought you just told me that people in Byzantium are so devout."

"So they are. But I'm not a Byzantine, am I?"

"Frankly, I don't know what you are, except that you're a very good-looking young man, very sure of yourself, and apparently very successful."

"Thank you, Domina." He chuckled. "What a different atmosphere there is here in Rome. People are still playing at being Romans. . . . "

"Playing?"

"Of course, Domina. We're all playing. Nothing wrong about it. What matters is the part we play. Take your noble husband, for instance. He is playing the ancient Roman philosopher, a Christian Seneca to a Gothic Nero."

"That's silly."

"And you, Domina? You *are* a noble Roman lady, but you play the part of one tolerating by her generosity the existence of the Goth, a rough intruder whose presence in the house is due to a lamentable misunderstanding. The Goth, the lady feels, should really be thrown out, but as her husband seems to be amused by his antics, one lets him stay and pretends not to see him."

"A delightful explanation", Rusticiana said, nettled. "And you? What part are you playing, if any?"

He had been waiting for that. "Oh, I . . . I've got a very bad part. I'm playing the disappointed lover."

"You! You probably had the most shocking success with the ladies of Byzantium. You left a trail of broken hearts behind you, I could swear to it."

"If I did," Peter said, "it would make no difference, because there's only one woman I love. Do you want to know her name?"

"Peter! You *know* it's in the worst possible taste to mention a woman's name in such circumstances."

"Not if the man's love is not reciprocated."

"Even then."

"And certainly only when he tells it to a *third* person."

"What on earth . . . "

"I fell in love with her many years ago. I was glad to leave the city where she lived, because I wanted to forget her. I have seen some of the greatest beauties in the world, and they couldn't make me forget her for an instant. Once more: Do you want to know her name?"

"But, Peter . . . "

"I have been faithful to her in my own way, Domina. It was of her I thought when I made love to other women. I am very frank with you, as you see. I won't try to appear better than I am. Her alone I desired, and other women only served to remind me of her, playing her part as a slave girl or a lowborn actress may play the part of a great queen. . . . "

"Peter, you frighten me. You . . . "

"Her name is Rusticiana."

She rose. "You have no right to say that."

"I know. I can't help it."

"What madness is this . . . "

"The madness I've been suffering from all my life, Domina. And you must have known it." Staring at her fixedly, he rose too.

"Peter! When you were a boy of thirteen you made sheep's eyes at me. Today you are a man and I . . . "

"You are the woman I love."

"You are talking to the wife of Senator Boethius", she said icily. "To the wife of your benefactor, your second father."

He nodded. "You don't think I haven't thought of that, do you? Tell me one thing, I beg of you. If you were free . . . would you marry me?"

"Peter, this is madness, absolute madness."

"If you were free, and I had a great position, a position of real power, would you marry me?"

"Don't talk like that, Peter, you mustn't. . . . "

"If I could free Rome and Italy from the Goth for you, would you marry me?"

"What will you say next!" Rusticiana shook her head. "My dear Peter, I am very fond of you, I always have been. But I cannot even imagine life without my husband."

He stared at her oddly. "I thought so", he said. "Yes, I thought so." He shrugged. "It is a great pity."

"I don't know what to say, Peter, except that I wish you hadn't told me."

"I'm glad I told you", he replied. "I couldn't keep it a secret any longer, and there was only one person in the world to whom I could disclose it. I have thought of this moment in Berytus, in Athens, in Byzantium, and on the high seas. It's been the great dream of my life. With you at my side there is nothing I couldn't aspire to, nothing. But you love your husband, or think you do. . . . "

"What insolence! What right have you . . . "

"None whatever." He began to pace up and down the room, and with a sudden pang of compassion she saw that he still limped a little.

"Once again I must ask you to forgive me, Domina", he murmured. "But it was you who taught me that the story of Helen and Paris was true; that a woman could bring about war and death and destruction upon whole nations. . . . just by being what she is."

"God forbid that I should ever . . . "

"It wasn't Helen's fault. It wasn't Paris' fault either. If there is a divine being at all, it isn't a god, but a goddess. . . . Ananke, Necessity, mistress of us all. She alone settles all problems and unties all knots." He picked up his goblet and emptied it. "Let's talk of other things", he said airily. "Old friends, for instance. What has happened to Senator Albinus?"

She decided to fall in with his new mood. "He is jealous of Boethius, but doesn't admit it even to himself."

"And Florentius? He became a priest, just before I left."

"Once a priest, always a priest. But his reputation is not of the best."

"Come to think of it, it never was. People don't change much with the years, do they, Domina? And Benedictus? Perhaps you don't remember him. He was my teacher for a short while and then rather mysteriously decided to leave Rome. I think he wanted to become a monk."

"As it happens I can tell you all about him, and it's quite a story, too. He did become a monk, and rather a remarkable one, it seems. He is living at a place near Sublacum and is building one monastery after the other. The last was the seventh . . . or was it the eighth?"

"He never struck me as being an organizer. A dreamer, more likely."

"They say he lived in the wilderness for several years, entirely alone. Some peasants or shepherds found him there. At first they mistook him for a wild animal."

"He was probably wearing a melote—that's made of animal skin, I know, I have seen so many of those people in Byzantium."

"He won the respect and even the veneration of the shepherds or whatever they were, by teaching them and settling their disputes . . . "

"Another Solomon."

" . . . so the monks of a nearby monastery, at Varia, decided to have him as their abbot, their own abbot having died suddenly. . . . "

"And Benedictus accepted?"

"At first he refused, I heard, but they pleaded with him until he gave in. But he warned them that he was going to be severe, and he was. They weren't accustomed to discipline and resented it. Then something happened. . . . It sounds quite incredible, but we heard it from a very reliable source. They decided to get rid of him by killing him."

"Charming monks."

"Yes, weren't they? They put poison in his wine. But when he raised the cup he made the sign of the cross over it, and it broke into small pieces."

Peter shook his head. "You don't believe *that,* do you?"

"I don't know what to believe."

"And what did he do?"

"He asked God to have mercy on them, reproached them—rather mildly, I think—told them to get themselves another abbot, and returned to his solitude."

"But you said he was building monasteries."

"That's right. There seem to be people who were not deterred by his severity—or what the monks of Varia called his severity. He found disciples and began to train them. A good many stories began to circulate about him, about strange things he had done. One is that he can read a man's thoughts just by looking at him. . . . "

Peter laughed. "Enough of him", he said. "Pious hermits and monks. We've got crowds of 'em in Byzantium. They are fashionable, too. Prince Justinianus, for quite a while, affected the robe of a monk. Not a melote, to be sure, but something that looked like one, only made of good cloth. What about Cassiodor?"

"Oh, he's still with the King."

"Happy in his position?"

"Frankly, I never ask myself whether Cassiodor is happy or not. It was he who dragged my poor husband into public life . . . "

"That was twenty years ago, but you've never forgiven him."

"I didn't say that. Mind you, he has his troubles these days. The old King is getting harder and more suspicious every day, they say, and Cassiodor never has had an easy task, not with all those flaxen-haired devils around him to whom every Roman is a degenerate, decadent remnant of a former era."

"The edict against the Arians . . . "

"That and a good many other things. My husband is rather worried, as I told you. He says . . . but that's his footstep."

"I couldn't believe it, when Cervax told me it was you", Boethius said, entering. "My dear boy, I'm delighted to see you back. Rusticiana, my dear, tell them to give us a specially good meal tonight. Peter comes from places where they know how to dine."

As they talked, Peter watched the wrinkled, sallow face, and the white temples. He has gone to seed, he thought. He can't be more than fifty, but he's old, old.

"I shall not be able to stay long, unfortunately", Boethius said.

Rusticiana frowned. "You don't have to go back to the Senate again, I hope?"

"No, but I must see a number of people. There is bad news, I'm afraid. I may even have to go to Ravenna. Can't see how they can possibly enforce it, but if they do, it'll be most troublesome; it may undo all my work."

"What are you talking about?" Rusticiana asked anxiously.

"The King seems to believe that we Italians are no longer trustworthy", Boethius said with some bitterness. "There is to be a general order to deliver up all arms to the Gothic authorities, helmets, swords, armor, shields, lances, spears, even daggers and knives above a certain length."

Peter whistled through his teeth. "They won't like that."

"No one could. They'll start with the Italian contingents of the army. There aren't many, but they will resent it most, naturally. Then comes the entire civil population."

"You don't mean to say that people like Papilius and Caesonius and Licinius will have to give up the swords of their great ancestors hanging in their trophy rooms, to some Gothic boor ransacking their houses?" Rusticiana asked. "Surely . . . "

"I'm afraid the new law states explicitly that there must be no exceptions", Boethius said sadly. "You mentioned one of many points I must bring to the attention of the King. I know they intend to search all houses."

"But this is frightful, Boethius. . . . "

"Yes. Yes. Very disagreeable. As I said, I shall probably have to go to Ravenna to argue with the King, though he does so hate it when one comes to see him unasked."

"Don't go", Rusticiana pleaded. "The King's gone mad, obviously. He may do anything. He may even have you arrested."

Boethius began to laugh. "That he will *not* do", he said. "It would be like telling the whole of Italy that even the most loyal and conscientious collaborator is to him no more than a potential enemy. It would be worse than unwise, it would be extremely foolish. He's not as mad as all that. In fact he's not mad at all, just getting more and more suspicious."

"So you trust him?" Peter asked casually.

Boethius screwed up his face, wrinkling it even more. "Trust him? My dear boy, you always had a knack of asking rather surprising questions. Do I trust the King? He . . . he is alien to me, naturally. His mind works quite differently from mine, and his reactions can be sudden and totally unexpected. Even so, I must admit in fairness that he is usually what we would call high-minded, naturally noble. . . . "

"And so he burned the church of Saint Stephen", Rusticiana said acidly.

"That was a bad lapse", Boethius admitted.

"But do you trust him?" Peter repeated.

Boethius gave an embarrassed little laugh. "I'm afraid it is much more important that he should trust me, which I think he does, up to a point."

"Precisely", Rusticiana said. "But what is that point?"

Boethius sighed. "I can't say I relish the idea of arguing with him over this arms issue", he said wearily. "I know so well what I must say and what he will answer. And you can't argue with him for long. Perhaps . . . perhaps I ought to resign."

"I wish you would", Rusticiana said quickly.

"Wouldn't he regard it as a sign that his suspicions were correct and that no Italian can be trusted?" Peter asked.

"You're quite right, my boy; he might take it like that. I really don't know what to do. I must talk to Faustus about it, to Albinus, and to your wise father, Rusticiana. *Beatus ille, qui procul negotiis,* eh? Horace knew what he was talking about, although he was rather lighthearted about most major issues. What do they say in Byzantium, Peter? I wonder whether they expected their edict to have such grave consequences. Mind you, this is no longer a matter of religious discord, it is the general attitude of the King that seems to have changed."

"I don't think they bother too much about things over here", Peter said, with a shrug. "Not the people I met, anyway. They have their own problems to worry about. The Persian frontier . . . "

"Ah, yes, that's always been a trouble spot."

"However," Peter said, "if good old Justinus felt that the people here still cared about the old ties between East and West, he might try to placate the King . . . make him presents, send him flattering letters, suggest that his own measures were only transitory . . . that sort of thing."

Boethius looked at him sharply. "What makes you think so, Peter? Do you know him?"

"Heavens, no", Peter laughed. "He doesn't even know I exist. It just occurred to me as a possibility. Justinus is a peaceful old man, and if he's approached in the right way . . . "

"Listen to him", Boethius exclaimed. "He's got the makings of a statesman, a diplomat at least. There may be something in what you say, Peter. I know the King has been upset lately by the attitude of Byzantium. Cassiodor has hinted at it in his letters. If that attitude could be changed . . . on the other hand, it might be quite wrong to make a direct approach. Perhaps you'd better come with me to Albinus', after dinner, Peter, and we'll talk it over there."

"I must admit, I was looking forward to a long chat with my gracious hostess", Peter said, with an odd smile. But Rusticiana remained silent, and he went on: "I suppose there will be an opportunity for that later on. I am quite at your disposal, Uncle Boethius."

"I do so wish you would resign, my dear", Rusticiana said.

"There is always time for that", Boethius replied. "Let's see whether we can remedy the situation. We must think of Rome first, mustn't we, Peter?"

"Quite", Peter said, and for some reason Rusticiana felt more worried than ever.

Cervax announced that dinner was served.

As they were moving towards the dining room Rusticiana touched Peter's arm. "Promise me something", she muttered.

"What?"

"That you will watch over him. If anything of what you told me is true, do this for me. Watch over him. See that he doesn't come to harm."

"I promise", Peter said.

14

"AGENT 23—Italy: To the Illustrissime Master of the Sacred Palace of Byzantium, Narses, devotion, profound respect, and the assurance of prayer for copious assistance and grace from heaven:

"Report III: Since my last report my efforts to assess the loyalties of the Roman Senate have come to a conclusion. Of the three hundred and three members only seven can be regarded as definitely pro-Goth, and seventy-one as definitely pro-Byzantine. A list of the names of each group is attached to this report. All others are ready to change sides according to their personal advantage, and therefore not likely, at this time, to say, write, or do anything that might endanger their position. They will become the Emperor's most faithful subjects as soon as no risk to their property or their necks is involved.

"I have tried also to get as clear a picture as possible of the views of other sections of the population. Merchants, traders, and other businessmen are pro-Goth rather than otherwise, which is due, in the main, to the low taxation, the security of the roads, the lack of interference on the part of the Gothic authorities, and to some extent also to the fact that the army of occupation as well as the Gothic civilian population pay in cash for large quantities of consumer goods. The 'man in the street' is lethargic and uninterested in matters of government, although he still dimly resents the presence of a million foreigners. Discontent is strongly marked among landowners who had to cede one third of their land to the Gothic invaders.

"The new law requiring the surrender of all arms to the Gothic authorities caused a certain amount of indignation, especially when private houses were searched by Gothic soldiers, but no rioting took place and none is to be expected.

"Pope John and his bishops are taking great care to stand aloof from all political issues, although there have been several cases of rough treatment of priests suspected of sympathies for the East.

"The Gothic secret service, allegedly under the command of Count Bilimer in Ravenna, appears to be rather obvious and not too well informed, but some of its Roman agents, like Opilio and Gaudentius (both senators and listed under Group A, pro-Goth) are clever and quite observant. I might have encountered difficulties with the latter, if I had not been forewarned by our Agent Seven in Ravenna who informed me in time that the correspondence of a number of malcontents was watched. Mail leaving Italy by sea is frequently checked by Bilimer's men. This report will therefore be carefully hidden until my messenger's ship has left the port of embarkation.

"The group of malcontents in Rome, formerly known as the Young Lions (a name dropped many years ago) is led by Senator Albinus (Group B of the list attached), whose dossier is well known to you and whose sympathies are unchanged. At a meeting in his house I planted the idea of writing to the Emperor, asking him to intercede with the King in a diplomatic way, with the view of easing the present tension. Senator Boethius (see my earlier reports 1 and 2) was at first in favor of the idea, but changed his mind, when some of the former Young Lions composed a first draft in which they asked the Emperor to 'give back the freedom of Rome and of Italy'. Boethius became quite angry, and Albinus was intelligent enough to agree with him that such a step would go far beyond the original idea and would be regarded as treason.

"I shall have to see Albinus alone. He is the right type for the plan outlined to me in paragraph 5 of your instructions: clever, important, vain, and occasionally rather impulsive.

"There exists another group of malcontents, led by a priest by the name of Florentius. Their activities are so clumsy that they must be regarded as downright dangerous for our cause. Under the cloak of patriotism they work mischief for mischief's sake, using hired thugs to do away with those they regard as their enemies. The priest Florentius is leading a riotous life, associating with a number of ladies of bad repute, including one Lelia, who used to move in high society but is now reduced to hiring out a troupe of female artists, tumblers, acrobats, and the like for entertainment at parties. This Lelia proved to be my best informant about Florentius and his group, several members of which have been in trouble with the city prefect over the magic-and-sorcery paragraph of the law and extricated themselves only by the testimony of the priest Florentius who declared them to be good Christians. Florentius, too, is supposed to be interested in occult studies.

"As this group is of no use to us, I propose to sacrifice it in order to establish my position with the Gothic authorities.

"I shall need a few more months to bring about a crisis of the kind referred to in paragraph 6 and 7 of your instructions. If it is to produce long-lasting consequences and a definite rift between the Roman people and the Gothic usurpers, it must be of such a nature that there can be no forgiveness. Events must take place that history will never forget. Twenty years ago only a fool or a child could have thought of bringing about an event of that kind. Now however, the increasing irritability and suspiciousness of the aging King should make it possible."

"The Senator Quintus Gaudentius to the gallant and noble Count Bilimer in Ravenna, greetings and expressions of high esteem:

"That young man Peter, or Petros, sometimes referred to as

Peter of Salonica, from an estate he acquired there some years ago, comes to my house fairly frequently, and I feel compelled to revise my opinion of him. I have been able to ascertain that his wealth comes from an inheritance, formerly held in trust for him by, of all people, Senator Boethius, and increased by the young man himself in a series of fortunate speculations. Although he moves in the best circles, he does not entertain on a lavish scale. Politically, I find him very clear-headed. He just laughed at the childish ideas of some of my colleagues, like Domnentiolus and Albinus and tells me that in Byzantium the younger generation (by which I suppose he means Prince Justinian and his set) are interested only in Eastern problems and especially the question of succession to the throne in Persia, which is a vital one. He told me that sooner or later the Emperor must make war against Persia and that for that reason he is more than ever interested in peace and quiet in the West.

"Senator Boethius, whom he likes to call his uncle, he regards rather naïvely as 'a well-meaning old dodderer' who ought to stick to philosophical treatises. Here, as you know, I beg to differ, but Peter was brought up in the Senator's house and thus is almost bound to misjudge him. The very fact that Boethius is still on very friendly terms with Albinus speaks louder than all his professions of loyalty to our great and glorious King.

"I still maintain that Peter of Salonica is an agent of Byzantium as I pointed out to you before, but I now believe that he has come here to represent the good will of 'the younger generation', and of this he has given me proof. He pointed out to me that in the course of the doubtful pleasures most young men seem to find in nightly excursions to the less reputable places of the city, he had come across the activities of an occult group, strongly opposed to the regime, and he gave me names and addresses. I followed this up and planted two of my men in the Hecate Club as the group calls itself after the pagan goddess of the underworld. One of them has come to grief. His body was recovered in a horrible state in a derelict building in the Subura. The other, however, gave me a full report, including a list of fourteen people, six of whom are women. Apart from the usual orgies, the group has reintroduced the cult of Hecate, and in the course of their unhallowed activities, tried to put a curse on the King in the course of a magical ceremony. I at once informed City Prefect Cyprianus and action was taken last night. I am glad to inform you that all fourteen members were arrested. Under close interrogation they not only admitted their crimes, but also mentioned the names of further devotees of the cult, whose arrest is imminent. There were also a number of 'guests', but it is difficult to ascertain their identity, as they invariably came in disguise. Peter himself mentioned the name of one Florentius who is a priest, but his name does not appear on the list of members. He was not present when the city prefect's men arrested the group, nor could he be found at his house, so it is quite likely that he was involved in some way and has gone into hiding or left Rome altogether. In any case the horrible machinations of these people have come to an end. Please recommend me to the great King under whose reign Italy is flourishing as never before."

"Aulus Cyprianus, Prefect of Rome, to Count Bilimer in Ravenna, greetings:

"I regret to report that the order to put the Senator Albinus under arrest could not be complied with. The Senator has disappeared. His house and that of Fulvia Crispinilla, his mistress, were searched very thoroughly. Slaves of both households testified that the two left together in a litter. Ownership of the litter is unknown. It is not possible to say, at this stage, whether the Senator is still in Rome or whether he has left the city, but it must be regarded as certain that there has been a leakage of information. The Senator's flight appears to have been extremely well prepared. Neither money nor jewels were found in either house. All papers are being studied by my clerks, but so far nothing relevant has been discovered. This also clearly points to a leak. Here in Rome only three people had official knowledge of the imminent arrest: the Senator Boethius; the Senator

Gaudentius, and myself. I can vouch for Senator Gaudentius' discretion, as for my own."

"The Senator Quintus Gaudentius to the gallant and noble Count Bilimer in Ravenna, greetings and expressions of profound respect:

"I am sending this by special courier. The Senator Boethius left Rome half an hour ago, allegedly for Ravenna. He will be shadowed by the city prefect's men, so there is no need for worry. He left by the Salarian Gate. Still no news about Senator Albinus. Much perturbation in the Senate, where Senator Opilio said that he regarded its temporary closing as very probable and its complete abolition by the King as possible. Senator Decoratus asked for a declaration of loyalty, signed by all members, to be sent to the King. Old Senator Symmachus declared that he could see no reason for such action, as no one to his knowledge had put the loyalty of the Senate in doubt; if, however, the King did harbor such doubts, no declaration was likely to change his mind. Senator Symmachus, as you know, is Senator Boethius' father-in-law.

"Long life and a glorious reign to the King."

15

"SENATOR BOETHIUS has arrived, my lord King", Cassiodor announced. "He begs to be received in audience."

Theodoric turned his head and stared at his minister. "He shall have it", he said. "Let him come in." He watched Cassiodor walk back to the entrance. Getting old, too, he thought. Old before his time. But there is no treason in being miserable.

Cassiodor lifted the curtain, and Boethius walked in slowly, stiffly; another man old before his time. Still in his traveling clothes, crumpled and stained—not only the clothes, the whole man.

"Cassiodor," the King said, as Boethius made his obeisance, "leave us." Cassiodor retired in long-suffering obedience.

"I must apologize", Boethius said, "for appearing before the King in this manner. . . . "

Crumpled and stained. Tired, very. But there was no fear in the man's eyes.

"What do you want of the King, Senator Boethius?"

"Justice, my lord King."

"Justice", Theodoric repeated slowly. "Your wish is granted. Justice it will be. Not mercy. You may speak."

"My lord King, I received a royal order to have the Senator Albinus arrested for high treason."

"Yes."

"Attached to the order was a copy of the accusations made against the Senator by various people, including Senator Gaudentius, Senator Opilio, Senator Decoratus, and the Prefect of Rome, Aulus Cyprianus."

"Yes."

"I read these accusations," Boethius said, "and I regard them as a clumsily woven net of lies and calumnies. I have known Senator Albinus all my life. He is an honorable man, and I am happy and proud to call him my friend."

Theodoric leaned back in his chair. The fingers of his right hand played with the hilt of his sword. He said nothing.

"Some of the remarks quoted in the accusations were made in my presence", Boethius went on. "The accusers have twisted them almost beyond recognition."

"The Senator Albinus", the King said between his teeth, "has been in correspondence with the court of Byzantium."

"That by itself is no evidence of treason, my lord King."

"No?" The King's eyes contracted to mere slits. "You believe, then, that a Roman senator is entitled to correspond with foreign powers behind my back?"

"Assuredly . . . as long as his correspondence does not contain anything likely to be harmful to his own country."

"To his own country?" Theodoric asked in a low voice. "Or to me and the Goths?"

"The monarch's official title is King of the Goths and the Italians", Boethius said stiffly. "This implies that there can be no differentiation between the two."

"By God," Theodoric said, "I believe you're trying to remonstrate with me. What do you think I'd do to one of my nobles, if I found out that he was in touch with the enemy?"

"To the best of my knowledge there is no state of war between Italy and Byzantium, my lord King."

"There are ways of waging war without declaring it", Theodoric rasped. Almost casually he went on: "How do you know that the correspondence of Albinus is not treasonable? Have you seen his letters, or did he tell you what he wrote?"

"Neither, my lord King."

"Did he ask for your advice in the matter?"

"No, my lord King."

"I have heard differently", Theodoric said gravely. "But we shall let that pass . . . for the moment. How is it that my order to arrest Albinus was not executed?"

"Senator Albinus could not be found, my lord King."

"Did you warn him?"

"No, my lord King."

"Somebody must have", Theodoric said dryly. "Do you know where he is?"

"No, my lord King."

"Flight points to guilt", Theodoric said.

"Not necessarily, my lord King. A man may flee when he has come to the conviction that powerful enemies have decided to destroy him and are ready to commit perjury in order to achieve their aim."

Theodoric stamped his foot. "You are making common cause with the traitor when you talk like that, Boethius."

"If flight points to guilt, I cannot be guilty", Boethius said coldly. "I have come straight to the King."

"Then Senator Albinus will be put on trial," Theodoric snapped, "and it won't help his cause that he is not here to defend himself. If he doesn't turn up, judgment will be given *in absentia.*"

"I am ready to defend him," Boethius replied, "and as I cannot do so as one of the King's ministers, I must ask for permission to resign."

The King's fingers played again with the swordhilt. "Defend him, eh? What if I tell you that some of his letters to Byzantium have been intercepted and are in my possession? What, if in one of them he expresses the hope that Italy will be free again, as he puts it?"

"To hope for something does not constitute a crime", Boethius stated. "And to hope for the freedom of one's own country is natural and necessary for any man but a born slave."

"You dare to tell me that?"

"I would despise myself, if I did not", Boethius said. "You cannot forbid a man's hope, my lord King. You cannot forbid a man's thoughts. It is the fundamental difference between a ruler and a tyrant."

"This is rank insolence. . . ."

"Oh no, my lord King. It is simply the truth, and the ruler will endure it, indeed he will insist on it; only the tyrant will condemn it. If there is nothing worse in the letter of Senator Albinus than the expression of a hope, he will be fully acquitted. He must be." He was trembling. "I have asked the King for justice," he went on, "and the King has promised it to me. I have been the King's faithful servant for more than twenty years, because I have felt that by serving him I was serving Rome. I have deeply regretted a number of measures taken in answer to the Byzantine edict against the Arians. Two wrongs do not make a right. I warned the King against the law forcing all Italians to give up their arms. For suspicion must breed suspicion. But even then I went on serving the King. Now it seems that we Italians are no longer allowed to hope and to think. If that is so, I can serve the King no longer."

Theodoric roared. "Do you want me to grant a license to

conspiracy? Your friend Albinus is a traitor and will be punished accordingly. What's more, I shall find out how many more traitors there are in the Senate."

Boethius folded his arms. "If Albinus is guilty," he said, "then so am I—and so is the entire Senate."

The King rose. For one moment it seemed that he might strike Boethius in the face. Instead he walked past him and out of the room.

Boethius gave a deep sigh. He passed a weary hand over his forehead. He might at least have offered me a chair, he thought petulantly. Barbarians, all of them. Without exception.

Steps, loud and heavy. Clanking.

A beefy Goth towered over him, the officer of the guards. "King's orders", he said in atrocious Latin. Cold iron encircled Boethius' hands, a chain rattled.

"Follow me", the Goth said.

There were two more of them, with swords and spears, one on the right, one on the left; really, it was too ridiculous.

"Where are you taking me?"

"You see when you get there. Now you come."

"Wherever it is," he said, "at least I shall be able to sit down."

Walking between the two soldiers Boethius looked almost as small as a child.

16

"AGENT 23—Italy: To the Illustrissime Master of the Sacred Palace of Byzantium, Narses, devotion, obedience, and the blessings of the saints:

"The arrest of Senator Boethius caused widespread consternation. Everybody expected many more arrests to follow, and there were rumors that the King intended to have all senators put in jail and to declare the Senate itself abolished. The worthy fathers of the city were much relieved when Theodoric did nothing of the kind, but instead went through the ancient rigmarole of long-gone imperial times to make them try their famous colleague and former head, with all the formalities due his rank and position. They accepted their task with alacrity; feeling, no doubt, that the role of judge was much preferable to that of the culprit or of the potential conspirator.

"The King's move is a sly one, and Theodoric can be sly, except when he is in a rage. It may be hard to believe that a Gothic ox can have a sense of diplomacy, but Theodoric has it, and the worthy senators are fawning on him; most of them, anyway.

"Nevertheless the affair of Boethius has had the effect we desire. Unlike the spineless men on the Capitol, the people are thoroughly upset, astonishingly so, when one considers that the imprisoned man, far from being a man of the people, is a scion of one of the most ancient Roman families, a born aristocrat and a thinker and philosopher to boot. In the inns and on the market place one hears curses and maledictions against the Goths, uttered by men who have never read a line of what Boethius has written. The Gothic regime, needless to say, has never been popular. But never has it been as unpopular as it is today.

"Boethius has been taken to Pavia, where Count Pitza is royal governor, a brother or cousin of Counts Tuluin and Ibba . . . all three of them fiercely anti-Italian, I hear.

"Contrary to my expectations, Cassiodor has not resigned—nor has the King dismissed him. The man is a mystery to me, but I doubt whether it is worthwhile trying to solve.

"What will finally happen to Boethius is not easy to foretell. The only certainty is that the senators will not acquit him, as that would be tantamount to overriding the King's own judgment expressed by the order of arrest. They are debating now, not whether Boethius is guilty or innocent, but what exactly he is guilty of. The weirdest insinuations and accusations are cropping up, including those of sacrilege and of using magical arts, although hell alone knows how they could get their minds to dwell on such obvious absurdities. There is, after all, a difference between Boethius and the priest Florentius and his group.

"Senator Albinus has still not been found, and your devoted servant is about the only man in Rome whom that does not surprise. Yesterday I received the message agreed upon, announcing his safe arrival on the little estate in Sicily I bought from the Vandal prince, Sason. It is fortunate that only part of Sicily belongs to Theodoric's realm—though it's the much larger part. The Vandal, around Lilybaeum, may well serve for many more fugitives from the Gothic brand of justice.

"I have established a listening post in Pavia, so I hope to hear about the developments there early enough to take any measures that may become necessary. But I think it will be several months before the prisoner is brought to trial. In the meantime not only Count Bilimer and the Goths' secret service, but also some of the prisoner's former colleagues are trying their utmost to collect evidence, and there is some talk about certain letters, signed by Albinus, Boethius, and possibly others, asking for the Emperor's help by force of arms. The question is not whether these letters are forgeries, but who the forger is.

"To think that all this started with my remark, quite casually planted, that it might be useful to write to Byzantium, asking the Emperor to put in a good word for the harassed subjects of Theodoric! But then, as Your Illustriousness pointed out to me before I left, there is rarely the need to destroy a man one wants to be destroyed. All that is necessary is to give him a good opportunity to destroy himself. Like so many others, I am most indebted to your wisdom."

The cell in the gigantic tower of Pavia had only one small window and as there was no lamp, Boethius could write only during the day.

"How easy it is to acquire new habits even at my age, when one must", he said, looking up at the small square, crossed by iron bars. He could see it. That meant that the first gray of the morning was filling the sky. "I used to work through half the night and more, and sleep deep into the day. Now I await the dawn as a lover awaits the arrival of his beloved. It is bliss to see her come, slowly, as if hesitating, and yet with certainty. It is a new kind of bliss, a new joy. And thus again I defeat those who wish to take all joy out of my life. You are right, you are always right, my great Lady."

He had come to like talking to Lady Philosophy aloud, although she understood his mute thoughts just as well, and he spoke to her with all the love and deference due to an angel of God.

It was she who had given him the idea of writing his book, the book to console those in affliction, and as she came from heaven the idea was a divine one; and as it was divine, acting upon it consoled not only the reader but the writer also. For such is the nature of divine gifts that he who gives them away becomes richer instead of poorer.

The little square high up in the wall grew lighter and there was just a tinge of red in it, a pale red, chaste and yet warm and soft.

Soon, soon now he would be able to see enough to write for a whole, long day, to continue his dialogue with Lady Philosophy. Would God that they could read it, all those who needed the Consolation of Philosophy: poor Rusticiana, his sons, Albinus—everyone who suffered and had not yet come to clarity as he had; and above all those who caused the suffering of others.

He prayed for a little while, while the light grew stronger and clearer. When he finished he would sit down on the low, three-legged stool and take his reed pen and write. Parchment he had enough, the one favor Cassiodor had been able to obtain for him.

"Nowadays," he wrote, "lawyers endeavor to make the judges pity those who have suffered; whereas pity is more justly due to the causers of such sufferings. It is they who should be brought by compassionate accusers to judgment as sick men are brought to the physician, that their diseases and faults might be taken away by punishment. . . . "

The golden sentences poured out as the rays of the sun came pouring in.

" . . . To hate the wicked would be against reason. For as faintness is a disease of the body, so is vice a sickness of the mind. Wherefore, since we judge those that have corporal infirmities to be worthy of compassion rather than of hatred, much more are they to be pitied, and not abhorred, whose minds are oppressed with wickedness, the greatest malady that may be."

"Agent 23—Italy: To the Illustrissime Master of the Sacred Palace of Byzantium, Narses, most respectful greetings and deference:

"Pope John the First has been summarily ordered to appear before King Theodoric in Ravenna and Agent Seventeen has informed me that the King asked, or rather commanded the Pope to travel to Byzantium, as the King's special ambassador, there to request that all measures against the Arians be stopped, that all Arian churches be given back to that sect and that those who had abjured it and become Catholics, be asked to return to it. According to Agent Seventeen the Pope at first refused to go, but the King fell into one of his famous rages and uttered such terrible threats that the Pope accepted the mission, with the exception of the last demand—the re-conversion of Catholics to Arians.

"I cannot refrain from commenting that Theodoric is now ordering the Pope to do the thing for which he arrested Boethius and still wants to arrest Albinus!

"The rumor reached me today that Theodoric is going to ask the Senate to condemn Senator Boethius to death. It is as yet unconfirmed, but I am informed that old Senator Symmachus, Boethius' father-in-law, has left Rome for Ravenna, to ask the King for clemency."

Count Pitza, Governor of Pavia, was being visited by his brother Tuluin when the King's letter arrived. "That looks to me like the decision", he said, with a significant glance. "Well, we'll soon see. Hey, Trautmar, come here and read this thing to me."

Old Trautmar, former leader of a Hundred, had the functions of a secretary to the governor, because he could both read and write, accomplishments of which, to Pitza's amusement, he was quite proud.

"If only the old man hasn't weakened", Tuluin said nervously. "You never know with him. And the Runts must have their lesson. Bilimer tells me that they are more sullen and insolent than ever."

"Come on, Trautmar, hurry up", Pitza urged. The faces of the two brothers, eager, hawklike, were turned towards the elderly Goth who was moving his lips as he deciphered the letter.

"From the palace in Ravenna", Trautmar said ponderously.

"From where else", Tuluin exploded. "What's it say, you ox?"

"Shut up, brother", Pitza said. "Now then, Trautmar . . . "

" 'Order of the King' ", Trautmar read in a reproachful tone. " 'To the Governor of Pavia, Count Pitza, greetings: Know that it is my will and that of the senate of Rome that the prisoner Boethius be put to death forthwith.' "

"At last", Tuluin ejaculated with much relief.

" 'As he has sinned against us with his mind,' " Trautmar went on, " 'he shall be killed by crushing his skull which is the seat of his mind. Theodoric, by the grace of God King of the Goths and the Italians.' "

"That's a new one", Tuluin said, laughing. "Not a bad idea, though. If a man runs away from the enemy, cut off his legs. If he has spread lies, tear out his tongue. Well, I'm glad the old man has not turned soft."

"Right, Trautmar", Pitza said. "Put that paper on the table and tell Wulfila I want him."

A few minutes later the jailer came in and received his

instructions. "Crush his skull?" he asked doubtfully, tugging at his beard. "How do I do that?"

"I don't know and I don't care", Pitza said impatiently. "You ought to know your business. Report to me as soon as it's done."

Wulfila departed, shaking his grizzled head.

"How the learned Cassiodor must have hated writing that letter", Tuluin jeered.

"The King has other secretaries", Pitza said, with a shrug. "He probably spared Cassiodor's feelings."

"Can't understand why he keeps that Runt with him all the time", Tuluin said. "It's the woman's doing, I'll bet."

"Amalaswintha? You may be right there, brother. She's a Goth only in name. And Cassiodor has taught her all the Roman tricks."

"She's the King's daughter", Tuluin said, "and his only child. If anything happens to the old man . . . "

"She can't rule!" Pitza exclaimed, horrified. "Her son will be King."

"Athalaric is a child", Tuluin said. "He's growing up, but who knows whether he will have grown up by the time the old man goes. Then what? We ought to call for a *Ding* of all the armed men and get rid of the Amalung dynasty by general vote."

"That's dangerous talk, brother", Pitza said, looking around nervously. "The King isn't dead yet. He may live for another ten years or more. Let the gods decide the issue."

"That's another good reason for getting rid of the Amalungs", Tuluin said in a low voice. "They've forsaken the gods and gone over to the crucified Jew."

"Many of our people have done that", Pitza said. "No good dragging that kind of thing into it. Let them believe what they like. Some worship Father Wodan, some Donar, some Ziu—why not let others believe in the Jew-God?"

"Because he's got nothing to do with our people", Tuluin said hotly. "And because he excludes all the others."

"You won't be able to bypass the boy Athalaric", Pitza

warned. "Most of our people will regard him as their lawful ruler, when the King has gone, and we can't risk disunity, not in this damned country."

"I know, brother; you don't have to tell me that. That's why I've been trying hard to make friends with the boy and get him over to our ways. But that woman found out about it and ever since she keeps him away from me as much as she can. She can't always." Tuluin grinned. "The boy likes wine, and his mother keeps him short. It won't be long before he'll have an eye for the girls, too. Uncle Tuluin is always ready to help a young prince. Well, we'll see. By the great Father of Victory, how long does it take that man of yours to crush a Roman skull?"

"I wish he would finish off a few others I could name at the same time and by the same method", Pitza said. "The King should have done away with those speechmakers in Rome altogether. From the way this country is run one would think any lousy Italian is as good as a Goth, when we proved that they're not. There isn't a single Runt I couldn't lick with my left hand alone."

"Nor I", Tuluin said. "Ah, there's Wulfila."

"Sorry if I look messy", the jailer said sourly. "Even with two of my men, it wasn't so easy."

"You do look a sight", Pitza said distastefully.

"Tried to carry out orders", Wulfila growled. "Tied a cord round the prisoner's forehead and we tugged, till his eyeballs started from their sockets. Never thought a Runt could have such a hard skull. Wouldn't break. So we clubbed him."

"He's dead, then?"

"That he is."

"Did he grovel?" Tuluin asked.

"Can't say he did. Very polite and civil he was, as always. When I told him why I was there, he said he was glad I had come today instead of yesterday, because it had given him time to finish his book."

"Mad, of course", Tuluin said. "Couldn't bear prison life after a life of luxury; went mad. All these Runts are degenerate."

"Then he prayed for a bit", Wulfila said. "It didn't take him long. Oh yes, he said would I take his book to the governor, so that it could be sent to Ravenna. Here it is." He put the manuscript on the table. "When we started on him he said nothing, just groaned a little. He didn't struggle."

"Oh, all right", Pitza said. "You can go to the office and get your five solidi."

"And one for each of my men", Wulfila reminded him.

"Yes, yes. Now, what are you waiting for?"

"The governor must view the body", Wulfila said morosely.

Pitza grinned. "Stickler for regulations, that fellow Wulfila."

"What are you going to do about this?" Tuluin asked, pointing to the manuscript.

"Send it to the King", Pitza replied. "No need for me to bother about it. Trautmar would take months to read all that stuff. Boethius must have been scribbling away all the time. Let the King have his fun with it. All right, Wulfila, I'm coming."

17

"CASSIODOR! Cassiodor . . . "

"Princess?" Cassiodor, pale and exhausted, waited until Amalaswintha reached him in the long corridor leading to the King's rooms.

She asked, in a whisper: "It isn't true, is it? It can't be. About Symmachus . . . "

"The Senator Quintus Aurelius Symmachus, former Consul, former Princeps Senatus, was executed this morning at the third hour", Cassiodor said woodenly.

Amalaswintha stared at him, horrified. "But . . . how can that be? There was no trial, not even an official accusation."

"No", Cassiodor said. "But the King gave the order. I did not know anything about it, until half an hour ago. Now, if you will forgive me, Princess, I must go. The King has sent for me."

"Cassidor, you don't think . . . you don't think. . . . I won't let anything happen to you. . . . "

"You won't be able to prevent it, if it is the King's will", he said, trying to smile. "I don't know why it should happen; but then I could have said the same thing of Symmachus." He bowed to her and walked on.

Sobbing, Amalaswintha returned to her rooms.

Cassiodor found the King alone in the smaller of the two audience halls, standing at the bay window. From there he could see a part of the fortifications of the city. Ravenna was the strongest fortress in the whole of Italy, in the whole world, perhaps. Theodoric himself had besieged it in vain, and entered it only when Odovacar agreed to discuss a peace treaty with him. Here in this room, big, merry, swaggering Odovacar had set his hand to the treaty. Cassiodor, then the Herulian's secretary and interpreter and only a little over twenty, had stood behind Odovacar. The next day the Gothic troops entered, and a great banquet took place in honor of the two leaders, both undefeated.

And at that banquet Theodoric had killed Odovacar with his own hand, the Gothic troops had attacked Odovacar's men, most of them unarmed, all of them taken by surprise. It was not a battle, it was butchery. The rest surrendered. Theodoric had allowed them to join his own army and treated them very generously . . . including Cassiodor who from then on became his secretary.

It has always been in him, Cassiodor thought.

The King turned towards him. "It was a long time ago, Cassiodor. More than thirty years. But you remember it well, don't you?"

Cassiodor said nothing. Theodoric often guessed other men's thoughts.

"I did a necessary thing then", the King said brusquely. "And I had another necessary thing done this morning."

"Necessary, my lord King?"

"Yes. If I hadn't killed Odovacar then, I wouldn't be here today. And if I hadn't had Symmachus killed . . . and Boethius . . . I wouldn't be here tomorrow. I . . . or my people, which to me is the same thing."

"I'm afraid I do not understand, my lord King", Cassiodor said coldly.

"Don't you? Then you're more of a fool than I think you are. Boethius was a traitor. Not because the noble Roman Senate said so—that band of cowardly lickspittles would say anything and do anything to save their own precious hides. Not even necessarily because of what he wrote to Byzantium. The letters they found may or may not have been forgeries. But he was a traitor in his heart. I have given Italy the best government it has had for centuries. Yet Boethius, and indeed old Symmachus too, looked towards Byzantium the whole time. If they did not commit treason, they were at least ready to commit it, and for that abysmal ingratitude I made them pay."

Cassiodor remained silent.

"Symmachus first begged for Boethius' life", Theodoric went on. "Then he demanded his acquittal. In the end he practically threatened me. I never liked that old man with his fish-face. This time he gave himself away. I asked him what he would do if he learned of a conspiracy against my rule. Would he come and tell me about it? In his fury he bluntly told me he wouldn't. That was enough for me. The man was very wealthy. I refused to have him spending his millions undermining the position of my people in Italy. And that goes for Boethius as well, and perhaps for others, too. I shall keep my eyes open. I could have asked the Senate to start proceedings against Symmachus. They would have complied, you know that as well as I do. But this time I wished to show them, and everybody else, that I need not do that when I don't want to. All power in Italy is mine."

Still Cassiodor remained silent.

"I don't owe an explanation to anyone," the King said stiffly, "but I wanted you to know my thoughts, because both Boethius and Symmachus used to be friends of yours. And because they were, I told you about their end . . . afterwards. I didn't want you to plead for their lives in vain."

"The King is gracious", Cassiodor said, his face a blank.

"Sit down at that desk", Theodoric ordered. "There is a manuscript there. Open it at random. Now read to me."

" 'If all things were moved by compulsion,' " Cassiodor read, " 'art would labor in vain. . . .' "

"Open the book somewhere else", the King ordered.

Cassiodor obeyed: " 'For it is impossible for any man either to comprehend by his wit or to explicate in speech all the frame of God's work. Be it sufficient that we have seen this much, that God, the author of all natures, directs and disposes all things to goodness. . . .' "

"Now the end, the last lines", Theodoric said.

" 'All that being so,' " Cassiodor read, " 'the free will of mortal men remains unviolated, neither are the laws unjust which propose punishments and rewards to our wills, which are free from all necessity. There remains also a beholder of all things, which is God, who foresees all things, and the eternity of his vision, which is always present, concurs with the future quality of our actions, distributing rewards to the good and punishments to the evil. Neither do we in vain put our hope in God and pray to him. . . .' " He could not read on. His eyes were filled with tears. "Boethius wrote that", he said in a strangled voice. "I know his handwriting."

"Yes", the King said. "Count Pitza sent the book to me. Nothing political in it, it seems. You may have it. I know I have caused you much pain, lately", he added gruffly. "Perhaps you will find some consolation in your friend's book. You may go."

18

"THE DOMINA can see no one", Cervax said uneasily.

The leader of the municipal soldiers grinned at the slave. "She'll have to", he said. "What do you think we're here for, to beg from her?"

"The Domina is in mourning. . . . "

"I don't care whether she's mourning, dancing, or having a baby. My orders are to enter this house. Out of my way, fat one, or you'll be sorry for yourself the rest of your life."

Cervax ran.

It was fairly early in the morning, but Rusticiana was up. She was sitting in the study, her husband's favorite room. She had been sitting here day after day, ever since the terrible message came. The freedwoman Marcia, an old retainer, was the only one who dared to enter. But the food she brought was left untouched, except for a few morsels, and at night Marcia had much difficulty persuading her mistress to leave the study and go to bed.

But this time Cervax rushed in: "Domina . . . the soldiers have come."

The slim figure in black sat bolt upright. "I thought they would."

"Oh, Domina, what will become of us?"

"That you must ask the King of the Goths", she said stonily.

Then Marcia came in, trembling. "Domina, there are soldiers in the house. . . . "

"Yes, Marcia."

"They'll be here any moment, too."

"There is nothing I can do about it, Marcia."

"Domina, shouldn't I run and tell Senator Faustus?"

The Senator lived next door.

"I have no dealings with traitors and murderers", Rusticiana said.

"Or the Lady Serena . . . or the Lady Varria?"

"I have no friends", Rusticiana said.

The door flew open and disclosed two men. One was an official of the praetor's office, a flabby individual, bald, with small, darting eyes. The other man, more than a head taller, had very blond hair and a fair moustache. Around his tunic he wore a leather belt with a long sword. A Goth. They had sent a Goth.

"I am the Decurio Corvinius", the official said. "This is the noble Count Tota. I take it you are Rusticiana, the widow of the late Senator Boethius." He seemed to regard Rusticia's silence as a confirmation, produced a document and put it before her on the desk. Boethius' desk. "Read this", he said.

The large black letters danced before her eyes, but she forced them to stand still and give an account of themselves. "Order of the Prefect of Rome, Aulus Cyprianus" . . . *He and Opilio and Gaudentius and Decoratus had given the most hostile testimony against Boethius. . . .* "As the judgment of the august Senate of Rome against the former Senator Boethius was death and the confiscation of all his property, the house in the Trans Tiberium district, generally known as the Anician Palace, will be taken over by the government forthwith, with all that it contains, money, valuables of any kind, furniture, slaves, horses." . . . *They were murderers. Why shouldn't they be thieves and robbers? . . .* "The same applies to the properties of the former Senator Boethius in Tibur and Bajae. The widow Rusticiana is herewith ordered to leave the Anician Palace at once, taking with her nothing but her personal effects, the value of which must not exceed fifty solidi. Given in Rome, at the calends of November of the year one thousand, two hundred and seventy-seven of the founding of the city."

Marcia, standing behind her, was sobbing. So was Cervax. They did not have to read. They knew.

"I . . . shall . . . come . . . with you, Domina", Marcia said. "And please don't tell me not to . . . I'd just run after you. . . ."

"You can't", the official said. "All slaves are to stay here."

"I'm a freedwoman, I'll have you know", Marcia flared up. "I'll show you my letter of manumission. You can do nothing to me."

"Very well", the official said. "Show me the letter and you can go."

"And I'll take my own belongings with me, too", Marcia told him energetically.

"Right. Go ahead and pack your things, then, both of you. But first: Where are the keys to desks, cupboards, and all the rest?"

"Give him the keys, Marcia", Rusticiana said. "And pack two black robes for me, day robes. I shall not need anything else. Sandals, too. And a veil. Farewell, Cervax. I know the master was going to free you, you and Diocles and little Vibia. It is a great pity. Whoever your new master may be, I hope he'll be good to you all."

"Domina . . . oh, Domina. . . . "

"Until Marcia has done her packing," Rusticiana said, "may I stay here? It won't take her long."

The official said doubtfully: "There may be valuables here."

"There are", Rusticiana said. "My husband's books."

"They must stay here, too", the official said. "I don't think . . . " But the tall Goth suddenly took him by the arm and shoved him out of the room, with irresistible strength.

"I regret much, lady", he said in a guttural kind of Latin. "We Goths do not make war on women never. That man is lout. You are beautiful lady. Perhaps if you write letter to King Theodoric, ask for clemency, he let you have some part back."

"Never", Rusticiana said.

The Goth nodded. "Understand. But you stay here till woman comes back." He raised his arm, heavy with golden bracelets, in solemn salute and walked out.

Alone, Rusticiana looked around. His study, his beloved study, part of him, almost. The Myrrhine vase he loved. The little bronze statue of the Apostle Peter. The carpet, woven in faraway India. She would not forget anything about this room, she would root it in her very soul. Memory too was possession—

he had said that once. He had said so many good, wise things. Even Father said that there was no mind alive that could be compared with the mind of Boethius, Father who was so wise and good himself.

But when a man was wise and good, he had to be killed, he had to be murdered, clubbed to death, crucified.

Christ, she thought fiercely, tell me, Christ, was it worth saving a world like this? Would you do it again, if you had to? Look at them, just look at them, barbarians, trampling all that is good and noble underfoot, and Romans too cowardly to resist, ready to betray the best and deliver them to the brutes. They have learned nothing in five centuries, and they will never learn anything. Let them go, I say, don't cover them with your mantle. Let them go, let us all go to perdition. For that is where we belong.

His mantle. They had not left him his mantle, not even his hemless robe. They had stripped him of everything.... Valuables.

They were being more generous with her—she was allowed to take fifty solidis' worth with her to ... where?

She did not know. She had nowhere to go. Ever since Boethius' arrest no one had come to see her, not Senator Faustus, not Serena or Varria or clever Peter. They all knew better than to make themselves suspect by coming to the house of a man accused of high treason, so they had faded out of her life. Her sons, too, would have had to leave the house of old Paphanios, the Greek millionaire in Sicily, near Panormus. It had been considered an honor to have them as guests—consuls, both of them, despite their youth. Now it was an embarrassment. Where would they go? Where could they go? If only they did not commit any rash and foolish act, like coming to Rome. They were headstrong and fiery, especially Anicius ... they would be in trouble at once. But what about their future?

She could not think. She had tried so often to make plans for them, but she could not think; her thoughts ran in circles like rats caught in a trap. No way out.

The men would come back any moment now. "Your desk,

my Boethius, your dear desk where you did all your work for Rome, till Rome betrayed you, for mankind, till mankind turned away from you." She kissed the beautiful, polished wood. "Goodbye", she whispered. "Good-bye, my darling."

Then she rose.

The official appeared at the door. "Your freedwoman is ready", he said sullenly.

"Very well." She walked past him, through the small and the large reception room, through the dining room. In the front room she almost lost her self-control. There all the slaves were assembled, herded together by the municipal soldiers, and they stretched out their arms towards her. "Domina . . . Domina . . . dear Domina . . ."

Boethius had always been good to them.

She wanted to give them a word of comfort, of encouragement, but there was a lump in her throat, and she knew she could no longer trust her voice. The blond Goth was standing in a corner of the room, and the official was coming up behind her.

She raised her hand in a gesture of blessing and walked on.

In the atrium Marcia was waiting for her with a huge bundle. "I put your things with mine, Domina, if you don't mind", she said in a dry voice. "It's easier to carry like that."

The official behind her murmured something that sounded almost like an apology.

She gave no answer, but walked on, down the path to gatekeeper's lodge. The gatekeeper was no longer there. Instead, two soldiers were watching the gate. They crossed their spears, barring the way.

"It's all right", the official bellowed at them from the main door. "Let them go."

The soldiers stepped back.

The street opened up before them, white, dusty, and hot.

"Let me help you carry this, Marcia."

"The Domina carrying a bundle? What next!"

"You must promise to tell me when you get tired, Marcia."

"It isn't heavy at all. But, Domina, where are we going?"

"I have no idea, Marcia."

After a while the freedwoman said: "There is the little church of Saint Philip over there, Domina. Perhaps you want to drop in for a while . . . "

"I can't pray. And I don't want to. I want to go away, far away. That's nonsense, of course. I can't. We shall both be tired soon enough, and we have no money and no one to help us. I . . . I really don't know what to do, Marcia."

"If it's only money . . . we have that, Domina", the freedwoman said. "I've got sixty-five solidi in gold. Saved them up for a rainy day and this is it, I think. Besides . . . "

Both women stopped.

There was a carriage on the road, pulled up near the wall of the little church, and from the inside a hand was beckoning them to come nearer.

"Don't go, Domina", Marcia whispered, terrified. "They're trying to trap you or something. Don't go."

Trap her? There was no need to do that. Still, they might have decided to torture her by first robbing her of all she had, leaving her only her life, then picking her up again to kill her. If only they would . . . it would be the best way out. Then indeed she would go far away, where no one could harm her . . . and she would meet Boethius on the other side.

"I hope you're right, Marcia." She walked straight up to the carriage. A Gallic traveling carriage. Four horses. Leather curtains.

"Get in, quickly, Domina", said Peter.

"Peter . . . "

"Yes, yes, get in. There's no one on the road just now. Quick. That's Marcia, isn't it? Coming with you? Up you go, Marcia, next to the coachman. Here, give me that bundle. There. Now then, up with you. Comfortable, Domina? Good. Off you go, Myron."

Rusticiana touched her forehead. "I'm dreaming this", she murmured.

The carriage moved on, gathered speed.

The street rolled past, faster and faster. Peter drew the curtain. "Somebody might recognize you", he explained.

"But, Peter . . . what are you doing?"

"I was waiting for you, of course."

"You knew I was coming?"

"I knew they would occupy the house this morning, certainly. Cyprianus told me so himself, God rot his black soul. I'm on very good terms with him and with Gaudentius and all the rest of the scoundrels. I have to be. That way I can find out what I want to find out. And that's why I had to stay away from you. You know your house has been watched ever since . . . the arrest. Don't you? They're still watching the houses of some of your former friends, to see whether they will take you in. I have so much to tell you I don't know where to start. Greetings from your sons, by the way."

"My sons . . . "

"They're safe and well."

"Oh, Peter . . . where are they? With Paphanios?"

"No. Panormus is in the Gothic part of Sicily. I got them over to the Vandal side, near Lilybaeum. I have an estate there. Goths and Vandals are not on good terms, not since Thrasamund died and Hilderic became King. He's pro-Byzantine, heavens knows why, but it suits us. Splendid fellows, those boys of yours. I had the greatest difficulty in keeping them there; they wanted to come up here and save their father and save you and so on. They would have given King Ox an excellent pretext to treat them as he treated their father."

"Oh, Peter . . . Peter . . . "

"Yes, I know", he said almost roughly. "Don't give way now. Is that woman, Marcia, reliable?"

"As good as gold. Better. She's a freedwoman. She insisted on coming with me and was ready to help me with her savings."

"Good. Do you want to take her with you, then? We shan't remain in Rome, you know."

"Where are we going?" What a relief it was to leave decisions to someone else, not to have to decide anything at all.

"To Sicily. To Lilybaeum. To my estate there."

"My sons", she whispered. "I shall see my sons."

"Of course you will."

"May I tell Marcia? She . . . she has a right to know, I feel."

Peter hesitated for a short moment. "You said she was reliable", he said. "Very well, tell her." He lifted the flap of the leather curtain in front of him. "Hey, Marcia", he said.

She turned in her seat. "Yes, Master Peter?"

"We're going to Sicily, Marcia", Rusticiana said. "To my sons. Master Peter will get us there."

Marcia nodded. "The Lord has helped you, Domina", she said. "You didn't want to go into the church, so he made you find help at his very doorstep."

"That makes me an angel, I suppose", Peter remarked. "A somewhat unusual role for me, I'm afraid."

"I shall never be able to thank you enough", Rusticiana said. "I was just beginning to realize that everything was finished. No friends, no money . . . "

"But I told you, Domina, there was no need to worry about money", Marcia said.

"Because of your savings, I know. You are a dear, good woman, Marcia, and I'll never forget it. But I'm afraid sixty-five solidi would not have got us very far."

"Perhaps not," Marcia admitted, "but the bundle would have."

"What do you mean?"

The freedwoman grinned broadly. "You didn't seriously think I packed only those two robes, the sandals, and the veil, did you, Domina?"

"You put in your own things, didn't you?"

"Oh yes, a few of my rags are on top, in case they wanted to have a look. But underneath I packed all the dresses with jewels on them, the three little gold cases with all your rings and bracelets and the sapphire necklace—you wouldn't wear any of them these last weeks and you forgot to put them away, oh yes, and the large pearl necklace, too, that you gave me for restringing, and the belt with the sapphire clasp and the two Myrrhine vases you always liked best, I wrapped them very carefully . . . "

"Heavens above", Rusticiana exclaimed. "Woman, do you realize that you've taken thousands of solidis' worth, instead of fifty?"

"They won't know", Marcia declared contemptuously. "That official fellow is a fool, anybody could see that. I got little Vibia to talk to him sweetly, asking what was going to happen to her, and when he started patting her, ever so fatherly, I knew I would have time to collect your things without him nosing about too much."

"Marcia, Marcia, you could give one back faith in human beings", Rusticiana said, deeply moved. "You and Peter . . . "

"Somebody had to be practical", Marcia declared. "And you had other things to think of." She turned back, abruptly.

"She saved most of my jewels", Rusticiana said. "Now I won't have to go begging or be an encumbrance to some good soul."

"That's right", Peter said, somewhat tepidly, it seemed to her. He let the flap of the leather curtain in front drop back. "But you needn't have worried about such things. I have money enough and to spare and what I have is yours."

"Dear Peter . . . I don't know what to say. . . . "

"Then don't say anything, Domina. I am not such a fool as to start talking about . . . other things at this time. You have had the most terrible experiences, and my greatest sorrow was that I could not be with you, worse still that I had to let you think that I, too, had deserted you. But it was the only thing to do, believe me."

"I believe you, Peter."

"Good. I have arranged for fresh horses all along the way. In a few days we shall be in Sicily, on my estate, where your boys are waiting for you. There you will find rest. And a few months later we shall talk of other things."

"Peter," she said, "dear Peter . . . I shall be grateful to you till my dying day. But I'm only the shadow of the woman you knew. There's no substance left in me, no feelings. . . . "

"That will all come back. You must have a long rest first."

"It will never come back, Peter. I know now that you love

me . . . your action proves it. But what do you want with a woman who can live only for mourning?"

"You are all I want", he said in a low voice. "You are all I ever wanted."

"I'm nothing, I tell you. My life is finished."

"Is it? Are you so weak or did you care so little for Boethius that you will let him remain unavenged?"

She recoiled as if he had hit her. "*What* did you say?" she asked in a whisper.

"Theodoric and the Goths have murdered the best of men," he said, "the last great Roman. Your husband. They have murdered your father, the most honorable man in Rome, a man of almost eighty who had never done harm to anyone. And you, his daughter, and Boethius' widow, can talk about your life being finished? Have you no blood in your veins?"

"Vengeance. . . . " she whispered. "Oh, if I could . . . but what can I do, Peter? For just a moment I really thought there might be some purpose left in my life. But it is absurd. What can I do against that murderer on the throne, with his huge army?—a mere woman who must be glad that she can pay for her daily bread and a roof over her head by selling her jewels, one by one."

"Why do you think they confiscated your riches?" he asked. "And those of your father and all the property of Albinus they could get hold of? Because they were afraid all those millions would be used to avenge their crimes."

"Perhaps you're right, Peter. But they've got the millions. And even if they hadn't, money alone would never suffice."

"It would be enough to hire killers," Peter said, "experienced men, not a little boy with a stylus."

"Oh, Peter . . . "

"But little boys have a habit of growing up", Peter went on. "And when they're clever enough they may create new riches. And when they are in love with a wonderful woman, a great woman, they will put it all at her disposal."

"Dear Peter . . . "

"All, I said", he interrupted her. "And that means considerably more than money. Do you want proof of that? You shall have it. You know they've been trying to find Albinus, don't you? They've been going over Italy with a fine comb, but they couldn't get him. Do you want to know where he is? On my estate in Lilybaeum. You'll meet him there."

"Peter!"

"He won't stay there long, mind you. He must go where he will be most useful to my plans, and I shall go with him."

"Peter, what are you talking about? Where are you going?"

His eyes were gleaming. "There is only one power on earth that can defeat Theodoric and his brutes," he said, "and that is the greatest power in the world today. Byzantium."

"Byzantium!"

"That's where Albinus will go. That's where I shall go. Byzantium is a giant, Domina, but like most giants it is lazy and slow and difficult to move. I know it well. I know almost everyone who matters there. I haven't wasted my time, Domina. I've studied them carefully, Prince Justinian, the man of the future, and Theodora, the woman of the future. Belisarius, the Thracian, whom Justinian has chosen to be his army commander, when the time comes; Tribonianus; John of Cappadocia; and that little eunuch, eaten up by ambition, who is bound to rise higher and higher, because his mind is as keen as a sword blade, Narses. I know them all and they know me. Nothing is likely to happen as long as the Emperor is alive. But Justinus is old and ill. He will die soon, and Justinian will be his successor. Then, from then on, things will happen. The new Emperor will have to prove his mettle."

"But . . . but didn't you say, once, that they were all looking towards the East, towards Persia?"

"I did, yes. And they do. That's exactly where I come in, Domina. That is my task . . . to convince them that Italy is waiting to be liberated from the yoke of the Goths. Shall I do it, Domina? Do you want me to? I can, you know."

"Vengeance", she said. "Vengeance . . . "

He saw the dark fire in her eyes. "Give the word", he

whispered. "Give it, and I'll move heaven and hell to make it come true. Give the word, and you shall see the fall of the murderer and of all his brood and all his people. Beothius and Symmachus will be avenged as no men were ever avenged before. That is what I planned to do for you. Shall I do it, Domina?"

"Do it," she said breathlessly, "do it, do it. And if you bring it about, if you can unleash those forces as you say you can, then you may ask me for anything you want, and by the memory of the dead, you shall have it. I will go with you to Sicily. I will sail with you to Byzantium. And I'll come back to Italy and Rome only when the army of our liberators has landed. Then I must be here. . . . "

"You look alive again", he said triumphantly. "More than ever. Magnificently alive."

"I have something to live for", she said. "I want to see them die, all of them."

"Is it a pact?" he asked, hoarsely.

"It is a pact."

His hands gripped her shoulders. "Then seal it", he said, drawing her towards him.

She did.

19

"WE SHALL SOON be there", Tertullus said comfortingly. "It can't be very far now. Are you very tired, Placidus?"

The boy on the donkey drew himself up. "I'm not a bit tired, Father", he said. "But I'm glad we left that house."

Tertullus reined his mule to a standstill. "Florentius' house?" he asked. "The priest's? It was a very nice house, wasn't it? And he was a very friendly man."

"I didn't like him", Placidus said emphatically. "And you didn't either, Father."

"Come to think of it, I didn't, much", Tertullus admitted. "But how did you know that, little man? We were only there a couple of hours." He rode on, slowly, and the boy kept at his side. The road was barely wide enough for the two of them. Equitius and Maurus behind them, both mounted on big mules, had to ride in single file.

"You talked alone with him in the garden," Placidus said, "you and Equitius, and something you said made him very angry, but he didn't want to show it and went on smiling with his mouth."

"It wasn't what I said," Tertullus told him, "it was something I didn't say. He wanted to keep Maurus and you with him for some years, and Equitius and I did not say yes to his suggestion."

"Stay with him?" Placidus asked, with a deep frown on his young forehead. "Father, I . . . I think I would have run away the next day."

"That's a nice idea for someone who wants to be a monk", Tertullus said with mock reproach. "I wonder whether Abbot Benedictus would approve of it."

"Abbot Benedictus isn't like that priest, is he, Father?"

"I only met him a few times in poor Senator Boethius' house," Tertullus explained, "and that's a long time ago. I doubt whether we will recognize each other, today. But from all I've heard about him, he isn't at all like Florentius."

"Good", Placidus said with such relief that his father laughed.

"I don't even know whether Abbot Benedictus will take you, son", Tertullus warned. "Or, if he does, whether he'll allow you to stay. We must see. But I would have never given you into Florentius' care."

"He greeted you as if you were an old friend of his, though", Placidus said.

"Well, I used to see quite a lot of him in my younger

years—at a time when he was studying for the priesthood. He was very different, then . . . or, perhaps not so very different, it's difficult to say. But I had no idea he was here in the Anio valley. He left Rome quite suddenly, nobody seemed to know exactly why."

"He said the Goths didn't like him, didn't he?"

"Yes. Whatever that may mean."

"He came up to us so suddenly, I thought at first he was going to attack you", Placidus said.

"Held up by a holy highway man, eh?" Tertullus joked. "Well, set your mind at rest about him. You're not likely to see him again."

"Maurus didn't like him either", Placidus stated.

"Did he say that?"

"No, Father, he looked it."

Observing little fellow, Tertullus thought. Always has been. Then he thought of his own observations, the dirty floor in the priest's house, that slave, or whatever she was, with her hair tinted a reddish brown. Yet there had been good things in Florentius' house, some very pretty citrus tables, nice vases. He must have money. Placidus was quite right, the man had been very angry when he heard of the plan to take the boys to Abbot Benedictus. Why have them shut in there with a bunch of raw, uncivilized monks . . . he had harped on that for quite a while. He should have known better, surely. Even in Rome it was known that some of the best families sent their sons to join Abbot Benedictus, yet Florentius pretended that Placidus would be rubbing shoulders with slaves and fugitive criminals. It just couldn't be true. However, he would keep a sharp lookout. For the hundredth time he thought of what the boy's mother would say, if she were still alive, and as always, drew comfort from the thought that she would be glad because the boy was safe there, safely away from what was going on in Rome and elsewhere in Italy. Arrests, confiscations of property. No one could feel safe after what had happened to Boethius and old Symmachus. And Equitius, too, felt confident that he was doing the right thing. . . .

Looking down he saw that Placidus had folded his hands and was praying. In the middle of the day, and in the middle of a donkey ride, too. He opened his mouth to tell him that he would do better, for the time being, to look where he was going, when he realized that the boy was doing just that. He did not look up or down but straight ahead.

There was a lake in front of them, calm and of the clearest blue, with gently sloping hills rising all around it. Very near the lake was a fairly large wooden building, half-hidden by trees and crowned with a cross.

"This looks like peace", Tertullus wanted to say, but the thought remained silent. There was a great stillness, and, dimly, Tertullus understood why the boy was praying.

The road made a turning. From behind a group of rocks a young monk appeared and greeted them courteously. "The Father is awaiting you", he added. "He bids you welcome. He has sent me to lead you to him. I am Brother Secundus."

"How did the Abbot know we were coming at this hour?" Tertullus asked. "I only wrote we would arrive today or tomorrow, but I didn't mention any hour. And you couldn't possibly have seen us."

"I don't know how the Father knew", the monk replied with a slow smile.

"I must ask him", Tertullus decided, and he saw the young monk's smile broaden a little, then vanish, as he welcomed Equitius and Maurus with the same joyful courtesy which was almost solemnity and started walking ahead of them, with long, purposeful strides.

Neither raw nor uncivilized, Tertullus thought with satisfaction.

Equitius looked at his son. "It seems we have arrived", he said slowly. "How do you feel?"

Maurus' deepset eyes beamed back at him. "As if I were entering Canaan", he said.

Equitius crossed himself. "I hope to God you're right", he said, and he sighed a little. He, too, had been a little upset by Florentius' warning. The priest seemed so sure that it was a mistake, to say the least, to take a well-bred boy to this settlement of monks.

"This is Saint Clement's", Brother Secundus said, pointing to the building with the cross. A tall, white-bearded man appeared in the entrance and stood, awaiting them, wearing a melote and sandals like Secundus'.

"Is that the Abbot?" Tertullus enquired, almost shyly.

"No," the monk replied, "it's Brother Gudila."

As they approached, Tertullus saw that the man's hair and beard were not white, but so fair as to appear almost white; and his eyes were blue.

"But, Brother . . . Brother Secundus. Surely that man is . . . I mean, he looks to me like a Goth!"

"He is", the monk confirmed calmly. "We have three of them here. The other two are in the Monastery of the Angels. That's a good bit farther down, on the shore of the lake. The building up there on the hill is Saint Blasius, and the one below is Saint Cosmas and Saint Damian."

"But . . . but the Goths are Arians!"

"These three aren't any more", Brother Secundus replied, smiling.

Tertullus and Equitius exchanged uneasy glances.

Brother Gudila came up to them, greeted them gravely in somewhat halting Latin, helped them to dismount and managed to lead all four animals away together.

"Very efficient", Equitius remarked.

"He commanded a hundred horsemen in the Gepid war", Brother Secundus said lightly.

"Did he really? Well, he no longer behaves like a conqueror, I'll say that for him. You should see those barbarians go swaggering through the streets of Rome", Tertullus said bitterly.

"A man who comes here doesn't want to swagger", Brother Secundus replied.

"I suppose not. All the same it's a strange thing to meet a monk who is a Goth, or, if you wish, a Goth who is a monk."

"Incidentally," Equitius interposed, "what about yourself,

Brother Secundus? You speak Latin without an accent, but there is an inflection of your voice that tells me you are not a born Roman. Where do you hail from? What were you before you became a monk? Who is your father?"

"I was born and bred in Byzantium", Brother Secundus replied. "I was supposed to study law. My father's name was Skoras."

"Skoras?" Tertullus repeated incredulously. "Not the Patricius Skoras who used to be Imperial Master of Ceremonies under Emperor Anastasius?"

Brother Secundus affirmed the question with a slight bow and at the same time beckoned them all to enter the building. "We shall go first to the oratorium", he told them in a low voice. They walked along a spotlessly clean corridor with a number of rough doors right and left. The monk opened one of them and let them enter.

The chapel was tiny. It contained an altar with a white cloth on it, a crucifix and two simple candlesticks, a pulpit, and six benches, three on each side, with a narrow aisle between them.

Brother Secundus shepherded them to the first bench and knelt beside them.

He looks like a dead man when he is praying, Equitius thought. As if he had gone on and left an empty shell behind him.

A Byzantine and a Goth, Tertullus thought. I wonder whether they've got a Persian, too, or a Briton. Then the stillness of the room embraced him, his thoughts stopped chattering, stopped altogether. Little Placidus was looking at the crucifix and praying, with an expression of such joy that his father felt tears welling up in his eyes. Dear God, he thought, don't let him be disappointed.

Maurus was praying with his eyes lifted up to the ceiling, like those of the wooden Christ on the crucifix.

After a while Brother Secundus rose and, very softly, walked out, so the others, too, got up. Tertullus and Equitius smiled at each other a little sheepishly. As they turned towards the door, they saw a monk standing there, a man almost as tall as the

Goth. Brown eyes with strong eyebrows under a domed forehead, and with a brown beard.

Maurus and little Placidus were walking up the aisle. The two boys stopped before the strange monk and . . . knelt together, at the same moment.

The monk gave the children a grave bow, then stretched out his arms, drew them up and towards himself, as if he were their father. Turning, he left the chapel, taking them with him.

Tertullus and Equitius followed, stiff and embarrassed.

Outside, the monk bowed to them too. "Welcome, Tertullus", he said. "Welcome, Equitius. Stay with us as long as you wish."

"You are the Abbot", Tertullus said. "You are Benedictus. You must be."

Later he told Equitius: "Would you believe it? I felt like kneeling before him myself. Absurd, isn't it?"

"Quite absurd", Equitius agreed dryly. "You were a little ahead of me, so you couldn't see me. I did kneel."

20

THEY STAYED ON for several days.

There were two guest rooms at Saint Clement's, where fathers and sons spent the nights. The monks—there were twelve—slept together in a dormitory, in which a single, tall candle burned all through the night. They remained clothed and girded, but had to take their knives out of their belts, a new rule, due to an accident; one of the brothers had cut himself during a nightmare.

"Straw mattresses", Tertullus had said, wincing.

"But also blankets, coverlets, and a pillow," Equitius pointed out.

"And only one meal a day!"

"Except from Easter to Pentecost, yes. But it's a good meal and well-cooked. Two dishes always and a pound of bread."

"No meat—except for invalids."

"My dear Tertullus, the gladiators of former times were trained on an almost meatless diet, and they were the strongest men in the world."

"I wouldn't like to live without it."

"You don't have to. Or are you by any chance thinking of joining yourself?"

"Toyed with the idea", Tertullus admitted. "But I'm afraid I'm too old for such a change of habits."

"Habits . . . that's right. Maurus will get accustomed to the change within a few weeks and so will your boy."

"What I like about these monks is that they all seem to be cheerful", Tertullus remarked. "They don't laugh much, but one can feel that they have a zest for living. Even so . . . going to bed at sunset and getting up in the middle of the night. . . . "

"Meaning that they wake you up with their chanting in the chapel. Also a matter of habit, I suppose. I didn't like it either, at first, but then I discovered that it's rather beautiful. It's . . . it's like a new language. We'll miss it, when we're back in our own noisy, chattering, yelling, drivel-talking world."

"I asked Benedictus what was the object of the singing", Tertullus said.

"What did he answer?"

"Well, he looked at me for a moment, as if I had asked him what he had a head for or why he was walking upright instead of crawling on all fours. Then he reminded me that a prophet of the Old Testament had said, 'Seven times a day I praise you, and in the middle of the night I rise to give you thanks.' "

"It gives a definite form to their day", Equitius mused. "The way they live can't leave them much time to be bored. That's another thing about them, I haven't seen one who looked bored. Always going about some business with a kind of cheerful determination. They're building a new monastery up on the hill, Saint Victorinus. . . . "

"What, another one? They have eight already."

"Nine. Each with twelve monks and an abbot, and with Abbot Benedictus supervising the whole thing. It's all his idea, down to the smallest detail. He's worked it all out."

"He's still doing that, he told me", Tertullus said. "Says this is his testing time for certain rules. What I appreciate most is that he won't go to extremes. He won't overdo anything. It's all well-balanced and it's moderate. Yet he keeps an iron discipline. He's, er, quite a remarkable man. . . . Why are you laughing?"

"Quite a remarkable man", Equitius repeated, grinning. "That's like calling a king a fairly high dignitary."

"A king?"

"That's what he is, Tertullus, a king. The man's royal. And *that's* only part of him. He's a sage, too, and a teacher and a philosopher—the one and only philosopher who lives his philosophy. He's a father, too, in fact, he's *the* father. There's no end to the man."

"You may be right. . . . What a pity that such a man should withdraw from the world and live here with a hundred monks in the Anio valley, instead of taking a hand in the great affairs of the state—There they go, chanting again."

"Maybe that is what really matters", Equitius said.

"What? The chanting?"

"Yes. Constantly getting in touch with God. Getting others to do it, too. They sing with their hearts, these people. For all I know they may keep the world alive by what they're doing."

Tertullus shook his head. "What on earth do you mean?"

"Rotten senators", Equitius said. "Murderous Goths. Cheating merchants, whores, scoundrels, adulterers, thieves, and cut-throats. Barbarian robbers, perverts, pleasure-seekers, charlatans, and time-wasters . . . why should God go on caring for such a world? So a man called Benedictus builds a place where everything is done for the sake of God alone, with a constant stream of prayer going up in this chant of theirs; where men don't own a thing and therefore have everything. He can't build that kind of place on Palatine Hill or in the middle of Subura—only in solitude. But he's still on earth, and that chant of theirs is like a living cord, a rope he throws up to heaven, and God takes it and holds the earth in balance with it."

"You've been talking to Benedictus this morning", Tertullus stated. "While I went up to see Saint Cosmas and Saint Damian's, you were talking to Benedictus, admit it."

"Yes, I was, but he didn't tell me what I told you. Not in so many words, anyway. I'd say he . . . he made me feel it. I don't know whether you see what I mean."

Tertullus said, oddly: "I've spent time with him too. That's how I know, don't you see? He's a dangerous man to talk to. Makes one very impatient and very angry . . . "

"What!"

" . . . with oneself."

"Ah well, once you start comparing yourself with him. . . . "

"I can't help doing that, can I?" Tertullus snapped. "He's going to be the abbot of my boy, and that means he's going to be my boy's father, instead of me."

"You've made up your mind about leaving your boy here, then?"

"Of course I have, and so have you."

"Then why don't we tell the Abbot and leave?" Equitius asked innocently.

"We shall", Tertullus said. "But there's no particular hurry, is there?"

"Well, you did complain about the straw mattresses. . . . "

"I didn't complain, I only said . . . "

"And about meatless cooking. . . . "

"Leave me in peace, Equitius. Where is Maurus?"

"In the chapel. So is Placidus. They've caught the rhythm of these people."

"It is a kind of rhythm, you're right, and I don't mean the chanting only. It's the same when they work or eat or pray. There's nothing in the least sentimental about them. They are so . . . reasonable."

"He is making new men", Equitius said. "He's building up a new society, for the service of God."

"With a hundred men!" Tertullus exclaimed.

"Great societies have started with less than that."

"So they have. But do you realize that Benedictus is no older than you and I, and probably a few years younger? Forty-five, I should say. Yet not only my Placidus, but I myself feel that he is my father rather than my brother. There is a mystery about this man, a secret, and I don't want to leave here before I have found out what it is."

They did not see him again that day. He had gone to help the brothers who were building Saint Victorinus and then to talk to the abbot of Saint John up the hill, who was having trouble with the water supply.

But the next day he approached the two parents, early in the afternoon, inviting them to join him in his room. "You have seen something of our life here," he said, "and I have talked to Maurus and Placidus. If you will entrust me with them, I will have them, and gladly."

They murmured their assent.

"Very well", Benedictus said. "Neither of the boys is of age. Each of you will have to draw a document that dedicates your son to the service of God. In that document you must promise under oath that you will never make a present to your son or allow anyone else to do so. You will go with your boy to the altar of the oratorium and offer him up, his hand clasping the document and both resting on the altar cloth. This will be done tomorrow."

"I hope Placidus will persevere", Tertullus said, suddenly anxious. The Abbot's words had brought home to him the finality of his decision.

"He will", Benedictus said simply. "Banish fear from your hearts, both of you."

Tertullus gave a sigh. "That's easier said than done. We have so many causes for fear in these days. The lawgivers themselves are no longer to be trusted; they, too, are full of fear, and ready to do wrong, any kind of wrong, to please the tyrant. . . ."

"The Gospels are our law," Benedictus said, "and the Lord told us to be afraid not of those who kill the body but cannot kill the soul, but rather of him who is able to destroy both body and soul in hell."

"My Maurus", Equitius interposed, "once said to me: 'Why should I fear God, when I love him and he loves me?' I didn't know what to answer. The things children will ask. . . . "

"No mere man", Benedictus said, "can regard himself as safe from temptation. The more he loves God, the more he will be afraid to lose God's love through sin. Even in human relations we are afraid to hurt those we love. A man who loves his wife, a wife who loves her husband will be most anxious not to lose the love of the beloved. On a lower plane a man may fear to lose someone else's love because in that case he might lose his position or his money; and a man may fear God because of the punishment he will incur if he sins. And that fear also is good."

"These thoughts", Tertullus said, "remind me of a book I read very recently, and I believe no more than three people have read it so far, the author included. Here it is." He drew the manuscript from the folds of his mantle. "It's poor Boethius' last book", he added. "He wrote it in prison, and sent it to Cassiodor, who read it and sent it to me with a short note saying that this is the original text and that no copy exists. I think he was afraid to have it copied in Ravenna. He's the last Roman in the entourage of the King, and he must have many enemies."

He put the manuscript on the table, and Benedictus let his hands rest on it and closed his eyes.

Was he praying, without warning? Tertullus hesitated for a moment and then went on, somewhat uneasily: "Frankly, I didn't much want to give it to anyone for copying either. All publishers in Rome are under supervision by the authorities, lest they should spread pamphlets or manifestos against the Goths. There isn't a word against the Goths in the manuscript; it's all pure philosophy and very moving and beautiful, but the very fact that it was written by a man supposed to have been the King's enemy—" He broke off. "So I thought I'd bring it to you", he added lamely. "It will be safe here."

Benedictus nodded. Tertullus' voice was coming to him from a far distance, heard, understood, and registered by some tiny fraction of his mind. Streaming into his consciousness came the picture of a cell, a prison cell and a lonely man writing away with a will and finishing his task, and three men entering and tying a cord around his head and tugging and clubbing the man to death; yet the book remained—books do remain—so many, many books, essence and heart blood of thinkers and poets, thoughts of truth and beauty, Saint Basil's writings and Cassian's, Saint Augustine's *City of God* and *Confessions* and *Letters* and *Sermons,* Saint Jerome's work and Saint Leo's, and golden in the flood of silver and turquoise and ivory, the Gospels themselves and the psalms and the great books of the Old Testament, a flood of wisdom and revelation, the human spirit trying to find its way up to the world of the divine and God himself descending to the human world through the Word. . . .

"So I thought, maybe you would safeguard the book . . . " came the voice of Tertullus. "Surely it would be a great loss to many, if it were destroyed. . . . "

Safeguard. Save. Build a treasury, treasuries for the great writings of past and present, the writings of those who lived before the Lord came to walk on earth, so many of them men groping and striving for truth, wrestling with truth, so many of them revealing the folly of man, describing the course of history, recording the work of great physicians, the recipes against ailments and diseases. Who would think to save all that in a time when emperors and kings did not know how to read or write, when barbarians ruled over the major parts of the world and threatened to conquer the rest of it?

Here was a task. Not the main task, for that could only be the Praise of God, seven times a day. But this, too, God wanted done, and therefore it would be done.

"I shall keep this book," Benedictus said, opening his eyes, "and I will have it copied a number of times, to make sure that it survives."

"I am glad", Tertullus said. "Here it will be safe, as far as anything can be safe in a world where emperors and kings do not know how to read or write and barbarians rule the major part of the world and maybe soon the whole of it."

Benedictus nodded. It did not surprise him to hear Tertullus say, almost to the letter, what he had been thinking. It had happened to him too often before. Besides, there was another thing, large, as big as a hill, almost a mountain. . . .

"There is another thing", Tertullus said. "I haven't come to you with empty hands. I own some land, south of here, near the town of Casinum, in the Liri valley. It includes a large hill, you might almost call it a mountain." Tertullus' face broke into a smile. "If you go on building monasteries here in the Anio valley at this speed, you will soon run out of space. Will you accept the land at Casinum as my gift?"

"I will, gladly", Benedictus said after a moment. "And God will reward you. It is a great gift."

A great gift. A gift. There was another gift coming, swift feet were carrying it, and it was not a blessed gift, but a cursed one. Two abysses were always open, the abyss of sin and the abyss of the enemy's malice.

"May I ask a question?" Equitius enquired. "I have heard that you lived as hermit, years ago. What made you give it up?"

"God sent me a messenger", Benedictus said. "A priest who was preparing his Easter meal when he was told that another servant of God, a hermit, had nothing to eat. He went out and searched for me. It took him a long time, but he found me and told me to stop fasting as no one must fast on Easter day. I said, 'I know it is Easter, because I was allowed to meet you.' But he assured me that it really was the greatest feast of them all, and so we ate together. It became clear to me then how far away I was living, not from God, but from the liturgy he gave us through the Church, and I began to think that God wanted me to make a change in my way of living. Then shepherds came to me, and peasants, and wanted me to tell them about the Lord and to give them advice in many things and to judge their quarrels. . . ."

"And so you were drawn back into the company of men."

"Of some few men, yes. I had taught children at Enfide. Then those shepherds and peasants. Then monks came, from the monastery at Varia, evil men, their tonsures a lie before God. They wanted me to be their abbot. From their ways I learned about the dangers and traps of community life."

"I've heard of that", Equitius said. "They felt you were too severe and tried to poison you, didn't they?"

"Yes." Poison. Tried to poison you. Poison was coming, running on swift feet, it would soon be here. "I withdrew again, to my cave. But others came, good men who really wanted to ascend and were ready to bear all the hardships, and I accepted them and taught them what I knew. Their number grew. . . . " Two, three, ten, fifty, a hundred, a hundred and seven. A hundred and seven today, but more were coming and more, keen faces, boys, youths and men, many hundreds, thousands, and still they came, the cadres of an army, a huge army, stretching across the years, the centuries, thinning out and growing again. . . .

"I have one more question", Tertullus said. "You sent Brother Secundus to receive us and lead us here. How could you possibly know we were coming at that particular hour?"

"I was told", Benedictus said gently, and he rose and bowed a little, the sign that he could give them no more time.

When they had left the Abbot's room, Equitius said: "I wonder why he never mentioned that the cup with the poison broke when he blessed it. That's the story I was told in Rome. Maybe it didn't happen that way."

Tertullus said nothing. He was thinking of his first meeting with Brother Secundus, and of the young monk's slow smile when he put the same question to him as he had just now to the abbot. Brother Secundus must have known that the Abbot would give no answer to that question, or an answer that wasn't an answer at all. Or . . . was it?

After a pause he said: "Remember what Florentius told us? About this being no place for a well-bred boy, only for raw and uncivilized fellows, slaves, or fugitive criminals and the like?"

"Florentius is a fool."

"A scoundrel, more likely", Tertullus declared. "Even that Goth, Gudila or whatever his name is, is a decent enough man. I talked to him yesterday. He told me it's a rule here that every guest must be received as if he were Christ himself. He even said, 'Every guest *is* Christ himself', but I suppose that's due to his faulty Latin, I mean that's why he expressed it badly. Brother Secundus is the son of a Byzantine patricius. Brother Gregorius, Brother Speciosus, and Brother Sextus are the sons of men of nobility, Brother Valentinian . . . "

"My dear Tertullus, what does it matter? A year in the company of Benedictus will make true nobles out of slaves."

"And slaves out of nobles, eh?" Tertullus grinned. "I've never seen men work as they do here. They seem to thrive on it, though. I tell you one thing, Equitius. It was a blessed hour when we decided to bring our boys here. This is the safest place in the world."

A swift-footed messenger arrived the day after Tertullus and Equitius left. He delivered a little parcel to Brother Doorkeeper, Brother Sextus, "For the venerable Lord Abbot with the best wishes of the priest Florentius", and departed as quickly as he had come.

Brother Sextus unpacked the parcel and found a eulogia in it, a piece of bread, round as if it were a Host, but thicker, the customary present on some special occasion from one Christian to another whom he wished well.

Brother Sextus hesitated. The Abbot and the brothers were having their meal. Should he wait till it was over? He decided that a eulogia was a joyful thing and that a joy should always be served up immediately, like a hot dish. He put the bread on a plate and walked into the refectory.

He could not at once draw the Abbot's attention. Like all others he was eating and listening to the reader, who, this week, was Brother Gregorius of the deep, booming voice. It was not his fault that he had a deep, booming voice; and like every reader he had first, after Mass and Holy Communion, asked the whole community to pray for him that God would turn away from him the spirit of pride and then prayed: "Lord, open my lips and my mouth will proclaim Thy praise", and the whole community repeated the prayer three times. Then the Abbot had given him his blessing, and thus he became reader for one week.

"Chapter fourteen", Brother Gregorius boomed. " 'But him who is weak in faith, receive without disputes about opinions. For one believes that he may eat all things; but he who is weak, let him eat vegetables.' "

Which they were doing at this very moment, though one could hardly call them weak.

" 'Let not him who eats despise him who does not eat, and let not him who does not eat judge him who eats; for God has received him. Who art thou to judge another's servant? To his own Lord he stands or falls; but he will stand, for God is able to make him stand. . . . ' "

The Apostle Paul's Letter to the Romans, Brother Sextus thought, was pleased with himself for knowing, and at once displeased with himself for being pleased with himself. And still the Abbot would not look up.

" 'He who regards the day, regards it for the Lord; and he who eats, eats for the Lord, for he gives thanks to God. . . . For none of us lives to himself, and none dies to himself. . . . "

The Abbot looked up. Brother Sextus pointed to the plate he was carrying and received the sign to approach and did.

The Abbot gave the eulogia a casual glance and gestured to Brother Sextus, to put it down on the table next to him.

Brother Sextus obeyed, opened his mouth, remembered just in time that he must not speak during the meal, and closed his mouth again. He stood for a moment or two, waiting; perhaps the Abbot would ask him about the sender of the gift, but the Abbot did not, and Brother Sextus retired, feeling dimly that he might as well have waited until after the meal.

" 'Therefore let us no longer judge one another,' " came the reader's voice, " 'but rather judge this, that you should not put a stumbling block or a hindrance in your brother's way. . . .' "

Closing the door behind him, Brother Sextus winced a little at the aptness of the passage. He *should* have waited. What had been the good of taking in the eulogia and not being able to tell the Abbot who sent it!

In the refectory, Benedictus was looking at the piece of blessed bread, he raised his right hand to bless it in turn and stopped and dropped his hand again. He saw the blight, deep inside the bread, the dreadful disease of the corn, like an army of tiny demons, some moving, others motionless like spiders waiting in their web.

Brother Gregorius read: " 'If, then, thy brother is grieved because of thy food, no longer dost thou walk according to charity. Do not with thy food destroy him for whom Christ died.' "

The gift was here, brought by a messenger, and it was poison. Blighted corn, the devil's manna, the very opposite of blessed bread, ergot that sent a man raving mad before he died in spasms. Yet the hands which sent this gift were consecrated hands.

" 'Do not for the sake of food destroy the work of God' ", the reader read. "All things indeed are clean: but a thing is evil for the man who eats through scandal.' "

There came a fluttering sound and the shadow of dark wings. A large raven had perched on the windowsill, turning its eyes right and left. Spreading its wings, it flew into the room, circled the table and dropped upon it, directly in front of the Abbot.

Some of the brothers smiled, but most of them took no notice. The raven was an old friend and rarely missed a meal. His nest was somewhere in the wood behind the monastery of Saint John, but he always came to Saint Clement's where the Abbot talked to him and gave him bread crumbs until he had had his fill.

Benedictus leaned down till his eyes were level with the bird's. "Take it", he whispered. "Take it and fly away, far away, and drop it where no one can find it."

The raven opened its beak, approached the eulogia, hopped back and looked at the Abbot from unblinking eyes.

"Take it", Benedictus whispered again. "Come, take it, but do not eat it; fly away and drop it where no one can find it."

The raven's wings began to flap wildly, it croaked, looked at the bread, croaked again, and would not move.

For a third time the Abbot whispered to it. Making angry noises, the raven hopped back to the eulogia, circled it, took it in its beak and flew whirring out of the window.

"Chapter fifteen", the reader's voice boomed, " 'Now we, the strong, ought to bear the infirmities of the weak. . . .' "

21

YOUNG ATHALARIC was sitting at the King's banquet table for the first time in his life, and enjoying himself hugely. The fact that his mother was angry added to his joy. She never wanted him to have any pleasure. She said he was too young for everything he really liked to do. Too young for hunting parties. Too young for drinking wine without water. But not too young for endless lessons about the greatness of Rome, about Roman culture, and all that stupid nonsense. She had forbidden him to be present at the banquet, too, but Uncle Tuluin and Uncle Witigis talked to the King and they chose a moment when Grandfather was in a good mood and so he said yes and once he had done that, he would never revoke it and he did not, although Mother went running to him and complained.

And this was a really great banquet, in honor of the young

nobles who had come of age and proved it by winning the necessary tests: three throws of the spear; jumping; riding an unsaddled horse; shooting a three-foot arrow at a moving target; the long run; and finally the sword fight with a hero of renown, like Godimer and Bitulf and Strong Visand. They used blunted swords for that, but a good many were wounded anyway; and young Riggo, who fought against Visand, had lost three teeth. Visand picked them up after the fight, put them in a little case of pure gold, decorated with pictures of some gods and goddesses, and given the case to his opponent as a gift of honor. "Part of my booty from the Gepid war", Visand said. "And here's wishing you a lot of booty of your own." Everybody had cheered, and young Riggo grinned happily.

But the real heroes of the day were the two young nobles who not only surpassed all the others in the preliminary tests, but who had won their sword fight. Such a thing happened perhaps once in ten years, but today it had happened twice in succession. Young Totila, Count Tota's son, won all four rounds of his fight against Gundaris, an experienced warrior, showing an agility and strength that made Gundaris look almost ridiculous. And Black Teja, whose opponent was Count Burimer, second only to Strong Visand in size and strength, won his fight with a single blow that drove Burimer's helmet, steel, leather, and all, down over his nose and ears, so that the fight had to be stopped.

"Those two will make their way, Prince", Tuluin told Athalaric. "The King will see to that."

"*I* shall, one day", Athalaric said aloud, and Tuluin darted a quick glance at Theodoric who was sitting a few yards away, between Prince Theodahad, his nephew, and Count Witigis. The King seemed to be absorbed in thought, but one could never know with him, Tuluin thought. Seventy-one he was—or was it seventy-two?—but he could be as sharp as ever. Witigis was gaining in influence, Tuluin thought, a sound enough man and a good leader in war, but new nobility, made a count on the battlefield. As for Theodahad—Tuluin's lip curled under the flowing moustache—Theodahad, in a way, was a living example of the theory that birth alone was not enough. An Amalung prince, spending his life cheating his neighbors out of their land—he owned more than half of Tuscany by now—buying and selling statues, vases, villas, and slaves, reading books on philosophy and poetry; why, the man was as bad as the King's daughter and not half as masculine.

However, he counted as an Amalung and despite his character he was a man, and there was something to be said for the fact that no woman was present at this assembly . . . and no Roman, not even Amalaswintha, or her favorite, the noble Cassiodor. Eight hundred guests, including the three hundred young heroes who had passed the tests of warriorship, eight hundred Gothic fighters, leaders of men, nobles, a match for three times that number of Visigoths, Gepids, or Vandals and ten times that number of Runts, Buffoons, or whatnots, may the gods blast them all! Count Tuluin had drunk a little too much, but he knew it; he allowed himself a little patriotic elation, and why not? He must be sure, though, that little Athalaric did not get too much, he thought.

Theodahad got up to toast the King, but for quite a while no one paid any attention to him. He was of slight built, and his movements nervous and fussy. It looked as if he had got up only to rearrange the folds of his richly ornamented state robe. In the end he had to appeal to the chief steward, Count Otharis, who grinned, crashed his fist on the table and bellowed for silence.

"Long life to the King", Theodahad said in his brittle, uninspiring voice. He looked almost frightened when eight hundred voices roared their traditional "Hail the King!", and quickly sat down again.

Then Count Witigis proposed the toast to the army, and Count Leuthari raised his cup in honor of the new warriors. They wanted young Teja to answer, but he declined almost angrily, so Totila rose in his stead and made a good speech about all young men being proud to be led by so great a king and hoping that he would lead them to more victories.

Tuluin jumped to his feet. "Down with the King's enemies," he cried, "whoever and wherever they are!"

"Hail the King! Hail the King!"

Sixteen hundred feet started stamping under the long rows of tables.

"Uncle Tuluin," Athalaric asked in his high-pitched boy's voice, "why did Grandfather kill the Pope?"

Tuluin looked about quickly. There was a good deal of noise, so the King was not likely to have heard the amazing question, but those sitting nearer almost certainly had. "Hush, Prince", he said. "No one killed the Pope. He just died, as old men must."

The boy shook his head. "Brinda must have lied, then", he said. "She said Grandfather had the Pope put into jail and that was as good as if he had killed him. Why . . . "

"Hush", Tuluin repeated. "Not so loud, Prince. Who the devil is Brinda, anyway?"

"Brinda is Lady Brinda, one of Mother's women. I don't like her. I thought she was lying. She's always for Mother and against me. She isn't a Goth, either, the dirty old liar. Did Grandfather put the Pope in jail, Uncle Tuluin?"

"Well, yes, Prince", Tuluin said in a low voice. "And he was quite right, too. He had sent the Pope to Byzantium as his messenger, to demand certain things from the Emperor. The old fellow stayed away a long time, and in Byzantium they dined and wined him and kissed his feet and so on, but they wouldn't do what the King wanted them to do, so the Pope came back empty-handed. It's a very difficult story to tell, Prince, and a very long and boring one. . . . "

"I'll give you the answer, boy", said Theodoric.

Tuluin smiled apologetically, hunching his shoulders.

"I gave the Pope his orders", Theodoric said aloud. "He came back and had carried out none of them. He said he couldn't, because the Byzantines refused my demands. I had reason to believe that he never seriously tried. So I put him and all the members of his embassy in jail; I was going to have him tried. But he died before the trial could start. Learn this, boy:

when the King gives an order, it must be carried out. When a man fails to do so, the King must decide whether he tried to do his best or not. If he did, he cannot be blamed. If he did not, the King must punish him, whether the man be a simple warrior or a royal prince, a Roman or a Goth, a slave or a pope."

"Hail the King! Hail the King!" roared Count Tuluin and the sixteen hundred feet stamped again.

Theodoric sank back, into his reverie. He had been watching the testing of the young warriors for seven solid hours. Leaders, that was what he was looking for. Sharp eyes, sharp reactions, speed of thought, the ability to change tactics when necessary. Resistance against odds... Such a wise old rule, to let these young cockerels fight against experienced men, instead of fighting against someone of their own ilk. Romans would sneer at such a way of discovering leaders. Learned Cassiodor would want to test them for knowledge of history, of philosophy and rhetorics. None of these could teach a man how to stop an army from fleeing. Leaders. War-leaders. No politics. Heaven forbid that a Goth should have to be a politician. Not even Theodahad was one. No instinct; and thinking of himself only, greedy little intriguer, royal pickpocket, no good at all. Among these youngsters only two outstanding, Totila and Teja, but not for the reasons all these idiots supposed. Not quite. Not because they had defeated Gundaris and Burimer, but because they were the only ones who refused to be intimidated by experienced warriors of great repute. They really set out to win, the others did not. And so they won. The idiots were right, but they didn't know why. How hot this confounded country was in August! Never make war in Italy in summer. Or in Greece. Those Vandals in Africa... several generations there, ever since Genseric.... Were they still the men they used to be? They were sure to ask that question in Byzantium. That fellow Hilderic was a fool, trying to hobnob with the Buffoons. Only one policy possible with them, be strong, keep them at arm's length. Twenty years ago one might have tried to smash them. Alliance with the Persians, double attack, from West and East. Too late now.

That woman Brinda must be removed from the retinue of the Princess. A Catholic, of course. He had killed the Pope, she said. No one, not even Cassiodor knew why the Pope had been arrested. They all thought old Theodoric had fallen into one of his rages. None of them understood that this was a test case, to see how they would react, the Runts, what would they do about it, how deeply did they believe in this successorship of Saint Peter, would they defend him? They hadn't defended Boethius and Symmachus, but would they defend the Pope? Well, they did not. But kill the old chief priest? Certainly not. Stage a big trial in public, for all to see. Old John the First had cheated him out of that by dying.

No Roman could be trusted, not one. And the better a Roman he was, the less he could be trusted. That's why Boethius and Symmachus were the two most suspect Romans of them all. How could a Goth rule Italy, when there were good Romans about, real Romans? They must wish every Goth throat cut, even if they didn't admit it, even to themselves.

A man could rely only on one people, his own, and lucky if he could do that. And to be King of the Goths meant to love one's own people's faults more than other people's virtues. They were quite right, the Tuluins and Ibbas and Pitzas and Leutharis, but a king could not afford to tell them so, or there would be riots everywhere and all the time. The King must think for his people. And for the sake of his people the King must kill. And regret nothing. Odovacar now . . . he had had to be killed. A country, like a man, could not have two heads. And Theodoric was a better head than Odovacar. Even Cassiodor admitted that. Seven hours watching tests was a long time. Especially in August. Never make war in summer, not in Italy.

Was this banquet ever coming to an end?

Here they came with another dish, something elaborate, it seemed; some of the men were applauding.

Fish. Stupid Roman custom to serve up some great, big fish course at the end of the meal, turbots fed with goose liver, *muraenae* fed with slave-flesh, all grouped around a center piece, a huge fish head, a dolphin's head. Huge. Fish. Eyes staring like a man's. That's what the old man was like, eighty, with his pleading voice, the obstinate old man. Another test case and didn't know it. Same guilt as Boethius'. Can't have Boethius killed and leave you alive, can I? Not justice. Boethius wanted justice and he got it, didn't he? Roman spiders. Comes the moment when one must crush them. No torture, just kill him. You can't complain, you had a full life, eighty years, that's enough for any old fool, so stop staring at me, do you hear?

Such a lot of blood, yet he went on staring.

"Stop staring, Symmachus", Theodoric shouted. Then he slumped in his seat.

They were all around him at once, Witigis and Tuluin and Leuthari and Ortharis and half a dozen others, they lifted him out of the chair and carried him away.

Prince Theodahad followed, ashen-faced, on trembling legs.

Everywhere in the huge room the chieftains and warriors had risen to their feet, wordless, thunderstruck.

Only little Athalaric sat still, watching it all. Suddenly he jumped up and ran after the men carrying his grandfather.

Tuluin came back, looking for Ibba.

"What is it?" Ibba asked in a whisper. "A stroke?"

"Seems to be. Don't know for sure. Babbling incoherently. I don't think he'll last long. Better send a messenger for Pitza right away. We may need him. I must talk to Leuthari. Where's the little man?"

"Athalaric? I saw him running away."

"Gods and devils, if only he were ten years older . . . or had had a stroke, too. We'll need a king soon, Ibba."

The huge dish of turbots and *muraenae* was still on the table, in front of the empty royal chair. In the middle of it, the great dolphin's head stared up at the ceiling like a tragic mask.

"I want the truth, and all of it", Amalaswintha said harshly. "Is my father going to recover or not?"

Elpidius, the Greek physician, bowed, as usual before answering a question. "There is always the possibility of a miracle, Princess."

She nodded, stony-faced. "Go on, man, speak up."

Elpidius bowed. "The King is suffering from an ague, Princess. That accounts for the bouts of high fever and the sudden sensations of intense cold. He has also suffered a slight stroke. I did warn against too much exposure to the sun, Princess, but the King would not listen to me and was present at the testing of the young nobles all morning and well into the afternoon. Then he sat down for a heavy meal." The physician's slim hands fluttered in eloquent regret. "It would have been dangerous for a man twenty years younger", he murmured.

"There is nothing you can do to cure him?" Amalaswintha asked.

"I can give the King some relief", Elpidius replied, bowing. "But there is no cure against the ague. The patient either resists the fever or succumbs to it. In this case . . . " Elpidius' hands fluttered again.

"There is something you're concealing from me", she said tersely.

"I assure the most gracious Princess . . . "

"Out with it. What is it?"

"Nothing . . . nothing tangible, most noble Princess, no more than an impression, a purely personal impression. . . . "

She stamped her foot. "Talk", she snapped. "I command you."

Elpidius bowed twice. "The King . . . speaks occasionally", he said. "It is a sign that his mind is working. He . . . he always utters the same words. And I have come to the conclusion that not only his body is suffering . . . "

"You mean . . . he is out of his mind?" Amalaswintha asked, terrified.

"No, not that, not that at all, Princess. Quite the contrary, if I may put it that way. There seem to be things *on* his mind, things he cannot forget, and they are sapping his strength. He . . . he no longer puts up much resistance to his illness, and when a man stops doing that. . . . "

"What are the words he speaks?" Amalaswintha asked.

Elpidius gulped. "N-names, most noble Princess, just names."

"What names? By God and the saints, I'll have you jailed, if you don't tell me."

"Boethius . . . " the physician stammered unhappily, "Symmachus . . . Odovacar . . . the Pope . . . "

Amalaswintha's expression did not change. "How long do you expect the King to live?" she asked coldly.

"Impossible to say, Princess. He may live for another week or even two. On the other hand, he may go quite suddenly."

"And will he regain full consciousness?" There was a slight tremor in Amalaswintha's voice, but the physician was too frightened to notice it.

"It is barely possible", he said. "I should doubt it very much."

"Thank you, Elpidius", the Princess said. She turned away from him: "Let Hargund come in", she ordered.

The official at the door beckoned an old woman to enter. She was almost absurdly ugly, her face a mass of sharp wrinkles, and her figure shapeless with fat.

Elpidius paled with indignation. That was the old Goth harridan whom some of the stupid women at the palace liked to call in for remedies against freckles, warts, or other blemishes. She was said to be an expert on herbs and poisons and, which seemed likely, a witch. "Princess," he stammered, "surely you do not intend . . . you cannot be thinking of . . . "

"Come with me to the King, Hargund," Amalaswintha said.

The physician's professional pride got the better of his prudence. "In that case," he stammered, his hands fluttering wildly, "I can no longer assume responsibility."

Amalaswintha gave no answer. Old Hargund belched with great gusto.

Theodoric lay trembling with cold under the heavy rugs, the great, round lion's eyes were staring glassily, but consciousness broke through in irregular spurts, sometimes lasting a few seconds only, at others for several minutes.

He knew that he was dying. He knew that there were certain things he must do before he died, but he could not think of them in an orderly fashion. Who was that woman?

"Father, I have brought old Hargund with me."

Hargund. Clever old witch. Better than a Buffoon any day.

Hargund stared at him from red-rimmed eyes. For a long time she said nothing. Amalaswintha stood watching her anxiously.

"Don't stare, Symmachus", the King said. "You're dead. Don't stare. You had to go; they all had to go."

Hargund moved forward. Squatting down, she pushed her face close to the King's. Then she began to mumble inarticulately.

Theodoric's eyes flickered. "Hargund," he said. "What have you done to Boethius?"

The old woman rose and looked at Amalaswintha. "He won't live", she said. "Be like this six days. I can make him think clear, sit up, talk. But if I do, he will lose three of his days. Want me to do it, Amalung's daughter, hey?"

Amalaswintha looked at the King. "Yes", she said.

Hargund nodded. Rummaging in the wide folds of her gown she produced a small phial. From the low table beside the King's bed she took a decanter and poured a little wine into his golden goblet which was shaped like a tower. She added a few drops of colorless liquid from the phial, and stirred the mixture with her dirty finger.

"I will give it to him", Amalaswintha said, breathing hard to overcome her disgust.

Hargund sucked her finger. "You can't make him take it", she said. "I can." Cup in hand she sat down heavily on the King's bed and stared into his eyes. She began to mumble again.

Horrified, Amalaswintha saw her father open his mouth in wooden obedience while Hargund held the cup to his lips and tilted it. Withdrawing it, she pushed up his lower jaw and held it closed.

After a minute she released it, slid down from the bed, and put the cup back on the table.

"Your reward?" Amalaswintha asked.

The old woman shook her head. "No cure, no reward", she said. "But I'll throw the runes for you, Amalung's daughter. Want me to?"

All the women said that everything Hargund foretold came true.

"No", Amalaswintha said.

Hargund grinned at her. "The crown is heavy", she said, nodded, and walked out.

"Wine", the King said suddenly.

Amalaswintha stared at him.

The King's eyes were clear.

She gave him half a cup of wine, and he drank greedily.

"You did right to accept Hargund's remedy", he said.

"What do you mean, Father?"

"Three days awake is better than six the way I was before. I heard it all, daughter—or something in me heard it and reported it. I know why you did it, and you were right."

"Thank you, Father."

He seemed to have shrunk a little, and his nose looked pointed. A few strands of gray hair half-covered his forehead. "Death is a good strategist", he said. "He made a surprise attack against me, and it succeeded. Or almost. Help me to sit up—no, don't contradict, do as I tell you."

As she propped him up with cushions, she could feel that his body was giving out much less heat than before. The fever, for the time being, was gone.

"Do you want Bishop Agilus to come?" she asked. The Arian bishop had arrived at the palace half an hour after the King's collapse and was holding himself in readiness.

"I shall meet enough bishops in heaven, I suppose", Theodoric said wryly. "Now, I must think of my people and their future. Are the leaders still here in the palace? Witigis? Leuthari? Valamer? Tuluin and Ibba?" He did not bother to mention Theodahad.

"Yes, Father. Some are still here, others went home and then came back. They're all waiting. . . . "

"For my death, I know."

"And some are plotting", Amalaswintha said calmly.

Theodoric nodded. "Who?" he asked casually.

"Tuluin and Ibba and their uncle, Leuthari. They have sent for Pitza, I hear. They are the core of the intrigue."

Again the King nodded. "You have kept your eyes open", he said. "But none of these would make a king. In fact, none of my leaders would. You are more of a king than any of them, and you are a woman. What a pity, what a terrible pity, that you are a woman."

"Semiramis was a woman", Amalaswintha said in a hard voice. "Queen Hophra was a woman. Cleopatra was, and so was Zenobia."

"Never heard of any of them", Theodoric said. "Cassiodor taught you a lot of history. How many of them died on the throne?"

"Semiramis did, I think", Amalaswintha said sullenly.

"One out of four, eh? And she wasn't a ruler of Goths." The King sighed. "Odovacar cursed me before he died", he said, almost in a whisper. "So I never had a son. The best of daughters cannot replace a son."

"I've felt it often, that curse", Amalaswintha said. "I see it every day, in the eyes of men, but it never really hurts me except when you mention it, Father."

"I told you, you're more of a king than any of my leaders", Theodoric said, impatiently. "What more can you want? I want them all here in one hour. Outside, in the anteroom. Give the order and come back to me."

She was back in a few minutes. Everything depended upon the King's next action, everything she had been praying for, hoping for, all these years. If her prayers were answered now, she would give Hargund her weight in gold.

"Listen, daughter", Theodoric said. "You know about the system of alliances I've built up over the years. With the Franks, the Sueves, the Visigoths, the Vandals. And the friendship pact with Byzantium."

"Yes, Father."

"None of them is worth anything", the King said. "They'll be on our side when all is going well. They'll turn against us when it isn't. You can rely only on your own people, and your people are the Goths, not the Italians. Don't say anything. Keep your tame Roman if you wish . . . there isn't much harm in Cassiodor. But don't let him make your decisions for you. Ask yourself what I would have done and then do it. The Runts are finished. Nothing of importance will ever come from Rome again. They had their time. This is ours."

It will happen, she thought. It will happen. . . . She said nothing.

"Never show weakness towards Byzantium", the King went on. "Avoid their love as much as their hatred. Never talk longer to a Byzantine ambassador than the fourth part of an hour, or he will prove to you that black is white and white is black. Avoid all priests, in matters of state. A good one will serve his God first and a bad one himself. Keep an eye on two young nobles who have just commenced their careers: Totila and Teja. They aren't leaders yet, but they will be and you will be able to make good use of them . . . if you live long enough. Now help me to dress. . . . "

"Father, you're not thinking of getting up!"

"I shall get up. The King must give orders, not an ailing old man on his deathbed. My coat, daughter. My cloak. Sword and helmet can wait until they are assembled, out there."

An hour later King Theodoric, in full regalia, received the Goth leaders in audience. With his hand on the head of little Athalaric he proclaimed the boy his rightful heir and successor.

"The law of the Goths does not provide for the rule of a woman," he said, "but there is no law against a regency. The Princess Amalaswintha will be regent with the title of Queen, until my grandson has come of age. She will choose her own advisers, and I know she will choose them well. Swear to me here and now, the oath of loyalty to Prince Athalaric as my rightful heir and successor and to his mother as regent in the case of my death."

"What shall we do?" Ibba whispered.

"Swear, of course", Tuluin replied without a moment's hesitation. "He's looking at us, you oaf. Swear."

Three hundred Gothic chieftains and nobles swore the oath, the Christians among them with their right hand on the hilt of their swords—the warrior's cross—the others with the naked sword held high.

"Look at the woman", Tuluin muttered. "Bursting with pride and satisfaction under that mask of serenity. And the way she puts her hands on young Athalaric's shoulders. . . . "

Ibba nodded. "As if she were trying to stop him from growing."

"Hail the King!" Tuluin shouted with the others. He added in a whisper: "You're right, brother. She would, if she could. But she can't."

Amalaswintha had taken up rooms next to the bedroom of the King so that she could be present at once, in case of an emergency, and she slipped in time and again to make sure that he had everything he needed. Two of her ladies were posted at the curtain in front of the King's bedroom.

The Princess was working day and night, most of the time with Cassiodor. She gave him the basic ideas for a manifesto to the Italian population and for the text of the oath all officials of the civil service would have to swear. All the slaves in the palace who were capable of writing copied and recopied these documents so that there would be one for every town in Italy.

Count Segimer, chief of the Royal Chancellery, made notes of a number of orders and promotions that would go out when the moment came: the order to all the principal cities of Italy to have a monument of King Theodoric made in bronze or marble by the best local sculptor and to give it a place of honor on one of the main squares. The order to the city authorities of Ravenna to have an Arian church built in memory of the King. The promotion of three old Gothic nobles as instructors of Prince Athalaric; it was not easy to decide on them, as they must be men on whom Amalaswintha could rely. Count Segimer suggested Leuthari as one of them and was taken aback when the Princess struck his name out at once with a sharp "Quite out of question." The promotion of Magnus Aurelius Cassiodorus to Chief Minister of the Queen.

When Segimer had left, she said to Cassiodor: "I want you too to take certain notes... notes of a highly confidential character."

"In that case," he replied, "I had better carve them on my mind. In times like these there are too many curious people about."

"You are right. It would be fatal if these matters were known—too soon. An amnesty is to be granted to all political prisoners. And the possessions of the late senators Boethius and Symmachus, confiscated by the state, are to be released and returned to their legal heirs."

Cassiodor trembled with joy. "That should win you every heart in Italy, most noble Princess."

"I want to win their hearts. And I want to right all wrongs... where I can."

"The legal heir of both Boethius and Symmachus would be the Lady Rusticiana", Cassiodor said. "She left the country about two years ago. No one seems to know where she is."

"Find out," Amalaswintha ordered, "and I will write to her. It is essential for my reign to regain the love of my Italian subjects. I need them against—I shall need them."

King Theodoric died on the third day of his illness, just before dawn. All the Gothic members of the royal household wherever they were, commenced the ancient mourning songs. The dark, monotonous sounds, wailing rather than singing flooded the palace.

Amalaswintha had been called into the King's bedroom half an hour before the moment of death, when it was reported to her that the King was suffering difficulty with his breathing. He had lost consciousness and never regained it.

The body was prepared for burial.

It was almost noon when Cassiodor was summoned to the room that had been the King's study.

Amalaswintha was in mourning. She was very pale, but her eyes were dry.

"I greet the Queen of the Goths and the Italians," he said, with a deep bow.

She nodded. "He was a great man", she said. "I think I am only just beginning to realize how great he was. It is all quite . . . different." Her voice was higher than usual, it sounded like a very young girl's, and Cassiodor felt his heart go out to her.

"I would gladly die for my queen", he said almost in a whisper.

She looked at him. "Live for me", she said. "I need you more than ever, now that my reign begins."

22

FAR FROM ALL affairs of state, the monasteries in the Anio valley were flourishing. Their number had grown to twelve, each a community of twelve monks under an abbot.

Twice both Tertullus and Equitius had come to inquire about their sons and each time they rode home with the one regret that they could not stay on themselves, although, at least politically, the atmosphere lately was much less tense. Instead of a rough old king who seemed to become more bloodthirsty instead of milder as life advanced, Italy now had a young queen as regent whose sympathy for her Roman subjects was well known.

"I don't say she's not making mistakes", Tertullus told

Benedictus. "This new idea of hers about putting a number of Gothic nobles into the Roman Senate is almost ludicrous, and most of the monuments erected in memory of her father are in extremely bad taste. But that amnesty of all political prisoners was a noble gesture. . . . "

"It came too late for Boethius and Symmachus", Equitius interposed.

"But not for Rusticiana", Tertullus retorted. "I've heard she is coming back to Rome to live again in the Anician Palace."

Benedictus remained silent when his visitors tried to draw him into a discussion of political matters.

"I wonder why", Equitius mused when he and his friend were on their way back to Rome. "A man of his great intellect must have opinions of his own. And he has no reason to think that he cannot trust us."

Tertullus shook his head. "I thought at first he had given up thinking about such matters", he admitted. "But somehow I don't believe it's that at all. Most people will talk about politics, knowing nothing about it at all. Men like us talk about it because we know something about it. Benedictus won't talk about it, because he knows too much."

"Well, yes, there are visitors coming to see him every day and from all parts of the country. From abroad, too . . . "

"I don't mean that either. He's got his own way of knowing too much. That raven of his . . . "

"Oh, come, you don't believe in such superstitious nonsense."

"I don't believe in superstitious nonsense, but I'm not so sure about that raven. Elias had a pet raven, didn't he? And Elias was a prophet. And then there's that story Placidus told me. . . . "

"What story?"

"Well, there are a couple of monasteries high up on the hill, who had trouble with their water supply. The poor monks had to go down to the lake for every drop of water they needed. The path was steep and dangerous, and you can imagine what it meant to carry heavy pitchers all the way up again. You know how they are, they take hardships as something to be borne not only with patience, but with joy, but even so it became a little too much for them, and their abbots came to see *the* Abbot and complained."

"Can't see what he could do about it, except try to comfort them. . . ."

"Which is what he did. He also told them to come back the next day. But that same night he went up the hill with my boy. . . ."

"At night! You just told me that the way up was steep and dangerous."

"Placidus is a good climber", Tertullus declared proudly. "Anyway, they got right up to the top, and the boy told me the Abbot went about there, quite slowly, with his hands stretched out as if he were giving a blessing to the rocks. Then he stopped, knelt, and began to pray. The boy says he's never seen anybody pray like that in his life. He says it was as if the Abbot became one with the rock on which he was kneeling, as if his knees must have penetrated the very stone so that in the end both the Abbot and the rock seemed to be praying together to high heaven. In the end he got up again and put three stones, one on top of each other, on the place where he had been kneeling. Then he called Placidus, and they descended again. Next day, when the monks came back as he had told them to, he said: 'Go to the top of the mountain and look for a place where three stones are piled up. There dig a hole in the ground. Almighty God can produce water even on a mountain top if it is his will to lighten your burden.' "

"Don't tell me they did and found water!"

"They did and found water. Not just moisture, Equitius, but a spring, a strong, merry spring, and it's been running down the mountain ever since."

"Like Moses with his staff . . ."

"Exactly. That's the point I'm making. A raven like Elias'. Water from a rock like Moses. And for years he lived in the wilderness like John the Baptist. Would it be surprising if such a man had the gift of prophecy? And if he has, is it surprising that he doesn't bandy it about when ordinary people are talking about what they think things are like and what they hope for or dread and what they think things will be like in a year or two? You and I, we've been worried and more than worried about the trend of things under Theodoric. Now we feel that things are easing up. But Benedict sees ahead, maybe five, maybe twenty or a hundred years. So he won't talk at all."

"Write, Brother Maurus", the Abbot said. "And mark it: *Further notes to the chapter about the appointment of the Abbot.*"

"... about the appointment of the Abbot", Maurus repeated, writing.

"Let him who has been appointed Abbot always bear in mind what a burden he has received," Benedictus said, "and to whom he will have to give an account of his stewardship, and let him know that it befits him more to profit his brethren than to preside over them."

"... preside ... over them."

"He must therefore be learned in the Law of God, that he may know whence to bring forth things new and old: he must be chaste, sober, merciful, ever preferring mercy to justice, that he himself may obtain mercy."

"... may obtain mercy."

"Let him hate sin and love the brethren. And even in his corrections, let him act with prudence, and not go too far, lest, while he seeks too eagerly to scrape off the rust, the vessel be broken."

"... be broken."

"Let him keep his own frailty ever before his eyes, and remember that the bruised reed must not be broken. And by this we do not mean that he should suffer vices to grow up; but that prudently and with charity he should cut them off in the way he shall see best for each, as we have already said; and let him study rather to be loved than feared."

"... loved than feared."

"Let him not be violent nor over anxious, nor exacting nor obstinate, not jealous nor prone to suspicion, or else he will never be at rest. In all his commands, whether concerning spiritual or temporal matters, let him be prudent and considerate.

In the works which he imposes, let him be discreet and moderate, bearing in mind the discretion of holy Jacob, when he said: 'If I cause my flocks to be overdriven, they will all perish in one day.' "

" . . . perish in one day."

"Perish in one day", Benedictus himself repeated wearily, and he passed his hand across his forehead, as if to brush off a fly. "Taking then the testimonies born by these and the like words to discretion, the mother of virtues . . . "

" . . . discretion, the mother of virtues . . . "

" . . . let him so temper all things, that the strong may have something to strive after, and the weak nothing at which to take alarm."

His hand touched his forehead again. The fly was back and it was not a fly, but a thought, and it was not a thought but a picture, the water, the lake, the boy. . . .

" . . . at which to take alarm", Maurus repeated. Looking up he saw, startled, that the Abbot was staring past him, his eyes wide open, he could see the white around the iris. What was he staring at? There was nothing but the wall of the cell . . .

"Brother Maurus!" The Abbot's voice cut like a whiplash. "Placidus is drowning in the lake. He's carried off by a current. Run to save him. Run!"

Maurus ran. He raced along the corridor—two of the brothers only just managed to step aside—bumped against the door, tore it open, and rushed down to the lake. His mind was a blank. He was the Abbot's command incarnate and put into motion, nothing less. He flew forward as if he were blown by a gale.

He could see the boy's head, a round black thing, bobbing up and down far away in the lake, and he rushed towards it, a dog after its quarry, a heron pouncing on its prey.

The boy's head grew, it was near, it was in front of him, he need only bend down. Bend down? In a flash his mind came back to him, and he knew, in a panic, that this was impossible, that he was on the water and yet not in it, and at once the water came up and he felt it splashing over his body, cold and numbing and full of enmity; and at the same moment the boy's head disappeared.

But it bobbed up again, and Maurus knew that the command was still in force, and he leaped forward like a salmon and seized the boy by his hair; he threw himself on his back, and the boy's body came to rest on top of him, so light that it seemed to have no weight at all, and now only he began to swim, gasping and bewildered, towards the shore.

A quarter of an hour later he and Placidus reported to the Abbot, both pale and feeling rather dizzy.

"I have lost one of our pitchers", Placidus confessed. "Brother Cellerarius sent me to fetch some water, and the pitcher slipped through my fingers. When I tried to grasp it, I fell into the lake."

Benedictus nodded. "The fear you felt was penance enough, but you must learn to concentrate your mind on the task given to you."

"Yes, Father Abbot."

Maurus tried to speak and could not. Again he tried and failed. In the end he managed to say: "Something happened to me, Father Abbot."

Benedictus waited patiently.

"I . . . I . . . walked . . . " Maurus made a tremendous effort. "I . . . walked . . . on the water", he blurted out.

Benedictus said nothing.

"You made me do it", Maurus stammered.

"You were obedient", Benedictus said. "God rewards merit."

But Maurus raised protesting hands. "I couldn't have done it," he said, trembling, "not alone. There's never been . . . I never have . . . well, I couldn't and I didn't; I know I didn't, because I knew nothing at all about it till it had happened. It wasn't me at all, Father Abbot, it was you. You commanded me to do it, you must have. . . . "

Placidus said in his high young voice: "I know it was you, Father Abbot. I can't swim. I was drowning, and you dragged me up. I could see your melote over my head all the time."

They both looked at Benedictus, their eyes shining.

He put a finger to his lips. But they saw, for a brief moment, what few people were allowed to see: his smile, full of warmth and joy.

Florentius was sitting in his favorite chair, his arms over his paunch, grinning broadly at the woman standing before him.

She was in a towering rage, which was the only state in which she could still amuse him.

"Seven cats," she shrilled, "seven cheap, tawdry, misbegotten sluts. So that was what you had to send to Rome for! At your age! And you a priest, too, and a married man, with two children. . . . "

"My dear Lucina," he drawled, "you would do well to leave my family out of your argument. The fact that I have a wife hasn't made much difference to you in the past, has it? Nor my priesthood. And as far as my age is concerned, it's an argument for me, not against me. I've given you the best years of my life. Why, then, such unnecessary anger against these poor girls? Seven of them, you counted quite correctly—one for each day of the week."

"The best years of your life", she fumed. "If that's what they were, what kind of life had you been leading before? In Rome you were, and you had a life of luxury and pleasure. I know! I inquired! I'm not as dumb as you think. Me, I was just good enough to share your exile with you, when things began to be too hot for you in Rome. Sublacum! Where people look into each other's pots and pans, where nothing ever happens. And me at your beck and call, year after year, doing everything for you, even taking part in those horrible incantations of yours . . . "

"Silence!"

". . . and ceremonies, too. If the magistrate knew about what's been going on here—"

"You'd better forget that", he interrupted coldly. "You can't blab about it. You're in up to the ears yourself."

"And that's why you wanted me in. As if I didn't know!"

"Not entirely", he contradicted. "You . . . had your own merits at the time."

"There was nothing I wouldn't do for you", she whined. "I even baked the eulogia for you, for that monk—"

"And bungled it", he snapped. "The most terrible poison in the world, infallible, absolutely deadly. Madness first and spasms, then painful death. I can still hear you telling me. Like a fool I believed you, and what happened? The monk is as well as ever."

"I don't know how he can be", she said, sullenly. "I never heard of a case where it didn't work. It must be magic of some kind. You ought to know."

He nodded. "Maybe he's immune," he said, "like King Mithradates of old. Maybe he's immune to all dangers. But even if he is, and mind you, I don't believe it—even if he is, the others aren't. And that's what I want the girls for."

"That's what . . . those girls? Those painted strumpets? I don't know what you're talking about."

"Wine", he ordered. "Must have some wine. Then I'll tell you, Lucina, Lucinina, my dove, my sweet, innocent Locusta. . . . "

"What a hateful name! Do I look like a locust to you now?"

"You ought to feel honored", he told her. "Locusta was a famous woman in the time of Nero. She poisoned Emperor Claudius. She poisoned Prince Britannicus. Her poisons worked, my sweet, bungling Lucina. And so do mine, as you will see, so do mine. I've got them here, seven doses of undiluted poison, all wrapped up nicely with gay rags and cheap jewelry and sent to me by my once lovely, but now somewhat dilapidated friend, Lelia. Let's see whether the great Benedictus and his monks are immune against *them.*"

She stared at him. "You mean . . . you want to turn them loose on the monks?" She giggled, much relieved.

"By the three-headed Hecate, you are waking up, my Lucina", he said. "Where's the wine?"

"I'll get it, I'll get it", she said, ran off and returned in no time with a decanter and goblets. "How are you going to do it?" she asked, still giggling. "There are almost a hundred and fifty of them living in the Anio valley. I mean . . . what can you do with seven girls?"

Florentius roared with laughter. He emptied his goblet and held it out to her for more. "You little fool", he said. "What do I care about those idiots? Benedictus is the man I want, him and those directly around him, at Saint Clement's. I'll try the sweetest poison in the world on him. I'll give him dose after dose, until he and his idiotic disciples are driven to distraction and their wonderful reputation is a stench in the nostrils of men. More wine."

She gave it to him and filled a goblet for herself. "I've often wondered why you hate him so much", she said.

"Oh, but I told you. I have an old account to settle with him. Over Lelia."

"If it's such an old account, that Lelia can't be very seductive now", Lucina opined.

"And she isn't, my beloved. I told you so."

"I thought it was because of the people coming to him", Lucina said. "So many important people, senators and . . . "

"Quiet", he snapped. "If these people are crazy enough to send him their saplings and listen to his advice as if he were a . . . I don't know what . . . that's their own business. He certainly knows how to pull the wool over their eyes. By Hercules, what a charlatan! But this will hit him, I know it will. I should have thought of it much earlier. Wine, Lucina."

"But those girls", she persisted. "You've let them take quarters with old Mother Syra. . . . "

"What of it? I couldn't very well take them in here, could I? I would like to have seen your face, if I had."

"Mother Syra is going to talk. . . . "

"Of course. That's exactly what I want. She will talk, and the whole town will talk, and the saintly monk will soon have the reputation I want him to have." Florentius rose and walked over to the balcony. "There," he said, "there's the road away from the valley. That road he must go, when he leaves." He walked out onto the balcony. "That's what I want to see", he said fiercely. "And I'm going to see it."

"Come back", she called. "I don't like you standing out there. It's not safe."

"Isn't it?" Florentius stamped his foot. There was a crunching noise, and he stepped back. "You're right", he said. "Curse this ramshackle old house. Tell you what, Lucina; when I've settled my account with that monk, we'll leave and go back to Rome. Things are different there now, I'm told."

"With you . . . to Rome?" she stammered, her face flushed. "Then . . . you still love me?"

"Of course", he said, wincing a little when she embraced him wildly. "You're the one woman who understands me", he added, grinning sardonically over her shoulder as she clung to him.

"And we'll go to Rome", she whispered.

"Yes. I'm as sick of Sublacum as you are and more so." He freed himself. "But the monk must go first."

When the seven girls left for Saint Clement's, Florentius went with them. He thought first of taking lamps with him, but then remembered that the moon was almost full.

He took some wine with him instead, which was just as well, as the girls were frightened by walking through open country in the middle of the night. They began to complain. It was asking a lot from a girl to tramp through such a solitude for hours, with nothing better in view than a few monks shut up in their monastery, and all that for a piece of gold. He gave them sips of wine. "A piece of gold for each of you every day," he reminded them, "and I doubt whether my purpose will be achieved very quickly. They'll try to hold out against you. Mind you, if you succeed within three nights, I'll give each of you another three golden solidi." At that they all embraced him, and he began to feel a liking for one of them, a soft brown-eyed creature from Samos, one Eutyche, and kept her at his side, talking to her in a whisper and making her laugh.

When they got near Saint Clement's, he led them to the back of the building where the dormitory of the monks was, and the garden. "Off with your clothes", he whispered. "Leave them here with me."

"Can't we keep our sandals on at least?" one of the girls asked plaintively. "The ground is so rough and . . . "

"Keep them on, then, curse you. Now then . . . wake them up, my girls. And as soon as something is stirring in there . . . dance!"

They began to sing one of their songs, the delight of their clients at parties in Rome, and after a while they linked their hands and danced.

23

IN THE MORNING, the abbots of the eleven other monasteries were called to a conference at Saint Clement's.

Benedictus, dignified and serene, told them about the attack of the enemy. "Before they departed they made an attempt to enter the monastery", he concluded. "They did not succeed. But I feel sure that the attempt will be repeated, and it may well be repeated again and again."

"A complaint should be launched with the town authorities of Sublacum", one of the abbots suggested.

Benedictus shook his head. "I cannot demand that they give us a guard", he said. "And I do not want to." The decurio of Sublacum, Barbatus, was the type of man to whom the incident would appear not as outrage but as a rather amusing affair, to be talked about with fat guffaws at his favorite tavern. Besides, he was a friend of Florentius.

"I know who instigated this thing", he went on. "It is a man who wishes to harm me personally, as indeed he has tried to do before. It is most unlikely that he will attack one of the monasteries in your charge. It is very likely, it is in my opinion certain, that he will attack Saint Clement's as long as I am here. We cannot fight this type of attack. Any move we might make would play right into the enemy's hands. The rumor will arise—and spread—soon enough that the settlement of the monks in the Anio valley is the scene of nightly orgies. There is only one thing I can do. I shall close Saint Clement's and leave, taking the twelve monks and the novices."

The silence was like a long-drawn cry of anguish.

At last one of the abbots spoke up. "Venerable Father Abbot, would not *that* be playing into the enemy's hands? Surely what he hopes for, is that you should leave and cease to be the cause of his horrible envy."

They all knew who the enemy was. He did not have to warn them.

"It does not matter what the enemy wants", Benedictus replied. "What matters is that God is served well, by men of poverty, chastity, and obedience. We shall leave today."

"But . . . where will you go, Father Abbot?"

"To Casinum", Benedictus said. "It's in the Liri valley. The noble Tertullus, the father of our novice Placidus, has given us land there . . . and a mountain."

"It is wild country", the abbot of Saint John warned. "I've heard of it. There used to be a bishop's See in Casinum, but now the town is in ruins and the few people living there are supposed to have gone back to pagan cults. . . . "

"A reason more to regain it for our Lord", Benedictus said.

Florentius was having his first meal very late that day, yet it was the very first thing he had done. He would take his bath some time in the afternoon, and his shave too. What he needed now was his morning wine, sweetened with honey, his *pulsum* with bits of meat in it, fresh bread, and fruit. It was served to him in his study on the upper floor, because from there he could watch the road, and it was not impossible that the monk might leave this very day. The monk was not stupid. He must know, by now, that there was a regular war on against him—

the kind of war against which he had no weapons. Why should he wait for another attack?

He grinned to himself, chewing his bread. They could say what they liked against the old pagan gods . . . Venus was still irresistible, and she had been the Mistress of the Night. All through it, when one came to think of it. He began to giggle. Little Eutyche was an artist, an artist in every way. When the task was done, he would have to talk to old Lelia about the girl. She could always get someone else to make up the seventh. Dancing girls were not so hard to find, although the import from the East was scanty. She'd have to get a Gaditan girl instead. He was going to buy Eutyche. She would have to go back with the others first, though. No good having her in the house, as long as Lucina was still around. It was a mistake keeping the same woman so long; they all grew sentimental and then thought they had rights simply because they felt sentimental.

The *pulsum* was all right, but the bread wasn't fresh, he must speak to Lucina about it.

He gazed at the road. A couple of carts, peasants, old Fabrio, drunk as usual. No monks yet. Maybe they would need a second dose after all. This time he would take the girls there in a cart, with a couple of mules, and the girls wouldn't get tired. Rather a nuisance to go there every night. One could send six of them and keep Eutyche. If she could slip into the house once, she could do it again, without Lucina noticing. What a pest that woman was. Better not have too many scenes, though. She wasn't a slave or even a freedwoman, but freeborn and she could make trouble. Unnecessary. In a few weeks he would be in Rome, and there no one knew her. Easy to get rid of her. Those bags under her eyes and that belt of fat. . . .

He felt a headache coming on and grinned ruefully. We're no longer as young as we used to be, he thought.

An hour later, Lucina came to fetch the tray. She looked terrible, pasty, with deep shadows around her eyes. What could he ever have seen in that creature? "What's the matter with you?" he asked. "Are you ill?" He tried to make his voice sound compassionate, but she saw the disgust in his eyes. She saw, too, that his hands were twitching aimlessly.

"Not I", she said. "But how do *you* feel, Florentius?"

"I've got a headache", he said, wincing. "And no wonder. Been up most of the night. But I bet you the monk is feeling worse than I do, he and his precious sons."

"I wonder", she said, staring at him oddly.

"The bread was not fresh enough", he told her. "You know I like it fresh. Tell them in the kitchen. I won't have such negligence."

"I'm sure you're mistaken", she said, with a ghastly smile. "It was quite fresh. I baked it myself, while you were up here with that slut."

But he did not hear what she said. His eyes were fixed on the road. A monk, a monk carrying a bundle and a staff. And behind him another and a third.

He jumped up and ran to the window. "Benedictus," he said softly, "are you there too, my Benedictus?"

Four monks . . . five . . . one could not see them clearly from here. He walked to the balcony, pushing a heavy chair out of the way with his foot.

On the balcony he could see them all, almost a dozen monks, each carrying bundle and staff. And there he was, there he was, the great man himself. . . .

Throwing back his head, Florentius roared with laughter. "I won", he exclaimed. "I won. Go elsewhere, most venerable saint, go wherever you like as long as I don't have you at my doorstep. Going south, are you? Fine, fine. Thought you could do what I couldn't do, eh? Make yourself a big figure, live in a spiritual citadel with people making pilgrimages to you. Well, I sent you some pilgrims, didn't I? How did you like 'em, you dog?"

They walked on. Couldn't they hear him?

"Can't you hear me?" he screamed. He was trembling all over, his legs were twitching convulsively; he seemed to dance. Pain shot up his body, a tearing, burning pain. The road before him rose and sank and rose again. Shrieking, he staggered forward and back. "To hell with you", he screamed, "to hell with the devils you sent me. I'm giddy. . . . I can't stand this. . . . "

He no longer heard the crunching noise around him; he was too far gone to feel the floor falling away under him.

"What's that?" Placidus asked when they heard the crash.

"Never mind what it is", Maurus replied. "Come on, we must catch up with the others. . . . Good Lord in Heaven! The balcony of that house has fallen down."

"That's the house of that priest, surely," Placidus said, "that's Florentius' house. We stayed there for some hours on our way to Saint Clement's . . . "

"Yes", Maurus said. "And there's a body amongst the debris— Don't look, Placidus. Stay where you are, but turn away. Don't look, I tell you. Wait for me."

He ran towards the house. One look at the dreadful face, bespattered with blood and brain matter was enough to tell him that the man was beyond help.

A strange, cackling sound made him look up. A woman stood in the doorway that had led to the balcony, a pasty-faced woman with reddish hair, that housekeeper or whatever she was. And she was laughing.

Horrified, Maurus turned away and ran back to Placidus. "We can't do anything", he said. "He's dead." Suddenly his eyes widened. "Dead", he repeated. "I must tell the Abbot. . . . Come quickly."

He raced on, Placidus following as fast as he could.

When he caught sight of the others, Maurus began to shout: "Father Abbot! Father Abbot!"

Benedictus stopped and turned. The whole group of monks came to a halt.

When Maurus reached them he was so much out of breath that he could not speak coherently. "Dead . . . " he gasped, " . . . your enemy . . . is dead. . . . F–Florentius . . . fallen to death . . . with the balcony of . . . his house." He took a deep breath. "Now we can return", he said, beaming. "He can persecute you no longer."

"May God have mercy on him", Benedictus said, visibly shaken. He traced the sign of the cross. Then he added severely: "And may God have mercy on you, who call yourself a monk and yet rejoice at the news of a man's death, who call yourself a Christian and yet have no love for an enemy."

Maurus hung his head.

"For your penance you will pray the penitential psalms every night before going to sleep, for seven weeks," the Abbot said, "and you will pray them for the soul of Florentius, a priest forever according to the order of Melchizedek, and for your own soul—both."

Then he turned and walked on, still towards the south.

They all followed. None of them dared ask him why, in the circumstances, he did not return.

But he knew that God had evil servants as well as good ones, and that he made use of the services of either in his own way and for his own purpose. If he permitted his servant Florentius to drive his servant Benedictus away from Sublacum; and if he permitted his servant Tertullus to give the land at Casinum to his servant Benedictus ... then that was his way to show his holy will, and there was only one place to go.

He had led his servant from Nursia to Rome; from Rome to Enfide; from Enfide to the cave; from the cave to the monastery at Varia; from there back to the cave; from there to the Anio valley and Saint Clement's; and now from Saint Clement's to the Mount of Casinum.

Was Casinum to be the last stage before heaven?

God alone knew.

But God's servant Benedictus knew that Casinum was to be the next stage. And thus there could be no question of returning to Sublacum, whatever happened.

Walking on he began to pray for the immortal soul of Florentius.

> O Lord, reprove me not in your anger,
> chastise me not in your wrath.
> Have pity on me, O Lord....

And as the great words were slowly gliding through his mind and soul, it came to him that he would pray for his dead enemy, not for seven weeks, like Maurus, but every day for the rest of his life on earth.

24

THEY REACHED CASINUM early on the third day of their journey.

"Quite a large town", Brother Secundus thought aloud.

Brother Gudila shook his fair head. "No life", he said.

"No walls, you mean, and no gates. But surely in those houses—" Brother Secundus broke off. The houses, white and dusty under the blistering sun, were empty shells. The street was full of rubble.

Penetrating deeper into the maze of ruined buildings and fallen masonry they saw an old woman scurrying away. A few children stared at them sullenly.

Benedictus went up to them, but another woman, dirty and ill-kempt, appeared from nowhere and dragged them off before he could talk to them.

Some kind of life was going on in the next street and the next; shadowy faces peered at them from behind ramshackle windows, a group of old men broke and dispersed in all directions at their approach. Then the houses were empty again, half-destroyed, three-quarters destroyed, heaps of stones and bricks and dust.

"This isn't a town at all", Brother Secundus said. "It's a village within the remains of a town." He spoke in a whisper.

There was something ghostly about the place, ghostly and malevolent. They were glad to leave it behind.

Then they saw the mountain. They had seen it before, as they approached the town, high and proud, a step towards the throne of God, but now it looked quite different.

"Cyclops built a fortress", Brother Secundus murmured.

The mountain soared up steeply to a height of more than fifteen hundred feet and on its very top the ruins of gigantic walls rose, threatening heaven.

The little group of men stopped, as the vanguard of an army will halt at the unexpected sight of the full force of the enemy. Then Benedictus walked on, and they followed.

An old man came running after them. "Wait," he cried, "please wait. Surely you are Christian monks?"

Benedictus turned towards him. "We are."

The old man said pleadingly: "You are not going to leave us again, when you have just arrived here, are you?"

A number of people came from behind the last houses, both men and women, a dozen perhaps or a few more, they did not dare to approach, although the old man was beckoning to them.

"They're all Christians", the old man said. "There are many more of us, hundreds more, and no priest. There used to be three churches in Casinum when I was young. Now they're all in ruins. We teach our children as best we can, but there is no one to hear confessions, no one to give us Holy Communion." Tears welled up in his rheumy eyes. "I haven't been to the Blessed Lord's table for twenty-seven years", he said.

There were by now at least fifty people in the group waiting at a distance, and still more turning up, singly or in pairs. Perhaps it was their number that gave them courage: they began to advance, though still somewhat timidly.

"We are going to build a church", Benedictus said.

The old man threw up his arms. "They're going to build a church", he shouted, beaming all over his face, and now they all came running and formed a circle around the monks.

"Will you tell us your name, venerable Father?" the old man asked humbly.

"Benedictus."

"Benedictus est qui venit in nomine Domini", the old man said, the tears running down his cheeks. "You will need help, venerable Father. There are artisans among us, smiths and masons and dyers and workers in copper and silver. We'll help you build; it's the least we can do."

"We did not expect such kindness", Benedictus said, deeply moved. "When we were passing through the town the people ran away from us. . . . "

"You must have gone through the pagan district", the old man said. "We Christians all live in the eastern part of the town. The pagans keep apart; there are many empty streets between us, and we rarely see anything of each other. They still worship the old gods, venerable Father, and they have a priest, one Hermophilus, who renders sacrifice to Apollo, up there." He made a shy gesture towards the mountain.

"That is where we shall build our church", Benedictus said, and the old man recoiled as if he had been struck.

"Up there?" he asked. "But that's where the old temples are. They go up there at night for their sacrifices, one at midnight and one at dawn. The place is accursed, venerable Father, it's unclean with the blood of . . . of what they have killed there."

"It is time that it should be cleansed, then", Benedictus replied. "The mountain belongs to our community, it was given to us by the noble Tertullus, who owns the land. All pagan worship there will cease forthwith."

"Venerable Father," the old man stammered, "the priest Hermophilus will. . . . He is a dangerous man; they say he is well versed in magic, and the demons he worships. . . . None of us dares to go up there even in daytime."

"We are going there now," Benedictus told him. "And we shall accept your help only when we have driven out what is pagan and when the mountain has been dedicated to the one true God and his angels and saints." He raised his hand in a blessing and walked on, and his monks followed.

An elderly woman said bitterly: "We won't see any of them

again. Hermophilus is sure to know about their coming and then . . . "

The old man sighed deeply. "With Christian priests or monks here, that fight was bound to come", he said. "We can only hope . . . "

"Hermophilus will think that we called the monks in", the woman whined. "There'll be another plague of rats, just as there was five years ago, when he was angry with us. There may be worse. As for those monks, they are as good as dead."

The ascent was steep, but there was a path snaking up the mountain through olive groves and across stony patches, where brown and green lizards slipped away, almost from under their feet.

"Apollo", Brother Secundus muttered. "Strange that they should build a temple for that one on top of a mountain. Jupiter would be more likely—they like to build his sanctuaries high up, near to his lightning."

"All demons are one to me," Brother Martinus said, "but whoever it is, Father Abbot will know how to deal with him. And if he doesn't, God will, as he did with that fellow Florentius."

"Brother Martinus," Secundus said, "you don't speak often, but when you do, you are worth hearing."

They were nearing the summit. Before them rose the remnants of gigantic walls, and behind the walls the columns of the temple, covered by a half-destroyed roof.

"Watch out!" Benedictus called, and he stepped back and pressed himself against the wall.

When the others saw the gray cloud coming down the path, they followed his example very quickly. There were leaping things in the cloud, round and square and of all sizes, small as an orange, big as a man's head, stones and rocks, and behind them with a rumbling, thunderous noise came heavy boulders, rolling and pounding downwards in thick, choking swirls of dust.

When the avalanche was gone, Benedictus asked curtly: "Is anyone hurt?"

No one was, and he calmly walked on.

"Not a very friendly reception", Secundus murmured.

Brother Martinus shook his head. "A demon should know better than that", he declared.

Secundus tried to smile and found that he could not.

They were right in front of the temple, and dust, still rising thinly from part of the destroyed stairs, showed where the stone avalanche had started.

Benedictus knelt and began to pray, so they all did.

The air was preternaturally still.

Into Placidus' prayer winged a thought: this is the way the Father Abbot prayed on top of the hill in Sublacum, and later they found the spring. Something is going to happen. Something is going to happen. Then the thought left, and he could pray as he had been taught to pray.

After a long time Benedictus rose and turned sharply to the left. There, white and gleaming in the sunlight, set above the temple itself, was an altar.

He began to walk towards it.

From behind it a dark figure appeared.

The monks stopped. But as they saw their Abbot walking on, they also continued to walk forward.

The dark figure by the altar stretched out an arm, and a thin, high-pitched voice cried out: "Benedictus!"

The Abbot did not seem to hear. He walked on.

"Benedictus!" cried the voice again.

Still the Abbot walked on, and his monks, following him, saw that he was holding a small wooden cross in his right hand.

The dark figure spread lean arms as if to protect the altar. "Maledictus!" it screamed. "Not Benedictus! What do you want with me? Why do you persecute me?"

There was no answer. Inexorably, the Abbot walked on. As they drew nearer the monks could see that the figure was that of a tiny, wizened old man, dressed in the dark, manifold robes of a flamen, a pagan sacrificial priest. The veil on his head could not entirely conceal that he was bald. His face was a maze of deep, yellow wrinkles, the open mouth was toothless, but the eyes were large, black, and fiercely alive. The top of his head was level with the altar.

Benedictus began to ascend the stairs without paying the slightest attention to him.

"That must be the priest Hermophilus", Secundus murmured. "Unless it is a demon."

"Demon or no demon," Brother Martinus grunted, "if he's trying to harm Father Abbot, I'll throw him down the mountain."

But the fierce eyes of the wizened figure stared at him, and he paled and froze in his tracks.

Amazed, Brother Secundus saw all his companions stop, as if they had run against an invisible wall. One more step and he, too, met the terrible eyes and felt his will ebb away and his bones turn to water.

When Benedictus reached the altar, the priest leaped aside, mouthing curses and clawing the air with both arms.

At last the Abbot looked at him. Their eyes locked.

At the priest's sudden movement the veil had slipped from his head. With his hairless skull stretched forward on a long, thin neck he threw out his right hand, pointing with the first two fingers at the Abbot's head.

Benedictus stood upright, and motionless. A slight tremble ran through his body, but his right hand, holding the wooden cross, lifted, moved forwards, and met the challenge.

Time's passing slowed. There was no time.

The priest's hand wavered and fell.

When the Abbot made one step towards him, he shrank back.

Benedictus secured the wooden cross in his belt. He turned to the altar, with both hands seized the large sacrificial stone vessel, lifted it up and threw it down with such force that it broke into a hundred pieces.

A bestial howl broke from the priest's throat, he staggered, fell, scrambled to his feet, and ran. He ran past the group of monks and down the path towards the plain, in wide leaps, raising flurries of dust.

Benedictus looked at the altar. A shallow groove crossed it; all around the place where the stone vessel had been the surface was mottled with brown stains. The pagan gods liked blood, even Apollo who was not only the effeminate idol of poetry and music but the slayer of heroes and the cruel killer of Marsyas. The blood of doves and cocks, of goats and calves. Sometimes the blood of man. Vicious things had been done here throughout the centuries and to this very year, despite all edicts against pagan sacrifices. Cults of older and still darker gods had been mixed with the cults of Apollo and Jupiter; Samnitan gods, Pelasgian gods, satisfied only with the hearts of virgins and the bodies of newborn children. There was nothing worse on earth than that perversion of the worship of God that was the worship of demons, love changed into cringing self-abasement, reverent awe into shrieking terror, holy joy into orgiastic rites.

Benedictus swung around to his monks. "Come up here", he ordered. "This altar must be overthrown."

Recovering themselves, they swarmed up the steps and set to their task with a will. There were spades, hammers, chisels, and other utensils in their bundles, and they all knew how to use them. Even so it took the major part of three hours to loosen the altar from its foundation. Then they toppled it over, and it crashed down the steep slope with a noise that could be heard as far as Casinum.

"We shall build a chapel in honor of Saint John the Baptist here", Benedictus said. "And the temple of Apollo will be transformed into a chapel in honor of Saint Martin."

They cheered as if they were soldiers instead of monks, and he had to silence them with a gesture. "There will be two other chapels," he announced, "one in honor of the Blessed Virgin, the other in honor of the Holy Cross."

When he wanted to build a monk's first thought was for chapels and church. All the rest of a monastery would be built around them.

There was space enough up here for many large buildings. One for the monastery proper. One, perhaps even two, for guests. A special building for the novices. Good use could be made of the remnants of the old tower. A hospital. A garden of medicinal herbs and another for vegetables. A bath house, too. And all in quadrangular form, protected by strong walls, a true fortress.

Suddenly Benedictus realized why he had been allowed to see the villa of the Emperor Hadrian, that day, so many years ago, not far from Enfide. There the Emperor had tried to create a small replica of the Roman Empire. The monastery of Casinum would be a small replica of the City of God on earth.

A citadel of God.

Many would come to help him. Many would come as novices, to live in a world where God would be served as he should be served, in total submission to his holy will, in voluntary poverty, chastity, and obedience, with joy and continuous praise. All vestiges of paganism, however, must first be hewn down and rooted out. Then the great work could start. And as always in the work for God, the end would be the beginning, Alpha and Omega in One.

All this he saw and more, as he stood on the summit of the great mountain, and the beauty and majesty of God's world encircled him. He knew that his citadel would be like an island itself in danger, not once but many times, from the raging seas around it.

He must build it strong, and not only materially. The means to that were at hand, but there was only one true source of strength, and here it could flow freely into the hearts of men.

He would accept slaves, too, and make no difference between them and those born free. For in Christ all were one, rendering their war service under the same Lord, and God was no respecter of persons. Therefore he would give his love equally to all and keep them to the same discipline.

Here and here only he would be able to write what had been on his mind throughout the last years in Sublacum and yet would not take final form. Notes he had made, many of them, and some would prove useful, and others be discarded.

Here all this would come to fruition and become the instrument that one day he would leave to them as his last will and testament: the Rule.

Every novice would have to read it, and after some time, read it again, and still later a third time, so that no one could say he had not known what to expect. For his community was not a fraternity of initiates and adepts; it would have no mysteries except those Christ himself taught and was still teaching through his Church.

A slight shiver reminded him that evil was still near and would always be a danger. Hermophilus had lost the first battle, but he and those working through him were still active.

That war would always go on, and constant vigilance was essential. But as the prophet said: Unless God himself watches over the city, all vigilance will be in vain.

From near by came the sound of spade work and of hammering. They were only setting up camp for the first night. And yet . . . work had begun on the monastery on the Mount of Casinum.

Book Three

25

THE DAY was like most other days since her return to Rome and the Anician Palace. Little Vibia brought the morning wine, sweetened with honey, and some fruit from the garden. Marcia came in with the household list, a few things to be bought, two slaves to be punished for drunkenness, and the Persian chairs had been found, after all, in the cellar. Count Tota, apparently, had not liked them. All in all, he had not altered things much during the short years of his possession nor had he sold any of the slaves. But then, he had never been in Rome for more than a few days at a time, in some official capacity. Just as well, perhaps, that the government had put the house at his disposal; otherwise, half the things in it would have disappeared, as they had from Senator Albinus' house.

After breakfast, Rusticiana had her bath, Zindia did her hair, and Iris helped her to dress. The Lady Varria sent a messenger with an invitation to a party, the third one, and, as she had twice before, Rusticiana scribbled a few polite lines of refusal, although one might have picked up some news about the situation in Africa, where Byzantine troops were said to have landed. But Varria was notoriously unreliable, and Africa was far away. A Byzantine fleet had been at anchor in Lilybaeum, on "police action" against pirates, weeks ago, or was it months? —and at first she had had high hopes. But then the fleet was gone again; no one seemed to know where.

Meanwhile, life was very comfortable, very quiet, a very quiet, indeed, a very comfortable hell.

But after the noonday meal Marcia came in with the letter, and everything changed when she recognized the seal, the head of Pluto, god of death and of secrets, though Peter always pretended to others that it was the head of the Apostle after whom he was named.

"I am going to the study", Rusticiana said tersely. "No one is to disturb me."

"Very well, Domina."

In the study Rusticiana sat down at Boethius' desk, broke the seal, cut the strings, took the double wax tablet out, opened it and read:

"To the Lady Rusticiana humble greetings and admiration:

"It gives me much joy to inform you of recent events in this most wonderful city and elsewhere. Throughout the entire Empire the Emperor's new laws and measures are producing prosperity, and to such a degree that it is like the return of the Golden Age. What a difference! Only last week the Persian ambassador was heard to exclaim: 'Ever since Emperor Justinianus and Empress Theodora began their reign, Justice and Beauty personified, happiness fills the realm from the moon to the fishes.' Before you receive this letter, you will have heard of the great action undertaken against the brutal and heretical nation of the Vandals. There is no doubt here that their days are numbered and that the Emperor's general, Belisarius, the conqueror of the Persians, will come home victorious, his fleet laden with the booty the Vandal king, Genseric, won in Rome, when he looted the city only a few decades ago. But so great is our Emperor's love of peace that he would not have resorted to war even against the Vandals, had it not been for the fact that the usurper Gelimer most treacherously dethroned the rightful king, Hilderic, and made him a prisoner. Hilderic is—or most likely, was—the best ruler the Vandals ever had, and on terms of friendship with Emperor Justinian. It is to assist him against the usurper that our troops have been sent to Africa.

I was happy to hear that Queen Amalaswintha has set right the wrongs done to you and your family by her late father, and that you have been given back your possessions. Much is said here, at the imperial court, about the goodness, the noble ways, and the beauty of the Queen of the Goths, and I know that the Emperor and Empress regard her with great esteem. . . . "

Rusticiana smiled. There were many more such sentences, fulsome, treacly, full of her praise, of the imperial couple in

Byzantium, and of pious hopes for an alliance between "East and West" within the near future. She glanced through it quickly. Then she lit a small oil lamp, put it on a piece of cloth and held the wax tablet over it. The wax began to melt. Thick drops of Byzantine praise fell to the cloth. After a while the parchment underneath began to be visible and she stopped, put the lamp away and very carefully scraped the last thin layer off with a sharp penknife. The parchment was covered with writing.

"I love you, Domina, my great and only love." That was how he always started when the text of his letter was to be taken seriously. "This is my seventh report." Another of his measures, to make sure that she would know if one of his letters had gone astray. "The wax coating of this letter, now melted, should have pleased both the Imperial and the Gothic authorities, if by ill chance, it had fallen into their hands, which, however, was not very likely. It will also show you that I have learned to express myself in our new, Byzantine style. Our manners and mannerisms are sickly sweet, but we can speak a very different language too, as the Vandals are finding out. General Belisarius has only a small army, but makes up for that by taking his wife with him, the celebrated Lady Antonina who used to follow the same profession as our beloved Empress. She is as hard as nails and has managed to conquer the unconquerable hero of Byzantium so completely that he eats out of her hand. I beg of you not to be disappointed that this first campaign is directed against Africa. Regard it as a rehearsal for the real thing, for that is what it is. It would be most unwise to attack Italy with the Vandal kingdom intact in our rear. As for the fears you expressed in your last letter that the mild regime of Amalaswintha might convince the Emperor that there is no need to interfere on behalf of the Italian population: Domina, forgive me, but that is not politics. In politics mildness is weakness, and weakness invites attack. But I have something better to tell you than political axioms: I have become a full-fledged Byzantine official at last, and my services have found favor with both Their Clemencies (that's their new official title: Your Clemency!), especially since the little 'Nika' incident, which very nearly cost both Clemencies their throne. No need to bore you with an account of that rebellion, you must have heard all about it by now in Rome; even earlier I mentioned it in my fifth report, as you will remember, though only very briefly. It was a pretty desperate affair, but I had a feeling that our Clemencies might come out on top after all and, therefore, I was very conspicuously courageous and saved at least part of the situation by a timely attack on the rebels at the head of three hundred cutthroats I managed to hire. When all was over, my cutthroats were forcibly enlisted in the army—they are now fighting in Africa—and I found myself in the good books of both Their Clemencies, which is just as well, as Theodora's favor is at least as important as that of her imperial husband's. She, incidentally, behaved magnificently during the rebellion; if it had not been for her, the Emperor would have fled. Her enemies say that she is a vampire and has drawn to herself the strength of all her lovers, but I refuse to believe that. No one could be quite *that* strong. However, there is no doubt she is by far the stronger of the two Clemencies and that Justinian's position is not very different from General Belisarius' in that respect.

"I have had two audiences with the Emperor so far and one with Theodora. She is a bewitchingly beautiful woman but becomes a pale shadow when I conjure up your picture. It is more than possible, it is probable that I shall soon go to Ravenna, no longer as an agent, but as the official ambassador of Their Clemencies. My old friend and superior, Narses, has recommended me strongly. Can you imagine me at the Gothic court? And can you imagine for whom I shall really be working there? We have many reports about the Queen's difficulties with her nobles and with her own son. I study them zealously. From inside Italy I could do much more to bring about the situation we want, than here at court. Justinian is a diplomat—he may prove to be first rate—but he has the faults of the type, too. He wants always to be clever, and there are times when one must be direct. And he vacillates. It was not easy to make him decide in favor of the Vandal war. It will be even more difficult to make him decide for you-know-what. But if Belisarius succeeds, my task should be much easier. The taste for laurels is an acquired one, but once it has been acquired, a man becomes an addict.

"I am glad you took my advice and accepted the 'amnesty' granted by Amalaswintha. When a thief gives you back what he stole from you, you would be a fool not to take it, but there is no reason to love the thief, nor does it exculpate the thief of a guilt much graver than stealing. But, apart from such highly moral expositions, it is well that you should be in Rome. The reasons for that later. I need not remind you not to trust anyone. There is little need to go out much and still less to gather information. You are above that kind of thing. Whatever you may hear, and from whatever source, except myself—and with the code we agreed upon, you will always know whether a message purporting to come from me, is genuine or not—keep aloof and do nothing that could endanger your position, that of a widow, living quietly in retirement.

"You know how unhappy I was about having to go to Byzantium without you. Today I am unhappier still. And yet you may be right: I have no right to happiness as long as I have not succeeded in my task and fulfilled the promise I gave you. There could be no greater incitement. You sealed the pact—unforgettable moment. Now it's for me to win the prize, of which there is no like on earth.

"Your sons are well. They are both tribunes in the army and both rather upset because the Emperor would not let them join Belisarius' expedition as they wanted. They do not know I told Justinian that they would be too valuable elsewhere, one day, to expose them to unnecessary danger in Africa. If they knew they would bite my head off. You won't, I feel, so I tell you about it.

"They are fine young men, and I am very fond of them, although they sometimes upset *me* a little—by resembling in some curious way the woman I love. It is quite a disconcerting experience. Something haunting about it. And how can you have grown-up sons? It is not right, it does not make sense. I have decided to think of them as of your brothers. My love, my life, my heart, have a little more patience. I am preaching that to you, I, who am bursting with impatience myself. It is not easy to topple over that imperial colossus to squash with it the vermin that did you harm, but I will do it. Believe me. Believe in me. I love you."

There was a postscript: "You inquired about the Academy of Athens in your last letter, and I almost forgot to answer. Yes, it is true that Justinian has had it closed. No doubt a great howl went up in the schools and a still greater one in the ranks of aesthetes, rhetors, would-be poets, and other know-alls. But I think the Emperor was right. The Academy of Athens had long ceased to be a citadel of learning, of wisdom and philosophy, and had become the breeding ground for intellectual mountebanks, skilled in proving or disproving anything. Plato and Aristotle would have been the first to agree with Justinian's measure.

"There is an ancient and rather curious prophecy, going back to the good old days of the famous oracle of Delphi, I believe, that the end of the Academy of Athens would come only when a new great seat of wisdom was built elsewhere. Of that, however, I have heard nothing; nor can I imagine such a thing happening in these times of ours. Where could it happen? And who could found it?"

The one who could have founded it, was murdered, Rusticiana thought. Peter was right. This was not a time when anything great could be constructed. Too much must be first torn down.

She reread the letter with great care. Then she burned it over her oil lamp.

Three days later news came to Rome from Sicily, where a Byzantine warship had taken shelter from a storm: General Belisarius had taken Carthage, the capital of the Vandal kingdom.

Marcia picked up the story on an errand in the city and quite casually reported it to her mistress. To her utter astonishment, Rusticiana threw back her head and laughed with joy.

26

"BAD NEWS?" Amalaswintha asked, as Cassiodor entered. She did not have to wait for his slow nod—his face gave enough away. "It will be difficult to bear", she said bitterly. "I've been studying bad news all morning. Here . . . " She gave a despairing tap to the papers on her desk: "He's drunk every night. He's consorting with the worst type of woman. Four times within three weeks he attacked and wounded some of his so-called friends. Here . . . a report about orgies in Verona; some of the incidents are so disgraceful I can't talk about them even to you. And it harms his health! At the reception of the civic authorities in Milan he fainted, and it took them two full hours to bring him back to consciousness. And I can't do anything! Not as his mother and not as his queen. How is it going to end, Cassiodor?"

"My news, too, is about Prince Athalaric", Cassiodor said gravely.

The Queen stared at him. "He . . . isn't . . . has anything happened to him?"

"They want to make him King", Cassiodor said.

The beautiful face became rigid, masklike. "They can't. He's not yet of age."

"They're going to change the law."

"Only the general *Ding* can do that, and they can't convoke a *Ding* without the permission of the Regent."

"They have done it, noble Queen."

She sprang to her feet. "That is rebellion."

"Not yet," Cassiodor said, "but it's the prelude to it, I'm afraid."

"Who signed the decree for the summons?"

"The Prince himself. Count Tuluin countersigned as the 'King's Count'. The Sajons are underway with their white staves."

"And they are being obeyed?"

"Most of those summoned won't know that it is not the Queen Regent who is convoking the *Ding*. They will see the white staff, hear about time and place, and obey. Once they are there, they have already broken the law, by appearing at a *Ding* summoned unlawfully. It will be easy for the conspirators to convince them that they can't back out after that."

"That's Tuluin's idea. It's just like him. When is this *Ding* to take place and where?"

"At Regeta. In three weeks' time."

"I shall be there, too", she said grimly. "With my guards."

"Heaven forbid that you should expose yourself to such danger", Cassiodor said. "I couldn't get all the information I wanted, but it is more than likely that at least the troops in the North . . ."

"Don't say it", she snapped. "The plague on Tuluin, Ibba, Pitza, and Leuthari and all the rest of them. I should never have let them get hold of the boy."

"You couldn't help it", Cassiodor said sadly. "They planted the idea that the Prince must be brought up among young men so very cleverly, and they themselves kept in the background, and let Count Witigis do the work for them. I am sure he knew nothing about their real intentions. . . ."

"Witigis is a political fool," Amalaswintha said, "but I am not, and I should have seen through it."

Cassiodor said nothing. He remembered only too well what had really happened: how they had taken the young Prince away in the middle of the night and then sent a deputation of army commanders to her, insisting that the people of the Goths as a whole wanted their young prince brought up among the Gothic youth and not in a palace; among warriors and not among women. It had been a very humiliating experience. Obviously, the Queen wished to remember it differently.

"The rule of a woman is too mild for some of my commanders", Amalaswintha said between her teeth. "But now at least we know what the effect of *their* education is. They have ruined the Prince. And if they make him King now, he'll ruin everything. All *they* could teach him was what they know themselves: hunting, riding, the use of arms, the company of low women, and drinking oneself into a stupor. They have made a brute out of him. How can he rule? And Tuluin and his set have taught him systematically to hate everything foreign. To them, only a Goth has the right to live; other peoples exist only to serve him. They have sworn fealty to me—now they are ready to break their oath. If that is manly, I thank God I am not a man."

Cassiodor remained silent. They had been over all this so often before.

She turned towards him. "Athalaric can't rule", she said hotly. "If he could, I would abdicate in his favor this very minute. As it is, I won't. Never."

"Don't go to Regeta, noble Queen", he said in a low voice. "I beg of you, don't."

After a pause she said tonelessly: "I may have to go to Dyrrhachium after all."

Dyrrhachium, in Epirus, was in Eastern territory, but the Queen had secretly bought a house there, and no less than forty thousand golden solidi were buried in the cellars. Cassiodor's most trusted agents had made the arrangements, two years ago, when things had looked dangerous then, too, though not as bad as they did now.

Her sudden change of mood was no surprise to him. After all, she was a woman, the most wonderful woman, a thousand times too good for a barbarian people. He said: "Everything is ready for . . . Dyrrhachium. But first you should hear what the Byzantine ambassador has to say."

"What ambassador?"

"A ship arrived this morning from Byzantium, a very fast bireme, and on it a special envoy of the Emperor. He is asking for an audience."

A shiver went through her body. This was fate itself, showing the way. Her last letter to Justinian had not been answered. Even Cassiodor did not know that she had written. He might have disapproved. But she had felt compelled to write as she had. Now the answer had come. A special envoy, not merely a letter. The horizon was suddenly ablaze with hope.

"The formal reception", she said, "will take place in the large audience hall. I want all the commanders and nobles to be present. Six of my ladies. No other women. And there will be a state banquet tonight. The reception will be two hours after noon."

She was again the Queen.

"Who is the envoy?" she asked. "Did you see his credentials?"

"Yes, and they are in order. He is the Illustris Peter of Salonica."

The Illustris Peter of Salonica, resplendent in a tunic and cloak of gold cloth, marched with cool composure through the assembly of Gothic chieftains. He bowed to the Queen. He had come, he said, to bring the great and noble Queen the affectionate greetings and expressions of warmest love from Their Clemencies, Emperor Justinianus and Empress Theodora. Both Their Clemencies wished to state how happy they were that the relations with the great House of the Amalungs were better than ever before and that they would do everything in their power to maintain the state of sincere friendship now existing between Byzantium and Ravenna, a friendship due in great measure to the wisdom and the breadth of vision of the Queen of the Goths.

Amalaswintha gave a gracious nod and then looked sharply at the Gothic nobles.

She was still phrasing, in her mind, the right answer to so much praise and good will, when, unexpectedly, the ambassador went on. He was happy to inform the most noble Queen that peace had been restored in Africa.

This was news indeed, and the Gothic audience grew tense.

"A negotiated peace?" Amalaswintha could not abstain from asking.

A question asked by royalty could never be answered in the negative. "Yes, most noble Queen, inasmuch as short negotiations took place before King Gelimer surrendered unconditionally with the remnant of his troops."

The Gothic listeners gasped.

"There could be no other outcome", the ambassador went on. "As the most noble Queen will surely remember, the war became necessary because Gelimer imprisoned the rightful ruler of the Vandals, King Hilderic, who was a friend and indeed an ally of the Emperor. King Hilderic appealed to the Emperor for help against the usurper, and help was sent immediately. The usurper Gelimer then committed the most dastardly deed: he had his own rightful king murdered. After that there could be only one aim: to punish the murderer. The Emperor's general, Belisarius, defeated the Vandal army in the battle of Decimum, conquered Carthage, won the decisive battle of Trikameron, and chased the usurper into a mountain fortress on Moorish territory, where he finally capitulated. He and his nobles have been sent to Byzantium in chains, and Africa has become again a province of the Roman Empire."

Again Amalaswintha looked at her nobles. "We are happy indeed", she said, "to have the assurance of friendship on the part of a great Emperor, who has proved that he is ready to come to the help of his friends in the hour of need; and to avenge them, if they are harmed. And the Emperor may rest assured that this is our conception of friendship, also. As long as Byzantium and Ravenna are allies, there will be peace all around the Mediterranean sea."

When the audience was over and Amalaswintha alone with Cassiodor in her study, she said triumphantly: "That was exactly what I needed. Did you see their faces when the Illustris told us about the punishment of the usurper? It made them think."

"I hope so", Cassiodor said. She was so beautiful when she was happy.

"Of course it did. They didn't enjoy that bit about being dragged in chains to Byzantium. I like that ambassador. He said just the right things; he couldn't have done better."

"They're going to claim Sicily", Cassiodor said. "The Vandal area."

"Do you think so?" She frowned thoughtfully.

"I am sure of it. We haven't been able to get any news out of Africa for weeks. Why not? Because Byzantium wanted to present the story of conquest dramatically during this audience. Now will come their claim."

"Ah," she said, smiling, "but there may be another reason for such dramatic procedure. I wrote a personal letter to the Emperor, asking for his friendship and protection."

"Protection?" Cassiodor's face darkened. "A potent word, noble Queen, a dangerous word. And a personal letter . . . "

"I didn't tell you about it," she interposed gently, "because I didn't want you to be involved. No, don't ask questions. But the Byzantine ambassador's words were the answer. The Emperor has declared his friendship *and* made it clear what happens to those who dare to harm a friend of his."

"The protection of Byzantium", Cassiodor murmured. "Noble Queen, don't you see that the matter is very different in your case? They are convoking a *Ding.* That's a plebiscite. The ordinary Gothic warrior won't pay attention to any warning from Byzantium. Neither will Count Tuluin and the other irresponsibles. Besides . . . "

"Go on, speak."

"Byzantium has sent help to King Hilderic. Massive help. But it came in time only to acquire a new province for the Emperor. It did not come in time for King Hilderic."

Amalaswintha bit her lip. "What is your advice, then?" she asked almost brusquely.

"Dyrrhachium", he said. "And a life of peace."

"And let the crown go to my son?"

"That would be necessary in any case, when he comes of age."

"Many things can happen before then. And if they can rebel against me, they can rebel against him as well. Ah, you've thought of that, too, haven't you? And then? King Tuluin, perhaps? And bloodshed all over the country. You have called them the irresponsibles. I, at least, have a feeling for responsibility."

"Forgive me", he said in an unsteady voice, "for thinking of your own safety first. No one else seems to do so."

"I can't", she exclaimed. "I mustn't." With a somewhat forced smile she added: "The *Ding* will be in three weeks. There is still time."

She used it. The Illustris Peter of Salonica was summoned to a private audience that very day, a few hours before the state banquet was to begin. He proved to be a perfectly charming man, well-read, clever, and extremely well informed. One could talk to him on any subject. When she mentioned Sicily, he said he had no instructions about it. "That is not likely to be a troublesome question anyway", he said, with a boyish smile. "It's such a small thing, in the first place, the Vandal . . . I mean the ex-Vandal part of it. Lilybaeum. I know it quite well. I have a small estate of my own there. A villa. Such a pretty view. Have you ever been in Sicily, noble Queen?"

"No. I should have gone there long ago, but it's far and I couldn't leave Ravenna for more than a few days."

He nodded. "Crowned heads cannot move freely. A pity, of course. Sicily is lovely. Much more Greek than Roman. Quite similar to Epirus. To the region around Dyrrhachium, for instance."

Amalaswintha looked at the ambassador fixedly. "Dyrrhachium", she repeated. "Perhaps I should visit there also . . . someday."

"If you do," Peter said, "you will be received with open arms. You know that, noble Queen. But like Sicily, it would mean leaving Ravenna for more than a few days. . . . "

"For many more than a few days", she said slowly.

Peter leaned forward. "My instructions are to help you in every way, noble Queen. The Emperor is fully aware, believe me, of the difficulties a wise and peaceful regime is bound to encounter with a people of . . . warriors. Dyrrhachium is only a refuge. There should be other ways to meet the situation, whatever it is."

"No ruler is without enemies, I suppose", Amalaswintha said. "But it's hard when one cannot rely on one's own son."

"The Prince", Peter said, "is very young. And when one is very young, one is inclined to listen to those who talk very loudly and aggressively. Men like Count Tuluin, for instance."

"You are well informed", Amalaswintha said. "Count Tuluin is the type of man I have loathed all my life. Crude, brutal, insensitive, narrow-minded. He and three other nobles, all relatives of his, are the misfortune of my reign."

"I take it", Peter said, "that the usual measures are not likely to succeed with such men. Gold, for instance . . . "

"No. My cousin Theodahad would sell his immortal soul for gold—if the sum were big enough—but not Tuluin, Ibba, Pitza, and Leuthari."

"Honors?" Peter asked.

She shook her head. "A dukedom would mean increased power. And it's too late for that anyway. They . . . "

"They will strike soon, you mean, noble Queen?" Peter asked.

Amalaswintha hesitated. Then she shrugged. "As you know so much, I see no reason why I shouldn't tell you the rest", she said. "They will strike in three weeks. And I don't know what to do."

"It is not for me to advise the Queen," Peter said, "but I know what I would do. I would strike first."

Again she shrugged. "I no longer know on whom I can rely", she said bitterly. "That's why I wrote to your Imperial Master."

Peter nodded. He had been present when the Emperor told his counselors about the Queen's letter. Theodora, too, was present. "She asks for my protection", Justinian said, smiling. "If that letter were shown to the Gothic warlords, they would have her killed. She is asking for my help, too. That means I can make her or break her. Which is it to be?" They hemmed and hawed, trying to ascertain what Their Clemencies themselves wanted to do. But the face of the Emperor resembled nothing so much as that of a coldly calculating sphinx, and the face of Theodora that of a beautiful and sardonic sphinx, so the counselors could only try to guess the right decision, or do that still more dangerous thing: say what they thought. Perhaps it was symptomatic of the state of affairs at court that the first person who dared to take the plunge was a eunuch. "Don't break her now, Clemency", said the Praepositus Sacri Palatii Narses. "If you do, the Goths might elect a strong king. You don't want a second Theodoric." That broke the ice. John of Cappadocia, Minister of Finance, warned against anything that might lead to a war in Italy, because like all financiers he preferred to keep all the money in the treasury. The great lawyer Tribonian gave a learned exposition on the difficulties arising from the differences between Roman and Gothic law, all very lucid, beautifully put, and entirely beside the point. Theodora said sweetly: "I don't think this is a matter of either finance or the law. It's a matter of a woman and a woman's instinct, so Narses and I are much more likely to have the right approach. I agree with him entirely." She and Narses had always been enemies, although no one seemed to know why. His answer was as poisonous as hers: "I am glad Her Clemency agrees with me, although for different reasons. I want to keep beautiful Amalaswintha in power, for the time being. The Empress wants to keep her in Italy. I don't want her to fall; the Empress doesn't want her to rise." The innuendo must have been clear to everyone present, yet no one dared raise an eyebrow . . . not even Justinian himself, who, as usual, did not divulge at the end of the council what he intended to do. Instead, he did it, and the Illustris Peter of Salonica received his instructions—from *both* Their Clemencies. . . .

Picture and sound of all this went through Peter's mind like a flash. The latest secret reports given him on his arrival at the port of Ravenna had told him a good deal about the weakness of the Queen's position. He had known about the *Ding* to be convoked in three weeks' time before she told him. But the Queen's last words indicated that she was no longer sure of the army. Drastic action was necessary under the circumstances and her chief adviser, dear old Cassiodor, was not the man to know what action was needed and even less carry it through.

"What would happen to the rebel movement, if the four leaders you mentioned were to die, noble Queen?" he asked. "Surely it would die too, would it not?"

She looked up sharply, to meet a courteous, unconcerned smile. "Why think of anything so unlikely?" she retorted.

"I don't see why it should be so unlikely", he said. "In fact, there are conditions in which it might be very likely; as good as certain, I should say." He saw the revulsion, the first signs of indignation, and knew that he would have to be quick. Her next words might end the audience. "Listen to me, noble Queen", he said, dropping the mask of indifference. "These men are rebels. You know they are. You know they are going to strike. When they do, it will be too late for countermeasures; nothing will prevent their crime, because the royal power will then be no longer in your hands but in theirs. Therefore you must punish them for their crime before it has been committed. What is the punishment for rebellion against the King or Queen according to the law of your countrymen, noble Queen?"

"Death", she said. "But what you are advocating is murder. I can't . . . "

"Not murder, noble Queen. Execution. Have you never had to sign a death warrant?"

"Yes," she said, "and I've felt wretched each time for days. I try to be merciful wherever I can, but there are cases . . . "

"Exactly. There are cases when one can't show mercy without defying justice, perverting it, making a fraud of it. Now think of these men and what they intend to do. You have managed, in the course of your reign, to keep the peace, to rule justly, to enter into close friendship with the greatest power on earth—and in this you have achieved more than your great father ever did. What are your enemies going to do when they have succeeded? We in Byzantium also know what they are like. Your son will be a puppet in their hands, and if he does not comply with their wishes, they will know how to eliminate him. They will tyrannize and torment your Italian subjects; and sooner or later they will drive your people into war, most likely against us. Streams of blood, of innocent blood, will flow, and why? Because Queen Amalaswintha did not have the moral strength to have four rebels killed before they could wrest all power from her hands. Can you take the responsibility for that?"

She said nothing. He saw her hands, folded in her lap, pressed together so hard that the knuckles were white. One more effort and she would do it. He remembered the dossier he had read about her, pages and pages of it, things overheard by ladies-in-waiting, by guards, by servants. "Of course," he said gently, "this is very difficult for you. A queen, even a great queen, is still a woman. . . . "

Her hands separated. "You are mistaken, my lord Ambassador", she said coldly. "I am aware, I hope, of the difference between mercy and weakness. If I hesitated, it was only because I could not think of anyone whom I could trust to carry out such an order—and carry it out successfully."

Peter bowed. "In this, as in everything else, I am the Queen's humble servant", he said solemnly.

She stared at him. "You mean . . . "

"The Queen will need four messengers", he said. "One for each of the four culprits. They will be mercenaries, Herulians, who closely resemble Goths. When and where does the Queen wish to give them their orders?"

"Tonight at the banquet," she said, "you will be sitting on my right. I shall tell you then."

27

A WEEK LATER the first Gothic demonstrations took place before the royal palace. A couple of thousand warriors assembled, shouted slogans like "Theodoric, where are you?", "We want a King", and "Long live King Athalaric", and then broke into the old Gothic war songs. The Queen sent for the head of her guards, Count Rudigar, to order them off the square, as she was working and the noise disturbed her; and, a little to Rudigar's own surprise, they obeyed. But they came back a few hours later and this time Rudigar had to disperse them by force. There was a free-for-all that cost the royal guard four dead and seventeen wounded and the demonstrators seven dead and at least thirty wounded. Ravenna was seething.

Amalaswintha summoned the Illustris Peter of Salonica to tell him that she had information about unrest in other parts of the country, that the possibility of an attack against the royal palace had to be considered, and that in the circumstances her advisers regarded it as dangerous if the personal representative of Their Clemencies of Byzantium remained there.

The ambassador expressed his profound regret that the Queen should have such a harrowing experience, his hope that the present difficulties would soon be overcome, and his readiness to be of service in every eventuality. Personally, he was quite prepared to stay at the palace and share with the Queen whatever dangers might arise, but if the Queen preferred him to leave, he would of course do so and take up quarters on his ship. "The *Adelphia* is an excellent vessel", he stated with some emphasis. "It has a picked crew and is quite capable of any service that might be required."

He could not say more as the audience was taking place in the presence of a dozen Gothic officials, all rather nervous and worried, but he felt sure the Queen understood the hint.

Back on board, Peter had arms distributed to the crew of seventy, doubled the sentries, had a short conference with the captain, and gave orders to report anything unusual to him personally and at once. Then he withdrew to his cabin. A report from Agent Six arrived soon afterwards, and two hours later Agent Four arrived in person, a thing strictly against the rules and excusable only because the man was badly wounded. He made his report, collapsed, and died shortly after sunset. Two more reports arrived before midnight.

Ravenna was quiet. The royal palace, just visible from the ship, showed no lights.

The first carriage drew up one hour after midnight, with an escort of six men. Four veiled ladies alighted and were taken on board immediately and led to the ambassador's cabin: the Queen, Princess Mataswintha, and two ladies-in-waiting. Peter received them with the greatest courtesy, bade them welcome in the name of Their Clemencies and apologized profusely for the cramped space.

"That is a small price to pay for safety", the Queen said with a weary smile. Princess Mataswintha said nothing. She was a girl of fifteen, whose beauty equaled that of her mother and might well surpass it in a year or two. "The last news we had", Amalaswintha went on, "was that troops from the North are marching on Ravenna, and will reach the town at dawn."

Peter nodded. He was all solicitude for the ladies, sent for choice food and wine, and managed to persuade them to partake of both, except for the Queen who drank only a goblet of wine.

"We are ready to leave whenever it pleases you, noble Queen", Peter said. "And when we do, no one is likely to catch up with us, certainly none of the ships I have seen in port here. But from what you told me there is no need to hurry, and in a few hours we may have further news."

"Cassiodor must come with us", the Queen said. "He should

be here any moment." She looked slim and forlorn, a helpless girl rather than a ruler going into exile. Peter thought of Theodora's mature beauty, aided and abetted by a hundred artificial tricks. No wonder she did not want Amalaswintha in Byzantium, to say nothing of the Queen's daughter. An ambassador who took these two women to the court of Justinian would have Theodora for an enemy for the rest of his life, and that life would not be a long one.

Two carts with luggage arrived.

The Queen refused to go to bed. "I have forgotten what sleep is like", she said in a strained voice. "I watched the demonstrations at the palace. How brutal men are and how ungrateful."

Peter murmured the right things. On the Queen's orders Mataswintha and the ladies-in-waiting retired. None of them had spoken a single word. "They had been asleep, poor things", the Queen said. "We had to wake them up, tell them to get dressed at once, and go down to the courtyard. I am afraid they haven't fully realized what is happening. The news about the troops in the North—" She broke off, shaking her head. "Your Imperial Master will get a bad impression of the people of the Goths", she said almost fiercely, and once more Peter murmured reassuringly.

"I am worried about the Princess", she said. "She is not very strong. I hope we won't encounter a storm." Her hands kept folding and unfolding. "Neither of my children is very strong", she went on. "It's their father's heritage, not mine. He died very early, you know. His heart . . . " She went on talking, jerkily, about Prince Eutharic, Prince Athalaric, the problem of training a young prince for kingship.

But Peter knew that all the time her mind was elsewhere, and that she did not dare to talk about the one thing she really wanted to know. He knew the answer. Agent Four had not died in vain. He knew even more than that. But she would have to hear about it from her own sources. It would not do to let her see that Byzantium was better served in Italy than the royal house of the Goths.

Two hours before dawn another carriage arrived, and a minute later Cassiodor was announced.

Peter went to welcome him.

"Illustris," Cassiodor said, "I have important news for the Queen. Will you lead me to her without delay?"

"Most certainly. The Queen is expecting you."

He showed Cassiodor the way, announced him and let him enter the cabin alone.

"Great heavens," Amalaswintha exclaimed, "Cassiodor! You look like a ghost. What has happened?"

"Noble Queen," Cassiodor said, "the troops from the North are led by Count Witigis, and he says he comes to safeguard the throne of the Queen."

She rose. "But . . . what about Count Tuluin?"

"Count Witigis has arrived with a vanguard of a thousand men", Cassiodor went on, disregarding her question. "He has asked me to tell the Queen that there is nothing to prevent her safe return to the palace. He asks for an audience tomorrow . . . today, that is . . . in the afternoon or at any other time convenient to the Queen. He gave me his word of honor for the Queen's safety."

"Tuluin", Amalaswintha urged. "What about him and the other conspirators?"

"Count Tuluin is dead", Cassiodor said woodenly. "So are Count Ibba and Count Pitza. They were murdered."

He saw the triumph in her eyes and looked down.

"Who did it?" she asked.

"No one seems to know. The murderers, too, are dead, cut down by the retinue of the nobles, except for one who was taken prisoner; but he managed to swallow poison and died almost instantly. Count Witigis thinks they were Herulians, not Goths, but he is not sure."

"And Count Leuthari?" Amalaswintha asked.

Cassiodor looked at her with deep sorrow. "What made you think that something might have happened to Count Leuthari too, noble Queen?"

She bit her lips. She said nothing.

After a pause Cassiodor said: "He, too, was attacked and wounded, but help came before the murderer could finish his work. It was the man who wounded him who was taken prisoner and poisoned himself."

There was a pause.

"Most noble Queen," Cassiodor said in a trembling voice, "I have had the honor to be your servant for so long that you will permit me say what is in my heart. And that is: Give up the throne."

"What? Are you mad?"

"Give up the throne", he repeated. "Don't return to the palace. Tell the ambassador to give orders to the captain to set sail. Go to Dyrrhachium."

"Now?" she asked. "My enemies are dead; my father's and my best general asks me to return. And at such a moment you want me to flee into exile? What madness is this?"

"It is the voice of one who cares for nothing so much as for your happiness," he said, "and it is speaking to your conscience and your heart, not your pride and your mind. There will be no peace and no happiness for you on the throne from now on. You must regain your peace with God, and that you cannot do without a sacrifice."

"I don't know what you mean," she said harshly, "and I don't want to know. I will hear no more about it."

All light went out of his eyes. "So be it, then", he said tonelessly. "Many years ago you made me promise that I would never leave your service. My answer was: I never shall as long as you love what is beautiful and noble and right. Most noble Queen, I can serve you no longer. Thank you for letting me stay at your side for so long. From now on I shall serve no one but God."

"Cassiodor! Don't go. Don't leave me like this. Think! Surely you must understand . . . "

She broke off, as there was a gentle knocking at the door. A moment later Peter came in.

"I am sorry to interrupt, most noble Queen," he said, "but a Gothic commander has come to the pier with a carriage and an escort, to take the Queen back to the palace. His name is Count Witigis. He says the rebellion is over, and he guarantees the Queen's safety. My crew and my oarsmen are ready. We can defy him and sail. What is the Queen's command?"

.Amalaswintha saw the flicker of hope in Cassiodor's eyes and turned away so as not to see it die. "I am coming", she said. "Illustris, I have much to thank you for. I shall expect you at the palace this afternoon. Count Witigis has brought a carriage, you said? Only one? What fools men are. I shall send another for the princess and my ladies." She swept out, and the two men followed.

The Byzantine crew was standing in readiness, helmed, and armed. No man moved, as the Queen went down the gangway to the pier, where Count Witigis was waiting, huge and shadowy in the gray light of the dawn. He greeted her respectfully and led her to the carriage, flanked by a small escort.

"There goes another chapter of history", Peter said airily. "But aren't you returning with the Queen, noble Cassiodor?"

"I am returning," Cassiodor said, "but not with the Queen. I have resigned my office."

"It grieves me to hear that", Peter said. "The Queen always spoke very highly of you. On one occasion she said you were her guardian angel."

The cavalcade on the pier was moving away briskly.

"I tried to be", Cassiodor said. "And I cannot help wondering what *you* are. Farewell, Illustris."

His gait, as walked down the gangway, was that of an old man.

Peter smiled.

"There will be no *Ding,* Frau Queen", Witigis said. "It should never have been called. Quite wrong."

Amalaswintha was again in the little audience room. She had had a bath and changed her dress. The Princess and the ladies-in-waiting were in their rooms, resting. There was no rest for her, but that did not matter; she could not have slept if she had tried. She was sitting again in her father's chair, with the Amalung crest, a gilded lion rampant, cut into the dark wood, and she felt strong.

"Things should always be done in an orderly fashion", Witigis went on. "Bad enough when some young firebrand oversteps the mark, but these men were old enough to know better. It was Count Tuluin's idea, of course, always a great one for ideas he was, and where has it got him?"

"Were *you* going to the *Ding,* Count Witigis?" Amalaswintha asked curtly. She had never had a great liking for the beefy hero of the Gepid war, although her father seemed to have thought much of him.

Witigis rubbed his fleshy nose. "Tell you frankly, Frau Queen, I was", he admitted. "But then I thought you had ordered it. Who else could have? I thought; the Queen alone has the right to do it. They pulled the wool over my eyes, they did, I must hand it to them, what with the Sajons going about, white staff and all, in the name of the Queen Regent, they said, so what was I to think? Still, the fellow who summoned me and my men seemed to come from the wrong direction, should have come direct from Ravenna, without making a detour, but hadn't. There were rumors, too . . . I didn't like it much. Then Count Pitza came to see me and sort of talked around, all kinds of veiled hints about dynasties and whether a woman should be allowed to rule and suchlike, and I decided I would attend in any case, as there might be some mischief. Frau Queen may be a woman, I thought, but she is my old king's daughter, too, and I was one of those who swore fealty that day just before the King died."

"So did Count Tuluin, and the others", Amalaswintha said sharply.

"So they did, Frau Queen," Witigis agreed, "and now they're dead. Kind of justice, one might say, but I'd still like to know who did it."

"Cassiodor told me they were either Goths or Herulians," Amalaswintha said quietly. She was sitting bolt upright in her chair.

"Herulians, more likely", Witigis said. "But who sent them?

It was a good choice. There are Herulians serving under Gothic command, Frankish command, and Byzantine command, they don't care much for whom they fight, those boys, as long as somebody pays them. Good fighters, too, very reliable. I've seen one of the bodies. Not a thing on it that would help, no letters, no badges. All four of them kept a tiny bladder with poison in their mouth, only had to bite on it and they were beyond reach of anyone who tried to interrogate them. Well prepared, Frau Queen. And that's why I don't think *you* sent them. No, no, don't look so angry, Frau Queen, I mean no offense, but women just haven't got the accuracy, everything just right, every detail calculated. Planning, that sort of thing takes. I really would like to know who worked it out, I could do with a man like that in the army. Any number of hotheads we have, but few men who can work out a good plan in detail."

"In any case," Amalaswintha said, "we seem to agree that Tuluin and the others deserved their fate. And as the men who killed them are dead, we can now discuss things worthier of our attention." But she was baffled by the workings of his mind.

"They had a good many enemies, naturally", Witigis said. "That sort always has. Ah well, no good brooding too much over it. We can leave that safely to their kinsmen. Let them ferret out who is behind it, if they can. Now then, Frau Queen, order has been established again in Ravenna and elsewhere. I have seen to it that the Sajons are informed that there will be no *Ding.* There are a number of small points on which I need your agreement and signature. Promotions, mostly. All in order. Then—"

"There is one matter of far greater importance", Amalaswintha interrupted. "I am extremely dissatisfied with the reports I've had about Prince Athalaric. His companions have had a very bad influence on him. I have not seen him for months, and I do not intend to tolerate this state of affairs any longer. He must come back here, where I can keep an eye on his activities."

"I was coming to that", Witigis said, looking rather embarrassed. "Only I would have preferred to tell you about it after—Ah well, I suppose it must be done. It is bad, Frau Queen, very bad, but there it is and nothing can make it any better. I only had the news an hour ago. . . . "

"What do you mean?" Amalaswintha asked, bewildered. "What news?"

"About Prince Athalaric." Witigis was quite red in the face, and began to perspire. "He has been overdoing it lately, I fear. One can have too much of the good things of this life, they say, and so it is, it seems. And his heart wasn't very strong."

She leaped to her feet. "My son! What's happened to my son?"

"I am sorry, Frau Queen, but he's dead. He died yesterday in Milan after a drinking bout."

She stared at him as if he were a monster. She opened her mouth to scream, but no sound came and she fell in a heap to the floor.

Much dismayed, Count Witigis bent down to lift her up, found that he did not dare touch her, and bawled for her ladies. When they came and crowded around their mistress, Witigis slunk out of the room.

28

THE AUDIENCE of the Byzantine ambassador had to be postponed. The court was in mourning. The mortal remains of the young prince were transported to Ravenna, but it proved impossible to have the body laid out in state. Decomposition had progressed too far, and the Goths knew nothing about the arts of embalming. The Arian bishop of Ravenna conducted a solemn service in the chapel of the palace, and on that occasion Peter saw the Queen again and proffered his condolence in the names of Their Clemencies and in his own. The Queen was heavily veiled, and her only answer was a slight bow.

Three days after the funeral she sent for him. He found her looking pale and haggard, but at least outwardly serene and confident. She told him about Count Witigis' visit. "He is a very primitive man, but honorable", she said. "His father was a peasant, but I suppose now I shall have to give him a dukedom. I have had to let Cassiodor go, you know. He was getting old and rigid, but I shall miss him. There are not many people here with whom one can have intelligent conversation, Illustris."

"There are a considerable number in Byzantium, noble Queen", Peter said. "Which reminds me that I had mail from there, yesterday. I must tell you about it, but I wanted to wait until you called me. In my reply I could suggest that a few of my friends there might be sent to Ravenna, if that would please you. Generals and the like are poor company for a noble and erudite mind, even when made dukes."

She gazed at him steadily. "I am very much indebted to you, Illustris."

"I cannot remember any service I have rendered the Queen", Peter said blandly. "Only that I had the honor to have her as guest, for a few hours, on my ship. But I do hope I shall be of use in the future."

She gave a slight shudder. "I trust . . . I sincerely trust I shall never again have to . . . resort to such measures."

He nodded. "That is my hope also. And the new instructions I received point to my Imperial Master's desire to strengthen your position as much as he can."

"You can tell the Emperor that it is more secure than ever before", she said with a sad smile. "Now that my poor son is no more, I am no longer Regent. I am the Queen."

"That is exactly the point that troubles me a little", Peter told her. "The rule of a woman, however highborn and noble of character she may be, is a novelty to the Gothic people.

They accepted it because King Theodoric asked them to; but it was supposed to be a temporary measure, lasting only until the young prince came of age. Now that the Prince has passed away, any of those bullnecked generals may be tempted to seize power. And first he would try to acquire the confidence and trust of the Queen."

"Witigis?" Amalaswintha asked incredulously. "Don't tell me you have reason to suspect that he has ambitions so far above his station. No, I refuse to believe that. I have studied the reigns of many rulers, and I don't wish to make the mistake so many of them committed, being suspicious of everyone."

"I have no evidence against Count Witigis and I have not mentioned his name", Peter said. "But the danger of further rebellions certainly exists. Last time, a Byzantine ship gave you shelter. Next time your protection should be stronger. You must have a powerful guard whose proximity or, better still, whose presence, will make any potential rebel think twice. I am happy to inform the Queen, that Byzantine troops have landed in the formerly Vandal part of Sicily."

Cassiodor, she thought. He had warned her that Byzantium was going to claim that part of Sicily. Now they had not merely claimed it, they had taken it.

"But this is little more than a gesture," Peter went on, "and it would not help much in the case of a real emergency. We must do better than that. What my Imperial Master has in mind is a state treaty, and I have been ordered to suggest it and to discuss its various points with you. The main point and the basic reason for the treaty is the safeguarding of your throne. Therefore an alliance should be made with you personally. The Emperor would come to your help against *any* enemy, from within or without. And the world must know that no one may dare to attack you or rebel against you, without the immediate danger of war with Byzantium."

Amalaswintha closed her eyes. This was almost too good to be true. Vandal Sicily did not amount to much, and Justinian's claim on the area was not without justification.

"You will need a bodyguard", Peter went on. "Men absolutely

devoted to you and free from any absurd prejudices about the rule of a woman. The Emperor will arrange for it. A Byzantine fleet could come to Ravenna, for a friendly visit. A few thousand men would be landed and given quarters within the precincts of the fortress. When the fleet sails away, the men simply stay on. In that way you would be safe against any surprise attack from within."

"The Gothic commanders wouldn't like that", she said, and her brows contracted a little.

"Let them dislike it then", Peter replied cheerfully. "You are the Queen. There's no need to tell them beforehand, and once the men are here, they won't be able to do anything about it. And you will be safe."

"It *is* an excellent plan", she admitted. "But surely . . . your Imperial Master has wishes of his own. . . . "

"No more than tokens, noble Queen", Peter said. "Thus he would like you to come to *his* assistance in any wars of his with a token force of three thousand Goths. . . . "

"Conceded", she said at once.

"And that way," Peter said, smiling, "you could get rid of any unruly elements in your army. Another point is: the withdrawal of all Gothic garrisons from Sicily."

She sat up. "But why?" she asked warily.

"To enable my Master to come to your help, in case of need. The troops in Lilybaeum could not land on Italian soil if mutinous Gothic troops barred their way at Rhegium, at the end of the Straits of Messana. I must show it to you on the map. And land they must, in such a case, or your guard, here in Ravenna, would be isolated. I need not tell you, most noble Queen, that my very frank exposition of the treaty we are planning, is for your ears alone."

"Of course. But this is too great an issue to be decided on the spur of the moment. I must think about it."

When the ambassador had gone, she paced up and down the room. The plan was magnificent. But it could be dangerous. So far Justinian had showed himself a true and loyal friend, ready to assist her in every way. And it was clear that he must prefer a civilized ruler in Italy to some Gothic chieftain who might make war tomorrow just for the male fun of making war. Something of that was in every one of those men. Hunting, drinking, brawling, that was all they were good for.

And yet: if she withdrew the Gothic garrisons from Sicily proper, what was there to stop Byzantine troops from marching in, now that they had a foothold and a port on the island?

That Illustris was a charming man. He was also a very glib talker. She remembered her father saying that she should never give a Byzantine ambassador an audience for longer than a quarter of an hour. What would *he* say to this treaty? But then, of course, no one had dared threaten *his* position from within.

She needed protection. It was good, it was excellent, to have a guard. But who would protect her against the guard?

Several days passed. She saw the Illustris again, on two occasions, but purposely only for a few minutes. Once he suggested that statues of Justinian be erected in Ravenna and in Rome, to accustom the Goths to the fact that the Queen had a powerful protector.

Meanwhile the secret reports coming in from all parts of the country were far from reassuring. There was a great deal of grumbling about the deaths of Tuluin, Ibba, and Pitza, and many nobles believed that the Queen Regent had had a hand in the affair. And time and again there were mutterings of dissatisfaction with the rule of a woman. The walls of houses in many towns were defaced with inscriptions: "A woman should stick to her cooking pots", or "A woman should serve and not rule." Not many Goths could read or write, so the effect of the scrawlings should not be great; but, on the other hand, they proved that there was opposition at the top. It was galling, infuriating. Her guilt, her real guilt, was not the death of the rebels. It was the fact that she was a woman.

Count Ortharis announced Prince Theodahad, and she lifted her eyes to heaven in exasperation. The Prince never came to see her except on official occasions, unless he wanted royal influence exerted against some legal opponent. He was always involved in lawsuits—especially against neighbors. He hated neighbors, they were to him nothing but a limitation of his own property. The man was a miser and a bore, but he was also an Amalung and her cousin and therefore had to be received at once.

"Sorry to disturb you again, fair cousin", he said in his grating, brittle voice. "But after all, you're the Regent, I mean you're the Queen, and where else can a man find his rights?"

Amalaswintha sighed. "And who is it this time, cousin Theodahad?" she asked. "You have taken all the land in Tuscany. What more do you want?"

"Oh, nothing, nothing much", he said. "But that fellow Optaric is really quite intolerable. I wanted to buy some of his estate, and he wouldn't sell. Wouldn't sell to me, an Amalung. His father was a cowherd. Got a lot of booty in the last war, bought up that land before I could. It's just what I need for a deer park. Recently the fellow forgot to pay some debts, and I thought I could get him that way, but when I sent over to remind him, he drove away my men by force, wounded two of 'em. Nasty fellow. Next day he sent me the cash he owed. But he had put himself in the wrong, you see, attacking my men and wounding two. Anyone who hits my men, hits me, isn't that so? And anyone who hits an Amalung . . . what does he deserve? So I got a couple of hundred of my men together and we seized his estate—punishment for his attack. So he goes and complains to the court, saying all kinds of things, quite frightful. Now it stands to reason that we can't have all this spread out before the court, doesn't it, cousin? Optaric is a really nasty fellow, he might say anything, does so even now, about some of my men having, er, insulted his two daughters and all that sort of thing, quite ridiculous, but it's a bore, and it sounds so bad, can't expose the name of our family to such things."

"Cousin Theodahad," Amalaswintha said sternly, "this is not the first time you have come to me with a story like that, but this is one of the worst. I really don't see what I can do about it, except let the law take its course."

"Now don't be so rash, cousin Amalaswintha", he said nervously. "You could always ask Optaric to appear before you and order him to reach a settlement. I'll even pay the price for his damned estate, if he insists on it. Trouble is, he won't take it from me. But he'll have to from you. You're the Queen, aren't you?"

"I can't force him to sell, if he doesn't want to", she said angrily. "Why do you always have to do such shabby things, cousin? I can't think of anything worse than to be your neighbor. And you an Amalung." It was at that moment that the idea came to her, and she looked at the fussy little man with cold appraisal. He was accustomed to have women look at him with anything from indifference to dislike and even contempt, but this long, icy stare was too much for him; he wilted under it. One never knew with women. She might have him arrested and thrown into jail. She might do something still worse. She had had Tuluin, Ibba, and Pitza killed, great nobles, though not of royal blood. Perhaps she felt he was in her way.

"Cousin Theodahad," Amalaswintha said, "will you marry me?"

He sprang to his feet. "Amalaswintha, for God's sake . . . you don't think I'm aspiring . . . you don't think I've been trying . . . "

"Calm yourself," she ordered, "and sit down." She laughed harshly. "Your first reaction to my proposition was scarcely flattering", she said.

"Amalaswintha," Theodahad stammered, "you are still a very beautiful woman, you're of the blood royal, and you're the reigning Queen. What do you want with an elderly fellow like me. You must be joking. I . . . I . . . "

"Set your mind at rest, cousin", she said coldly. "And listen to me. Our marriage would be one in name only. In every way. You don't think for a moment I would allow you to touch me? I'd die first. I would go on with my reign as before. You would have no say in affairs of state. But you would have the title of King and be present at all official ceremonies. And you would receive a private allowance as high as my own."

"How much is it?" he asked quickly.

"I really have no idea," she said contemptuously, "but you can look it up in the household books. I'll tell you why I am offering you all this, cousin. It will save you much unnecessary thinking. The people of the Goths would be perfectly satisfied with my reign, if it were not for the fact that I happen to be a woman. So now they will get a king as well as a queen, and all will be well. After all, cousin Theodahad, you happen to be a man."

Theodahad giggled.

"Now you know my motives as well as my proposition and my conditions", she said. "What is your answer?"

He grinned. "I accept, dear cousin Amalaswintha. I am most honored. Oh yes, oh yes, I accept."

"The official proclamation will be made tomorrow", she said. She added irritably: "Why are you laughing, cousin?"

"Oh, well . . . I couldn't help thinking what a bad day this is for Optaric."

29

THE MARRIAGE of Queen Amalaswintha and Prince Theodahad came as a surprise to everyone, not excluding the Byzantine ambassador.

She's panicked, Peter thought. The pace I set must have been too fast for her. He was in a black rage. All his plans were upset. The worst was that Justinian could no longer play the part of the Queen's protector. This might please Theodora, always on the alert for potential rivals; it would not please the Emperor. And a displeased emperor might recall his ambassador and send someone else. Or he might change his mind about the conquest of Italy altogether. He always needed moral grounds for his actions, the imperial hypocrite, and now Amalaswintha was no longer in need of the kind of help Byzantium could give her. She had a husband. Her position among her own people was secure. That was why she had done it, of course. She could not have fallen in love with Theodahad, of all people. Why, she despised the man. He remembered her remark that he would sell his own soul for money. But he was a royal prince, an Amalung. No Gothic chieftain was likely to rise against him.

He began to feel a little better when he studied the dossier, carefully compiled by a number of agents in the course of many years. Weak-willed, cowardly, greedy, rapacious. Such a man was not likely to be a popular ruler. Such a man was going to be a puppet in her hands, and that was another reason why she had chosen him. To her Goths she could now point out that they had what they wanted: a male ruler. Yet it was she who would go on ruling them. Neat.

He went to the wedding, of course, a monstrous affair with two thousand guests, whole oxen turning on spits, Gothic girls and youths performing tribal dances, and most of the men getting drunk.

The Queen was a little cooler than before, and he thought he could detect a note of mockery in her voice when she introduced him to her husband: "The Illustris is a most reliable friend."

Theodahad, in a purple cloak and with a diadem on his thinning hair, looked like the king of weasels.

The Queen left early, and Peter used the opportunity to lose two thousand solidi to Theodahad at a game of dice. The King cheated shamelessly.

The negotiations did not get any further. The Queen was evasive, the audiences were short. The King had no part in them, not even as an onlooker, but one could always meet him late at night, at the dicing table, as long as one was prepared to lose money to him, and Peter was. He used the opportunity to speak of the wealth of Byzantium, and mentioned that the

Emperor was buying up Lesser Armenia. "A little deal of forty thousand pounds of solid gold", he drawled. "Enough for the monarch of that country to live in royal splendor without any of the troubles of kingship."

"Pretty sum", Theodahad agreed. "Buying the whole country, eh? Took a lot of haggling, I suppose."

"Not much", Peter said. "The Emperor regards haggling as undignified. He is very generous. The Empress is . . . a little more careful about money."

"So's the Queen", Theodahad said. "And that's putting it mildly. Very . . . accurate in such things. Got a regular sermon from her the other day. The money of the country, responsibility towards the people, and so forth. Always the little patriot. *She* wouldn't do what that Armenian man did. Oh no. Rather go on ordering everybody about, endless conferences, work. Strange, for a woman. Me, I prefer collecting really good vases and rare furniture."

Peter only just stopped himself from saying: "Strange for a man, especially when he happens to be a Goth." Instead, he said, "I understand you, most noble King. When one has to go through all those wearisome ceremonies, one would prefer to give the orders, too."

"The treasury now", Theodahad said, fussing with his coat sleeve. "Can't get anywhere near it. Can't even get the figures. I'm very good at figures, you know. But no, keeps everything to herself. Really, sometimes . . . "

"After all," Peter said, "now that Prince Athalaric is no more, you are the nearest male kinsman of the late King Theodoric."

"So I am", Theodahad agreed. "So I am. Quite right. Oh, I see, you mean it's really me who ought to . . . that's good, that's very good. Ought to tell her that one day, when she starts again yapping about this, that, or the other."

"*Telling* her won't get you any nearer to the treasury", Peter said tersely, and the King's watery eyes protruded a little. "Your throw next", Peter went on, handing over the dice.

Theodahad took them. He began to giggle. "You're a subtle

one, Illustris", he said. "I wonder what's going on in that sharp mind of yours."

"No need to tell that to a man of your intelligence, most noble King. My Imperial Master has certain ideas he would like me to suggest to the ruler of this country, ideas that would lead to *very* great advantages to both. Now you are not obstinate, not over-ambitious, and above all not a woman, who changes her mind from one day to another. You are, on the contrary, a thinker, a philosopher, and what you really care about is the ideal life, without worries and troubles, in an ideal climate, and in complete security. With whom, then, do you think, my Imperial Master would prefer to deal?"

"Bold, very bold", Theodahad said, far from displeased. "You're right, Illustris, there is no need to tell me. There is only one thing I'd like you to consider."

"And that is?"

"Italy", Theodahad said, "is worth more than Lesser Armenia."

Ever since Prince Athalaric's death, the Queen had made it a habit to drive once a week to the Arian church containing his tomb and that of her father, to pray there, and she preferred to do so in the evening, when her visit would remain unobserved, to go in an ordinary carriage and to take only one lady-in-waiting with her, usually the Lady Brinda.

This evening the weather was sultry and the church stuffier than ever. She found it difficult to pray. It was as if the dead did not care for her prayers. Perhaps they really did not. Perhaps what the priests all seemed to hint at was true, that love alone could be the measure of prayer. And how much love did she have for father and son? More today, perhaps, when they were dead, than when they were still alive, and . . . in the way. Useless to try to push away the thought, it always returned. It was the same with Eutharic and Cassiodor, who had loved her all his life and was now somewhere in the South, in Scylacium, where he was building a monastery of some sort. Had she ever loved anyone at all?

Morbid thoughts, unworthy of a queen. She rose from her

knees and beckoned Lady Brinda. Silently the two women walked back to the portal and the carriage waiting for them.

The groom, who helped them to enter it, closed the carriage door with a crash.

"Badly trained", Amalaswintha said. "I must speak to Count Bodila about it. Why is it so dark in here?"

"They have drawn down the leather flaps against the sun," Lady Brinda said. The carriage was moving away.

"That's absurd. It's stuffier in here than it was in the church. Knock and tell the driver to draw the flaps back."

The carriage was moving so fast and jerkily that Lady Brinda was almost thrown off her seat when she tried to get the attention of the driver. He paid no attention to her knocks and calls. "He doesn't seem to hear me", she said. "No wonder, when he's going at such a pace."

"He shouldn't", Amalaswintha said, frowning. "Why, the man must be mad. Listen to those hoofbeats! Galloping horses. Brinda! We didn't take an escort with us when we left the palace, did we?"

"N-no," the Lady Brinda stammered. "You d-don't want one when we're driving to the church, so I didn't order one."

"We have one now," Amalaswintha said. "I hear more than the hoofbeats of two horses. Something's wrong. Did you recognize that groom who held the door for us?"

"N-no, I didn't. There're many new servants now, since the King has come to stay at the palace and . . . "

"Was he a Goth? I didn't look at his face. Was he?"

"I d-don't know." Lady Brinda's teeth were chattering. "He might have been. Or a Herulian. They may have sent one of the King's carriages by mistake. His stable people are mostly Herulians. What I don't understand is, surely we should be back at the palace by now. They must have taken a wrong turning. Oh God, why are you looking at me like that?"

"I am sorry, little Brinda", Amalaswintha said. Her voice seemed to come from very far away. "We shall never see the palace again. We are going to our death."

"Fifty thousand", King Theodahad said very firmly. "And not an ounce less."

"I shall pass it on to my master," Peter replied, "but it's the largest sum ever paid to one man. With a single pound of solid gold one can buy . . . "

"And a country estate of no less than eighty square miles, of my own choice in either Cappadocia or Cilicia", Theodahad interrupted. "And the title of King for life."

Peter gazed at him with admiration. "No one's ever going to get the better of you in a bargain, my lord King", he said.

"I hope not", Theodahad replied calmly. "Don't forget that as things are I shall have to fulfill most of my part of the bargain, before Justinian can fulfill his; and that means a very dangerous time for me. The withdrawal of the garrisons from Sicily is easy, I grant you that, and so is the concentration of Gothic troops on the Frankish frontier. I have merely to give the orders. But once your troops are on Italian soil it'll be ticklish. I don't want to risk my life for nothing."

"The Franks are always a potential danger, so your move won't cause any suspicion", Peter said. "The only real danger I can see is that a certain person is still alive, as you told me . . . "

"Oh, don't worry about her", Theodahad said. "It is all nicely arranged. She is . . . well, never mind, where she is, but she's safely hidden away, and she would have to have wings to leave the place. I . . . I'm not the kind of person who—I don't like blood. Fact is, I can't even look at blood, makes me feel funny. Who's going to command your army?"

"The conqueror of the Vandals, General Belisarius."

"He's good, isn't he? He'll have to be. These people of mine are first-rate killers. Just love it. Used to despise me when I was a boy, for not being like them. Never liked brawling. But I got the better of them in my own way." Theodahad gave a short giggle.

"The lady we were talking about is remarkably free of your scruples in that respect", Peter said.

"Oh. Ah, you mean the fate of Tuluin, Ibba, and Pitza, eh? I always thought she was responsible. Fact is, everybody knows, but nobody can prove it. Old Leuthari is the only one who got away. He's coming back here soon, I believe."

"He is back", Peter said indifferently. "I saw him, just before I came to you. Incidentally: How long do you think you'll be able to keep up that story you gave out—about the Queen being on an inspection tour?"

They looked at each other in silence.

"Just as long as it's necessary", Theodahad said, sullenly.

Peter nodded. "Just one more matter, my lord King. There are nineteen thousand Goths on Sicily proper. They will be withdrawn within three weeks."

"That's right. The order will go out today, now that we have come to an agreement."

"Can you see to it that they are not used for the defense of either Neapolis or Rome?"

"They'll be needed farther north", Theodahad said, grinning. "In fact, here in Ravenna."

"Thank you, my lord King." Peter rose.

"My respects to your Imperial Master, Illustris, and I rely on him, as he relies on me."

Peter bowed and walked to the door. There he turned. "Count Leuthari is in the anteroom", he said. "I wonder whether the King will permit me to tell him to come in."

Theodahad gulped. "By all means", he said somewhat nervously. "Certainly. Must congratulate him on his escape."

Peter smiled, bowed again, and withdrew.

A moment later Count Leuthari entered, a haggard giant of a man, gray-haired, fully armored. His bow was a threat rather than a courtesy.

"Very welcome, my dear Count Leuthari", Theodahad said, fussing with his sleeves. "You have recovered from your wounds, have you? What a dastardly deed that was, to be sure."

"Lord King," Leuthari said, "as you well know, the law of our people makes the husband responsible for the actions of his wife."

Theodahad leaped to his feet. "Stay away from me", he shrilled. "Are you mad? What have I to do with any action of my wife, committed before I married her? Nothing. I repudiate it. I will have nothing to do with it."

"I will not speak of the attack made on me", Leuthari went on, quite unruffled. "But my three kinsmen have been murdered, and I am the head of the clan. The murderers were sent by the Queen. Your own words prove that you know."

"I know nothing", Theodahad stammered.

"We are neither Runts nor Buffoons", the terrible old man went on. "We are free Goths. No king or queen may commit murder and be exempt from accusation, trial, and execution. The *Ding* and its decision is above royalty and nobility as well as above the ordinary man. But the *Ding* will want proof; and the only proof I have is the certainty of my mind."

"Not good enough", Theodahad said. "And you know it."

"I know it", old Leuthari said stolidly. "Also it is true that a husband cannot be made responsible for an action committed by his wife before he married her . . . unless he wishes to accept such responsibility. You tell me you do not."

"Indeed I don't", Theodahad exclaimed, much too relieved to be annoyed by the old man's look of open contempt.

"Therefore I must see the Queen", Leuthari said. "Where is she?"

Theodahad looked at him fixedly. "No one knows where she is", he said. "She is away on a tour of inspection." He was sweating.

"You know better than that", Leuthari said. "If you won't accept responsibility, you must not protect her. Do you think this is easy for me? I carried her father's shield for many years. But a blood feud is a blood feud and comes first. Where is she?"

"Lake Bolsena", Theodahad said in a whisper. "There is an island in the middle of the lake."

Leuthari nodded. "How many men has she with her?"

"Twenty Herulian guards."

"Lord King," Leuthari said, "I hope for your sake that you have told me the truth." He gave a curt salute and stalked out of the room.

Theodahad wiped his forehead. "God," he said, "God,

you're my witness: I didn't tell him to kill her. I'm not responsible."

He sat down heavily. What a people they were, these Goths. But it would not be long now before he would be rid of them. Bullies, both men and women. He began to think of Cilicia and the palace he would have built for himself there.

30

ACROSS THE BLUE SEA came the ships, five long lines of them, the five long, white, fingers of Emperor Justinian, clawing their way towards the West. His other hand, filled with gifts, stemmed the onslaught of the Persians.

Uniremes, biremes, and triremes they were, many of them veterans from the Vandal conquest, others newly built on the imperial wharves, and each one filled with a mass of men and arms and siege engines of a dozen kinds, battering rams, onagers, pyro-ballists, group-shields, and several new machines for the spreading of Greek fire.

The flagship carried the Magister Militum per Italiam Belisarius, Count of the Roman Empire, Patricius, and his wife, slender Antonina, about whom the soldiers sang rather bawdy songs, her six women servants, her present lover Theodosius, and part of the guards, picked soldiers in the personal service of the Commander-in-Chief.

Staff officers were distributed throughout the fleet so that there would be no lack of commanders, if some of the ships were to go down in a storm. Most of the officers were Greek. Of the soldiers only every sixth was a citizen of the Eastern

Roman Empire proper. Five-sixths were mercenaries and adventurers from three continents. Sarmatian and Bulgarian detachments, Egyptians and Syrians, Moors and Sudanese, Abasgi and Isaurians, Lazians, Franks, Burgundians, Gepids who had an old account to settle with the Goths, Huns who slept with their heads on their horses' bellies, and Italian refugees, tight masses of aggressive virility, trained killers.

The wind was favorable.

The official reason given for the presence of an imperial fleet in West Mediterranean waters was the quelling of a Moorish rebellion in Africa and the destruction of pirates' nests all along the coast. Only a fool could believe such a story when he saw the size of the fleet, but no one was likely to see it before it arrived in Lilybaeum, and after that it would not matter.

But if the force sailing towards Sicily was too large for the mere punishment of Moorish mutineers and North African pirates, it was small indeed for greater aims; no more than twelve thousand men.

Eight thousand more were marching at that moment across Dalmatia towards the northeast frontier of Italy, under General Mundus. Their aim was not conquest, but a diversion, a feint that would give verisimilitude to the idea that the real danger was not coming from the south.

Steadily, majestically, the fleet sailed on, a forest of white sails, a thing of strange, spectral beauty, at once graceful and ominous.

In the whole of Italy only one man saw it coming; a monk in his cell high up on the Mount of Casinum. He saw it in a dream, or so most people would say.

"She is dead", said Agent Six.

Peter jumped from his bed. "You are sure?"

"Quite sure, Illustris."

"Who killed her?"

"A Gothic noble, an old man, named Leuthari. A count."

"Where did it happen?"

"On a small island in the middle of Lake Bolsena. She was there with only one woman and twenty Herulian soldiers."

"What happened to them?"

"The Goth had them all killed on the spot."

"How do you know all that?"

Agent Six grinned. "My assignment was to ferret out where the Queen was. You told me to look for the whereabouts of an ordinary carriage that went through Ravenna at great speed, escorted by Herulian riders, in the evening of a certain day. There weren't so many of them. So, in due course, I arrived at the shore of Lake Bolsena. There's a ferry to the island, but the ferryman was dead, killed, and his boat gone. The boat came back after a few hours, though, with some Goths in it. Ten of them. The boat would not carry more. Most of the men were wounded. The two who weren't took the boat back to the island and returned to the shore with another eight men. That was the beginning of a regular service, lasting several hours."

"I see. And you?"

"I thought, under the circumstances, it would be better not to show myself. But there were good, thick trees enough, and I listened. The Goths were all nobles, and in some way related to each other. A clan of sorts, I think. One of them said it was horrible to kill a woman with one's bare hands, and she of royal blood, so another told him off. 'You didn't have to do it. Uncle Leuthari did it himself, didn't he? And she deserved it ten times over.' A third said he could not be sorry for the Queen, but he was for the lady with her, because she had killed no one and was pretty. They all agreed that the Herulians had put up a stiff fight. Then more of them came over, including Count Leuthari himself, and they stopped talking. They had lost four dead in the fight and took their bodies with them. When they had gone, I took the boat and rowed over to the island. There is a small villa there. After what I've seen, I wouldn't take it if somebody gave it to me as a present."

"You saw the Queen's body?"

"Yes, Illustris, and it wasn't a pretty sight. They hadn't troubled to bury her, or anyone else."

"We shall see worse sights than that soon", Peter said. He paced up and down the cabin, the very cabin in which she had made her decision not to go to Dyrrhachium . . . much to his relief, at the time. But then, if she had gone to Dyrrhachium, she wouldn't have lived long either. Theodora would have seen to that. Ananke, inexorable Fate. Yet within its iron laws a man could still plan and act and see his plans succeed.

Now, the Emperor had the moral pretext he cared so much about. He had assured Amalaswintha of his protection, and the Goths had murdered her. And there was no need for Justinian to keep the pact with Theodahad. . . . Even if the King survived the next few months, which was extremely doubtful, the Byzantine ambassador could prove to the Emperor that Amalaswintha had been killed either on the direct order of the King or at least with his connivance. . . .

One thing remained: to give the signal for the attack.

"You have done very well", Peter said.

Agent Six grinned. "I'm paid well, Illustris."

"There's better in store for you than a bag of gold here and there", Peter told him. "Now listen. I am sending you to Sicily. Get there as quickly as you can. Here are five hundred solidi for your traveling expenses."

The agent smiled. "With a sum like that I could get to Byzantium."

"Go to Messana first", Peter went on. "Visit Iskander Girgios, the shipowner. Tell him to lead you at once to the Commander-in-Chief of the Byzantine troops. That's General Belisarius of course."

The agent whistled through his teeth.

"You might find it difficult to get to Belisarius on your own", Peter went on, "that's why I want you to see Girgios first. Tell Belisarius just the one word: *timoria.* But you must say it four times."

"Timoria", Agent Six repeated. "Vengeance. Four times."

"Right. Later you can tell him about the death of the Queen and anything else he may wish to know. But your message from me is that one word. And don't come back here. Try and get to Rome. We'll meet there, I think—you know where to find me. Can't tell you exactly when it will be, though. There should be some rather interesting developments here, soon, and I must watch them as long as I can."

"There is no letter to take with me?" the agent asked.

"No. You may be searched. All kinds of things may happen between here and Neapolis within the next few weeks. I have given you your message. There is no need for you to know more. If they are sufficiently suspicious, they may put you to the torture; and there is a point when a man breaks down under it."

The agent winced. Then he laughed. "They'll have to catch me first", he said. "Don't worry about me, Illustris. I'll get through to Belisarius."

31

NO ONE COULD ENTER or leave the monastery on the Mount of Casinum without passing the Tower. And no one could pass the Tower without being seen by the Abbot. For in that Tower, two-storied, massive, the most ancient building of them all and yet the one that needed the least restoration, Benedictus had his own cell. He saw them all arrive, parents bringing their sons as oblates; artisans not only from Casinum but from places all over the country, offering their work and often enough staying on as novices and monks; guests who wanted to be beggars of God and beggars who wanted to be guests of God; erudite priests who would discourse about the great problems of theology and philosophy; and men at the point of despair who felt dimly that these men on the Mount were nearer God and therefore might be able to show a way out of what to them seemed to be a labyrinth, a vicious circle or a bog of quicksand. The ill were carried in, and the possessed; travelers, who had heard about a great man of God residing on top of a mountain with his spiritual sons, came from afar, some out of sheer curiosity, others to verify strange things they had heard, and again others because they were searching for God.

What they found was a place unlike any they had ever seen. It was teeming with life, but all life was directed towards an aim; yet there was nothing antlike about it, nothing that remotely resembled military barracks. There was no barking or bellowing of commands, yet the discipline was sterner than that of a crack army unit. The monastery was a living organism, the mystic body of a man in perfect command of all his faculties and functions, of a man who seemed to have overcome the Fall. There was constant movement and yet there was repose; there was little food, and yet great strength. Everything was simple, nothing was ugly. All things served a purpose, but none was drab. And the jurisdiction of the Abbot, the head of this mystic body, combined the justice of a father with the mercy of a mother.

No monk could remain idle for a single moment, but none was driven.

Their work was such that it made the monastery practically self-supporting. They were millers and bakers, blacksmiths and woodcarvers, masons and marble-polishers, gardeners, tailors, and shoemakers. They copied and illuminated manuscripts, they studied and taught. And seven times a day they assembled to praise God in song, as they praised him in their work.

By now Benedictus had put down in writing what he regarded as the Rule for beginners, the minimum of what was to be expected from a monk, and the seventy-three chapters of the Rule were being copied and recopied. For one copy would have to be sent to the abbot of Sublacum and another was to be put in readiness for a third monastery planned at Terracina.

A minimum. A Rule for beginners. But also one long Act of Loyalty to "the Lord Christ, the true King".

The citadel of God that was the monastery on the Mount of Casinum was as good as ready. Work was still going on on one building, which served as a storeroom. The Abbot had given the order to have it enlarged.

Brother Gregorius of the booming voice was supervising the work. A wall had to be made higher; a cellar had to be dug. To some of the monks, and especially strong Brother Martinus, it felt like old times again, digging, uprooting things; the novices knew nothing about those times, they had found their beds all made. "It was dangerous in those days", Brother Martinus said, working away with his spade. "You never knew what you would come across next, all kinds of pagan stuff, you know. We threw the altar of Apollo down the mountain, we burned the groves of Venus and chased old Hermophilus off the grounds. How he leaped! Like a goat, like his own horrible old god Pan, horns and all."

"Hermophilus? He's still alive, they say", Brother Gregorius boomed. "But his community, or whatever they call it, has dwindled to almost nothing. That's one who doesn't love us much."

"What is he like?" asked young Vitus, shoveling bravely. He was the son of a *curialis,* an official in Rome, and he had never done any digging before he joined the brothers a few months ago.

"Nasty", Brother Martinus replied somewhat curtly. He felt a little uneasy for having brought up those old stories. Besides, there was work to be done. Then his spade struck something hard and he saw a gleam of metal, brass it was, and he called out and together with two other monks he unearthed the head of a statue, as large as that of a cow and far less agreeable to look at, the head of a huge brass woman with brass snakes coiling around it. "Talk of the devil", he said, peering up at Brother Gregorius, who did not like the sight much either.

"Take that thing out of the way", Brother Gregorius boomed. "Put it . . . put it in the kitchen."

The brass head was hollow, yet it took the combined strength of four men to carry it over to the kitchen, and the monks there did not seem to be particularly happy about it.

A few minutes later Brother Sextus in the kitchen gave a shout: "Fire!" and the brothers outside saw thick smoke coming out of the kitchen door. The first man to recover from the shock was Brother Gregorius: "Get pails", he boomed. "Get water. Form a chain."

When the Abbot arrived he saw the monks hurrying hysterically to and fro with pails of water, and Brother Gregorius roared: "Get back, Father Abbot, the building is going to collapse."

Benedictus raised his hand: "Stop, all of you", he said, and in spite of the excitement which possessed them they obeyed at once. He bent his head and prayed, not very long, just about the time it takes to say the Lord's Prayer. Then he looked at his sons. "Put down those pails," he ordered, "and make the sign of the cross over your eyes."

They obeyed. And they saw that there was no smoke and no fire. The building was untouched.

Benedictus walked into the kitchen, where Brother Sextus and three others were trying to take cover behind a heavy table from a fire that did not exist. He gave them the same order, and they rose sheepishly. The Abbot pointed to the idol. "Take that thing to the smithy and tell Brother Valentinian to have it melted," he said, "but let him, too, first make the sign of the cross over his eyes."

Then he returned to the Tower. The enemy was active again, as a volcano, after a long period of quiescence, might erupt all of a sudden. Aping God in his own, brutish way, he tried to work through matter and through people. He could never create, but he could pervert and corrupt that which was created. Constant vigilance was the only answer.

Brother Secundus, who was something of a physician, went down to Casinum to see what he could do for an old woman who had broken a leg, and young Vitus who was interested in all things medical, received permission to accompany him.

When they returned, they reported that groups of fugitives were continually passing through the town, some on foot, some on carts drawn by mules or donkeys. They said there was war, but they did not seem to be quite sure who was making war on whom. Some said they had been besieged by Greeks, others that the Goths had burned their houses, and some even that the Huns were after them. Surely there had not been a Hun in Italy since the days of Attila! Yet one cartload of refugees insisted that an army, half a million strong, was marching on Neapolis, all of them barbarians whose language no one could understand, and others told of small Gothic detachments marching in a great hurry towards the north—away from the enemy.

As for the old woman's leg it was a perfectly ordinary fracture, but her relatives had called Hermophilus in and young Vitus had to shoo him away before they could start setting the leg. All the old heathen had done was to prescribe an amulet the woman was to wear over the place where the leg was broken.

"I told Vitus to take it away at once", Brother Secundus reported. "Hermophilus had gone by then. *He* could not have set the leg in any case. Both his hands were thickly bandaged. He seems to have burned them badly."

"He looked very old and very ill himself", Vitus added. "I felt quite sorry for him."

The Abbot nodded and let them go back to their work on the wall. The dreaded time had come. He had seen it coming, not once, but many times, armies streaming up and down the Via Casilina, cities burning, fields ruined; and all because one thief wanted to keep his loot and another wanted to take it away from him—unless it was that other and more powerful forces were making use of the two thieves for their own ends. There was no ascent towards God without the constant awareness of the abyss. He began to pray. But almost at once he knew a presence hostile to his prayer, a brutish presence, except that brutes had blood in their veins. There was cold mockery, a poisonous malice, an almost childish desire to frighten and to hurt. There was a threat, spitefully and monotonously repeated, the threat of an attack, today, this very hour, any moment now. . . .

The Abbot jumped to his feet. He cried out: "Brother Maurus!"

The young monk came racing up the stairs to the upper room and was stopped, halfway, by the Abbot appearing on the narrow platform above. "Run to the brothers working on the new wall, behind the kitchen. They are in danger. Tell them to be on their guard."

Maurus ran as fast as he could, downstairs first, and across the court and past the hospital building and the guest house, around the main building, around the kitchen, and there they were, working on the wall, young Vitus standing on it and one brother just beginning to climb up the ladder.

"Come down", Maurus yelled. "Father Abbot says there's danger, he wants you to be on your guard. . . . " But the sound of his voice was drowned by a grating, crunching noise. The wall trembled as if hit at its base by a huge, invisible fist, young Vitus screamed, threw up his arms in a futile attempt to regain his equilibrium, fell off, head forward, and the entire wall came crashing down on him. For a few moments the world was blotted out by a cloud of gritty dust. Then it began to clear, and the clarity was more desolate than the darkness. Brother Gregorius stood unhurt beside the broken remnants of his ladder; the other monks, too, were frightened but unhurt. But from under a huge pile of rubble a young hand stuck forth, its fingers spread out as in terror.

"Get him out", Brother Gregorius groaned. "For the love of God, get him out." But they were already on their knees, clearing the rubble away as fast as they could.

"There's no hope", Brother Martinus gasped, working feverishly, "Look . . . there's no hope."

Brother Gregorius looked up to Maurus with a little gesture of despair. "Tell Father Abbot", he sobbed, and once again Maurus ran.

When he came back, they had managed to free the boy's

body. It seemed impossible there could be a single bone in it that was not broken.

Maurus said in a trembling voice: "Father Abbot w-wants you to c-carry him to the Tower."

They stared at each other helplessly. Brother Martinus pressed his huge fists to his eyes and cried like a child. Brother Gudila walked over to the kitchen and came back with a large piece of sackcloth. It took a long time to do what they had to do. Then Brother Martinus and Brother Gudila carried it to the Tower. Brother Gregorius, Brother Secundus, and Maurus followed.

The Abbot was awaiting them on the platform of the upper story. "Carry him into my room," he ordered, "and put him on my *psiathium.*" The abbot's *psiathium* was a small mat in the middle of his cell, on which he used to kneel when he prayed alone.

The brothers looked up to him for a word of comfort, but all he said was: "Go back to your work. The wall must be built." And they slunk down the stairs, half-blinded with tears. Martinus and Gudila followed a moment later.

Work was resumed immediately. The debris had to be cleared away first, and that alone would take several hours. They worked in a grim silence, communicating with each other only by signs. They had been fond of the boy, and prayer came slowly to their hearts for they must purify it first lest it contain a tinge of reproach and be unacceptable to the One who could give and take as he willed it.

When a fresh young voice behind them exclaimed: "Whatever has happened here?" they stopped short, and for a moment or two not one of them dared to turn around. They knew that voice, and they knew that it could speak no more.

There was the grinding noise of a spade, a lone spade working, and they turned, slowly.

The boy Vitus was shoveling away the debris with a will. Feeling that they were staring at him, he paused, looked at Brother Gregorius, and explained innocently: "Father Abbot has ordered me to help you." Then he went on shoveling. But they still stood staring at him, at the strong movements of his arms and shoulders, the healthy texture of his skin, and after a while he paused again and looked up questioningly, as if to ask them whether anything was wrong, and they nodded and smiled back at him and started to work again; and of a sudden Brother Martinus burst into the *Te Deum Laudamus* in a curiously hoarse voice, and first Brother Secundus joined him and then Brother Gudila and Brother Gregorius with his booming voice and others too, so young Vitus chimed in, wondering a little why they should praise God with that most exalted of hymns at a moment when they needed their breath for shoveling away all that debris.

By himself in his cell Benedictus, too, was singing the *Te Deum;* having started a little earlier, he was a few lines ahead of the brothers at the wall, but it mattered little, because he could not hear them at that distance.

That night the old priest Hermophilus died in his ramshackle house in Casinum. He died in his sleep, but it seemed that he must have had a nightmare, for his tiny, shrunken face was contorted with fear and hatred. The few pagans left in the town gave him a burial in accordance with the ancient rites.

Perhaps it was just as well that he died that night, for on the next day his house suddenly collapsed, as if a huge, invisible fist had knocked it over.

Two weeks later Abbot Benedictus saw, from the window of his cell, a long gray snake slowly crawling along the Via Casilina in the direction of the north, its back glittering in the light of the sun. The Byzantine army had conquered Neapolis and was marching on Rome.

32

"THE CITY is in an uproar", Marcia reported to her mistress. "I've never seen anything like it. I gave Helvidius the bracelet for repair. The King of the Goths is supposed to be dead. I bought the vase you wanted, and it was only a hundred and eighty solidi, not a hundred and ninety. The Pope has told the Goths to leave Rome at once, and they are, I saw a lot of them leaving; they say there won't be a single one left by nightfall, but they must have done the most frightful things, there are hundreds of wounded people in the streets, women and children, too. Everybody is either laughing and singing, or crying and praying, and some of them are doing both at once. And the Byzantine army is coming, they say, either today or tomorrow. . . . "

Rusticiana pressed her hands to her temples. "Rome free", she murmured. "Rome . . . Roman. Do you realize that we have never been free, Marcia, you and I? Always, as long as we've lived, there has been a foreign tyrant lording it over us. Odovacar . . . Theodoric . . . O God, if only Boethius were alive; and Father. . . . "

Cervax entered to announce Senator Albinus.

"The Senator is very welcome."

"I'm glad to hear it", Albinus said, gently pushing Cervax out of his way. "You've heard most of the news, Domina, I suppose. It looks as if from now on you and I are no longer forgiven criminals, but free citizens."

"It is true, then. The Goths are leaving?"

"Oh yes. But I have some news for you which I think you know nothing about yet. Look at the door."

She turned. Her eyes widened. "Boethius!" she screamed. She staggered and would have fallen if Albinus had not caught her.

"Only Anicius", said the young man at the door sadly. "I'm sorry to have frightened you, Mother."

"Anicius," Rusticiana stammered, "of course. But you are so much like your father. . . . "

He approached slowly as if he were going to the altar to receive the Lord's Body. "I am glad if I am like him, Mother", he said, embracing her reverently. "But I'm afraid you will find me a dullard in comparison with his genius. All we can do, Manlius and I, is to see to it that he will be avenged, and to protect you from that brood of murderers."

"You always resembled your father a little," she murmured, "but now . . . it is almost uncanny." She rallied at last. "Manlius," she said, "is he here with you, too?"

"Here I am, Mother", Manlius said, appearing from behind Cervax' broad back. "I'm not a bit like poor father, but I love him no less for it."

"Come along, Cervax", Albinus said, taking the old majordomo by the arm, as Manlius ran up to his mother. "But it's just as well we did it this way, isn't it? Even so, your mistress almost fainted."

"No, stay, Albinus, stay, dear old friend", Rusticiana cried. "If you go I shall believe that it's all a dream. My sons here in Rome and with me and in this house!"

"We may be staying with you for quite some time", Manlius said. "Do you think I can have my old room? And Anicius, too?"

"Of course you can. But . . . how did you get here? From what Peter told me you were in the army and . . . "

"We are", Anicius said. "We are both tribunes."

"We helped conquer Neapolis", Manlius said. "Anicius killed a Goth, the lucky dog. A big one."

"But . . . how is that you are here, then? Surely Belisarius can't have entered the city yet and . . . by the saints, there are still Gothic troops here, they're leaving, but they haven't all gone. If they see you . . . "

The two young men laughed.

"We aren't dressed as what we are, Mother", Anicius said.

"But even if we were, I doubt whether the few Goths left here would be much of a danger. They'll be glad if they get out of the city without being stoned to death."

"There are a couple of hundred of us here," Manlius added, "all Romans in Byzantine army service, Sporianus, Licinius, Paeto, Salvianus . . . quite a number of names you know, and we have been busy under the very noses of those Goths, getting our old friends together. Rome has risen, Mother. You ought to come with us and have a look for yourself."

"I will", Rusticiana said proudly, her hands on the shoulders of her sons. "Let us go. Are you coming with us, Albinus?"

"I wouldn't miss it for anything", the Senator said, beaming. "But I advise you to take a carriage . . . an open one. The streets are crowded with people."

"Cervax", Rusticiana cried. "An open carriage and a dozen slaves."

The city was teeming with excitement. Driving slowly through the streets they saw groups of wildly debating and gesticulating people, flowers in windows, and troops of young men armed with knives and even swords that must have escaped the watchfulness of the Gothic authorities by some means or other.

"The sons of the She-Wolf", Albinus said, grinning. "Remember the days of the Young Lions, Rusticiana?"

But remembering meant Boethius to her, and she could not return his smile.

"Lots of arms were hidden away", Anicius said, "I think we shall be able to form a number of Roman units."

The Forum was black with people.

"Believe it or not," Rusticiana said, "this is the first time in ten years that I have seen the Forum and the Capitoline Hill."

The carriage had been slowed almost to a standstill.

"Make room, friends," Senator Albinus shouted, "make room for Domina Rusticiana, the widow of the noble Boethius!"

The crowd began to cheer, and Rusticiana wept unashamedly.

"By the Furies," Manlius exclaimed, pointing to a statue near the Rostrum. "Who is this?"

The statue was not a very big one, only a little more than life size; made of bronze. It showed a bearded warrior in Gothic armor, the helmet circled by a simple crown.

"Old Theodoric", Albinus explained. "Queen Amalaswintha had that kind of horror erected in every town. I don't think it will remain with us much longer."

"Down with it", Rusticiana said. "Anicius, Manlius . . . get somebody with a hammer or an axe."

The two young men looked at each other.

"You're right, Mother", Anicius said. "Stop the carriage, you! Down with Theodoric. Hey, friends . . . we need half a dozen axes to smash that fellow there."

"I want an axe", Rusticiana said, and her sons laughed uproariously at the idea; they could not help it, uproariousness was the general mood. No one had an axe, but half a dozen hammers appeared as if by magic together with a surprising number of swords. A few men started raining blows on the head and shoulders of the statue.

"Get the carriage nearer," Rusticiana ordered, "and let me have a sword, somebody." She rose and looked about.

"She means it, by God", Albinus said, half-admiring, half-amused. "A sword for the Lady Rusticiana!"

A big man held one up to her, and she drew it out of the scabbard as the driver edged the carriage as near to the statue as he could. The weapon was too heavy for her, but she managed to hit the King straight in the face.

"Careful, Mother", Manlius said, ducking a little. "You'll behead us all."

"She's magnificent", Albinus murmured.

The crowd roared enthusiastically and applauded, but suddenly the clapping ceased and there were wild shouts and curses.

"Heavens above!" Albinus ejaculated. "Look at them! They must be mad to come here."

"Goths", Anicius said, startled. "A small troop only. That must be the last of the garrison."

"Fifty or sixty men", Albinus said, "What lunacy to lead them across the Forum. They'll be massacred."

But although the crowd yelled and shouted abuse, no one seemed to think of attacking them. The little troop marched on stolidly behind its leader, a young officer with brand-red hair and a hooked nose, riding a black horse.

"They certainly don't lack courage", Albinus admitted grudgingly.

The Goths passed by at a distance of no more than fifteen yards, a thin double line in the dense crowd. The woman with a sword in her hand, standing in a carriage at the foot of Theodoric's statue, was so conspicuous that they could not ignore her, as they did the rest of the crowd.

Rusticiana saw the officer look at her. Staring back at him, she deliberately raised the sword once more and let it come down on the statue's helmet. Half a dozen men were slashing and tugging at it, and it was beginning to shake.

The red-haired officer took the reins into his shield-hand, and drew his sword, but a stone hit his horse and it reared, neighing, and more stones came flying at his men. He rapped out commands, and the Goths raised up their shields with the terrible spike in the center and pressed on vigorously. Around the officer the Romans fell back to escape the hooves of the black horse. He got the animal under control, and his strong, young voice cut across the din in guttural Latin: "We'll be back, woman!" Then he followed his men, hitting out right and left.

"If they stay together they'll get away", Manlius said coldly. Anicius nodded. No mob was a match for trained soldiers.

There was a shout of hundreds of voices and a crash. The statue of Theodoric had fallen. The men who had toppled it looked around, proud and beaming victors, and the crowd applauded wildly, leaping and dancing. The Gothic soldiers were gone.

"Let's return home", Rusticiana said curtly.

Albinus told the driver, and the carriage began to move.

Halfway back Rusticiana discovered that she was still holding the sword the big man had given her; she looked at it with disgust and threw it out on the street.

33

THE MAGISTER MILITUM PER ITALIAM Belisarius, Count of the Roman Empire, Patricius, was riding his favorite horse, Phalion, a bay with white fetlocks, full mane and tail. He wore the golden cuirass a grateful emperor had given him for his victory over the Vandals, a golden helmet with a horsetail dyed blue, and a short blue mantle, trimmed with ermine. He did not like the trimming, but Antonina had sewn it on with her own hands and thought it looked gorgeous, so he did not want to disappoint her by criticizing it. The great general's size was such that he would have dwarfed any man of his army riding beside him, and Antonina was a small woman, riding a little white filly, so her head came about to his knee. She had an extraordinarily mobile little face, with a sensitive nose and a wide mouth. She could ride like a Hun and swear like a cavalry instructor, and for such reasons was popular with the troops who had half a hundred nicknames for her, the mildest of which was "the General's General".

A strong detachment of guards preceded them. Behind them came a glittering swarm of commanders, then another detachment of guards, and after them, the many contingents of the army, the infantry in files of six, the cavalry in files of three.

A deputation of senators came out from the city to meet the liberator and to assure him that there was not a Goth left in Rome. Belisarius replied: "You had a garrison of four thousand until yesterday morning. The last detachment left the Flaminian Gate in the early afternoon, led by Count Blidin." The accuracy of his statement did not fail to impress the worthy fathers of the city. Belisarius smiled benevolently. "Thank you all the same for trying to help the Emperor's cause. I wish the Neapolitans had behaved as wisely. If they had, they would have fared better." Then he rode on, leaving it to the deputation to find a way back into the city—not very easy, since the troops filled the entire road.

At a mile's distance from the Asinarian Gate a single man rode up, unarmed, and dressed in the style of a Byzantine high official, gold cloth, jeweled belt and all.

"The Illustris Peter of Salonica", Belisarius said, surprised. "Joy to you, Illustris. What makes you travel without retinue? I thought I'd find you in Rome, but I didn't expect you to roam the countryside all by yourself."

"Joy and more victories to you, great Magister Militum and to you, most beautiful Magistra. I am going to Rome, as a member of *your* retinue. I did have twenty men with me, but I sent them back to my ship when I saw you coming. The *Adelphia* is at anchor in Ostia. Will you permit me to join you? I have a great deal to tell you."

"You may ride on my left", Belisarius said, "and be my guest at the Capitol tonight. As for your news, it will keep. All I want to know is, where is the Goth army?"

"Twenty-four thousand are marching from Regeta to Ravenna. They are the nearest Gothic troops. They include the four thousand that left Rome yesterday, and they are commanded by the new King."

"From Regeta to Ravenna?" Belisarius asked incredulously. "Going *north?* Are you sure?"

"Absolutely certain, Magister Militum."

"There is a mystery here", Antonina said suspiciously.

"And a new king", Belisarius said. "One never knows what to expect from new kings."

"There are half a dozen mysteries here, Patricia", Peter said. "Fortunately I think I know the answer to all of them, including the one about what to expect from the new King. But as you said, Magister Militum, my news can keep."

His curiosity thoroughly aroused, Belisarius wanted to ask more questions, remembered in time that this would be in contradiction to his earlier attitude and therefore would entail a loss of prestige. He settled down to a self-enforced silence.

Peter, reading him like a book, concealed his amusement and looked straight ahead. It was always good to keep the military in its place, and he was satisfied with his first encounter with the great man.

The Asinarian Gate came in sight, with its portcullis up and huge flower arrangements right and left, and here another deputation was waiting on a hastily erected dais.

"More senators", Belisarius growled.

"You will be given the keys of the city", Peter told him.

"The deputation is headed by a woman", Antonina remarked. "Fancy that! Couldn't they find a more suitable representative for such a ceremony?"

"No, Patricia, they could not", Peter said gravely. "This is Domina Rusticiana, the widow of Boethius." His eyes were shining.

"And who was he?" Antonina asked superciliously.

There was an awkward little pause before Peter answered: "Anicius Manlius Severinus Boethius, former Consul, Princeps Senatus, scholar, philosopher, and poet, was falsely accused, wrongly condemned, and brutally executed on the order of King Theodoric."

"He was the father of our two young tribunes", Belisarius added innocently. "Don't you remember them, Antonina? They're there, standing to right and left of her."

"Oh yes, of course", Antonina said airily.

The vanguard passed the Asinarian Gate and Belisarius halted his bay in front of the dais. The commanders behind him halted too, and behind them the second detachment of the guards, the Illyrians, the Huns, the Lazians, the Isaurians, and all the rest of the army, stretching over miles and miles.

A bevy of senators, the city prefect, and other dignitaries

filled to capacity the space behind Rusticiana and her sons. She was wearing a dark red robe and the Anician family jewels.

She has never been more beautiful, Peter thought, gazing at her as he used to when he was a boy. What kind of an age was this, when they chose her as the city's representative for the sake of a late consul, a dead senator, a half-forgotten philosopher, instead of choosing her, jubilantly, for her own sake, as the veritable symbol of the Eternal City!

"*Ave,* Belisarius", Rusticiana said, "Rome welcomes her liberator from Gothic tyranny."

That's what they asked her to say, Peter thought. They would. And as it was fulsome and stilted, it would probably be just right for Byzantine ears. But there was no joy in her voice, and her smile was ceremonial, put on.

Belisarius took the golden keys from her hands, bowed lightly in the saddle, said a few polite words, bowed again, and rode on. He had done that kind of thing so often, in Persia, Armenia, Vandal Africa, and Sicily. Either they gave him the keys of the city, or he rammed in the gate. Peter had time only for one last look and a wave, and she saw him; their eyes met. Here I am, Peter thought, I kept my word, didn't I? Smile at me, goddess, I have a right to ask for that, if ever a man had. Smile! But she would not smile. The beautiful face was without expression, an enigma, a mystery to which he did not know the answer. And he had to ride on.

"Quite an attractive woman", Antonina said, watching him out of the corner of her eye, and he agreed lightly and pointed out the decorations of carpets and flowers in the windows of the forest of houses going up the Caelian Hill. Perhaps the goddess was right not to show any emotion at that particular moment.

The municipal soldiers were out in force, and for most of them arms had been found in cellars and attics; units of patriotic youth cheered the Emperor's general as he passed the Flavian Amphitheatre, and on the Forum the majority of the senators was awaiting him, a large white blob in the middle of the huge crowd.

That's where I was standing, when King Ox came in, Peter

thought, and for one strange, wild moment he almost expected a boy of twelve—or was it thirteen?—to come rushing out at him with a writing tablet hiding a sharp stylus. . . . He could feel something of that terrible determination, that absolute readiness to die for . . . what? The glory of Rusticiana? The glory of Rome? His own? Whatever it was, it had ended with an almighty kick.

"You look amused", Antonina said. "May one know what you're thinking of?"

"I am thinking of a very large foot", Peter said. "A foot that kicked me once, a very long time ago."

Antonina was annoyed, but Belisarius grinned. "What did you do, Illustrius? Kick back, I hope?"

"I couldn't, then," Peter said, "but I'm doing so now."

Then they had to listen to an eloquent, flamboyant, extremely flattering, and much too long speech from the Princeps Senatus. Belisarius' answer was a single sentence of thanks. Now he could ride on to the Imperial Palace that had been the residence of so many and such different men. But as Peter tried to take his leave, the General shook his head. "I shall have to make a tour of inspection presently", he said. "Must get a look at the fortifications. From what I've seen so far, they'll need modernizing. Must see how my men are looked after and half a thousand other things. But before I do that, I want your news. Antonina, you and I. No one else. Wine, somebody. Maxentius! Get guards posted. No one enters this room until I give the word, not even you."

"I want a bath", Antonina said.

"So do I, dear heart. But I think we ought to hear first what the Illustris has to tell us." Belisarius took off his helmet and put it on the nearest table.

"Oh, very well", she said, shrugging. "I hope it'll be worthwhile." She sat down, crossing her legs.

"Well, he did say something about the Goths having a new king", her husband reminded her. "What about it, Illustris? What's happened to the old one?"

"King Theodahad", Peter said, "died rather miserably. It was due, to some extent, to his lack of tidiness. He left some of his papers about, and they were seen by some underling or other who was curious enough to read them and disloyal enough to steal them and pass them on to Count Ortharis, the King's chief steward. Count Ortharis read them too, and informed three other nobles who in turn ..."

"Make it short, Illustris", Belisarius snapped.

"As you wish, Magister Militum. The papers in question were letters, or rather copies of letters the King had written to Emperor Justinian, reminding him of the arrangements they had made, stressing the fact that Theodahad had carefully seen to it that the Emperor's general would find little resistance on his arrival on Italian soil, and suggesting that the Emperor should let him have, in addition to the other grants of their agreement, one quarter of the Gothic treasury."

"Good Lord in Heaven", Belisarius exclaimed. "I knew you made some sort of a deal with that man, they told me something about it in Byzantium, but this ..."

"*Most* untidy to let a document like that lie about", Peter said. "The nobles decided to convoke a *Ding,* one of their grand assemblies, you know. Ordinarily this is a prerogative of the King but under the circumstances they couldn't very well ask him, so they called it themselves and invited him to attend and to defend himself against an accusation of high treason. When he received that information he knew of course that his only hope was to escape from his own country. He wanted to come on my ship. Fortunately I found out in time and sailed before he arrived."

"Why?" Belisarius asked, frowning.

"Because he was no longer of any use to us", Peter said. "We may wish to deny that we ever made a deal with him. Well, we couldn't do that very well if he was given shelter on an imperial ship. I was ready to provide refuge for Queen Amalaswintha, for such were my orders, and in fact I did so. But it's different with Theodahad. The Emperor can't appear as the protector of a man who sold his people to us."

It took Belisarius some time to grasp the idea, but in the end he did. "I hope the Emperor will agree that you did the right thing", he said ponderously.

"I think His Clemency will agree", Peter said cheerfully. "It saved him fifty thousand pounds of gold, apart from other advantages. I myself wasn't too happy at the time, because it was clear to me that the Goths would now choose a warrior-king, and that would mean more work for you, Magister Militum."

"I don't mind that", Belisarius said simply, meaning it.

Peter bowed to him. "They *did* choose a warrior-king", he went on. "A fellow called Count Witigis, one of King Theodoric's trusted army commanders. That was the outcome of the *Ding.* It was held at Regeta. They declared Theodahad as deposed and condemned to death—*in absentia,* naturally. By then Theodahad was fleeing north as fast as he could, but they caught up with him, and a man of the name of Optaric cut him down. He had some kind of a personal grudge against him, Theodahad had wronged his daughter or sister or somebody."

"Most men are pigs", Antonina declared surprisingly.

"No doubt," Peter agreed politely, "but King Witigis is more like a bull, or perhaps a bear, large, beefy, and not as slow as he seems to be. I'm told he is a good tactician. How much of a strategist he is, remains to be seen. The Gepid war in which he acquired laurels did not give too much scope for strategy."

"Why did he go north?" Belisarius asked. "You did not make a deal with him, too, did you?"

"He's not the type for that", Peter replied. "I had to use other means."

"He should have thrown his twenty-four thousand men into Rome and let me try to storm it", Belisarius said. "Even a Goth must know that much about strategy. Why didn't he do it?"

"Because he wants to marry", Peter said.

Antonina gasped. Belisarius' large face flushed. He rapped the table. "Stop joking, Illustris, and give me a sensible answer, if you have one."

"Oh, I'm far from joking, Magister Militum", Peter said cheerfully. "King Witigis really wants to marry. I should know.

I put him up to it, in a way. You see I was sore about the untimely fall of Theodahad. He served us well. Most of the Gothic army is still near the Frankish frontier, although now they will return. I had to think how I could undermine King Witigis' position a little. The *Ding* at Regeta was a relatively small affair. What if Witigis' election was not recognized by the rest of the army? So I had my agents in the North hammer away at the fact—the indisputable fact—that Witigis comes from simple stock. His father was a peasant. Some of the highborn Gothic dukes and counts couldn't be very happy about the choice, and my men did their best to kindle the flames."

"Oh, oh", Belisarius said. "Maybe there's some sense in this after all. But what is all that about Witigis marrying somebody?"

"He wants to marry Princess Mataswintha", Peter said, "Queen Amalaswintha's only daughter, the one surviving grandchild of King Theodoric. She is an extremely lovely girl, but I think he would take her if she were as ugly as a camel. She's an Amalung! As her husband, his kingship can no longer be questioned by anybody. *And that is why he's going north,* Belisarius! He wants to get to Ravenna as fast as he can, or somebody may spirit the girl away."

"By Venus and the saints", Antonina exclaimed, "I think the Illustris is right."

"So now, there are two possibilities", Peter said. "If Witigis doesn't reach Ravenna in time or the girl kills herself rather than become his wife, there may well be civil war. The name for Witigis which my agents planted among the nobles is 'the peasant-king', and it's having a good effect. Well, nothing could suit you better than a civil war! *Tertius gaudens!* But if Witigis succeeds in marrying Mataswintha, the Goths will obey him, and in that case he will come down on you with all the Gothic might. However, even then you will have a breathing space. He must wait until the troops are back from the Frankish frontier and until he has made sure that they'll be loyal. In any case, you can be fairly certain that there won't be a Goth anywhere near Rome for at least three months."

"Ample", Belisarius said. "Tonight I shall know what there is to be done, but three months will be enough to make the city impregnable. I'll put the entire male population to work, if it's necessary. Let them come."

"If they come, they'll be pretty strong", Peter warned. "You'll have more than a hundred thousand men against you and maybe as many as a hundred and fifty thousand."

Belisarius gave a slow smile. "I have yet to meet a general capable of moving that many men well. *That* part of the business you can safely leave to me, Illustris. But otherwise I must say you have done quite extraordinarily well, and I shall not fail to tell His Clemency so."

"Thank you, Magister Militum."

"Yes", Antonina said. "I've never seen anybody who could cheat so many people in so many different ways." Her smile took some of the venom, not all, out of her words. "And now, I hope, I shall be allowed to have my bath", she added.

"We shall see you tonight at the state banquet", Belisarius said. His nod was just a trifle condescending.

Peter gave the couple a courteous bow and withdrew.

34

SHE WAS ALONE as he hoped she would be. Both Anicius and Manlius had had to return to their units and no doubt would be duly inspected by their general on the walls of the city. She had changed into a simple dress. No jewelry. There was nothing to detract from her beauty; all this radiance was her own—jewels could do nothing to enhance it.

"Here I am, my lady", Peter said, "to report to you that the most difficult part of my mission is accomplished. The destruction of the Gothic people has started. And Rome is free." Why did she look so frightened? "When I saw you on that dais I felt like falling down and worshipping you", he went on. "You looked like the soul of Rome. You were the soul of Rome. Do you realize that you stopped twelve thousand men? You were magnificent. But you did not look happy."

"I wasn't", Rusticiana said.

"How can that be? At long last I have succeeded, we have succeeded. The one enemy who can and will beat the Goths has landed, has taken Neapolis and Rome! You should be jubilant."

"Jubilant", she repeated. Then she burst into tears. At once he was on his knees before her, he seized her hands. "My love, my great love, what is it? What can it be? I did feel there was something I couldn't fathom, out there at the gate, when you wouldn't smile at me. I wanted to come to you at once, but I had to stay with that peacock of a general, Belisarius, and with that slut of a wife of his. She is his evil genius, I think. I had to deliver my report. Tell me, my love, what is it?"

"Belisarius", Rusticiana said, "is not the only man to have an evil genius. You, too, have one."

Could it be that she was jealous? "Who is my evil genius, my Lady?"

"I am. No, I'm not mad, Peter. I mean it. I know now that I have been your evil genius all your life. It started here, in this very room. You were a boy, a child, yet I planted in you the idea of murder. I poisoned your mind. How can I ever be forgiven for such a sin?"

"My dearest," he said, smiling, "we were both children at the time—yes, you, too, although you were a married woman. And no murder was committed. Come now, you've been alone for too long, and it's made you give in to all kinds of morbid thoughts. We're children no longer."

"No, we aren't," Rusticiana replied, "and so we have committed murder . . . and a hundred other crimes as well."

He shook his head. "What's come over you, all of a sudden? What *do* you mean?"

Her eyes were haunted. "Neapolis", she said. "Do you know that there are several thousand refugees from Neapolis here in Rome? I've been told that the Goths had ill-treated them in the most dreadful manner. I've been told that the Gothic garrison leaving Rome brutally wounded hundreds of people. I found out it wasn't true. I talked to the people themselves. They told me."

"What did they tell you?"

"That our great and noble liberator's troops were the criminals, when they conquered Neapolis. I couldn't believe it. Why should they do such things? Why should Romans hurt Romans? Why should the victorious troops of the Emperor murder women and children, yes, women and children, Peter! Why should they loot and burn and rape? But these people did not lie. Such grief does not lie. When the Senate asked me, through Albinus, to receive Belisarius at the gate, I accepted. I wanted to see him and his army. Peter, Peter, what have these people got to do with Rome? Have *you* seen them? Those Huns? Those horrible little men with their slant eyes and cruel mouths? It's not so long ago that the great Pope Leo risked his life to keep them away from Rome . . . and now we have brought them here. . . . "

"Killer Hun against killer Goth", Peter said. "We don't have to weep for either of them."

"I wept when I saw a little boy of six with his eyes put out," Rusticiana said. "*He* could no longer weep. A Hun had done that to him, to extort from his parents the place where they kept their jewels. They didn't have any, poor things!"

"So there will be a blind man more in the world", Peter said. "Aren't many people born blind? You believe in God, I think. Then why don't you blame him for that?"

"Don't blaspheme!"

"Listen to me, Rusticiana", he said sternly. "I promised you vengeance . . . vengeance against the people who murdered Boethius and Symmachus. We both knew that this would mean war. I have been working for years to bring it about. I lied. I cheated. I planned and brought about the murder of three Gothic nobles. I planned and brought about the downfall and death of Queen Amalaswintha and of King Theodahad. It was I who gave the signal to Belisarius to cross over to Italy and start hostilities, and the word I chose was *timoria*... vengeance. Have you forgotten what they did to Boethius? To your father? To the honor of Rome?"

"Vengeance", she said. "I did want it. Now I am beginning to think that there is no such thing."

"I don't understand you."

"How can it help Boethius or my father or me when others die? Their death is just another wrong. Nothing is set right by it. Even if Theodoric himself were still alive and I could kill him with my own hands, it would not help. It would be futile, as futile as what I did yesterday, when I helped to smash Theodoric's statue in the Forum. I felt so stupid afterwards, so childish. What would Boethius have said, if he had seen me standing there, with some man's sword in my hand, hitting away at a statue! What would he say to this war, Peter? Think of it... can you imagine him happy that we brought this to Italy in his name? He was the best, the mildest of men.... "

"He was a Roman. Don't forget that."

"But he refused to ask for armed help from the Emperor", she replied. "He was so wise. He knew what kind of men would come to liberate us. This is nothing else than another invasion. And we caused it, Peter. A war!"

"The war has only started", Peter said, with sullen vehemence. "So far I've made it easy for the great Belisarius. But the great clash is still to come, the real hecatomb on Boethius' grave. It is going to happen here. The decisive battle will be that of Rome. It will be better for you to go to Sicily again. You may not be safe here. Or, worse still, you may have to thank a Hun for saving your life."

The haunted expression was back in her eyes. "I don't want to be safe, Peter. I shan't leave Rome. You know my sons. Anicius looks so much like his father now, doesn't he? Perhaps he, too, will be killed in this war, perhaps they both will be part of that hecatomb. I dreamed just that, last night."

"It is as I thought", Peter said. "You're overwrought. You, my evil genius! I've told you what you are: the soul of Rome and the woman I love."

But she avoided his embrace. "Strange man," she said, "terrible man! Don't you see that the things we've done are too big for us? That we have started what we can no longer control? What are we making of ourselves, Peter? Demons . . . monsters . . . "

"Whatever we are," he said hoarsely, "we belong together. And we made a pact. Or have you forgotten that, too, now that you have discovered that there is 'no such thing as vengeance'? We made a pact, Rusticiana. This is what you said to me: 'If you bring it about, if you can unleash those forces as you say you can, then you may ask me for anything you want, and by the memory of the dead, you shall have it.' I can still hear your voice. Well, I have brought it about."

"Ask, then", she said. With her head bowed, her hands hanging lifelessly, she was like one condemned, waiting to be told the measure of her punishment.

"You know what I want", he said. "I want you."

She said nothing. All power had gone from her.

"Look at me", he ordered. She obeyed. He was smiling bitterly. "What do you expect me to do?" he asked. "Behave like a Goth or a Hun?"

"You can do much better and much worse", she said.

"What I want is Rusticiana," he said, "not her shadow. My great and lovely lady, my queen . . . not an overwrought little girl who has seen for the first time in her life that war means suffering, the suffering of both the guilty and the innocent, and who can't bear what she has seen. Just now, I think, you took me for a merchant who has delivered his goods and promptly demands his payment. But then you always underestimated me, Domina. You don't know what I am. And much less what I shall be."

"What do you mean, Peter?"

"This morning," he said, "a few hours before I met Belisarius on the Via Asinaria, I was in Ostia, on the *Adelphia.* A ship arrived with mail for me from Byzantium. The Emperor has made me Patricius. There is only one other man of that rank in Italy, and that is Belisarius. I didn't tell him that I am of equal rank with him. He still thinks I'm nothing but the former Byzantine ambassador for Italy and an excellent source of information for him. He is fairly friendly and just a little condescending. His wife seems to sense that there is more to me, but she doesn't know what. If I told them, they would want to see the letter from Byzantium. They know that there is always a letter sent with the document of high appointment. And that letter I can't show them. It contains a secret they mustn't know for some time, six months perhaps or maybe longer." Peter rose. "When the war is won," he said, "Belisarius will be given other work to do, probably at the Persian frontier. Justinian doesn't like a general to be in charge of a province, and that's what Italy means to him. He wants to restore the entire Roman Empire, but Byzantium is to remain the capital. So he will appoint a governor, a viceroy."

"You mean . . . he will appoint you?"

"Yes. And then I shall be able to rebuild the whole of Italy, not, like Boethius, as the minister of a barbarian king, but in my own way. Justinian cares little about the administration of his provinces, as long as he gets the revenues he wants. I shall be the ruler of Italy. And then I shall remind you again of our pact and ask you to be my wife. Good night, Rusticiana."

"Good night", she said softly. She watched him walking out, saw him limping and felt compassion flooding up in her. Poor Peter. Strange Peter. He still felt that Boethius was his rival, a rival he must outdo. Governor of Italy. Viceroy. I am not really a woman to him at all, she thought. I'm a symbol, a symbol of achievement. She was right, then; she really was his demon, the spur to his actions. She shivered. She tried to pray. But Christ had shrunk to the size of a little boy of six, with red, empty eye sockets; Marcia found her stretched out on her couch, sobbing her heart out.

35

THE NEXT DAY Belisarius exploded into action. Battlements were set at sharp angles, moats and ditches dug at the foot of the ramparts, and war engines placed on them in support of the archers. A triple chain closed the Tiber to navigation, and measures were taken to close the aqueducts as well. Neapolis had fallen to him because four hundred of his Isaurians had crawled through one of the city's aqueducts, killed the Gothic sentinels, and opened the nearest gates from the inside. No one was going to play the same trick on *him.* Fifteen thousand Romans were pressed into service and had to dig under the watchful eyes of Byzantine officers. The Tomb of Hadrian became a heavily armed fort. Belisarius himself was everywhere, correcting, scolding, cursing, and praising. His pride was a watchtower he had built near the Milvian Bridge. It was built, by his best engineers, all of stone and mortar, so it could not be burned. Two hundred men up there, and no enemy could make use of the bridge or even get anywhere near it alive. The Goths would have to build another bridge and that would take them at least ten days and probably more. Thus the element of surprise was eliminated. Six weeks after the General's entry into the city things had begun to take shape.

"One more month and they can come," Belisarius said, "and I don't care how strong they are. In fact the stronger they are, the better I shall like it. It'll only increase their forage problem and the number of our targets. Goths are Germans, and Germans are at their best when they attack. Their first attack is the worst. Then, gradually, they get weaker. They make one last mighty effort, and when that doesn't work they break. That's how they were when old Marius fought them, six hundred years ago, that's how they are now, and that's how they always will be."

But the Romans cared very little about the Byzantine general's knowledge of German psychology. They had welcomed him and his troops enthusiastically, they had wined and dined him, but they expected him to leave the city and pursue the enemy towards the north. He had taken Neapolis and Rome; why stop here? It was bad enough that half the male inhabitants had to dig ditches and carry stones. But the idea of becoming the center of attention of the entire Gothic army did not appeal to them at all. A siege was at its very best an extremely disagreeable affair. Quite apart from the actual fighting, there would be shortages of all kinds and there might be epidemics. Why could not all these foreigners fight it out elsewhere?

"It's the Pope", Antonina exclaimed, when report after report came in mentioning the lack of enthusiasm on the part of the Roman population. "The Pope is a traitor."

"Of course", Belisarius said mechanically. He was studying the plan of the whole net of fortifications as it now was. Then he frowned. "*What* is that you said?"

"I said the Pope is a traitor", Antonina declared. "I bet you it's that old fellow with his silvery beard and his pious eyes who's behind all this dissatisfaction."

"The cause of the dissatisfaction, my dearest, is the cowardice of the Romans. The more I see of them the more I am convinced that they're not worth liberating."

"It's the Pope", Antonina insisted. "I know what I'm talking about. It was he who persuaded the four thousand men of the Goth garrison to leave, wasn't it? He wanted no bloodshed in the holy city, he said, the hypocrite. You would have either killed them or captured them, isn't that true? There you are. He let them slip through your fingers. It would have been a nice report to Their Clemencies: 'I have conquered Rome by first assault and killed the garrison down to the last man.' And who was it wrote you an insolent letter about the conquest of Neapolis? The holy Silverius. The Pope."

"Well, our Huns did behave rather badly in Neapolis", Belisarius said. "I didn't mind the looting so much, but they killed a great many civilians and there was a most unfortunate incident at that nunnery. . . . "

"Yes, and that's all old Silverius would write about", Antonina interrupted. "And in what terms! Who does he think he is, the Emperor?"

"I wish you wouldn't say such things, dearest", Belisarius said, somewhat ill at ease. "After all he is the Pope and he is also the Bishop of Rome and as such—"

"As such he makes statements that are downright heretical", Antonina interposed. "The Empress warned me of that before we sailed. It's something about Christ having two natures. I don't quite get the gist of it, but the Empress *always* knows what she's talking about. How can one person have two natures, anyway?"

"I'm no good at such arguments, my dearest," Belisarius said, "but, so far, I haven't a shred of evidence that the Pope has anything to do with treason. However, if you wish, I can have him watched. . . . "

"Don't bother", Antonina said, smiling. "I'll have that done. You have enough to do with the Goths. Leave the Pope to me."

When Peter announced to Belisarius that the Gothic army was approaching, the General grinned: "So King Witigis has managed to marry that princess . . . I forget her name. . . . "

"Mataswintha. Yes, he did. She didn't like it much, and I can't say I blame her. It's like a match between a bear and a gazelle. The bear's army will be here by tomorrow, Magister Militum. One hundred and fifty thousand men."

"One of my best men arrived half an hour ago from Ravenna. He left there with the army, as a sutler, and he was with the Gothic vanguard until yesterday evening. Then he stole the commander's horse and raced ahead."

"Hundred solidi for that man", Belisarius said. "How are they coming?"

"Down the Via Flaminia."

"Just as I thought. Thank you, Illustris."

In the afternoon of the next day Belisarius took one thousand Moorish cavalry with him on reconnaissance. "Just in case a few hundred Goths should have swum across the Tiber", he told Antonina. "I can mop them up then. The main army is still on the other side of the river, held up by my tower at the Milvian Bridge. I want to see where they're making their camp and get an idea of their distribution."

An hour later he knew better. Large squadrons of Gothic cavalry came rushing up from the east, and just as he was ready to give the order to face them, more squadrons appeared out of a small wood on the western side. He had less than half a minute to make his decision. The Goths must have managed to get hold of the Milvian Bridge after all. That meant that the two hundred Abasgian archers on the newly built tower had capitulated, overwhelmed probably by the mere sight of the huge Gothic forces. The sensible thing to do was to gallop back to the Flaminian Gate at once. But the sensible thing did not always win battles, and Belisarius was the Emperor's best general for good reasons. He maneuvered his men so skillfully that he not only got them out of the seemingly inevitable clash with the two Gothic forces, but did so too late for the Goths to rein up their heavy horses, with the result that they ran into each other. At once Belisarius swung his men around and attacked the mass of disorganized cavalry. He cut through them like a knife, wheeled round, and attacked again. His thousand men were like one, they were a sword in his hand, stabbing, withdrawing, stabbing again. Their small African horses were twice as fast, and had been trained for the desert warfare of hit and run. The Goths never had a chance. "What's the matter with those black flies," the Gothic commander bellowed, "can't you swat them?" The man on his right was an Abasgian deserter; they had forced him to come with them in order to explain what he knew about the fortifications of the city. "Get the big man on the bay", he shouted. "That's the Magister Militum himself. Get him, and the war is over."

"That would be a pity", the Goth said. "It has only just started. So that is Belisarius, is it?"

But the Abasgian could not answer, there was a Moorish arrow in his throat.

"Hi, Belisarius", the Goth roared. "Come and fight me, if you're a man. I'm Count Visand."

The Magister Militum saw a man seven feet high with the neck and shoulders of a Hercules, riding a horse half the size of an elephant. It was nonsensical, stupid, and perhaps criminal, but he could not resist the temptation. He shook off two of his guards who tried to hold him back, galloped straight at Visand, parried a blow that would have split his head, let his sword glide around the enemy's, cut his right arm open, wounded his horse with a downward stroke, swerved away, and rode a half circle around the Goth, looking for an opening. "Good," Visand shouted, "but not good enough." He drew a short club from his belt and threw it. Belisarius ducked and the club killed a Moor fifteen yards farther back. By now all fighting around the two had ceased. Everybody was watching the duel. At the second attack, Visand had his helmet knocked off; at the third, his horse broke down under him with a gaping wound in its throat. They tried to hoist him on another horse, but Belisarius killed two of the helpers and slit Strong Visand's left cheek. They got him on a horse finally, and he was in a towering rage. He managed to get one tremendous blow home, and it smashed Belisarius' shield and grazed the bay's back, but the counterblow cost Visand his left ear and a moment later Belisarius knocked him off his horse, cut through his shield-arm, nicked his neck, and, giving up all pretentions of scientific swordwork, clubbed him massively over the head. Strong Visand crumpled up in a heap and that sight was too much for the Goths. They fled, howling, taking Visand's body with them. He was not dead, in fact he recovered after a few months, but with no less than fifteen fresh scars on his body and a healthy respect for his opponent. "There wasn't a thing he didn't do to me, except bite me", he told King Witigis who came to visit him.

Having fallen for the first temptation, Belisarius promptly fell for the next. He pursued the fleeing Goths right to their camp, and his Moors who had had almost no losses, cut down the enemy by the hundreds. But when the camp began to spout Goths from a dozen gates, sweet reason returned to the General's mind, and he ordered the retreat to the city. However, this was one of those days when nothing worked out the way it should. When he arrived at the gate it was just beginning to get dark and he was not recognized when he shouted up to the men on the rampart to let him in. He had lost the horsetail from his helmet, he was grimy and spattered with blood, his voice was hoarse from shouting orders; besides, there was a rumor that he had been killed. They would not open the gate for him. And the pursuing Goths drew nearer and nearer.

Belisarius, dead tired, half-lame and beside himself with rage, ordered his men to turn around. "Seems we've got to prove to those asses on the rampart which side we're on", he said, "Charge!" He was riding ahead of his Moors. They met their pursuers before they had time to close their ranks. An attack was the last thing they could expect, in the circumstances, but then it was that kind of a day. The Moors killed and killed; they were drunk with killing. It was getting too dark to see clearly, and the Goths began to believe that the Byzantine army was coming out in force. They wheeled away, fled back to their camp, and Belisarius led his Moors once more back to the Flaminian Gate.

From high up on the rampart came the shrill voice of Antonina: "Will you hurry up and open that gate, you misbegotten apes? That's my husband!" There was a roar of laughter, and the portcullis went up. Such was the beginning of the siege of Rome.

36

JOY OVER THE INITIAL SUCCESS gave way to uneasiness and even fear when the real might of the enemy became evident, and the huge preparations made for the first general assault. The Goths were building fascines to fill the ditches and moats, scaling ladders by the hundreds, battering rams, and gigantic turrets on wheels, each drawn by twenty or thirty oxen and rising as high as the ramparts. The work went on within sight of the defenders, and the hammering sounded throughout the nights for the Goths were working in shifts. "Driving nails into our coffins", someone said, and the word went round very quickly.

The great attack started on the nineteenth day on a broad front from the Praenestine Gate to the Vatican. Belisarius killed two Gothic commanders with as many arrow-shots and then told his men to shoot at the oxen drawing the turrets towards the ramparts. After four consecutive attacks the Goths ran out of oxen. The attack was repulsed. It was repeated and repulsed again, and again, and again.

Once the Goths broke through, near the Tomb of Hadrian. The defenders who ran out of arrows had to hurl the priceless statues by Praxiteles, Polycletus, and Lysippus on the assailants, an Apollo Musagetes, a Diana, a Hercules, Bacchus, Venus, Mars Repulsor, and half a dozen fauns; somebody said that the ancient gods of the pagans had thus proved themselves effective after all. Once the Goths made a breach in the wall near the Vivarium, the great stables where wild animals were kept for the Games, and Belisarius ordered them opened, to let the brutes loose on the enemy, until he could appear in person, with five hundred of his guards, to push the bewildered Goths out again. He had armed contingents formed of Roman citizens from the seventeenth to the thirty-fifth year of age. They were not much good for fighting in the open, but did quite well on the ramparts and as sentinels.

As time went on, and food became scarce, Belisarius managed to evacuate the greater part of the civilian population by way of the Via Appia, the Via Latina, and Via Ostia.

But the Goths also began to suffer from a shortage of food. Their forage parties found less and less in a countryside ravaged by war, and the very size of their forces increased their difficulties. Their losses were tremendous... the first great attack alone had cost them almost thirty thousand men... and they had little or nothing to show for it. They became sullen and bored.

Meanwhile Antonina had all the time she needed to launch her campaign against the Pope. "Get rid of that man", the Empress had told her the day before Belisarius set out for Sicily. "Get rid of him somehow, and we'll see to it that his successor will be the kind of person I want on the throne of Saint Peter. If you can do it, you may ask me for whatever you want, and by heaven, I will get it for you." Antonina went to work very carefully. A letter, allegedly intercepted by her agents, proved to the hilt that Pope Silverius was in secret communication with the King of the Goths and had promised to have the Asinarian Gate opened to him on a certain night. It was a good choice, as the Asinarian Gate was quite close to the Lateran Church. The Pope's style and handwriting were forged to perfection.

Confronted with what seemed to be undeniable evidence, Belisarius still felt very ill at ease about having to sit in judgment over the head of his own Church. "Then *I* will preside", Antonina declared with every evidence of exasperation. "But I demand that you be present." The hero Belisarius agreed meekly, and the Pope was summoned "to appear before the Emperor's representative" who by now was residing in the Pincian Palace on the hill of the same name. Antonina had everything prepared. The Pope's retinue found itself separated from him and made to wait "behind the first and second curtain", just as would have been the case if Silverius had come to visit Justinian himself.

The scene that followed was an absurd travesty of the trial of Christ, with Antonina playing Caiaphas and Belisarius a sullen and silent Pontius Pilate.

Antonina started by asking in the grand manner of a tragedian: "What have we done to you, Holy Father, tell us, that you should wish to deliver us into the hands of the Goths?" When the old man indignantly denied any such intention, she put her "evidence" in front of him. When he denied, even more indignantly having written the letter, she told him that he was lying. Without further ado the Pope was led to an adjacent room, where he was forced to put on the habit of a simple monk. His retinue was told brusquely that the Pope had been deposed and had become a monk. The poor ecclesiastics withdrew as quickly as they could.

During the "trial" Antonina reclined gracefully on a couch, with Belisarius sitting at her feet.

Pope Silverius was sent under escort to Patara in Lycia and later to the island of Ponza, where he was systematically starved to death.

Under Byzantine pressure Deacon Vigilius was elected Pope, a Roman of noble family. Antonina was jubilant and so was Empress Theodora, until she discovered some time later that the new Pope likewise would not yield to her theological theories.

One attack after another failed before the walls of Rome and almost every night the Romans could hear the monotonous chant of the Goths, burying their dead. But the Byzantine losses also mounted, and Belisarius was forced to send a desperate plea to Justinian for reinforcements. At long last they arrived. First, sixteen hundred Huns; then three thousand Isaurians under Paulus and Conon and eighteen hundred Thracian horses under their general, John, known in the entire imperial army as Bloody John. They had the sense to bring huge food transports with them, and Belisarius made a few skillful sorties to give them the chance to enter the city.

Heartily sick of the siege, King Witigis sent three of his commanders to negotiate. He was ready to cede the entire island of Sicily and to support the Emperor in all his wars with a strong contingent of Gothic warriors.

The Illustris Peter of Salonica who was present when the Gothic commanders delivered their king's proposals grinned to himself on hearing those concessions, the same he had once proposed to Queen Amalaswintha. Magister Militum Belisarius grinned openly and widely. "Nice of the King to give me Sicily which I've got and he hasn't; I'll offer him as my present the island of Britain. The climate isn't very good, but it's much bigger than Sicily."

After some bickering about the causes of the war the Goths went away, and the siege continued.

A few weeks later Peter came to see Belisarius. "Do you want to end the siege, Magister Militum?"

Belisarius gave him a keen look. "D'you have an idea how?"

"I've had my best agent out for some time. He's back. There are epidemics in two of the Goth camps. The ague. Swamp fever."

"I know that", Belisarius said. "We've got cases here, too."

"My agent was very proud of his discovery", Peter said, smiling. "So much so that he almost forgot to tell me about Picenum."

"What about Picenum?"

"It seems the Goths have chosen that province as a resort for their families. Good air, you know, and enough to eat. All the commanders have sent their wives and children there. Little Mataswintha is there as well, still very angry about having been forced to marry the peasant-king."

Belisarius listened attentively. "So?" he asked.

Peter shrugged his shoulders. "It just occurred to me, that it might be a good idea to send a capable commander, a sharp one, say Bloody John, with a few thousand horse into Picenum. The Goths here will know about it soon enough. They won't like it much, will they? Here they are, bashing their heads against our walls, and there Bloody John is chasing their wives and daughters. The King won't like it either, especially when he hears about Bloody John and Peter of Salonica getting in touch with his queen. All that *and* swamp fever *and* half his army either dead or incapacitated. I think in the circumstances he might give up the siege, don't you?"

Belisarius jumped to his feet. "Guard", he roared. A huge guard entered. "Get me Blood . . . get me General John at once."

Three weeks later the night sky over the city was red. The Goths were burning their camps. When day came they were seen marching along the Via Flaminia towards the north. After one year and nine days and sixty-nine battles the siege of Rome had come to an end.

The way to Ravenna was not easy. And when, after much fighting, a strongly reinforced Byzantine army surrounded the royal city of the Goths, the specter of another endless siege loomed. But King Witigis' spirit was broken. With his army reduced to a fraction of its former power, his granaries set afire, and the wells of the city poisoned by enemy agents; with a queen beside him as hostile as she was beautiful, he despaired, not of his people, but of his kingship. And in that black hour the simple, decent, luckless man had something he had never had before in his life: an original idea. He offered the Gothic kingship to . . . Belisarius.

It was a Gothic idea. Belisarius was what a Goth respected most: a hero. He had defeated Strong Visand in single combat. He had held Rome with twelve thousand men against a hundred and fifty thousand stout fighters. He was worthy of being King of the Goths. It was as simple as that and Strong Visand, now fully recovered, was the first to agree wholeheartedly.

For Belisarius the offer of the crown, the treasury, and the support of the Goths was a far more formidable blow than any Strong Visand had delivered. To him there was only one possible end to the war: to take Ravenna and lead the King and Queen of the Goths in chains to Byzantium. Everything else was for his gracious Emperor to decide. He was beside himself. This Witigis was an idiot, a criminal, a devil, and a simpleton. The whole thing was preposterous. He called in his commanders who looked bland and noncommittal. He asked them for their opinion about a general attack against the fortress. One after another the Generals Bessas, Demetrius, Paulus, Edrax, Zorlas, and even Bloody John declared it to be hopeless. Belisarius raged. What could he do except attack? He was in the same position as Witigis before the walls of Rome. There was swamp fever here as well.

"There is just one other thing you could do", suggested the Illustris Peter of Salonica. "You could accept the proposal of the King . . . "

"I forbid any mention of such treachery", Belisarius roared.

" . . . enter the city, occupy the strategic points, seize Witigis, and send him and his crown to the Emperor", Peter said.

"That's treachery too", Belisarius said after a moment of utter stupefaction.

"Maybe," Peter said airily, "but I think you'll find it easier to commit against the Goth than against your Imperial Master."

Belisarius looked about helplessly. "What do you think?" he asked.

Bloody John grinned. "I wish I'd thought of it myself."

And thus Ravenna fell. Close to starvation, with their king and queen in enemy hands and Byzantine troops in command of all the strategic points of the city, the Goths were too dispirited to renew the fighting.

Belisarius had the men disarmed, and they suffered it dully, bewildered, thoroughly dejected. Not so the Gothic women. When they saw that most of the enemy soldiers were much smaller than the average Goth and much weaker in numbers, they jeered at their men, they spat into their faces, and beat them with their fists, like the women of the Suevi six centuries before, when Caesar's army of small Romans had beaten King Ariovistus.

The Magister Militum did not feel happy about his conquest,

but it was due to natural clemency at least as much as to an attempt to assuage the pricks of his conscience, that his very first orders were to send every available ship into the port of Ravenna laden with foodstuffs. King Witigis and his queen were heavily guarded, but treated with royal honors and allowed to keep their suite in the palace. Deputations from small Gothic garrisons in a number of towns arrived almost daily. They could not believe that Belisarius was serious about his refusal of the Gothic crown. "What," exclaimed the burly Ildibald, King Witigis' commander of Liguria, "would you rather be a slave than a king!" There were a number of such Gothic garrisons in the north and west, but none of them was strong and none would be difficult to subdue, if any of them showed signs of resistance. This at least was the opinion of Emperor Justinian. A fast ship arrived from Byzantium and with it the great Logothetes Alexander with a personal letter from His Clemency. Belisarius kissed the imperial seal, opened the letter, read, and retired for the rest of the day into his rooms. He spoke to no one, not even to Antonina.

"It's a very nice letter", the Logothetes Alexander told Peter of Salonica. "The Emperor expresses his impatience to reward the great Belisarius for his great services and wishes to consult his wisdom in matters of far greater importance than any he could find now in Italy. There is no doubt in my opinion that he will be given the Eastern Command again. Persia always seems to get restless when Belisarius is too far away."

"Quite", Peter said, "and generals are not necessarily the best civil administrators."

"Oh, I agree entirely, especially when they start to play about with a crown. A strange story, don't you think, most noble Peter? So unlike the straightforward, simple character of the man to conceive such an idea." Alexander caressed his silky little beard and smiled sweetly. "I mean Belisarius, of course, not Witigis."

"I am sure he didn't conceive it", Peter replied dryly. "But he did carry it out. And it worked. Which is what matters."

"I agree again. Nevertheless one can't help feeling that our

Imperial Master cannot be entirely happy about it. But why talk about Belisarius? His time here is over. I have a letter for you as well, most noble Patricius. Here it is . . . and if I am rightly informed, it contains your nomination as Imperial Governor of Italy and Sicily."

Peter kissed the seal. With Alexander present he could not afford a breach of etiquette. He knew that shrewd eyes were watching him as he read the fulsome phrases. "I see that you will be my colleague, most noble Alexander", he said, evenly, "and of equal rank with me."

"Ah, yes," Alexander said amiably, "but that need not worry you in the least. Our activities are parallel, so to speak, they do not overlap. You are the head of the government. I am merely the tax-collector."

Peter frowned. "Taxes", he said. "You will have to be very lenient at least in the first years, I fear. The country is ravaged. A great deal of rebuilding must be done, and of course the peasants are in dire straits. Either the Goths took away their cattle and destroyed their fields, or we did."

"Oh, certainly", Alexander said. "But the war was expensive for the imperial treasury too. And the Emperor wants his revenues." He smiled agreeably. "Don't let it worry you", he said. "I'll get them. I always do."

Three days later Belisarius and Antonina embarked for Byzantium. On their ship were King Witigis, Queen Mataswintha, a number of Gothic commanders, and, the best part of the Gothic treasures and trophies, including the regalia.

The same day Peter of Salonica, Imperial Governor of Italy and Sicily, Patricius, took up quarters at the royal palace. The Logothetes Alexander contented himself with a row of houses, where he began to install his offices.

37

THE MONASTERY on the mount of Casinum had suffered no damage during the war. After the conquest of Neapolis all major fighting had taken place farther north. Once a large forage party of Goths came to Casinum, where they found very little. The commander thought of sending some of his men up to the monastery, but he made some inquiries first and, when he heard that the monks had only one meal a day, he decided they must be near starvation and that it was not worthwhile climbing a mountain to take away the last of their food.

Fugitives came, especially during the siege of Rome, peasants whose farms had been burned, men and women searching for missing relatives and friends. Tertullus came to bid farewell to his son Placidus, who, with several other monks, was to build a small monastery in Sicily. He was deeply impressed to find his boy transformed into a strong and vibrant personality. "It's an amazing thing," he told Benedictus, "despite all the severe discipline here, he gives the impression of being a freer man than I am."

"And so he is, Tertullus, not despite but because of that discipline."

Tertullus sighed. "We Romans have lost the ability for it; yet it's one of the old Roman virtues."

"There was much that was good in the Roman world," Benedictus said, "and we are trying to recreate its substance."

"In that case, these monks of yours may well be the first new Romans. According to your Rule you elect your abbots. That makes you a republic . . . a republic of saints, or rather a number of such republics, since each monastery is an independent unit. Those in Sublacum are flourishing, Placidus told me, and so is the new one in Terracina. When I arrived I saw a building at the foot of the mountain; it wasn't there when I came the last time. . . ."

"It is a convent. The nuns there live in a way similar to ours."

"And you founded it?"

"No. My twin sister, Scholastica."

"How many nuns are living there?"

"I don't know."

"Will you ask? I know of a relative of mine who may wish to join them. Rusticiana, widow of Boethius."

"She should enquire herself or send another lady to do so for her. No man may enter the convent."

"But surely you must meet your own sister from time to time?"

"Yes. We meet once a year on a nearby farm, run by good and devout people."

"To talk of old times, of memories of your childhood?"

"To talk of God."

Tertullus nodded. Here was the answer to a question he had often asked himself. A saint was a lover; he was in love with God. A true lover was happiest when talking to the beloved, and next to that, when he could talk about the beloved. Whatever he did, said, or thought would always encompass the beloved or be encompassed by the beloved. Lesser men were like the moon, reflecting the divine fire as light, but the lover, the saint, was like the sun, lit up by the divine fire, burning and yet not consumed. It was the light of that fire that made the monastery what it was, a radiant place full of happy expectation. Only the best could live here all the time. He could not. I wish I could die here though, he thought.

"You will", Benedictus said and walked away. Only when he had gone did Tertullus realize that the Abbot had read his heart.

The siege of Rome lifted, Tertullus came back to the monastery twice. The second time he fell ill and within two days he died, with his hand in that of the Abbot and the monks chanting the great prayer, triumphant rather than sad, recommending to God, and all the good powers serving him, the Christian soul going forth to find its true home.

Ravenna had been conquered, the power of the Goths broken, and after a while there was word that an imperial governor was ruling Italy and Sicily, now provinces of the Great Roman Empire of the East, one Peter of Salonica. But fugitives still came from time to time, some Goths, some Roman, and a few fell in love with God and stayed on to become monks. There was no doubt that the new governor was a man of great power. No fewer than eleven generals had to carry out his orders to subdue what remained of little Gothic garrisons.

The day came when Brother Maurus was sent, with three companions, to Gaul, a sad day, because everyone loved him and there was little chance that they would see him again, except in heaven. When he knelt before the Abbot to receive his blessing Brother Maurus wept, and Benedictus, too, had tears in his eyes, a thing so rare and awesome that the brothers spoke of it only in whispers.

The Abbot was no longer young, but it was impossible to think of him as an elderly, far less an old man. Brother Sextus was old, and so was Brother Ludgar, the Goth, and Brother Corvinus. They walked slowly, and their eyesight was failing a little; Brother Sextus had lost all his hair and Brother Corvinus most of his teeth. But the Abbot seemed to be untouched by age, except for the silver sprinkling his hair and beard, and that did not make him look old. He was timeless, an entity, near and yet aloof. During his lifetime he had become a legendary figure, and the tales told about his sayings, the power of his prayers, and the miracles he performed were legion.

Complaints came first from the peasants of the Liri valley, then from other regions and from towns as well, about the terrible severity of the new regime. The tax-collectors of the Goths had been lenient under Theodoric, even more lenient under Amalaswintha, and harsh only during the short period of Theodahad's rule. Now they were three times worse. Peasants who could not or would not pay up, were arrested, their farms confiscated, their families sold into slavery. When there was a possibility that the man might have money salted away, he was put to the torture, and many died. In Apulia and Calabria, in Tuscany and Liguria, the peasants and their families often left their farms before the collectors arrived and fled into the woods, taking their cattle, if there were any left, to wait there until the soldiers had gone. But the collectors burned all deserted farms and ran down the fugitives with African hounds. Rioting occurred in a number of towns, the jails were full, and many Italians said openly that they preferred "to pay the Goths two to paying the Emperor five" and gave little or no assistance to the imperial generals who were trying to subdue the small Gothic strongholds still left intact all over the country; in some cases they even went so far as secretly to help the Goths.

Men who were trying to escape from rack and thumbscrew came to the monastery, men wounded, maimed, and ill, as if the war were still going on.

And then, all of a sudden, no news came at all. There was a strange stillness, as if loud and garrulous men had all fallen into silence, and people felt uneasy and worried without really knowing why.

It was during this period that Brother Doorkeeper announced to the Abbot the arrival of the Imperial Governor of Italy and Sicily, Peter of Salonica, Patricius, with a retinue of five.

"Somehow I thought you would recognize me, venerable Father Abbot", Peter said. "I hope I have your title right? You've got a lot of monks here, but I can claim the honor of having been your pupil long before any of them. Mind you, I don't think I would have recognized *you,* although I do have a good memory for faces. One must, in my position. Incidentally, when exactly did you recognize me? At the refectory table when you granted my wish to share a meal with you and your monks? When you showed me around? In the church, during the singing? No, not there, of course . . . "

"When I saw you", Benedictus replied.

"What, right away? Amazing. Do you know that very few people in Italy know that I'm not an Eastern Roman by birth? I'm called Peter of Salonica because of an estate I own there. I have another in Sicily, not very far from where your monks are building a monastery. The son of Tertullus is rather a young man to be an abbot, don't you think? But you know what you're doing, and in any case even the Governor of Italy and Sicily has no jurisdiction over your choice."

"No."

Peter looked about him. "So this is where you live when you're not with your community. A tower room. Magnificent view, too. A kind of eagle's nest, isn't it? A fortress, rather. D'you know what the great Belisarius said when he saw it? He was passing by down there, along the Via Casilina, on his way from Neapolis to Rome, and he asked why the fortress on the mount didn't appear on the Byzantine maps. So somebody told him that it was a new building and not a fortress but a monastery, and he said with great relief: 'Well, I'm glad I don't have to storm it.' "

"So am I," Benedictus said, "after what he did to Neapolis . . . and what he did to the Holy Father."

"As far as the Pope is concerned, it wasn't so much his doing as hers", Peter said. "Antonina, you know, his wife. He's really brilliant, a born leader. He could lead any army to victory. As for Antonina . . . well, they say in Byzantium that Belisarius will make men out of pigs and Antonina, like Circe, pigs out of men. But in the case of the Pope she practically conducted the trial, if one can call it a trial."

"She tried to destroy Pope Silverius", Benedictus said. "By doing so she gave him martyrdom. But she will suffer greatly, and so will her husband."

"It doesn't look like it", Peter said dryly. "The Emperor gave him the supreme command in the East. Justinian can be generous, at times. He was also very gracious to King Witigis and Queen Mataswintha. When they renounced Arianism and became Catholics the Emperor made his royal prisoner a senator and patricius. Success is what matters in this world. I seem to remember that we talked about that when I was a boy. I think I warned you then that I might turn out to be wicked, but successful."

"You told me you wanted to use others and not be used by them", Benedictus said.

"Yes . . . and that good people always lost and that I wanted to win. I only knew two people whom I could call good, at that time. One was Boethius. You were the other. I was only thirteen years old, but I wasn't stupid, was I?"

"Do you still think you were right?"

"Well, I have had a certain amount of success, using my own methods, venerable Father Abbot, you must admit that."

Benedictus said nothing.

"As for the good men," Peter continued after a pause, "we know what happened to Boethius. And when I passed through Casinum and saw your monastery on the mount, I wondered how things had worked out for you." He smiled amiably. "Strange, isn't it, how vividly one remembers the things one felt and said as a child. Such primitive things, too. Everything is either black or white."

"Things are like that", Benedictus said. "They appear gray only to our blunted senses, because the black and white elements are blurred."

"These men of yours seem to be happy enough," Peter said, "and so, I presume, are you. But if I had to live this kind of life, I suppose I'd be raving mad after six weeks."

"Not if you were living it," Benedictus said; "only if you had to share it without living it."

"I know nothing about metaphysics, but I can sense that there is some kind of meaning to what you say. I told you before, I don't doubt your happiness or that of your monks. But then it's easy, perhaps, to be happy when one has no ambition."

"There are no more ambitious people on earth than my sons and I", Benedictus said quietly. "We want to be friends of God, close friends, and we are ready to sacrifice everything, even our own will, for the sake of that aim. Nothing but God himself will do for us. Can ambition fly higher?"

"And in the meantime the world may go to pieces", Peter said.

"If it doesn't," Benedictus replied, "it is because we help to keep it in balance."

"*You* do? By praying and fasting and singing the dear old songs? Venerable Father Abbot! What you have here is a school. But the real school is life itself, with all its risks and fighting, its victories and disappointments."

"And what is it that you have learned in that school?" Benedictus asked evenly.

"A thousand ways to make people do my bidding", Peter said. "To move men like pieces on a chessboard, big men, much more powerful than myself. To make my enemies work their own ruin. To form their thoughts for them in their own minds, without their knowledge. To force them into a corner or give them rope, as best suits my interests. Some of that may not be to your liking, Father Abbot . . . "

"None of it."

"Maybe so. But it has led to results, hasn't it? I have made history, in my own inconspicuous way, and history is not made by singing psalms. After years and years of effort to undermine the Kingdom of the Goths and to make Byzantium move, I won. I made this war, Father Abbot."

"My poor Peter," Benedictus said not unkindly, "stop your boasting. It would not impress the youngest of my novices."

"Father Abbot! You seem to forget to whom you are speaking."

"No, Peter. I am speaking to a boy of twelve who has never grown up."

"I should insist on being addressed by my rank and title", Peter snapped.

"You were announced to me as the Governor of Italy and Sicily," said Benedictus, "but in truth you are a fugitive and in great fear of your life."

There was a pause.

Peter's face, drained of blood, became rigid, lifeless.

Benedictus did not seem to notice. "When I bade you farewell in Rome," he went on, "you thought we might not meet again, and I told you we would, when you needed me. You need me today and that is the real reason why you are here. You did not win, Peter; you lost. Your enemy is looking for you, and he is a very determined man."

"How do you know?" Peter whispered. "Who told you about . . . who do you think this enemy is?"

"Your real enemy is within you," Benedictus said, "and instead of driving him out you have allowed him to dominate you. But the one you are thinking of comes from the north, and he is very near."

"Who told you that?"

"You did."

Peter stared at the Abbot. "It is true then, what they say about you. I couldn't believe it. I'm not sure I believe it now. No knowledge of what happened has reached so far south. You say I told you, but I didn't."

"Not in words, no."

Peter passed a weary hand over his forehead. "Plutarch wrote somewhere that a dying man is like one initiated in the mysteries. He sees what the ordinary man does not see. Perhaps there are men who . . . never mind. You know. It wasn't my fault. I couldn't help it. But then, the Emperor will never trust anyone completely—that's why he gave Alexander equal rank with me, the great logothete, the financial expert. Do you know what they used to call him in Byzantium? *Psalidion.* The Scissors. He got that name for his ingenious idea of clipping the rims of all the pieces of gold in the imperial mint. By that he saved the Emperor a great deal of gold, yet without defacing the image of Justinian on the coins. The man's whole mentality is revealed in that one idea. I warned him. I implored him not to tax the population too heavily. But he could think only of figures and how to please Justinian by sending him the full revenue he demands. If it hadn't been for Alexander, I could still count on the Italian population. As it is, I can't. And thus that cursed new King of the Goths is finding allies where he ought to be finding enemies."

"A new King of the Goths?"

"Ah, then there is something you don't know after all."

"I only know what God allows me to know", Benedictus said. "Who is this king?"

"His name is Totila. A youngish man, they tell me. Not long ago he was nothing but a commander of a thousand and in charge of the little town of Treviso. There were a number of such pockets of resistance when Belisarius was removed." Peter laughed angrily. "I scarcely know how to tell you what happened", he said. "It's like a joke . . . a cruel joke played by destiny."

Benedictus said nothing.

"As the Regent of Italy I ordered my general officers to deal with those pockets", Peter went on grimly. "It should have been easy enough. The Goths were demoralized. Their situation was hopeless. Young Totila, too, regarded it as hopeless. He was quite ready to capitulate to my general, Constantinus. But all of a sudden he changed his mind."

"Why?"

"Because the garrison of Pavia had elected him King. They sent a delegation of twenty warriors to tell him so. A provincial garrison, if you please. Have you ever heard such nonsense? But Totila couldn't resist the offer of a crown. He gave Constantinus the slip, rode to Pavia, and found himself Lord and Master of five thousand men." Peter began to pace up and down the narrow cell. "When I heard about it, I knew I must act at once", he said. "I sent all available troops. Twenty thousand men. Trained soldiers, Benedictus, regulars, the very men who had beaten the Goths with the same odds *against* them! I could have no doubt about the outcome, could I? Could I?"

Benedictus made no comment.

"I'm not a soldier, of course", Peter said bitterly. "I didn't know that eleven commanders are worse than no commander at all . . . especially when each one of them regards himself as another Belisarius and the others as idiots. Totila came down on them like a whirlwind, and my twenty thousand heroes dispersed in all directions. For all I know they may still be running. That was the so-called battle on the hills of Mugellum." He stopped in front of the Abbot. "This Totila is as lucky as King Witigis was unlucky", he said. "That's all there is to him. But it's a great deal." He turned away and stared out of the window. "What could I do?" he asked fretfully. "I traveled south as quickly as possible to rally whatever troops were left there. But Totila, too, turned towards the south. He crossed the river Po, all the Goths came out of their hiding places and joined him, his army grew and grew like an avalanche. Twice he caught up with me, and I escaped only at the last moment . . . "

"He will come here", Benedictus said tranquilly. "He is very near now."

"I wouldn't be surprised", Peter said. "He's looking for me, of course. For me and for Alexander. He won't get *him,* though. As soon as the situation became serious, Alexander embarked on the fastest ship he could get hold of and fled."

He resumed his walk up and down the cell.

" 'Gone to Byzantium to report', is the official version. His real purpose is to save his precious skin while convincing the Emperor that everything that happened was my fault. He'll bribe people right and left to say the same thing and he'll probably be believed."

Peter stopped again. "If you're right, Father Abbot, and King Totila is on his way here, Alexander's little efforts won't do me much harm," he sneered, "for the simple reason that the Goth will have me killed. Do you see now what I meant, when I said it was all an absurd joke of destiny? For years and years I fought for power, real power. And as soon as I had it in my grasp, Alexander's greed, the stupidity of a few officers, and the incredible luck of a Gothic nobody tore it out of my hands. So you're right, Father Abbot. I lost. I'm a failure. Maybe you ought to pray for me."

"I have."

"You have? When?"

"Ever since the day you tried to kill King Theodoric."

"Ever since . . . do you mean to tell me that you've been praying for me all that time?"

"Every day."

"What? Year after year? You're mad. You must be. No one madder." Peter's voice rose shrilly. "Ye gods, how disappointed you must be. And how much more you would be if you only knew everything I did to get those damned Goths good and ready for the big slaughter. Maybe you kept me going with those prayers of yours. If you did, you have taken a lot on your shoulders, most venerable Abbot Benedictus. And a tender conscience like yours, too. How does it feel, tell me, to have prayed and prayed every day for years, for decades, and then find the man you prayed for the worst sinner in the world. Why, I've broken every law in your code."

"Poor Peter", Benedictus said. "Still boasting. Still flattering yourself. And all the while, time is running out. I told you your enemy is very near. I think he is here now." He walked to the window.

Six riders were coming up the hill. They were Goths.

"Stay where you are, Peter", Benedictus said. "Don't move."

From far below a voice called out in guttural Latin. Brother Doorkeeper answered in a few words. Then silence.

"What are you going to do?" Peter asked in a whisper.

Benedictus gave no answer. After a while there was a knock at the door, and Brother Doorkeeper entered. "There are six Gothic riders at the gate, Father Abbot. They say their king wishes to see you."

Benedictus nodded. "Tell them the King may come at his pleasure."

38

OUT OF SIGHT of the monastery, more than a hundred feet below the gate, a group of Goths clustered around a tall young man who was sitting almost naked on a boulder, dangling his feet, and grinning cheerfully. "Now we shall see two things", he declared. "Whether those peasants spoke the truth when they said that the Buffoons' governor was hiding up there; and whether Zalla is right about that monk."

"I'm right, lord King, I know I am," said a burly man whose beard covered more than half of his face, "and I wish you had listened to me. That monk isn't what he seems to be. He may be an *alf* or a *Wane* or even a god, I don't know, but he's not one to play tricks on."

"That's exactly what I'm trying to find out", the young man retorted. "You think he's something superhuman. The Runts seem to believe he's a prophet. In either case he ought to be able to tell that Riggo isn't the King of the Goths, even if he's wearing my clothes and my armor and has a retinue of three genuine nobles. As for your story about that encounter of yours, I think you must have been drunk."

"I wasn't, lord King", Zalla expostulated. "Hadn't had a drop, I swear it. No use getting drunk when one has to collect money, is there? I was furious when that yapping dog of a peasant told me he hadn't any and that he had given all he had into the care of the chief monk on the mount. Never liked Catholic monks *or* priests, being a good Arian . . . "

"An excellent Arian," the King affirmed, smiling, "believing in *alfs* and *Wanes*. . . . "

Zalla scratched his head. "That's as may be," he growled, "but I was very angry and I tied his arms together with a strong cord and led him up there by the scruff of his neck, and there was the old monk. . . . "

"So he is an old man, is he?"

"I don't rightly know, lord King. He's not one a man can look at for long. . . . "

"Ho," the King said, "this is getting better and better. Why can't one?"

Zalla shook his head. "Count Riggo's going to find out", he declared. "*I* couldn't say why not, but that's how it is."

"So then what happened?" the King asked. They had all heard the story several times before, but it was always amusing to hear it again.

"He was sitting at the gate, reading," Zalla said, "and I shouted at him to get up and fetch me the money he had got from the peasant fellow. So he looked up from his reading and looked at the peasant, and the cords fell off him. Just like that."

"You didn't tie him up too well, I suppose", the King said. But he frowned and put a warning finger to his lips, when his men broke into laughter. "Not so loud", he said. "One doesn't have to be a prophet to hear you when you roar like that."

"It doesn't matter", Zalla said. "There they are, coming back." It was his turn to grin now. "They don't look so happy", he added.

"What's the matter with you?" the King asked, as the four men approached. "Did he find out the truth? What's he done to you?"

"Lord King," Riggo said, "let's go and go quickly."

The King jumped off the boulder. "Give me back my sword", he said. "I hate to see it in a trembling hand. By God, if I hadn't seen you fight at my side in battle, I'd think you were a coward."

Riggo handed over sword, armor, helmet, and purple clothing without a word.

Totila shook his head. "Pull yourself together, man", he snapped. "I want to hear what happened. Did you tell that monk that you were the King? No? I *ordered* you to say that!"

"There was no time", Riggo managed to say. Then he began to blubber like a child.

Totila looked at the three nobles. "Wulderic", he said.

"Ruderic . . . Blidin! One of you must have some sense left. *Will* you tell me what happened?" He began to dress while they helped him.

"Nothing much", Count Blidin said sourly. "He was sitting on a bench. Saw us coming. Before Riggo could open his mouth, he called out: 'Take those things off, son; take them all off. They aren't yours.' And Riggo fell to the ground."

"So did you", Riggo blubbered. "All of you."

"I don't remember that", Blidin said sharply. "I don't want to. Anyway, we came back. The man's a magician, if you ask me, lord King."

"I'm not asking you or anybody else", King Totila said. "I'm going to see that man myself. I don't fall to the ground so easily."

"Don't go, lord King", Zalla cried out. "He'll do things to you, change you. He'll . . . "

"Shut up, you fool", Totila put on and adjusted his helmet with its huge swan wings. "No, I don't need a shield, Blidin. And I don't need a retinue either. Wait for me here, all of you."

"There may well be more than a hundred monks in that place", Count Ruderic warned.

The King shrugged and began to ascend the path to the gate. Despite his order they made as if to follow him, but he flung over his shoulder, "I told you to stay where you are", and they halted. He wanted to be alone. He felt he needed to do a bit of thinking.

So the old monk had seen through Riggo after all. But did that really make him a prophet? Somebody could have given him a description of the new King of the Goths. And perhaps that somebody was the Buffoon governor who in turn had it from one of his spies. Why, they hadn't even inquired whether that so-called governor was there! They just walked in, saw an old man, fell on their bellies, and then ran away. Whatever the old man was, he must be taught that he could not play tricks on all the Goths.

A magician, Blidin thought he was. Blidin was a good warrior, but a fool. This monk was not an Arian, so he had wrong ideas about certain points of theology, but he was still a Christian of sorts, and magic was forbidden to Christians. But if he was not a magician, how could he make men like Riggo and Blidin fall to the ground? I should have brought them with me, Totila thought. And all the others as well. Just to show them that one doesn't have to succumb to . . . whatever it is. All of a sudden he realized that he wanted them with him for a very different reason: he felt very much alone. No, he . . . he felt exactly as he had, when he was five, and his father told him to mount a horse three times as high as he was. He had gritted his teeth and done it. And yet . . . it was not like that, really. It was a feeling that he was in a dream: he was to be presented to King Theodoric, but he had no clothes on and the sword he carried was corroded with rust.

The monastery gate was before him, and the gate was wide open.

Totila gritted his teeth and walked through it.

A monk was sitting on a stone bench at some distance. There was no one else in sight. Totila found himself thinking of the killing of the relatives of Count Uraja, eight of them; he had ordered their deaths to avenge his uncle Ildibald, but he might have spared the lives of some of them, if he had had time to investigate their guilt. The two hundred Isaurians, seeking asylum in that church in Ariminum, Froda had it burned with all the men inside— He could have stopped Froda, but the Isaurians had fought like devils the day before, and he had felt tired and let it go. The old man in Pavia, who wouldn't get out of the way of his horse but had gone on pleading and sobbing about some wrong done to his son or daughter or somebody, and he had pushed him away with his shield, and the spike on the shield pierced the old man's gullet. . . . Why did he have to think of all those things? And why did this infernal armor seem so heavy? The old monk was sitting on a throne as high as a mountain, how could one ever get up there? He could see everything, the old one, one should never have gone near him, but now it was too late. No man could carry hundreds of bodies. . . .

The old monk said, "Get up", but that was impossible. The old man said it again and a third time, but it could not be done, he could not rise under the burden of all those bodies.

Then the old monk himself rose from his throne and came down, and as he did he grew in size, grew beyond human frame, but his hands were gentle and cool, and strong enough to get a man on his feet again despite the terrible burden. "You have done much evil," he said, "much wickedness. Now you should give up your iniquity. You will enter Rome. You will cross the sea. You will reign nine years, and die in the tenth."

The blood sang in Totila's head. He heard himself say, loudly and with a great urgency: "Pray for me, holy man." Then he turned and walked into the nine years of life that lay before him and the death that awaited him in the tenth. Outside the gate the first thought he had was that he might have known a prophet could see the past as clearly as the future. When he reached his men, they stared at him curiously, but none of them said a word. Only when he began to walk downhill, Count Wulderic asked: "He isn't up there, is he? The Buffoon governor?"

King Totila stopped in his tracks. "I forgot about him", he said, with mild astonishment.

Count Blidin took a deep breath. "Shall we go back and ask?"

"No", Totila said. "I know enough. Perhaps I know too much."

When Benedictus returned to the Tower room he found Peter standing by the wall farthest from the window; Benedictus nodded to him and sat down.

"Well," Peter asked, "what have you decided, you and the King of the Goths? Am I to be killed or must I become a monk, or what?" His voice was calm enough, but his eyes were those of a hunted animal.

"You were not mentioned at all", Benedictus said.

Peter laughed. "I have become a nonentity, it seems. He didn't come for me. What did he want, then?"

"Like you, he was concerned only with himself."

"Oh, was he? He came with a large retinue, I take it?"

"He came alone."

Peter stiffened. "Alone? The King of the Goths? Why, I could have . . . I have five officers with me . . . we could have taken him prisoner. He would have been a hostage. What an opportunity! Where is he now?"

Benedictus shook his head. "There is no war within these precincts," he said, "except the war against evil. All action here is for God alone. Everything else to us is no more than a dance of shadows. The King has gone on his way, as you will also, in due course."

Peter sighed. "I suppose it is too much to ask of a monk that he should think like a soldier."

"We *are* soldiers," Benedictus replied calmly, "fighting for the King of kings, ready to lay down our lives for him."

"In other words," Peter said bitterly, "you have no feeling left for the freedom of Italy."

"Did you fight for the freedom of Italy?" Benedictus asked sharply.

"If I didn't," Peter said, "it was not because I was thinking only of myself. But never mind, Father Abbot. You wouldn't understand. Perhaps it's your very wisdom that stands in the way."

"You did not fight for the woman either," Benedictus said, "although you told yourself so, many times, no doubt."

"I loved her", Peter shouted. "That's what you'll never understand, monk. I loved her and I still love her."

"You have never loved anyone but yourself, Peter. If you had loved her, you would have done everything for her happiness. But she was not free. She had a husband whom she loved. Are you sure, in your heart of hearts, that you never wished for his death?"

"I didn't bring his death about", Peter said quickly. "I swear I didn't."

"You thought of his death. You wished for his death. You killed him often in your soul. Perhaps you did not even stop others from certain actions that endangered his life. And when he had lost his life, you offered yourself to his wife as the avenger."

"How dare you say such things to me", Peter stammered. "Why, I have never—"

"You never gave yourself a true account of your motives, I know", Benedictus interrupted. "That's why I told you that you have never grown up. You did not fight for Italy. You did not fight for the woman. You fought, tricked, cheated, and killed for yourself, for your own greatness, and you wanted that greatness to be mirrored in the woman's eyes. Everything you did was no more than a repetition of your attempt to kill King Theodoric. That failed. And all the rest has failed now."

"This is murder", Peter said in a strangled voice. "It would have been better if you had delivered me in chains to the Goth."

"You are not ready to die yet", Benedictus said. "First you must overcome the illusion of power. Our only true freedom is to do the will of God, and the beginning of it is repentance and prayer. Pray, Peter."

"I can't. I haven't prayed in thirty years. To start now, just because I don't know which way to turn, would be nothing but cowardice."

"It is that thought that is the real cowardice", Benedictus said.

"Leave my thoughts alone", Peter screamed. "I can't stand this." He braced himself. "I must sort them out by myself", he said.

"Indeed you must. *Do.*"

There was a pause. "If all you believe in is true, how can there be help for me?" Peter murmured. "How absurd it all is! I don't even know whether I can leave here without walking straight into enemy hands. I don't know where to go."

"You will be able to leave tomorrow morning", Benedictus said. "You should go towards God. And there is help . . . for the asking."

"You know so much more about this than I do, Father Abbot. How does a man go towards God?"

"By going away from the self", Benedictus replied. "Watch out for an opportunity to do something for someone else, to your own disadvantage, for God's sake."

"I will have such an opportunity?"

"Yes."

"Shall I recognize it? I . . . I might miss it."

"You will recognize it", Benedictus said tranquilly. "There will be a great silence and a great emptiness. Then it will come."

39

WHEN CERVAX ANNOUNCED to his mistress that a nun wished to see her, Rusticiana looked up, surprised. "Did she say where she came from?"

"Yes, Domina, from Casinum."

"From . . . Show her in."

The nun's little face under the dark veil was free of wrinkles. She could have passed for a young woman if it had not been for her eyebrows, straight, bushy, and snowy white. The large clear eyes, the thin, sensitive mouth were at rest. Yet her whole being smiled.

"I am Mother Scholastica", she said. "I believe you have made some inquiries about our convent."

"Sit down, venerable Mother." Rusticiana pointed to the couch next to her. "You are the Abbess, aren't you? You must be."

"I am, noble Lady."

"I take it you have urgent business in Rome?"

"I came to see you."

"You mean to say you traveled all the way here, in times like these, just to see me?"

"Of course. I would have done so for a slave woman who wanted to join us; why should I not do it for the widow of the man who wrote the *Consolation of Philosophy?*"

Rusticiana's eyes filled with tears. "You have read my husband's last book?"

"I have had it read at our convent during meals."

He is still trying to look after me, Rusticiana thought. She closed her eyes. When she had regained control of herself she said in a low voice: "I am not worthy to join you."

"A Roman commander said something like that to our Lord", the nun said cheerfully.

"You don't know very much about me, do you, venerable Mother?"

"The noble Tertullus mentioned you to my brother, Benedictus."

"I asked him to inquire . . . there are times when I feel . . . "

"You have suffered greatly and you are longing for peace, but you know that that is not enough; and you are not sure of yourself."

"You read my heart, venerable Mother. How can I join holy women when I am laden with guilt?"

"Our Lord himself has answered that question. He has taken your guilt on his shoulders on the Cross."

Rusticiana took a deep breath. "If I could do as I want, I would come with you at once . . . if you would have me."

"But you cannot?"

"A nun should love God with all her heart, shouldn't she?"

"Everyone should."

"A nun should leave all other ties behind her."

"Yes."

"I cannot do that, venerable Mother. I have two sons fighting in this horrible war which I helped to bring about. They belong to the garrison of Rome. I can't leave them. I must wait until there is peace."

"Neither you nor I may live to see peace on earth", the nun said, looking past her into the void. She rose. "I must go back."

"What? At once? Won't you stay with me a few days . . . one day? You must be tired. I haven't offered you anything. . . . "

The nun shook her head, smiling. "I must go back to my daughters", she said. "As for you: God wants you, I believe. So you will come to us in his own good time. Until then . . . farewell and God bless you."

She was gone before Rusticiana could speak. She might have been an apparition in a dream. But strangely, the impression left with Rusticiana was very different; it seemed to her that everyday life was a dream and that the nun's world, still hidden as if by a veil, was the true reality.

40

KING TOTILA, ignoring Rome, attacked and conquered Beneventum, sent flying squadrons of cavalry to Lucania, Apulia, and Calabria, and forced Neapolis to capitulate. In striking contrast to the behavior of Belisarius' troops, the Goths not only avoided all looting, burning, and killing, but actually helped the famished citizens wherever they could, feeding them and helping them to rebuild destroyed houses. The young king's clemency astonished both friend and foe. It seemed almost inexplicable even to those who knew him best. Many believed he wanted to win the hearts of the Italian population, which he certainly did. There was only one thing he seemed to hate: fortifications. He had the walls of Neapolis destroyed and those of every other town he conquered. He told his Goths he did so to prevent the enemy from reoccupying them and using them as fortresses; he told the citizens he wanted to spare them forever the sufferings of a siege. But the truth was that he really hated walls. He had seen the finest army of his people bleed to death before the terrible walls of Rome, picked off by archers and smashed by engines of war, thrown from huge siege ladders, burned by boiling oil and pitch. He had sworn to himself that this must never happen again, not as long as he was King. Yet when he had conquered the South he could no longer afford to leave Rome in Byzantine hands. And thus the second siege of Rome began. But Totila did not attack the walls. He encircled the city and . . . waited. He did not make a single attack. Some said he had sworn that no Gothic victim should be sacrificed to those bloodthirsty walls. He had an ally he could rely on, a horrible, hollow-eyed, spectral ally: Famine.

Pope Vigilius was not in Rome. Because he had disappointed Empress Theodora, like his predecessor Silverius, she had persuaded Justinian to "invite" him to Byzantium. He was seized at the altar of the Church of Saint Cecilia and forced to board a Byzantine warship. But it was late in the year, storms were raging over the Mediterranean, and the ship had to remain in a Sicilian port until spring. The Pope used the opportunity to buy up all the wheat he could pay for and to send it to Rome. Bishop Valentinus of Silva Candida was in charge of the transport. The Goths intercepted it, despite a desperate sortie made by a part of the Roman garrison, and Totila, relapsing into his former cruelty, gave the order to cut off the bishop's hands.

In the sortie the two Roman tribunes, Manlius and Anicius, the sons of Boethius, lost their lives.

The famine in the city became intolerable. Deacon Pelagius, the Pope's representative during his absence, spent his entire fortune in an effort to alleviate it. Despite the terrible fate of

Bishop Valentinus, Pelagius dared go to Totila's camp and try to negotiate a truce. The King's conditions were so harsh that he had to return, weeping, to the unfortunate city.

Deputations of citizens went to see the Byzantine military commander, Bessas. Their speaker was Senator Albinus: "The people of Rome implore you", he said, "to treat them not as friends of equal descent, nor as citizens under the same laws, but as vanquished enemies and slaves of war. Give bread to your prisoners, then! We don't ask you to feed us, only to give us just enough to be able to serve you as befits slaves. If that is asking too much, permit us to leave the city so that we can spare you the trouble of burying us. And if you cannot grant us even that, well then, have pity on us, and kill us all."

Bessas' reply was short: "I have no food for you. I cannot let you go; it's too dangerous. I cannot kill you, it would be impious. Belisarius will come to relieve the city. That is all."

Yet Bessas and his men ate well and regularly. He confiscated all the foodstuff in Rome and resold it to the population, at a price. A small measure of wheat sold for seven pieces of gold; the carcass of an ox for fifty. The Romans pawned their best and soon their very last belongings for a meal. The poor ate nettles and grass. Suicides abounded.

It was true that Belisarius was returning, but the Emperor's avarice had let him go without an army. He was allowed to take with him only his guards, men who were in his private pay. He landed in Ravenna, where he found a few thousand men, garrison troops, demoralized and not too willing to fight. Even so, he tried to relieve Rome. But his plans failed by a concatenation of unfortunate circumstances, he was forced to withdraw again; that and an attack of swamp fever led to a complete collapse. He was ill for weeks, delirious, fighting Totila, Witigis, and the Persians on his camp bed.

Peter was in Rome. When he left the monastery on the Mount of Casinum he found that all the Gothic troops had gone south. The way to Rome was open, except for occasional small enemy detachments. Traveling by night he evaded them without much difficulty, entered the city and went at once to see the military commander. Bessas was the kind of general to whom a civilian was no more than a nuisance; besides, he was shrewd enough to know that the Governor of Italy and Sicily was not likely to retain his position for long. Justinian had little use for failures. Thus Peter found himself treated with barely concealed contempt. This should have been all the more difficult to bear since Bessas was one of the eleven commanders who had lost the first and decisive battle against Totila. But strangely enough, the Patricius Peter of Salonica did not seem to mind the soldier's boorish attitude. He began to protest only as the siege continued and it became obvious that Bessas was deliberately withholding all foodstuff from the population to drive up prices. Bessas' answer was as blunt as it could be: "Most noble Patricius and Governor, you misjudge your position. In peace time you can give orders as you please. Now there is war, Rome is under siege and I am the man responsible for its safety. I will have no interference from anybody. If that doesn't suit you, you are quite free to complain to His Clemency." Bessas sneered openly. His men were watching every gate. A letter to the Emperor would never get through.

Peter left without a word. For a while he tried to get food transports into the city by every way and means he could think of. Twice he succeeded, but the supplies were promptly confiscated by the military authorities and sold piecemeal to the highest bidders.

He never went near the Anician Palace. The idea of facing Rusticiana now was more than he could bear. He had promised to come back to her as the ruler of Italy. Now he was just that, yet with less power than a subaltern officer. He had promised her that he would rebuild the ravaged country; instead, he had to vegetate in the closed tomb that was Rome, helpless and despised by Bessas and his bullies. If only Benedictus had let Totila seize him! All would be over now, the bitterness, the shame, the hatred for himself.

When he heard about the death of Anicius and Manlius he felt like running to their mother to share at least her mourning;

but his limbs were leaden; he knew he could do nothing to help her. This was his war. He had killed those boys. She could get no comfort from the compassion of the murderer of her sons.

Albinus committed suicide, a few weeks after his speech, both eloquent and pathetic, as leader of the deputation of the starving people.

The next day Peter heard from one of his sources that several slaves of the Anician household had died of starvation and that Rusticiana herself was ill. Three hours later he went to see Bessas.

"I must talk to you alone", he said, and there was something about the way he said it that made the burly commander cock his eyebrows and dismiss his aides with a curt gesture.

"Listen well, Commander Bessas", Peter said. "For many lives will depend upon the decision you are going to take within this hour . . . including your own."

Bessas gave a short laugh. "Lives are nothing in wartime", he said. "As for my own, I know how to guard it."

"I hope so", Peter said coldly. "So far you have consistently refused to let the civilian population leave the city."

"Certainly."

"Your official reason was that it would be too dangerous. By that, I take it you mean that it would be too dangerous for *them.* Is that right?"

"Of course. I can't take the responsibility for such an exodus. They would all be butchered by the Goths."

"Things have come to such a pitch", Peter said, "that few of them would mind. My unfortunate old friend Senator Albinus told you that before, but you wouldn't listen to him. So he killed himself. Now it so happens that I am still the Imperial Governor and therefore concerned with the well-being of the civilian population, and in this capacity I must now *demand* that you let all civilians go. No, don't interrupt! You might say things you'd bitterly regret later. I know very well why you have kept the people here. You wanted to go on trading with them. Don't interrupt, man! I've collected all the evidence I need about your activities. Here, have a look at this list. It is probably more accurate than your own, because I feel sure that at least a considerable number of your middlemen are cheating you. Men like Afronius, Mimmas, Euphridion, and Gogas for instance. These are the quantities of meat and bread they sold; here are the prices they obtained. And here is the list of people who died from starvation within the last two months. Now what do you think would happen to you, Commander, if these lists should get into the hands of certain people in Byzantium who are not too kindly disposed towards you? The Patricius Narses, for instance, or the Imperial Protonotary Tribonianus?"

"Lies", Bessas said. "Concoctions. No one would listen to such nonsense. As for you . . . "

"Just one moment," Peter interposed, "before you give the order you're thinking of. I have other lists, including a great number of sworn statements from well-known citizens, all duly witnessed and in order. You don't seriously think that I would come into this lair of yours without protecting myself? A number of agents of mine—and I won't tell you the *exact* number, my Bessas—have copies of all these lists and each of them holds also several of the sworn statements I mentioned. If anything should happen to me, they will get their documents to Byzantium, and, my Bessas, *some* of them will get through, despite you and despite King Totila. I haven't been governor for very long, but I have been the head of Byzantine Intelligence in Italy for many years past and I know what I am talking about. If you now still wish to do something . . . shall we say, rash? . . . do it. The Emperor may well recall me, after what has happened in Italy. But he won't like it much, I'm afraid, if the military commander of one of his cities presumes to take the law into his own hands in a matter over which the Emperor alone has jurisdiction. Have I made myself quite clear, my Bessas?"

The commander glared at him. "What do you want of me?" he snapped.

"I told you. Revoke your refusal to let the civilian population go. Send trumpeters through the streets announcing that they may go if they wish to go. Announce the gates through which they may pass. Come on, man. You can afford it. You've sucked them dry."

"The Goths will massacre them. I can't take the responsibility for their lives."

"You don't have to. The responsibility is mine. Here, take this document as well."

"Order of the Imperial Governor, the Patricius Peter of Salonica to the Commander Bessas", Bessas read. After a few moments he looked up. "What about those other documents and lists?" he asked.

"They will be destroyed", Peter said. "I don't care much about your life, Bessas . . . either way."

Bessas nodded. "I'll do it. The trumpeters will go out in two hours. The people may leave by the Salarian, Praenestinian, and Asinarian Gates."

Half an hour later Peter arrived at the Anician Palace. The shadow of Cervax opened the door for him. There was little left of the man but skin and bones. He murmured a welcome. His smile was like the grin of a death's-head.

"How is the Domina, Cervax?"

"She is alive", Cervax murmured. "Such a wonderful lady, Most Illustris; always shares food with us. Equal parts, too. But there are only five of us left. No, four. Little Vibia died this morning."

"I must see the Domina at once, Cervax."

"Certainly, Most Illustris." The majordomo shambled off with tired little steps.

How often he had thought of this moment, with joy and triumph and fear and shame. Now there was nothing of all that, not even shame, only a strange urgency, it was something that had to be done before it was too late. She might refuse to see him, of course. She might . . . but there was Cervax again, beckoning.

The shadow of Rusticiana was still beautiful, in a strange, disembodied way. Her eyes seemed preternaturally large in the small face. "Ah, Peter. I thought you'd come one day. Poor boy, you look as if you hadn't eaten for a long time. There is a little bread here, Marcia bought it for one of my pearls. I still have seven of them left."

"My lady . . . " Peter said and then found his voice giving out. He touched his throat with a trembling hand.

"You'd better sit down", Rusticiana said, "none of us is very strong these days. You know about my sons, don't you? I thought you did. We sacrificed them, Peter; they're part of the hecatomb. Do you remember when I told you they probably would be? That's what happened to us for believing in vengeance."

Peter took a deep breath. "Listen to me, Domina", he said. "I needn't tell you how much I've wanted to come here, but I couldn't. I am a failure, and worse. I . . . "

"Oh, Peter," she said wearily, "what does *that* matter?"

"But now I had to", he went on. "I told General Bessas a pack of lies and bluffed him into letting the civilian population go. The permission to leave the city will be proclaimed in the streets. Have you any horses left? Pack your things, only the absolute necessities and leave at once, so that you can avoid the mobs of people that will congest the roads in two hours' time."

"Leave?" Rusticiana asked. "You asked me to do that last time. I won't leave. I'll let the slaves go, though, if they want to. Little Vibia died this morning. Glaucus and Elpis will probably leave and Cervax might, if I tell him to. Marcia won't. There's no one else, you know."

"My lady, my dear love, you must leave. I implore you to. There is no hope left for Rome. The Goths could have taken the city long ago, if they had attacked in force, but Totila knows that the city must fall soon, so why should he be in a hurry? Bessas is a stupid, obstinate brute who still believes that Belisarius will come to his help in time or that the Emperor will send reinforcements. He *wants* to believe that, because he cannot bear the idea that he might lose his loot. I *know* there will be no help for Rome."

"There is only one place where I would like to go," Rusticiana said wistfully, "but it's much too far away. I'd never get there."

"I'll get you there," Peter said, "wherever it is. I'll do everything. Where is it?"

"It's near a place called Casinum. There's a monastery high up on the mount, and the Abbot is Benedictus. Perhaps you remember him; he was your tutor when you were a boy, and it was he who . . . "

"I know Benedictus", Peter interposed. "I . . . spent some time at his monastery. You would be quite safe there, but he can't take you in, not even for a single day."

"Of course he can't. But near the foot of the hill his sister has built a convent. Our old friend Tertullus made some inquiries for me, and some time ago, long before the siege, the Abbess came to see me. She was a wonderful woman; and she said she would be willing to take me in. I would have liked to go with her at once, but my sons were still alive then, and I felt I could not. Now it is the only place on earth I can think of."

"A nun", he said in a whisper. "You . . . a nun. And you didn't think of me at all. You have never loved me, have you, Domina?"

"Dear Peter," she said softly, as if she were talking to a child, "I never loved you; and you never loved me either, though you thought you did. I have known that for a long time."

"Benedictus", Peter said. Then he bit his lip.

"What did you say?"

"Nothing. You are going to be a nun."

The tinny sound of a trumpet came from afar.

"Bessas is quick", Peter said. "They're already proclaiming the permission for the people to leave. When will you be ready, Domina?"

"I am ready now." She rose from her couch. "I'll tell Marcia", she said. But after two steps she faltered, and swayed. "It's nothing", she said, as Peter ran up to her. "I have been ill, you know, but I'm getting better every day. As a nun should", she added with the ghost of a smile.

"You can't travel", Peter decided. "Certainly not with the crowds that will be leaving today and tomorrow. We shall wait a few days. And you must eat. I'll get you food from Bessas' stores. He must have some left or he would have had to capitulate."

"Give me two days," she said, "and I'll be strong enough."

But it took a week for her to recover. Peter managed to buy a light carriage and an old horse from the military stores, for a price that at other times would have bought a country estate; he even provided a guard . . . three of his most reliable men whom he made swear that they would protect the lady in their care with their lives. "I can't come with you", he said. "Bessas would never let me go. I'm supposed to be his superior; in reality I'm practically his prisoner. But I'll come with you to the Asinarian Gate to make sure that you get out without trouble. As for the Goths . . . so far they seem to have let civilian fugitives through. I shall come and fetch you tomorrow morning at dawn. The farther you get on the first day the better."

41

WHEN RUSTICIANA CAME OUT of the house to enter the carriage, Peter heaved a sigh of relief. Old Marcia was holding her arm, but she was walking quite steadily. "Well, Marcia," he said, "are you coming with the Domina, as you did last time, when I picked you up a little farther down the road?"

"Certainly, Master Peter."

"It was difficult enough to make Cervax and the others leave on their own", Rusticiana said with a sad smile. "But Marcia is a freedwoman, and I have no jurisdiction over her. She wants to enter the convent too."

"Somebody must look after the Domina", Marcia declared.

"I don't seem able to convince her that in a convent we are all equals", Rusticiana explained. "She'll have to learn it, though. If the Abbess will take her, that is. I can only hope she will."

"The life of a nun can't be so very different from the one I've been living these last years", Marcia growled as she helped her mistress into the carriage.

"This is Barbatio", Peter said, and the driver raised his hand in a respectful greeting. "There was a time when he was my most trusted agent. Number Six, he was called then. My other two men are waiting for us at the Asinarian Gate. They live near there, and there was no point in their coming here first, across half the city. They have a long march ahead of them as it is. I couldn't get horses for them . . . or for me. Bessas is corrupt enough, but he won't sell a horse still capable of war service. He knows too well that he will soon need them. The poor brute dragging the carriage is no longer strong enough. My men will keep pace with it easily. Let us go, Barbatio." Slowly the carriage began to move, Peter walking alongside. "Just one thing, Domina," he said, "don't be frightened by what you'll see."

"What do you mean?"

"Rome, Domina. Dead Rome. I saw some of it when I came to fetch you. It's . . . it's bad."

"Rome has been dead a long time", Rusticiana replied. But she pressed her lips together when she saw the great Via Portuensis, cold and deserted in the pitiless clarity of the early morning. Not a single human being. No noise coming from the silent houses.

"That's nothing", Peter murmured. "Brace yourself, Domina."

The Sublician Bridge without carts, without milling multitudes; the yellow Tiber, passing under it, whispering and jeering. The way to the Forum and the Palatine Hill, the great temples, thoughts turned to stone. The Circus Maximus on the right, no chariots, no riders, no spectators. The dead are no longer curious.

The air was full of ghosts, spectral rhetors haranguing spectral listeners, the shadows of victorious legions parading before invisible crowds shouting inaudibly; a thin wind singing a song of mockery and derision; and the clap-clap of four tired hooves.

As they were passing across the Forum the wind ceased and with it all life.

"Oh my God," Rusticiana whispered, "it's like being dead. There is nothing left but stillness and emptiness."

Peter looked at her strangely. His lips were white. Stillness and emptiness, a great stillness and emptiness, someone had said that to him once, the monk. *And then it would come.* He shivered. This is a nightmare, he thought, I shall wake up and be somewhere else, in Ravenna, in Sicily, in Byzantium, anywhere that is not here.

But she was riding in a carriage at his side, she was going to be a nun, and the hooves of the old horse were beating time to a mute song.

There was no place in the world for love, ambition, and success. They were dead, these three, as dead as everything else, as dead as the past glory and the past beauty of thirteen centuries of Rome. They were skeletons, as Rome was a skeleton.

The sudden sound cut through the huge stillness like the shriek of a demon. The horse jerked forward. Rusticiana gave a scream.

"No," Peter stammered, "no. It can't be."

But there it was again, louder still, the sound of a horn, of a Gothic war horn and the distant clatter of many hooves, nearer the sounds came and nearer, a troop of riders thundering across the Forum, winged helmets, horned helmets, Goths.

They've broken through from the south, Peter thought in some niche of his mind; they've taken Bessas by surprise or treason; they're in, and it's all over. . . .

Barbatio gave a short, high-pitched yell and toppled over, with a long arrow in his chest. The horse reared and fell.

A bolt of lightning came down on Peter's head, the world was aflame and turned black, and he fell. But he could hear voices shouting above him in guttural Gothic, something about women, only women, no need to kill women—thank God for that, they wouldn't kill her, thank God. And they thought he was dead. There was a chance that he might escape, too, just a chance. . . .

But a new voice shouted in Latin: "Oh, it's you, lady, is it?" and Peter, peering from under his eyelids saw a tall, red-haired, hook-nosed Gothic officer on a black horse, his face contorted with rage. "I told you we'd come back, lady", the man snapped, and he dragged Rusticiana out of the carriage with such brutality that she stumbled and almost fell. "You are the woman who destroyed the statue of the great Theodoric. I saw you!" He drew a dagger from his belt.

"Stop, you dog", Peter roared. He was up on his feet. The earth was unsteady, he could hardly see for the blackness around him, but he must save Rusticiana and he staggered towards the Goth.

"You first, then," the Goth said, and his dagger came up and down in a glittering arc. Peter tried to catch the man's arm, the stab was deflected and cut deep into his shoulder. Peter reeled back, but he did not fall. With his right arm hanging lifelessly he threw himself before Rusticiana. "You're right, Goth," he said hoarsely. "You can't . . . kill her . . . before I am dead."

The second stab came at once, and his knees buckled under him.

A great voice sang out: "Room for the King!" and the Goths recoiled. A tall man, fair and in shining armor, swan wings on his helmet looked down from a huge, white horse. "Blidin . . . who is this?"

"I'm nothing," Peter murmured, "but the lady . . . is . . . Rusticiana . . . widow of Boethius. . . . " He heard the red-haired Goth say sullenly: "When we left Rome I saw that woman destroy the statue of the great Theodoric", and there was a pause, blood filled Peter's mouth, and he struggled for breath. Then the King's voice came: "She had a rightful grudge, Blidin. Let her go free."

Peter felt himself drowning in a cool stream that was carrying him—where?

A woman's voice, Marcia's: "My lady has fainted. We were going to a convent near Casinum."

Casinum. That was where Benedictus was, the monk, the great monk. Going away from the self. Going to Casinum. You there, on the mount, are you satisfied?

The voice of the King came from very far away: "It is a good place. Blidin! A new carriage and horses and twenty men for an escort to get the lady there safely."

Peter did not hear the clatter of hooves as Totila rode off on his way to his own final destiny. He was floating away faster and faster, and from high up, on the mount, Benedictus smiled at him.

42

THE WAR IN ITALY rolled back and forth. Belisarius, restored to health, recaptured the empty shell of Rome while King Totila was away in Apulia, and lost it again some time later. Twelve years of war, and still no end in sight. But only one end was possible. For the Goths were no longer as strong as they had been under King Theodoric; and Emperor Justinian hated their very name and had sworn an oath to destroy them utterly.

In the monastery on the Mount of Casinum Abbot Benedictus and his sons went on with their life of total service to God, war or no war. They built and studied, they taught and nursed, and above all they prayed and seven times a day they sang the praise of God in the words of the inspired royal poet of a thousand years ago. Roman, Gothic, and Byzantine fugitives found asylum in the sacred place where the ills of body and soul were cured.

Three days after one of his rare meetings with his saintly sister, Benedictus saw from his cell a vision of her soul flying to heaven. Soon afterwards the brothers at work heard the voice of their Abbot coming from the oratory, where he was singing psalms of praise all by himself. When he came out, he told them serenely:

"My sister has gone to heaven, and I have given thanks to God for her great glory." And he ordered them to bring her mortal remains to the monastery and bury them in the tomb he had prepared for himself, in the oratory of Saint John, built over the very place where he had destroyed the altar of Apollo.

"She was his twin sister", Brother Secundus muttered, as he and Brother Martinus were going down the mountain with four others.

"I know she was." Suddenly Brother Martinus stopped in his tracks. "You don't mean . . . you can't mean . . . "

"I don't know", Brother Secundus said uneasily. "But did you see his face just now, when he told us about her? Joyful and eager, as if he too were expecting . . . oh well, come along."

"I can't even think of it", Brother Martinus said, trailing after him. "Why, he's . . . he's . . . who else but he . . . "

"Yes, yes. Don't talk about it. Pray against it . . . if you dare."

Three more months passed. Then the Abbot suddenly gave orders to have the tomb opened again. He stood before it for a while, praying at Scholastica's coffin and returned with weary steps to his cell. An hour later Brother Secundus came to see him and found him in a state of fever.

For five days the brothers besieged heaven, begging for their Father's life. But the fever rose, and Benedictus grew weaker and weaker.

On the sixth day he desired to be carried into the oratory of Saint John, where he received Holy Communion.

"His eyes are much clearer", Brother Sextus murmured excitedly. "Perhaps the Lord himself has put new life into him, life of his own Life. . . . "

Brother Secundus gave no answer, but he, too, saw that there was a change. A moment later the Abbot whispered "Help me up, my sons", and they lifted him up and he stood, with their support. Once more he raised his hands to heaven, in the gesture they all knew so well, and he broke into song. The great words came only haltingly, and his voice was barely audible, but he sang.

None of his sons dared to join in, for this was holiness addressing the Most Holy God at the very gate of heaven, and at such a moment no other voice was worthy to be heard.

The singing sank to a murmur, and as it ceased, Benedictus died, standing upright and praising the Lord with his very last breath.

Epilogue

A Byzantine army under Narses defeated the Goths at Taginae, and in that battle King Totila fell, in the tenth year of his reign. The remnants of the Gothic army, under their new king, Teja, fled south and fought a last, grim battle with the Byzantines on the slopes of Mount Vesuvius. In the end Narses, on the advice of Bloody John, allowed the last Ostrogoths to leave Italy, free and unhindered and with their arms. There were not many left. And no one knows what became of them.

Little more than twenty years after Benedictus' death the Langobards invaded Italy and destroyed the monastery on the Mount of Casinum. As soon as they had gone, Benedictus' sons built it up again.

The Saracens came and destroyed it. The Benedictines rebuilt it.

Emperor Frederick of Hohenstaufen burned it down, but it rose again from the flames.

Troops of more than a dozen nations fought all around it and hundreds of planes destroyed it in the Second World War, but the monks restored it, and it stands. And each time Benedictus' sons escaped with their lives. They, and not one of the warring powers prevailed in the end. For fourteen centuries they have continued their great Father's work, dotting the world with citadels of God, sending up streams of prayer and carrying the ancient culture and civilization of Rome deep into barbarous countries. Scarcely a European country does not owe them a debt of gratitude that can never be repaid.

And everyone of Benedictus' sons is trained and lives by the great Rule of the founder of their order, that Rule of which Saint Bernard said that its real author was the Holy Spirit.